WHAT GOES AROUND

EDITED BY DAVID OWAIN HUGHES &
JONATHAN EDWARD ONDRASHEK

KnightWatch Press

Great British Horror Books
www.GreatBritishHorror.com

First published in the UK by KnightWatch Press,
an imprint of Great British Horror Books, 2016

CONTENTS

FOREWORD

If you look up 'horror' (a noun) in a dictionary, you'll find something similar to the following: an overwhelming and painful feeling caused by something frightfully shocking, terrifying, or revolting; a shuddering fear: to shrink back from a mutilated corpse in horror (I particularly like the dictionary's example of something horrific).

But I think horror, true horror, is something that is embedded deep within the human psyche and can be different from person to person depending on past experiences you've gone through. This also explains why some people like watching or reading scary stuff, while some do not.

Let me explain.

I think, at least to some degree, all people like to be scared. It is just part of human nature. Have you ever noticed someone cover their eyes when watching a scary scene in a movie? Sure you have. These people act like they don't want to see what is happening, but are still looking through the spaces between their fingers. Some people say we, as humans, are inherently good. Overall, I believe that is true. But at the same time we all have a 'bad' side. It is that bad side that comes out when we watch the news or marvel at the destruction that some madman just caused on the highway or in someone's living room. If we didn't like hearing about other people's misfortunes we would turn off the news, press the off button on the DVD player or put down the book. But… we don't. Instead, we just shake our heads and think (and never or rarely ever say out loud), "I am so glad that it didn't happen to me."

Personally, I like writing scary stuff simply because that is what I have always been into (I grew up watching the slasher films from the 1980s). I like how a horror writer can make pretty much anything into something scary.

For example, a horror writer can start a serene story about a man walking a cute dog down the street, enjoying the outdoors, his life, his dog. Now, you can make that scary by having a madman in a car jump the curb, taking them both out. Say the dog dies and the guy ends up in the hospital and has to fight for his life. Then after getting out of the hospital, perhaps the guy goes on a mission to find the reckless driver and put him out of his misery. See what I mean? Even the everyday things we enjoy (walking a cute dog down a nice quiet street in middle suburbia) can turn into someone's nightmare.

As far as those out there that say "I don't like watching scary movies or reading scary books" – you better check yourself at the door to your high school English class. Because if you like 'classic literature' then you've probably read horror before (Romeo and Juliet killing themselves in the name of love is pretty horrific – and pretty much just downright dumb) and might have even enjoyed it (those stories were always too tame for my taste). And if you watch your local news, guess what? You're watching horror in real life taking place, which is far worse than any writer could come up with. Maybe.

Horror is all around us. It doesn't matter if you actually enjoy watching or reading it. It's in your face in the media – the made-up stuff and true reports of unfortunate things that happen to innocent people on a daily basis. Some of it is fascinating in a macabre sort of way (the made-up stuff, of course… ha ha), while some of it is just downright sick. I guess when it comes down to brass tacks, horror means different things to different people, but really it's all the same thing: horror. These everyday type settings and events are what you'll find within this tome.

So get comfy in your favorite reading chair and get ready for some fun.

If you consider horror fun, that is.

Quit kidding yourself, you know you do.

~Ty Schwamberger
author of Last Night Out, DININ' & The Fields

CONQUISTADOR

JACK ROLLINS

Luke's prized silver Ford Focus ST-3 crunched over the gravel-covered track, and Luke prayed all the while that the skipping stones would not scratch his paintwork as they tapped and dinged under the chassis. Passing several farmhouses and cottages on the rugged track, he took his aviator sunglasses off and placed them in the hollow within the console, in front of the gear stick. Then he scanned the gates and walls, looking for Arion House.

Black gates topped with two ebony horse heads stood tall and solemn at the end of the track like two huge chess pieces. Between the bars of the gates, and stretching beyond the openings and behind the brick wall surrounding the property, a two storey house of elegant, angular timber and clean-cut stone awaited.

He pressed the control to lower the window, reached out and pushed the call button on the small keypad on the black post in front of the gates.

After a moment, a woman's voice came through the speaker. "Yes, who is it?"

"Luke Sharp." His name had served him well on nights out while studying at university and a Dizzee Rascal song had ordered them all to *fix up, look sharrrrrrp!* A ready-made anthem for the notorious young man about campus they said would fuck the crack of dawn if only he could get its legs apart. "I'm here to see a Ms. Demi Terrance."

"Just a moment."

Luke noticed the small camera eye set into the chrome panel and decided to suck his cheeks in to pronounce his cheekbones and bring out his angular jaw. He figured it was worth the little effort it cost him – you never knew who could be watching. He took in the landscape of sweeping moorland which surrounded Arion House. Such isolation was not his idea of a good time, but he could see its appeal for some, and perhaps as a holiday home or getaway for himself if the city became tiresome at any point.

"Ooh, you look as nice as you did on the website, Mr. Sharp," a different woman's voice purred.

Luke turned back to the camera eye and flashed a pearly-white smile. "Ms. Terrance, am I correct?"

"You certainly are. I'm buzzing you in. Come straight in to see me."

The gates slid open in utter silence – nothing could upset the peace of Arion House and its grounds, it seemed. Luke rolled the car forward, preserving the quiet and his paintwork. To the left stood a long stable block that he assumed opened out on the other side, into a field. Arion House loomed ahead. He parked next to a dark blue Vauxhall Astra and climbed out of his vehicle.

As he approached the front door, it was opened by a woman dressed in a knee-length grey pinstripe skirt and dark violet short-sleeve blouse, cut to show off her trim figure but buttoned high enough to maintain professionalism without attracting stares down her cleavage, which Luke could tell would be a rather pleasant sight. Shoulder-length brown hair framed her smooth, tanned face. He hoped this was who he had come to see, but suspected she was the first person to answer the intercom and likely the owner of the Astra rather than the house.

"Come on in, Mr. Sharp," she said, extending a hand.

"Luke, please." He shook the offered hand and noticed a rosy tint flushing the woman's tanned cheeks. The local government ID showed that she was a social worker, and from her youthful appearance, Luke guessed she was recently graduated and appointed. A year or two of service, no more.

He flashed the smile again and locked his piercing blue eyes on hers. Always on the hunt for new clients, he occasionally found someone he liked for his real life, too.

"I'm Jo Regan, Demi's social worker."

"I see," Luke lied. A frown crossed his forehead, revealing his false concern.

"Nothing to worry about," Jo said, leading the way through the house.

A dog barked and Luke heard the animal's scampering paws long before it appeared. He prayed the thing wouldn't jump up at him and mess up his smoky light blue-grey suit. He had just collected it that morning from the dry cleaners and had no desire to see the thing covered in pet hair. The yapping persisted and Jo addressed the approaching white West Highland terrier as "Rasputin."

"Cool name."

"I know, right?" Jo enthused, bending down to scratch the dog behind the ears. "Such a big name for such a little dog."

"Oy!" called a playful voice from a room just off the passageway. "He's a big, brave boy, is Rasputin. He protects his *mama*."

Rasputin capered off back to his *mama*, followed closely by Jo and Luke.

"Ahhh! Here he is," the woman Luke assumed to be Ms. Terrance announced. She was sat in an armchair with what reminded Luke of an old person's Zimmer frame, but this one had wheels and a tray a couple of feet away. Ms. Terrance wore her dark brown hair in a neat bob, and whereas the social worker's blouse was fastened for privacy, Ms. Terrance liked to put on a show, with her two full rounds of flesh and deep cleavage displayed with pride.

"Ms. Terrance," Luke said, stepping forward, offering a hand.

"Demi. Call me Demi." She took his hand and gently pulled, so Luke lowered his head and she planted a kiss on his cheek. "Mmm, you smell good."

"Thank you. So do you. Is that Viktor and Rolf?" he asked.

"Good nose."

"Flowerbomb?"

"Very good nose."

"I'm wearing Spicebomb. I know my V and R."

Jo cleared her throat, taking a seat. She grasped a notepad and pen. "If you please, take a seat, Luke. This will only take a few minutes."

Luke sat down then smiled at both women, waiting for one of them to begin.

"Would you like me to set the ball rolling?" Jo asked.

"If you don't mind," Demi said.

"Well, I'm sure if Demi would like to, she may well tell you about the accident she suffered and the repercussions of that. I think it's okay for me to say that while you don't want to live in a more built-up area, you recognise that social life is a problem for you, isn't it, Demi?"

"Absolutely. I can't really meet people up here, but this is my home. I don't want to give it up just to make it easier to get out to a pub only for people to ignore me while I'm there."

Luke nodded, wondering what the hell this had to do with him.

"Since Demi's husband left her…" Jo paused, looking for the correct phrasing.

Demi smiled at her social worker. "Look, that bastard left me for someone else. One of my friends – or so-called friend, as it turned out. I had an accident… I fell off a horse, actually. And I was left with crippling pains as a result of that. Some days are better than others, and I've got some pretty powerful pain relief so I can sleep on those bad days. Jo is here because, well, since I'm registered as disabled and I need some treatment, some adaptations were needed for the house and a vehicle, in the early days at least." Demi sighed. "What Jo is beating around the bush about is that I sometimes feel like I need" – she cast a mischievous glance at her social worker – "a good beating about my bush."

"You have such a way with words, Demi."

"Well, he's a man-whore! He's heard worse, I'm sure!"

Luke erupted into laughter. "Excuse me, Madam! I am a professional escort."

The two women laughed as well, and Demi said, "A professional *shagger*, more like."

"My job is providing company for people. I provide a vital service," Luke said, frowning in mock indignation.

"Essentially, as Demi has experienced periods of low mood, I have to ensure she has the capacity to remain in control of the decisions she makes regarding certain physical needs," Jo explained. "I'm satisfied that you're quite happy with your decisions so far, and I feel it's appropriate for me to withdraw from this particular aspect of your support, Demi."

"Thank you for helping me arrange this, Jo."

"No problem at all, Demi." Jo stood up with her pad and pen in hand. "If you need me for anything else, you know to give me a call." The social worker left, with little Rasputin trotting along at her heels.

"Close the door, Luke," Demi said.

Luke complied, then paused before her, letting her see his full form in his well-tailored suit. "What do you like?" he asked.

Demi blushed and giggled. "My God. You're direct."

"I want to please you. I want to make you happy."

"I don't want… *that* today."

Luke smiled. There was something girlish about the woman before him. At first appearance, she was a woman of confidence, humour and control, but it was becoming clear to him that her confidence had been crushed. Crushed by the accident. Crushed by her husband leaving her. Crushed by pain.

"I'm not really able to…to *do* anything today." Demi waved a hand over the little table at her side, indicating the shot-glass size medication pot with the remaining trace of some sort of medicine or suspension. The thick grey droplets clinging to the plastic pot reminded Luke of semen, but the large brown bottle on the table indicated that it was *oramorph*.

"Morphine?" Luke muttered. "Demi, your pains must be terrible."

"They are. But that does the trick. For a while, at least."

"Do you feel okay right now?"

"Yes, and if my pains start up again, I'll be laid out on my couch until the carers come to make my dinner and again until they come back to help me to bed."

"I see." Luke sat at the edge of the couch.

"Stand up."

Luke jumped back to his feet like a child who had done something wrong and been caught in the act. "Sorry… I thought you just wanted to talk for a while."

Demi bit her lip and narrowed her eyes. Her gaze seemed to radiate confidence now, the vulnerability of moments before eradicated with a single thought. "Show me your cock, Luke."

Luke's smile spread slowly across his lips. He grasped the lapels of his jacket and began to peel the garment off his shoulders.

"No," Demi interrupted. "Keep it on. I just want you to show me your cock. I want to see it just as you are, like that."

Luke unzipped his fly, reached his fingertips into the opening, and pulled aside his *Aussiebum Wonderjock*, releasing his genitals from the concealed pouch that kept everything pressed into a tight, neat, impressive package. He grasped his shaft and stroked, exciting the muscle to give Demi a little more to look at.

"Don't do that," Demi said. "Just show me it. Just take it out exactly as it is."

Luke raised his eyebrows and exposed himself. His flaccid penis hung in the opening of his trousers. Without the full erection to show her, he blushed and looked around the room, unable to meet Demi's gaze.

"Don't be embarrassed. Do you know how long it's been since I saw a man's cock just sitting there normally? If I want to see a massive, throbbing hard-on, I just need to turn on my laptop, don't I?"

Luke levelled his eyes on Demi's face once more, hoping she would instruct him to *do* something – *anything* – soon.

"Come here."

Luke positioned himself in front of his client and she leaned forward. Her warm breath tickled the flesh of his exposed penis. Demi reached into his fly and gently stroked his shaft with her middle fingertip.

A shiver of excitement ran through Luke's spine. He felt the throb as hot blood flooded his meat. Demi leaned her face closer, brushing his shaft with her lips. Her tongue flicked out, licking his flesh, tracing the engorged blue vein as his erection swelled and rose towards her mouth. She kissed the tip, then placed a flat palm against his shaft and pressed her cheek against it. She nibbled at his skin and tilted her head, his cock running beyond the width of her lips. She applied light pressure with her teeth, never hurting him.

Demi pulled her head away and shifted back in her chair. "You can put it away now."

Luke zipped himself up.

"It's a hundred an hour, isn't it?"

"Yes."

"The money's waiting for you on the kitchen table. Was *that* considered an extra? I know I'm paying for your time only."

"No, my time alone is fine today."

Demi looked him up and down. "I'll be in touch with the agency again soon."

Luke returned to his car. The moorland around him was cast in a wonderful orange glow as the last vestiges of the winter phase of afternoon sunlight washed the countryside and tinted the metalwork of his vehicle. He considered the woman living all the way out here on her own. Carers checked on her four times a day, as it turned out, but that only amounted to about two hours of contact time on most days, with extra time for shopping and domestic duties on two separate days in the week. Luke wondered why Demi hadn't just sunk a couple of bottles of oramorph and finished herself off in a fit of sheer boredom.

He was about to step into the Ford when a sudden snort startled him. He spun on his heels, crunching the gravel beneath him, and turned to the source of the noise. A bay stallion stood at the corner of the left-side north face of the house. The animal's eyes were fixed on him, as though weighing him up and forming an opinion of him.

Even standing perfectly still, the power in the creature's musculature was plain to see. Its tightly braided chocolate brown mane and tail set against its latte-coloured body perfectly. He knew nothing of horses, but he could see that this creature was exquisite.

The stallion snorted once more and turned away, disappearing out of view around the corner.

Luke drove to the console by the gates, wound down his window and pressed the button to open them. He glanced in the mirror and could see all along the north face of the property, but the horse was gone.

***

Luke's next appointment was not until the evening: one of his regulars, a woman in her sixties whose husband had suffered a stroke and couldn't get it up anymore with all the blood pressure medication he took. She was attractive in her advanced years; he thought of her as a MILF who'd turned into a GILF. Sometimes, when servicing older clients, he had to make use of Viagra to ensure a performance. With her he had no such problems, and he preferred that, preferred to find something he liked about the client, something natural that would give him the ability to perform. She was a good tipper, and all she wanted was to lay there and be fucked by someone she found attractive. Missionary, bareback, and he had to come inside her – that's what made her happy.

He trained at the gym for an hour, working his back, knowing he would need his arms and chest for the night's activity. Once his workout was done, he showered and wrapped a towel around his waist, collected his Speedos from the locker and slipped them on before entering the spa.

Resting the base of his skull on the lip of the Jacuzzi, he let his body float up to the surface of the water. The bubbles tickled his body, soothing his tired muscles. He closed his eyes, passing into a perfect state of relaxation. Focused on the bubbles surging against his flesh and the blackness behind his eyelids, he blocked out his troubles and let the moment take over.

The moment, however, was short-lived. Rough hands grasped Luke's head and pressed him beneath the water. The surface of the water erupted as his arms and legs thrashed. The downward force relented and Luke burst from the water, gasping for air, coughing and retching. He cleared his eyes and saw before him John Kelly, clad in a fine charcoal suit and pale blue shirt. Kelly's condescending laughter echoed around the tiled spa. A couple of curious patrons peered out from the steam room and showers, but ducked away when they saw the most feared and notorious member of their club.

"Sorry, pal, I thought you'd nodded off. I thought it safest to wake you," Kelly said, sneering.

"You're fucking unbelievable, John. Really you are," Luke managed to whine between gasps.

"Well, it doesn't do you good to rest for too long. Work's good for the soul, my friend. It's good for getting me the money you owe me, too."

"You said I had 'til the end of next month."

"You do, pal, but I don't think you're setting aside as much as you should be. Maybe you need to go and bang some more old women or something, eh… or maybe you'll need a good plastic surgeon to fix up *Luke Sharp*, when I've finished with you," Kelly said, almost singing the taunt. "Nothing quite like being debt-free, my friend, but some folk… well, the more they earn, the more they want. Isn't that true?"

Ignoring the question, Luke climbed out of the Jacuzzi and snatched up his towel, patting his body down, pleased to hide his almost naked form behind *something* while Kelly was present.

"Anyway, I'll leave you to it. I saw you come up here and couldn't resist. It's been so long since I last saw you, I absolutely *had* to come and have a little catch-up." With that, Kelly gave a patronising wave and left the spa, his message well and truly delivered.

Luke ended his spa session prematurely, his relaxation time spoiled. A flash of panic tore through his concentration: *the car!*

The chill air cut into his damp hair as he raced across the car park, his suit jacket crumpled over his left arm, gym bag flapping against his thigh. He paced around his cherished vehicle, braced for a dent or scratch in the paintwork to break his heart. To his relief, Kelly's spite, it seemed, did not extend as far as vandalising vehicles. Then it occurred to Luke that the reason may be that it would reduce the value of it should Kelly see the need to relieve him of it when the day of reckoning arrived.

He ran a hand over the rain-streaked roof and climbed in, throwing his jacket onto the passenger seat as he settled behind the wheel. He slammed his hands against the steering wheel in anger and frustration at Kelly catching him off-guard like that. The thing was, Kelly was *right*: he hadn't been setting aside enough to get the debt cleared. He hadn't been working as hard as he should. He'd been picky about taking on new clients, preferring instead to milk those he was established with. He'd taken on Demi purely because he'd known her age – she was mid-thirties – and if his luck was in, she'd be an attractive woman he'd happily fuck anyway and the money would just be a bonus. His luck *was* in, as it turned out, and he hoped he'd hear back from her soon. In all likelihood, he reckoned she needed companionship as well as sex. That could lead to lots of additional hours and a lot more money made with his dick alone.

Being an escort meant Luke made his money off the books, with no tax or national insurance payments, no student loan repayments and no paper trail with which to impress upon a bank his ability to repay a loan. When he had decided to take advantage of the property boom, he'd formed a limited company with his uncle Phil, who'd put in five thousand pounds. Luke had added the same amount, borrowed from the shark. They had then used the money as deposits on two homes, one of which they had let out immediately and the other which they'd discovered had serious foundation damage not highlighted in the initial survey.

Any money they had made from the rental had been quickly swallowed in the cost of the underpinning work on the other building, along with legal costs accrued from suing the surveyor for negligence.

And that was how in three months a five-thousand-pound debt had swelled to over twenty-thousand pounds.

***

Three days later, Luke received his usual email offering him some work. He knew immediately that the three-hour visit was with Demi, and he was correct in his assumption. This meant three hundred pounds basic, and whatever was negotiated for any sexual contact in that time. Had he not been so desperate for money, he might have given her that for free to secure frequent business from her, but time was of the essence and he needed to take as much as he could as soon as he could.

Everywhere he'd went, whether it was the shops or the gym, Kelly or one of his lackeys had seemed to be there, hovering around, watching him. Sometimes he had caught a glimpse of a knife, a club, and once even a power drill in their hands. A sense of desperation had risen like a flood tide within him – he couldn't even masturbate, which was, in his trade, most concerning. The urgency for money might just eradicate the only means he had to make it.

Stress burned in Luke's veins, tensing his muscles, making him push the car a little harder than usual on the moor road. Even on the track approaching Arion House, he sped along, sending gravel clattering up beneath the chassis to clank on the panels and his precious paintwork. He didn't care. *It's Kelly's fucking car soon, anyway!*

The speed rendered the hedgerows translucent as the gaps merged into one, opening up a view into the field to his right. Keeping pace with him raced the bay horse he had seen on his previous visit. A determined eye peered through the hedge, and although the animal must have been looking ahead as it ran, Luke had the odd sensation that the horse was observing him, or had at least recognised him.

The offside wheels of the Ford Focus thumped up onto the grass verge and Luke wrenched the wheel around to force the car back onto the track. His heart thudded in his chest as adrenaline sent his body and mind into overdrive, flooding him with thoughts of what would have happened had he crashed the car.

He didn't mind putting a few scratches on the paintwork for Kelly to inherit, but it would be no good if he wrote the whole thing off. Then he'd really be in trouble.

Demi opened the gates remotely. Within moments, Luke stood before her in the lounge. She sat with a table similar to those found in hospital, with a frame forming three edges of a rectangle so it could slip over her chair, with the main surface positioned over her lap. Upon the table stood an easel, a pack of charcoals open and at the ready.

"Strip," was all she said.

Luke smiled and did as he was told.

The first thing Demi did was photograph him as he lay across the sofa in a classic pose for a still-life drawing, with one hand supporting his head and the other arm draped over his midriff. "In case I don't get to finish while you're here," she informed him.

"I didn't know you were an artist," Luke said.

"I'm not a very good one, but you're such a nice thing to draw, I thought I would take advantage."

"I see."

"I used to draw my horse a lot."

"I suppose it's difficult if you don't get outside much. Plus, from what I've seen, he'd take some keeping up with."

Demi frowned and looked up from her work. "What do you mean?"

"He's bloody fast. He was racing me on my way in."

"Couldn't be my horse. Conquistador died not long after our accident."

"Oh. You're right then, it must have been another of your horses."

"I don't have any more."

"There was a horse bolting along the field out there – it must be one of your fields. Right next to the road approaching this place."

"Yes, that's my field, but I don't have any horses at all. Not since the accident."

"Bloody hell, then someone's missing a lovely bay racehorse."

Demi continued to work in silence for a long while. Eventually she said, "It's funny, you know, how you saw that bay horse. My Conquistador was a bay stallion. He was beautiful. Such an intelligent animal. He understood me more than any man could."

"Maybe you just haven't tried the right man. I think I understand what you need. Probably better than any horse could. I'd stake money on it."

"Really?" Demi grinned at him and wiggled her eyebrows. "Would you stake your fee for today on it?"

Luke groaned inside. "How do I know you'd be honest with me?"

"I'd be honest with you. If you can make me come, you'll be worth every penny. Not even my husband could make me come."

"It's a deal."

Demi slid the table away from her chair and grabbed her walking stick. "Right, then. Let's see what you're made of."

Luke excused himself and snorted a quick line of coke in the bathroom. Then he hurried to the bedroom where Demi had positioned herself in the centre of the bed. He undressed her gently but quickly. Her ex-husband had been an idiot, Luke decided. Even after a disabling accident, her body was toned and tight. Excitement coursed through him and he traced his fingers up her legs, working upwards slowly, deliberately. Demi shivered with the anticipation of one never touched sexually, or one who had gone without such contact for a long time.

Luke pulled Demi's legs apart and positioned his shoulders beneath her knees. She pushed her hips forward, squeezing his neck with her thighs, her shaven pussy only inches from his face. She giggled and so did he, finding her girlish excitement both funny and something of a turn-on. He slid his tongue along her right thigh, sending shivers of pleasure through her. As he reached the top of her thigh, he turned his head and listened as Demi took in a sharp breath, holding onto it, probably waiting for his tongue to make contact with her lips or clit. Instead he worked his tongue up her left thigh.

This time, he didn't make her wait. As his mouth moved closer to her opening, he found himself salivating and unable to resist a second time. He pushed his tongue inside her, making her gasp and squirm. He withdrew and brushed the tip upwards over her clit, tracing circles, altering the pressure, shifting to the blade of his tongue and back to the tip.

Demi came within two minutes, covering his mouth and chin with hot juices.

"Now," he said, shifting his weight on the bed as Demi released the pillow she had clutched throughout the trembling orgasm she'd enjoyed, "get on your hands and knees."

After her third orgasm, Demi doubled up on the bed. Luke slid his cock inside her again, but she moaned and wriggled away.

"Please – I'm sore. I can't do any more."

"Have I hurt you?"

"No," she whispered. "It's my pains. I should've known this would happen. Should never have done this."

"God, Demi, I'm sorry. I really am. If I'd known…"

"Don't worry about it."

For a couple of minutes, she rolled from one side to the other, onto her back, over and onto her front. Tears streamed down her cheeks.

"Please, Demi, let me get you something for the pain."

"Can you bring me my morphine and one of those little medicine cups, please?"

Demi described the location of the morphine in the kitchen and Luke hurried to collect it, still naked. He was glad she lived so remotely and had no little old lady neighbours to shock.

When he opened the cupboard where Demi's medication was stored, his eyes bulged. Six bottles of oramorph sat in a row before her blister packs of tablet medication.

He took the already opened bottle with a medication pot up to the bedroom and placed them on the bedside cabinet. "I see you're well-supplied. Plenty of morphine in that cupboard to keep you going, eh?"

She chuckled as she shifted into an upright position and twisted to see the medication. "What, those six bottles? That's a fraction of what I've got."

"Seriously?"

"Yeah, they've been trying to get it off me for years because they're saying the pains are all imagined. They say I'm just an addict, so I've been trying to take only tiny amounts over time to build up my stockpile. You know, just in case they eventually *do* stop prescribing it to me."

"So how many bloody bottles of this stuff have you got?"

"On your way out, have a little look in the old tack room in the stables. Then you'll see what's been going on. It's not all from the doctors, though. One of my friends is a pharmacist. Every now and then they claim a spoiled delivery box of them, break some of my empties, and give me a few bottles on the side." She poured herself 5ml of the liquid and knocked it back.

"Very clever."

"Well, they don't do it for free, but it beats dealer rates, put it that way." Demi lay back on the pillows once more and closed her eyes. "Hopefully that'll settle things down. Not a word about that stuff to anyone, okay?"

"My lips are sealed."

"Your lips have done quite enough for one day. Well… I suppose you've earned your fee. I forgot to ask, what do you charge for the extras?"

Luke ignored the question. He had a question of his own, and the coke seemed to insist that he ask. "What happened to you, Demi?"

"What do you mean?"

"What happened to you when you fell off the horse?"

A long sigh escaped her and she shook her head. "Did you take some of this when you were downstairs?"

"*That?* No! God. no. I had a little line before we got started, but that's it."

"Really?"

"Really. I swear."

Demi nodded, eyeing him with distrust. "If you really have to know, I lost a baby. I didn't even know I was pregnant. My period hadn't stopped or anything, but when I fell… that was that. Conquistador… he turned around in the middle of the track and stood over me, blocking the other horses. They collided with him, and one of his hind legs was broken. He collapsed next to me, but somehow pulled himself past my head to protect me. I was on my way to hospital, screaming the ambulance down. I remember them bringing the screen around him, and that was that. He was no longer worth keeping, as far as my dad thought, and… they killed him. My beautiful Conquistador."

Demi descended into a flood of tears, pressing her palms firm against her eyeballs. It occurred to Luke that the loss of the horse meant everything. The loss of a baby she hadn't known she'd carried meant nothing.

An idea bubbled away in Luke's brain. Demi's upset faded into the background as he turned over the possibilities. He didn't like the idea, but it would get Kelly off his back. And he might get to keep the car after all.

"Help me," she whispered, pointing to the bottle.

Luke poured another 5ml measure and pressed the cup into Demi's trembling hand, guiding it to her lips. When she had swallowed the syrup and collapsed back onto the pillow, Luke waited with her as her eyes grew heavy and she slipped off into sleep.

It was then he made his move. He raced down the stairs three at a time, then inspected the loops of keys on the hooks by the front door. He found one for the stables and a key labelled Tack Room. As he lifted the key, he heard a massive metallic thump. He thought, *I hope that wasn't my car!* Then, his shrill car alarm sounded to confirm the worst. Luke almost tore the front door off its hinges as he flung it open and leapt out onto the gravel.

He raised a hand to his mouth and cried out in anger as soon as his eyes fell upon his vehicle. A huge dent had appeared in the centre of the bonnet. "Who the fuck did this?" he shouted. "Who's out here?" He pressed the button on his key fob to deactivate the alarm.

Luke hurried around the house, finding nothing but empty garden and fields beyond. He returned to the car and looked around to see if any clues lay nearby. He expected to find a huge chunk of broken chimneypot, but there was no sign of what had damaged his car.

"Fucking brilliant!" he muttered. His anger burned hot and bright, but he managed to return his attention to his main purpose and approached the stables. He accessed the tack room easily. It held a dusty assortment of saddles, bridles and stirrups, and in one corner he saw the sort of locker one might use in a garden, to store tools or a lawnmower. A brass padlock held the locker door closed. The smallest key on the loop opened the padlock and Luke pulled back the thick plastic doors to reveal the contents.

Demi had not exaggerated. Luke guessed she had amassed about fifty half-litre bottles of oramorph in the locker. She really was worried they would take her precious pain relief away. He wondered if her pains were even real anymore. The jigsaw pieces began to slot together. The accident. Her love for that horse and her belief that it had sacrificed itself to save her. The pains that were no doubt real and intense enough to be prescribed some heavy duty relief. Her husband leaving her. Her ability to trim the amount of morphine she took in order to save it up in case they ever took it away from her. She was an addict, nothing more. A clever one with some level of control, but an addict nonetheless.

In a moment, the phone was in his hand, Kelly's contact details on the screen, and the tone was in his ear as the call went through.

"John, it's Luke."

"I bloody know that already. Your name came up."

"Whatever. Listen, is oramorph any use to you?"

John went quiet for a few moments. "Some. Why?"

"Some? How much? Is it any use to you or not?"

"As it is, it doesn't give a massive *high*, but I know some boys who'll plug anything up their arses and they'll have a fucking field day with the stuff. Why, like? Have you got your hands on a bottle?"

"How much would you give me for a bottle?"

"How big's the bottle, and what's the dosage?"

Luke grabbed one of the cardboard boxes from the locker and inspected it. "Says here it's five milligrams per ten millilitres and it's a five-hundred-millilitre bottle."

The phone went silent as John did the mental arithmetic. "I'll get a few quid for it, Luke, but it's going to take a lot of that shit to clear what you owe me. Why the fuck are you bothering me about this?"

"John, I'm looking at about fifty to sixty bottles of it here."

"Really? That's a bit more interesting. And would you care to tell me how you've come by that amount of this stuff?"

Luke proceeded to explain about Demi, the lonely woman on the moors, her morphine addiction and the stockpile she had built up.

"If you're doing this, Luke, you must be fucking desperate to pay me back. Now listen, you're looking at about ten grand for fifty bottles, right? I'll make more than that, but I have to split it right down to shots for these idiots to stick up their arses. That's a half of what you owe gone. We're still looking at the car and whatever else I can lay my hands on up there to clear the rest, yeah?"

"What do you mean, 'whatever else'?"

"There'll be some *ket* or something up there, I'll bet. All sorts of interesting shit I can use on horse farms."

"But don't hurt her. Just leave her alone, okay?"

"What do you give a fuck, Luke? You called here, inviting me to burgle the place right underneath her. Anyway, what if I give her for free what you charge her money for?"

"This is a joke, right, John?"

John remained silent.

"Tell me you're fucking kidding me."

"What do you take me for?"

"I know, but… don't say things like that." Luke's legs felt like jelly as he stepped outside into the orange-grey moorland dusk. "The car – it's got a right dent in the bonnet, John."

"Will it tap out?"

"Probably."

Another pause. "Well, I'll still take it."

"And what if there's no ket?"

"I'll take a gamble on that. There'll be something else I can take. She got any dogs?"

"A little terrier thing. Yappy, but not big."

"When will her next carers come?"

"They'll be here shortly for half-an-hour, then not again until nine, gone again about ten, I think."

"Lovely. Stay up on the moors. You know that ruined church?"

"Yeah."

"Park near that. I'll meet you up there and you can give me the guided tour when we see the carers drive off."

***

Luke did as he was told and waited by the ruined church. Its stone skeleton appeared black against the darkening sky as the last shreds of orange sunset slipped behind the Cheviot hills in the west. He saw the carers approach – two cars, both with their headlamps on, racing along the track with no regard for the condition of their vehicles. They were probably rushed off their feet with dinnertime visits, with little time to get from one place to the next.

He made a private joke to himself that he should stop them on their way back and give them some career advice, as he could be paid ten to fifteen times what they made in an hour and all they'd have to do is stop selling care and start selling themselves.

This naturally led him to thoughts of his time with Demi. Rarely was he gripped by excitement as he fucked a new client, but she had been different. He enjoyed her. She looked good, she *felt* good, she *tasted* good. Under different circumstances, she might have been good for a relationship, but once they were a client, it was difficult to see a woman as anything else.

The carers left after about twenty minutes at Demi's place. It seemed to be a short visit, but he imagined that if she was doped up, her needs would be minimal. Then he wondered who had let them in. It was a brief wonder, as he realised they probably had the numerical code to open the gates without the need for help from the inside.

The carers headed back for town on the road snaking off to the north, and they had barely slipped out of view before the lights of another two vehicles became visible.

Luke shook his head in disgusted awe when he realised that John Kelly had brought two of his thugs and a black Ford Transit van. He climbed out of his car as Kelly did the same.

"Jesus Christ, John. You planning on emptying her house?"

"Hey, you never know what there might be in there, lad. Out here, these farmer types like an antique, you know?"

Luke told Kelly about the problem he anticipated with the gate access.

"She never gave you the code?" Kelly asked.

"If she had, I wouldn't be saying it's a problem, would I?" Luke snapped.

"Wind your fucking neck back in, you silly twat. I'm doing you a fucking favour taking this shit in lieu of payment. Speaking of which, giz a look at this bonnet." Kelly stepped up to Luke's Ford Focus, activating the torch on his iPhone. "Aye, that'll tap out no bother. You didn't fucking miss it, did you? Got a pretty good smack on you, eh?"

"Miss it? I don't know how the fuck it happened." Luke stroked the metalwork. "Anyway, what about this gate?"

Kelly pointed over his shoulder with a thumb aimed at the van and its two occupants. "They can get into anything, those two. I'll be surprised if that lock will keep them out." Kelly turned to face the men in the van and nodded to the passenger, who emerged from the vehicle rubbing his stubbly jaw as he walked around Luke to the Ford Focus. "Since the car's mine now, he's going to drive it. You can ride with me. I'll drop you off when we're done."

Luke's face creased with concern. "I thought I was only showing you the way. I don't want to be there while you knock the place off."

"Tough shit." Kelly sneered and climbed into his car. "You think I'll let you call the fucking coppers on me while I'm in the middle of the job? I don't think so. Get in."

In minutes the vehicles idled outside the gate at Arion House as one of Kelly's men worked on the console. It took less than a minute for the man to override the system and the gate swung open, allowing them access to the grounds.

Kelly pulled his Subaru Legacy estate up outside the stables, stopping at the door Luke had told him led to the tack room. Kelly opened the car boot and withdrew his crowbar. He pried open the black wooden door with a quick and heavy downward jerk. Wood splintered and the locking mechanism tore out of the old door.

"Follow me," Kelly said.

Luke stepped into the tack room with the loan shark. Behind him, Kelly's men worked to breach the house.

"Silly cow, how was plastic ever going to keep anyone out?" Kelly muttered, smashing the locker open.

"I'm sure she didn't expect anyone coming up here to rob her."

"And then she met you, eh?" Kelly snarled. He had a way of ensuring Luke could not distance himself from the crime, reminding him that he was not only an accomplice, but the mastermind behind the whole caper.

"You'd better help me get this shit out into the car as quickly as possible."

They worked fast and lifted the boxed bottles of oramorph into the boot of the waiting Subaru. Kelly covered the packages with a thick grey blanket and slammed the boot shut. "Let's get over to the house."

One of Kelly's underlings, the grey-haired, moustachioed man who'd driven the van, stood in the front doorway. At his feet lay a pile of silver plates, Demi's laptop, a blu-ray player and her forty-inch TV. "Mark's upstairs," the man said, stepping aside as Kelly entered the house.

"He'd better not have hurt her," Luke cried.

Without warning, Kelly spun on his heels with the crowbar outstretched, striking Luke across the side of his head. A lightning flash of pain preceded a red shroud over Luke's vision. His legs wobbled and he fell against the kitchen door, which opened upon impact. He hit the slate tiled floor with a heavy thump. As his consciousness faded, he caught a glimpse of something small and white beside his head, but before he could focus on it, all was blackness.

***

Luke woke, cold and with the corners of objects jabbing into his arms and midriff. It took him a moment to realise he was in the back of the van surrounded by everything Kelly and his two accomplices had stolen from Arion House. He pressed his fingers to the left side of his head. Wet, sticky blood met his touch, and excruciating pain planted in him fears for the integrity of his skull.

Sitting up, Luke heard footsteps crunching over the gravel and the voices of two men grumbling about the raw deal they'd received.

"I don't know why he gets to have all the fucking fun. I tied the bitch up."

"Always the fucking same. We get the sloppy seconds."

"Well, you can have the sloppy thirds, you old fart. I'm not stirring your fucking porridge for you!"

Luke climbed to his feet and readied his fists, preparing to jump at the men as soon as they opened the doors.

"What the fuck's that?"

"Is there an animal loose or something?"

Luke couldn't hear what had caught their attention from within the van, but he noticed that their footfalls moved away from his position. He crept to the doors and pulled the handle, hoping the men were too preoccupied to hear the judder of the door when the catch disengaged.

He peered out into the darkness. Beams of torchlight cut across the gable end of Arion House as the men approached the rear of the property. Luke stepped down from the back of the van and left the door open in his wake, creeping to the cover afforded by Kelly's car, which remained parked at the stable block.

One of the men turned, flashing his torch back to the van doors. Luke kept his head down and waited for the light to pass once more before chancing another peek. He saw the two men disappear around the far corner of the house and considered calling the police. He checked his pockets for his mobile phone, but of course, they had taken that from him while he was unconscious.

Luke rushed from the cover of the car to the front door. The house lights burned bright and Luke stepped inside with hesitation, placing his steps as carefully and quietly as possible. Kelly could be anywhere and would see him once he entered the light. He needed the element of surprise – there was no way he could overpower the man in a straight fight.

As he passed the kitchen, he saw Rasputin sprawled on the floor, his tongue grey and limp and hanging from his head, which had been twisted around to face backwards. He saw a cordless telephone handset and considered using it to call the police, but the coward in him decided against it. What was he meant to say? I wanted us to rob her *nicely*? *They made it nasty!* He knew it wasn't a wise choice if he valued his freedom.

He instead grabbed a knife from the angled wooden block by the cooker and charged up the stairs.

"I'm almost done here, wait your turn!" Kelly barked upon hearing his approach.

"You're done!" Luke cried, plunging the knife deep into the loan shark's back. He felt the metal blade grind against bone.

Kelly writhed, trying to reach for the knife handle.

He slid off the bed, falling face first to the carpet, his bare backside pointing up to the ceiling.

Demi lay still and silent on the bed. Her lips glistened with what at first Luke thought was semen, but he then noticed the empty bottle of oramorph next to her and realised he'd been fooled by her medication. The bottle hadn't been full when he'd administered it to her earlier, but there had to have been about 400ml or so. He placed his ear over her mouth and could neither feel nor hear any breaths.

He pulled the quilt to conceal all but her head, covering her bare legs and torn knickers and exposed breasts, which were bruised from rough handling. Hot tears burned down Luke's cheeks as he considered the dead woman. *I did this to you. You gave me money because you were lonely, and because I wanted more money, you're dead.*

Luke's tears were not solely for Demi. They were for himself, too. He was a murderer and an accomplice in a second murder, as well as a number of other charges that could be brought against him in this whole affair.

He checked the clock and realised the carers would return soon. He might be able to flee the scene without issue, but he had no idea where his mobile phone was. He dragged Kelly clear of the bed and turned him over. The handle of the knife acted as a stand, propping Kelly up and keeping him from lying completely flat. Luke rifled through his pockets, finding Kelly's phone and wallet but nothing else.

That meant one of the two thugs outside had to have it. He rolled Kelly over once more. Pressing a foot into the small of the dead debt collector's back to stabilise himself, he applied the great force required to break the vacuum within the wound and yanked the knife free of his spine.

Luke crept out to the top of the stairs, straining his ears for sounds of anyone approaching. He glanced down the staircase, then found his attention drawn to the open doors of the ransacked spare bedrooms, one of which had been used as something of a studio for Demi's sketching and painting. Sketches, charcoals and tubes of oil paint lay scattered across the carpet. Luke remembered the sketch she had made of him. Then he thought of the photograph, or *photographs* – he couldn't be sure which it really was – she had taken of him. Not necessarily incriminating evidence, but certainly something to connect him to the place.

Then of course, there was the record of the appointments she had made with him, and her social worker's knowledge of the arrangement at the outset. No matter what happened, he would have questions to answer, but he could do his best to make those questions simpler and fewer by removing any traces of himself.

Staying low, he tiptoed into the room, careful not to stand on the oils, which would split the tubes and cause him to leave a lovely set of footprints at a murder scene. He leafed through the scattered notebooks, working frantically, desperate to get out of the house, off the moor and back into town where he could at least have time to think up the next part of the plan.

As his eyes flicked over every one of Demi's lovingly rendered sketches, he saw many of various horses and ponies, but the ones that really stood out were the ones she had marked *Conquistador XXX*. Those sketches were so lifelike, so precise, that even the knowing look in the animal's eye was captured there on paper. Luke had seen the look before. He knew those eyes. He had been in the presence of this horse more than once.

Impossible, he thought. *Conquistador is dead.*

In that moment, he heard a blood-curdling scream from outside. Grabbing the knife once more, Luke charged downstairs and made it to the kitchen door before he heard the scream again. He knew it was a man's scream, and for one of those men Kelly had brought with him to be screaming, they *must* be terrified.

His grip on the knife tightened and he pressed a hand against the open door, using it to steady his nerves, prepared to shove off from it should he suddenly need to turn tail and retreat. Luke peered around the doorframe, hearing footsteps kicking up gravel nearby.

He saw one of the thugs – the one referred to as Mark earlier – sprinting towards him, light from the house making the dark stain across his face glisten as he raced past the windows.

Luke stepped outside and raised the knife. "Where's my phone, you thieving bastard?"

The man skidded to a halt on the gravel and changed direction, turning towards the parked van. "Fuck the phone, get out of here! She's killed Terry!"

Then he heard the hoof falls, a casual trot somewhere in the darkness. The steps were solid thuds; no splash of gravel accompanied them. Luke peered out beyond the edge of the stable, to the fields where the horses would have been more comfortable than on the loose stones of the driveway. He could see nothing.

"The keys! The fucking keys!" Mark cried, dropping from the driver's side of the van.

Luke ran to the back of the van and grabbed the thief by his jacket. "What's going on? You said *she* – *she* killed Terry. Who do you mean?"

A wet snort sounded from the gate. Gravel crunched under heavy, steady steps.

"The woman! The woman who lives here!" Mark shoved Luke aside and broke into a sprint as he reached out for the open door, desperate for the relative safety of the house.

"She's dead, you fucking idiot!" Luke cried.

Hooves fell like thunder. Stones whipped up and struck the side panels of the van, clanging louder and louder, closer and closer. Mark froze in the space between the van and the house, turning his head to the source of the furious commotion. He screamed.

Luke clasped a hand over his mouth as the silhouette of a horse and rider cut across the light projected from the front door. He heard soft, wet crunches as Mark's ribcage and head collapsed, his organs and vital fluids bursting out of his smashed body in lumpy, glistening spurts.

Luke took his chance and ran for the door, jumping over Mark's tattered body as he went. He slammed the door shut behind him but didn't bother to lock it, suspecting that whatever Mark or Terry had done to the lock to get in there in the first place had probably rendered it useless.

He had no idea what to do next. There were three vehicles outside and he had the keys to none. There was photographic and sketched evidence of his involvement with Demi, and four corpses on the scene. The only thing he could do was make a run for it, but there was no way he'd outrun a marauding horse.

The knife thudded on the carpet and Luke paced back and forth in the passageway with his fingers clasped behind his head.

Finding no answers to his predicament in the confines of the short corridor, he burst through the lounge door like he was a narcotics officer on a drug raid. He scanned the room and saw, sat on the table where she had left it, the little easel, some charcoals and a sketchbook. He tore the book open and flicked through it, finding the nudes Demi had drawn when he'd posed for her. He ripped them out and stuffed them into his pocket.

It was then that he noticed the next picture in the book. Demi had drawn herself in a blurred, dreamy image, standing with one hand on the glass of a window, beyond which was the handsome head and knotted mane of Conquistador. The composition made it clear that the two were locked in eye contact, but the strangest thing of all was that Demi's other hand disappeared behind the thigh of her bent leg. It was unmistakeable: she was masturbating in this picture, and it looked like the focus of her desire was the horse.

Luke flicked through more and more of the images, finding more sketches of this kind. He wondered if they were fantasies, but considered that Demi might have been drawing memories. Conquistador lying in a bed of straw, Demi naked, sprawled across his back. Pages of rough sketches of what he imagined to be a horse's engorged phallus.

"Fucking hell," he muttered, wide-eyed. "She loves it. She loves the fucking horse."

Demi's voice came from the passageway and Luke turned to face her.

"And he loves *me*. He *never* left me. Everyone else did, but not my *Conquistador*."

Her naked body – supple, healthy, vital – sat tall and proud, riding bareback on the powerful stallion she had loved beyond its death. Her position was not one common to comfortable riding, as she seemed to sit forward slightly, closer to Conquistador's neck. The animal stared deep into Luke's eyes, transfixing him as it strode into the lounge, Demi ducking her head beneath the doorframe.

Luke gasped, backing away around the sofa. "This is impossible. This can't be real. *You* are not real. I saw you. You're dead. You're lying dead on your bed!" The sketchbook slipped from his hand.

Demi's weight shifted with each movement of Conquistador's muscles, shifts which Luke could see caused one of the braided mane knots to rub against her clitoris.

"I'm dreaming this! I'm dreaming all of this, surely to God!" Luke continued to back away and stumbled over a side table. He toppled, taking a reed diffuser with him. Passion fruit and coconut oil spilled across the carpet and soaked into his clothes, thick and cold, the scent – normally pleasant – now too strong, *cloying*. Before Luke could scramble back to his feet once more, Demi towered over him and Conquistador's muzzle hovered inches away from his face, nostrils flaring.

"Demi, I'm sorry! Please, Demi – I didn't know he was going to rape you. I didn't know he would kill you."

She said nothing, only smiled.

A shuddering sigh escaped Luke's lungs. He sobbed and wept as terror gave way to relief.

Conquistador snorted as its lips peeled back, revealing two great barriers of gum and teeth. Luke screamed as the teeth clamped down over his wide open mouth and white-hot pain consumed him. Tooth and bone snapped and crunched as the mighty animal's powerful bite crushed the escort's jaw, tearing his tongue and lower lip off.

Coughing on the blood racing to the back of his throat, Luke thrashed out, finding his left hand in Conquistador's mouth. Over the crunching bones, he heard Demi moan with pleasure, the same groans he himself had provoked from her with his fingers and tongue earlier that afternoon.

There was no fighting the warm, cotton wool cloud of unconsciousness as the horse clamped onto his left cheek and eye socket. The darkness pulled him down. As he departed, Demi screamed at the peak of her ecstasy and he realised that even in death, he'd fulfilled the purpose of his chosen trade.

TIDDLERS
RHYS MILSOM

Stinking. Absolutely stinking. Dunno what he does on the night shift but he don't do much. Probably sits there and wanks into the stars and moon all night. That's probably why he walks funny. All that hide-the-sausage can't be good for you. His bell-end must be raw, chafing all the time.

When I'm here, it's pristine. Floors mopped, mirrors spotless, taps shining, skidmarks gone, enough toilet roll for a small nation. Like Haiti or somewhere.

When I came in here this morning to take over for Pete from the night shift, the place looked like something from one of those TV shows where houses are in disrepair and the people who live in them don't give two flying fucks about it. Cubicles were flooded (but I've told Pete that's *my* job to sort out – if you stick a plunger down the toilets they erupt like projectile sick from a dying alcoholic), toilet roll was swamped to the tiled floor like cysts, and the sinks… well, they were full of spit, spunk and blood rags.

Honestly, I used to think blokes were the dirty species, but it's women who cause the most mess here. All you get in the gents is piss on the floor and urinals lashed with pubes (which are easy to remove with a bit of kitchen roll). But the ladies treat these toilets like a rubbish dump, which you'll get when they're free to the public, I suppose. Bet their houses are a fucking shit tip. Oh, well. The more mess, the better for me.

It's 7am now. Been here an hour and I've just given the ladies the once-over. Sorted the gents out, took about 10 minutes. Few cans and needles in there but that's all right. You've seen one, you've seen them all. No matter how much dried scum, blood or whatever else is congealing on it.

Few people realise how satisfying and pleasing this job is. I took it up after being a dole bum for God knows how fucking long. Those years were the worst. No pleasure, nowhere to get it. No idea how to achieve that ultimate thrill. Week in, week out, tramping down to the jobbies and a suit talking at me: "Now, Mr. Lockley, it's been a while since your last spell in employment and we can see you've applied for things but these jobs are, well, maybe too demanding for you after all your time away from employment. There is a different job opening which we think would be more suitable for you." Over and over again until the suits were just gnashing teeth, twitching fingers and coffee breath.

That is, of course, until this job came up. More suitable. Suitable? My arse! It's perfect. Joy! Satisfaction! Lust! Thrill! Orgasmic! Zen!

I have a little office, too, which I share with Pete. Well, not sharing really. He uses it as a wanking space and I float around in it, watching the screens and checking if the fridge is working because it's always on the blink.

I'm standing in the doorway of the ladies now. The lights are a dull amber, like old traffic lights, and they *zzzz* like a dying fly or a drink fridge in the local offy. There isn't really any smell in here, or perhaps someone with bright nostrils could pick smells out but I can't. Never been one for smells, really.

I step in and check all the cubicles. No one here apart from me. I knew that already. I'd checked the screens before coming in. Habit, I suppose. Habits are good. Habits are what keep me and everyone else ticking along at speed, however quick or slowly we like.

I splash the water on the floor with my feet and it reminds me of that scene in *Mary Poppins*. I grab a toilet brush and hold it up like an umbrella, like it's pissing down, and I start to sing the song from the film that everyone knows. I am Mary. It feels good to be Mary.

Once I finish the song, I put the toilet brush back and start to mop the floor. The puddles soon get soaked up by the dreadlocks of the mop and once that's done, I give the mirrors and taps and sinks the once-over. I then restock the toilet rolls, because even the worst human being deserves to feel less shitty after taking a dump. There's nothing worse than busting your rim and finding there's no toilet roll. Makes you feel really shit. Literally.

After that, I check the cisterns of the toilet. I plunge my hand into the cold water which submerges all the mechanisms. Everything seems in place in each one, so I do my thing and fold thin pieces of wire over the pieces of plastic and metal which allow the toilet flush to work properly. I ram each piece of wire between the tiny spokes and try the flush. It doesn't budge.

My heart flutters and I gasp. My stomach turns and the backs of my knees start to sweat. Oh, dear Lord. Lord, the all-conquering and omnipotent being. Lord, allow me to open the chasms wider and taste the wealthy pools of desire. I get up from my knees and unlock my praying hands. My heart is beating so fast that if I was to claw it out, it would writhe on the floor like a battery-filled dildo: *brrrrr brrrrr brrrrr.*

I dry my soaking hands under the dryer, wipe them on my trousers, and head to the office to fill my pockets.

I unlock the cupboard labelled 'LOCKLEY' and grab four boxes of the little tiddlers I bought online the other day. Have to get little tiddlers because the big ones won't fit. Of course they are far too big. (Don't. Don't argue with me, you prick. Bigger ones would be too obvious. They'd be seen easily. The tiddlers do the job fine. Just fine.)

I go back to the ladies, shouting "Hello, cleaning", so that if anyone's in there, they will know there's another presence about and we can sort ourselves out before it all gets too much. There's no answer. I loiter for a bit in the doorway, but there are no sounds so I head in. I open each cubicle and grab the bottles of bleach from behind the toilets. I know it's not protocol to have bleach on display, but no one knows about it and my higher powers never come to do the routine checks like they're supposed to.

I unscrew each bottle top and slide one tiddler inside. I've made tiny holes in the tops so that the camera, the tiddler, can see. I stick some insulation tape – a tiny smidgeon – to the tiddler so it feels safe and cosy, and then I switch each one on.. When I'm done with the last one I let out a little "Eeeeee," like my mother used to when her breathing apparatus wouldn't work. I'd wait until she went all red like a raspberry and I'd switch the machine back on, laughing so much I'd piss myself and get the floor all wet.

I check my watch. 8:45am. Primetime. I head back to the office and make myself comfy in the chair in front of the screens. The CCTV shows a woman – dressed real smart like a fucking lawyer or something – walking into the toilets. This one's gonna be good. Never had a rich one before, one who probably doesn't even know jobs like mine exist.

My eyes switch from the CCTV to the tiddler vision in the bleach bottle. She chooses cubicle number two and I enlarge the video so that I get every detail. She puts her bag on the floor and her trousers come down. I'm left with an image of her high heels and her calves as she sits on the toilet, and a rewarding *pssss* comes from the screen.

Ah, my fucking divinity. Burn the skies and let the sun full. Collapse the forests and let the animals take over us. Drain the seas and watch the creatures below squirm to their deaths. I'm hard. I tense my cock and feel its power. My sphincter grins and twists and I'm on the floor.

She's pissing the golden stream. It's floating like an ephemera; it escapes like a rat. I can see her, see it; I can feel it, taste it, hold it, smell it, hear it. The crows are singing their occult into my ears, the fingers wiping everything dry, the paper mottled with stains of the bladder's groans. It drips, drips, drips, swirling around the clear water like a hungry eel. This can be the end, the beginning, and everything else that matters and doesn't. The desert starts. The Amazon trees. Vultures circling a rotting corpse and swallowing the maggots.

FUCK MEEEEEEEE!

I open my eyes and see on the screen that lawyer woman has gone, disappeared. I get up from the floor, dust myself off, go to the fridge and grab a Tupperware container that Pete must have washed last night, as it's bone dry and no detritus is inside.

I run to the ladies and lock the door behind me. It clicks into place. I head to cubicle number two and I can smell her perfume, her existence now only believable by the lingering scent. My stomach tightens up and that lovely feeling of orgasmic power washes over me. I kneel down and look at her piss for as long as I can before I have to blink. She must have tried to flush, as droplets of water are crying out from the cistern into the piss. Before it gets contaminated by the fresh water, I drown the Tupperware in the sickly golden liquid, pull it out and lift it to my lips. I brace myself before swilling some around my mouth and feeling the warm saltiness trickle down my throat.

I have to have more.

I swallow and swallow it all like a baby with milk and collapse against the toilet door, feeling my cock spurt cum everywhere inside my boxers. I dream of an Indiana Jones film I saw, the goblet of liquid turning the Tupperware to gold.

A bang on the door wakes me.

I stagger to my feet, my sweaty palms leaning on the frame of the cubicle. I grab the Tupperware and plough it into the toilet, dragging it out and keeping it all intact with the top clicking on. Droplets run down the side of the container and smack on to the floor, making sounds like a hundred parched lips trying to blow kisses.

I unlock the toilet door, smile and barely whisper "Cleaning duties " to the granny waiting outside. Head to the office, open the fridge and store the Tupperware inside.

Pete will be pleased at that one. Plenty for him to wank about tonight.

I sit in my chair and feel the wetness from my cock leaking through my pants and onto my trousers. I put my hand inside my pants and touch it all, then smell it. It smells like how my duvet used to smell when I lived with my mother. She'd never change my sheets.

I text Pete and tell him he's got a little treat waiting for him when he gets here, just as I watch the CCTV and see the granny leave the toilets. I'm tempted to get up off my arse and taste her antique gold but I'm all spent. My phone beeps and I see a text message from Pete waiting to be read.

"GR8 STUFF M8. GOT SUM GD STUFF 4 U 2. CHECK DIS OUT"

As soon as I read the message, another one comes through but this time it's a video. I open it up and the video shows a woman in her 50s tied to a sink in the ladies. Here, at the job. She's crying and bleeding all over, with candles tracing her body like a runway. Next thing, Pete steps into tiddler-view and pisses all over the woman. She tries to flail and shakes like a scared dog. Pete then licks his piss from her body.

The woman is hysterical by then and Pete is laughing so much he pukes all over her. I'm laughing, too. It's great stuff. And it explains the extra mess in the ladies this morning.

Pete gives the camera a wave and then grabs a screwdriver from the sink. The video then switches off.

Probably thinks he's got one up on me now, but I'll show him tonight. It's gonna come around for Pete.

I find the wetness from my cock more or less flooding through my pants after this and I take them off and put them on my face, basking in my own glorious smell. I don't know how long I'm gonna stay like this but I all I can think about is: zen.

ROUTE 66

DAWN CANO

Matt sang "Hotel California" at the top of his lungs as he flew down Route 66 in his 1973 black Chevy El Camino. He had the windows rolled down and his long brown hair whipped around his face, making it hard to see, but he didn't care. Matt was a good-looking man and he knew it. He kept his beard short and neatly groomed despite living in his car, and his body always managed to turn a few heads whenever he stopped for gas or food. However, he did his best not to attract too much attention because he held a secret – a secret that would land him in prison for the rest of his life, if he didn't end up dead first.

He wasn't ready to go down either of those paths though. He wasn't done having fun.

***

As a child, Matt had been different from all the other kids he'd known. He'd taken great pleasure from getting into fights and causing other children pain. As a young boy, he hit, bit, or kicked the others hard enough to make them cry, and he'd laughed as he was dragged to the principal's office.

Matt had also been different in another way: his parents were fucking loaded. His dad was a civil attorney for a large corporation in Dallas and his mom was an OB/GYN at Parkland Hospital. Not only had Matt wanted for nothing, his parents had rarely been home before he went to bed, which had given him all kinds of free time to get into trouble.

Torturing the neighborhood animals that roamed the streets – animals that were safe until Matt became bored – had been one of his favorite pastimes. His favorite animals to torture had been cats, and he'd always tried to come up with new, inventive ways to make their lives a living hell before killing them. At first, he'd tried the usual – sticking firecrackers up their asses and setting them on fire – but those had become boring. What he'd really loved was skinning them with the pocket knife he always carried.

Before skinning one particular friendly black cat with golden eyes he couldn't help but admire, Matt had slit its throat then completely cut off its head, taking care to remove each eyeball, keeping both intact as a sort of trophy. As he'd completed these tasks, he'd imagined doing the same to people. Later that night, he'd taken the cat parts home and hid them in his room, and after his parents went to bed, he'd masturbated onto the cat's fur.

As he'd grown older and stronger, he became the bully everyone feared, and his desire to commit heinous acts likewise grew. He never gave a fuck about what others thought of him. By the time he was sixteen he was permanently kicked out of school and would have ended up in jail if not for his parents' intervention. A year later, in 2001, he left home; he'd had more than enough money to live comfortably out on the road thanks to the savings account his parents had started for him when he was born, and he'd been determined to make his dream of becoming a serial killer a reality.

He'd set out on the highway from Dallas, not knowing or caring where he'd end up.

His first kill had been an easy one, all things considered. When he left town, he'd headed out west on I-20 from Dallas, and a few hours into his trip he'd come across a female hitchhiker. Although she was a little on the chubby side, she'd still caught his attention with her long tanned legs and nice, round ass. He'd stopped in front of her and she'd run to catch up. She'd climbed into his car after seeing his handsome face and chiseled body, and it wasn't long before he had raped, killed, and dumped her body alongside some trees by the road. As is the case with many serial killers, Matt wanted a souvenir but had been undecided as to what to take. He'd removed all her belongings and before he left her, he'd remembered the thrill of removing the cat's eyes. So, using his pocket knife, he'd removed one of the girl's dark brown eyeballs. He hadn't had a chance to figure out what to do with it so he'd popped it into a large water bottle and laughed as it bobbed around in the clear liquid.

In 15 years on the road, Matt had killed 18 people throughout Texas, New Mexico, Arizona and California. Not once had he felt remorse for his actions. He always took one eyeball from his victims and was never choosy when it came to selecting those to kill. Male or female, it didn't matter. Police and the FBI couldn't place him at any of the murders because he was always careful to wear gloves and a condom, leaving little in the way of DNA or evidence to link him to the crimes. And even if they could they'd have a hard time finding him. Matt never stopped long enough for anyone to catch up with him.

Eventually Matt had found himself on Route 66, the 2,400-mile-long stretch of highway that runs from Illinois to California and has plenty of dead spots with very little traffic. Seeing a hitchhiker along this length of road always gave Matt a thrill, and as long as he didn't already have a victim in the car with him, he picked up anyone he saw. During this time of year it got so hot, almost everyone took him up on his offer of a free ride in an air-conditioned vehicle.

Today would be no exception.

***

Right after he passed yet another Indian reservation in New Mexico, Matt came across a man walking down the side of the highway. Even from a distance, Matt could see the man was tall, standing well over six feet, yet he was very thin. He took slow, lumbering steps as though he was tired or beaten down by life.

Matt slowed a few feet in front of the man, then stopped and got out of his car, sizing up his next victim. Not quite as thin as he'd appeared from the distance, but Matt still felt he would be an easy kill.

"Hey, where you headed?" Matt asked the stranger.

"California. You going that far?"

Matt had no intention of taking the guy all the way to California. "Yep. Want a lift?"

The man didn't think twice about accepting the offer. The road was deserted and the temperature was quickly climbing under the midday sun. "That'd be awesome, man, thanks. Name's Justin." Justin held out his hand and Matt took it as he introduced himself.

The two walked back to Matt's car and got inside. As Matt started the engine and turned on the air conditioner, he glanced at his passenger. "Hungry? There's some beef jerky around here somewhere, and you look like you could use something to eat."

Justin replied without looking at Matt. "Nah, I'm good. Thanks, though."

Without another word, Matt pulled the car onto the highway and they headed west toward California. The pair sat in silence except for the *Eagles Greatest Hits* blasting through the car's speakers. After a couple of hours, it was time for a pit stop; the fuel gauge was getting low and both men needed a bathroom break.

Pulling into a truck stop, Matt was first out of the car.

"I think I'm gonna take a quick shower and shave. You good?"

"Yeah, I'm heading in to get something to eat. Want anything? My treat."

"Nothing, man. I've got beef jerky. We need to get back on the road so let's make this fast. I prefer traveling during the night when it's cooler. Let me grab a shower and fill up, then we'll head out."

Matt grabbed the gym bag containing his clothes and toiletries from the back and headed into the store before Justin got out of the car. The last thing they needed was to be seen together, not with what Matt had in mind.

After Matt walked into the store, Justin began snooping. Nothing caught his interest in the glove compartment, so he started looking under the seats. He pulled out a large water bottle, intending to dig around behind it, but as he pushed it out of the way he noticed what was inside. Eyeballs. Eighteen various colored ones in different stages of decomposition. Justin removed the cap and sniffed the liquid. Formaldehyde. After taking another moment to admire its contents, he replaced the lid and put it back where he'd found it.

Where most people would have run or called the police, Justin simply smiled.

***

Justin got out of the car and walked into the store to use the bathroom while Matt filled the gas tank. The two were back on the road within 20 minutes, Matt freshly showered and shaved and Justin highly amused by his discovery. Justin knew exactly what Matt had in mind for him, but Matt had no idea he had picked up the wrong passenger.

After a few minutes, Justin asked, "So, why are you heading to California? Business or pleasure?"

"A little of both, I guess. I take care of business on the way to wherever I'm heading. You?"

"I'm currently unemployed, but hoping to find work in Cali."

Matt smiled to himself as he thought about how Justin wouldn't live to see California. He took his eyes off the road and glanced at Justin, who was staring at him. Justin's eyes were a bright blue, which made Matt happy: he only had two blue eyes in his collection. The two looked at each other for a moment before Matt reached over and turned on the CD player. Popping out the Eagles CD, he put in AC/DC's *Back in Black* and cranked it up.

As Angus Young belted out *Hell's Bells*, Justin thought about his life. Here he was, a forty-year-old man who killed people for fun. He hadn't made a kill in weeks and the more time that passed, the stronger his bloodlust grew. Ever since he was a boy, he had loved learning about the human body and studying various ways to cause pain. He was fond of all kinds of extreme horror and would fantasize about the limits a person's body could endure. Once he'd started killing, he knew he could run almost any experiment he could think of and, as long as he was careful, he could live out his fantasies indefinitely. Justin knew he'd go out in a blaze of glory before he ever spent time in a jail cell. His studies of death meant he knew what happened to a person when they died, and the prospect of death had never frightened him.

Justin had the advantage in the car that day. He knew who Matt was thanks to the bottle of eyeballs, but Matt had no idea what he was up against. Justin knew, despite being a few inches taller than Matt, he'd be outmatched in a fistfight, but he still felt like he had the upper hand.

Once the sun set, Matt pulled the car over to the side of the road.

"Need to take a leak," he said as he climbed out.

Justin suspected Matt had no intention of 'taking a leak.'

Matt walked around the back of the El Camino and Justin kept his eye on him using the passenger mirror. In his mind, this was where the fun would begin.

As Matt reached the passenger side, he was surprised when Justin flung open the door and hopped out. Justin withdrew a long, serrated knife from its sheath tucked into the back of his jeans, and in one swift motion brought it forward, slashing Matt's chest, instantly drawing blood.

Angered, Matt rushed forward, knocked Justin's arm to the side, and tackled him to the ground. The two wrestled, and each found his opponent to be tougher than he'd thought. Punches were thrown and Matt kicked Justin so hard in the ribs he was sure he broke a few. Justin scrambled around trying to find his knife, but on a cloudy night, the blade refused to reveal its location.

Bloody and bruised, Justin finally spoke, gasping for breath between every word. "Shit… man. Eyeballs… really?"

Matt stopped and stared at the other man, taking a moment to catch his own breath. "What the fuck are you talking about?"

"I found the bottle in your car… with the formaldehyde… you're the one who's all over the news! I was hoping I'd run into you, but never thought I'd get lucky enough to actually meet you."

The last statement shocked Matt and he quickly stood up. "Meet me? What?"

"Dude, you're a fucking legend! At least as far as I'm concerned, anyway. The way you remove those eyes from your victims and never leave a trace of DNA or other evidence is brilliant. I just open them up – "

"You… are you kidding me?" Matt interrupted.

"Nah, man. I do the same thing you do, only I don't keep the parts…I'm the one they call The Carver. Maybe you've heard of me."

Matt was still in shock. "So, why the hell would you want to meet?"

Justin smiled a wild grin – not that Matt could see it. "Because I wanna fucking kill you."

That statement made the hairs on the back of Matt's neck stand at attention. Justin tried to get up but Matt reached out and pushed him back down. "Not if I kill you first."

Justin tried again to get to his feet. "Whoa, hold on. Let's make a bet."

"A bet?"

"Yeah, a bet. Look, we both get off on killing people, right? What about this: we both find a victim and we take him or her…"

"Definitely a her."

Justin sighed at the interruption. "Fine, *her.* We both find a victim and take her to a hotel room. We torture and kill her and the one who kills his victim last, makes her suffer the most, wins. Torture has to be part of the plan and we have to have a good time with this. If your victim dies last, you get to kill me. If mine dies last, I get to kill you. We can both use the same methods we've used all along or mix things up a little. What do you say? Are you afraid I'm better than you?"

"How the fuck am I supposed to know what methods you use? I've never heard of you. The only killer I've heard about is the guy who– "

"Serves up his victim's hearts on a plate? That's me."

"Fuck. You still carve pictures and shit into their bodies?"

Matt couldn't see him smile, but he heard it in his voice. "Yep."

"You're on the news almost as much as I am, but they haven't seen you around here before. How do you…"

"Take me up on my offer and find out. My tools are in my backpack and I'm ready to go. There's a truck stop about 50 miles up the road. We can find someone to play with there. You in?"

Matt considered the offer and was confident enough in his abilities to know there was no way he could lose. He was making the news and this other guy wasn't – at least, not as often – which meant he was the better killer. Justin did have nice eyes to add to his collection as well. "Fine, let's do it. How will we know we won't kill each other in our sleep though?"

Justin smiled. "We don't."

"Fair enough. This should be a fun little game, and I can't wait to add one of your pretty blue eyeballs to my collection."

With a laugh, Justin said, "I guess I'll just have to win and see if your heart is red like everyone else's. Or is it black?"

Matt walked around the driver's side and opened the door. "Get your ass in the car before I leave you here. We have women to find."

Justin got up, wincing at the pain in his ribs, and opened the car door. He quickly took inventory of his injuries. Other than a sore fist that had repeatedly connected with Matt's face, his ribs were the only thing that hurt. He gingerly climbed in the car and shut the door.

Matt started the engine, and soon the serial killers were shifting down Route 66.

***

Forty minutes after making their bet, Matt and Justin pulled into the Route 66 Travel Center, a large, brightly lit truck stop right off the highway. Matt rolled up to the pumps and looked at himself in the rear-view mirror, making sure he didn't look too beat up after the brawl. He changed his bloody shirt as Justin got out of the car and walked inside the store to pay for the gas. To stay off the radar, neither man used credit or debit cards and always paid in cash.

Matt filled the tank and walked into the store to buy something to eat. As he entered, he noticed Justin talking to a short blonde with large breasts and tanned legs by the soda coolers. Matt walked past and stared at the couple, worried that Justin had found his victim before he had even begun searching. He picked up a bag of chips and a bottle of Coke and made his way to the counter to pay. Standing in line and looking around the store, he noticed Justin and the girl had gone, but as he waited he noticed one of the cashiers was staring at him. She was tall and thin, with short black hair and several piercings in her ears and on her face, and must have been in her early to mid-twenties. He took a chance and smiled at her, and she smiled back before looking away.

He was next in line and placed his items on the counter. The girl blushed when he smiled at her again. After he paid, she wrote something on his receipt before handing it to him. He waited until he left the store before he looked at it. "Off in 5" was all it said. Matt smiled as he walked back to the car, but as he approached it, he saw Justin and the blonde standing by the back of the El Camino, laughing. Matt had to give him credit: the dude worked fast.

He walked around to them. "What's so funny?"

Justin was still smiling. "Matt, this is Becky. Becky, my buddy Matt. Becky and I are just getting to know each other."

Becky smiled as Matt shook her hand, but neither said anything. Matt sneaked a glance at her boobs before turning around and facing the store, looking for the cashier. After a couple of minutes, she came out the door and stood looking around the parking lot. Matt walked up to her and smiled his best disarming smile.

"Hi, I'm Matt."

She smiled back, seemingly finding the confidence she had lacked inside. "Alex," she said.

Matt couldn't help but notice how cute she looked when she smiled. "Alex, short for…"

"Alexandra," she said. "I've always hated my name, but I can live with the shortened version."

"We're headed over to the... what's it called? Route 66 Casino, I think. I've heard there's a nightclub in there and I want to see how you guys party. Up for it? We can get to know each other a little better."

Alex hesitated before speaking. "Yeah, I'm up for it. I can even show you where it is. Where's your car?"

Matt turned and pointed to his El Camino. "Come on, I'll introduce you to my friends."

They walked over to the car where greetings took place. When it was time to head to the hotel, Justin and Becky sat in the back. It didn't take long for them to reach their destination, thanks to Alex's directions.

They entered the hotel lobby and Matt walked over to the front desk, leaving Justin with the girls. When he returned a few minutes later, he gave Justin an almost imperceptible nod and said, "You guys ready to have some fun?"

They walked into the nightclub where Matt kept the drinks flowing all night long. He told the girls to get whatever they wanted, and they took advantage of his generosity by ordering the strongest, most expensive drinks on the menu. Justin and Matt held back and only had two beers each, and they waited and watched as the girls quickly got drunk. Alex took frequent trips to the bathroom, looking sicker each time, and Becky seemed as though she couldn't stay awake. When the girls were close to passing out, each man grabbed hold of his and made their way out of the club.

Taking the elevator, they made it to the third floor and Matt found the room he'd booked. Using the card key, he unlocked the door and stepped inside, holding Alex's hand. Justin and Becky followed.

The room was nice, with two queen-size beds with red and white duvets against the left wall and a 37-inch wall-mounted flat screen TV opposite the beds. Matt and Alex took the bed farthest from the door and he eased her down onto it. As soon as she lay down, she bolted upright and ran into the bathroom to vomit.

Justin let Becky find her own way to their bed and said, "Damn man, this is a nice room! How much did you pay for it?"

"Enough," Matt replied, throwing the car keys to Justin. "I rented it for three days, which should give us plenty of time to play and get out of town. Go down to the car and get our shit so we can get started."

Justin walked out of the room without another word and came back a few minutes later, carrying his backpack and Matt's large black athletic bag. When he entered the room, Becky was passed out on the bed and Matt was helping Alex get under the covers. Both girls were fully clothed but wouldn't remain so for much longer.

***

Matt opened his bag, pulled out a roll of black duct tape and tore a piece off that was large enough to cover Alex's mouth. He turned to see what Justin was doing and found the other man staring at him. He looked at Becky. "What? You don't know how long she'll be out so you should probably hurry up."

Justin smiled. "Duct tape? Isn't that a little cliché for a serial killer?"

"Shut the fuck up. I don't see you doing anything but smiling like a retard."

Justin held up his hands. "Okay, man. No need to throw insults around." Still smiling, he opened up his backpack and took out twelve feet of thin, yellow nylon rope and began tying up his victim. He wound it around her ankles and tied them to her wrists. He ran the rest of the rope up the length of her body, opened her mouth with one hand, and ran the rope through her mouth, between her top and bottom teeth. He was done by the time Matt finished using the duct tape on Alex's hands and feet. Both men stood back admiring their handiwork.

Matt wondered what Justin could possibly have in his backpack that would enable him to torture and mutilate his victims, but before he could ask, Justin spoke.

"You're first. It's 1:20 am and the timer starts now. Do whatever you want to her, but keep her alive for as long as possible."

Matt turned and looked at Alex and realized he'd forgotten to check her eye color. He reached over and peeled back her right eyelid, but her eyes were rolled up in her head so he couldn't tell. He wanted to wake her up, so he dug around in his bag until he found what he was looking for. He held up a large vegetable peeler and showed it to Justin. "This is how you sober somebody up."

Matt sat next to Alex and picked up her arms, which were still bound at the wrists. He took hold of her index finger with his left hand and, using the vegetable peeler, dragged it down the length of her finger. Unlike peeling a carrot or potato, the skin didn't come off in one long sheet, but rather in small pieces. Blood immediately poured from the wound and despite how much it hurt, Alex didn't awaken. She moaned and tried turning over, but Matt held her in place and continued removing the skin on her finger as Justin watched. By the time he had removed all the flesh, Alex was awake, struggling to scream through the duct tape on her mouth.

Matt stood and stared down at her.

"Good morning!" he said with a smile. "I'm glad I finally have your attention. If you stop screaming, I'll tell you what's going on."

Alex's muffled screams died down to pathetic whimpers as Justin came over to have a look at the skinned finger. "Ouch," he said with a grin.

Matt ignored him and spoke to Alex. "As you know, this is Justin. Justin and I have a little bet going that you girls are going to help us with. I don't know how much time you spend watching the news, but given that you got in a car with a stranger, I'd guess not much. Justin kills people and is the guy who puts his victims' hearts on a plate. Heard of him?"

Alex couldn't say anything but her eyes widened in recognition.

Matt gave her a moment then spoke again.

"And I, well, the press know me as the guy who removes the eyeballs of his victims."

At that, Alex started screaming and struggling to break free.

Matt interrupted her but had to raise his voice to be heard. "You're getting all worked up and I haven't even told you about the bet. See, Justin came up with the idea that whichever one of us can keep his victim alive the longest during several *uncomfortable* procedures gets to kill the other one. Seeing as how I'm the best at what I do, I couldn't help but take him up on his challenge and kill him, but not before teaching him a few things."

Tears flowed out the corners of Alex's eyes and she stared at Matt and Justin pleadingly.

Matt didn't seem to notice as he sat back down on the bed and picked up her hands once again. She tried to sit up which only pissed him off, so he elbowed her in the face, breaking her nose. "Better turn your head to the side, princess. Wouldn't want you choking on all that blood."

As she dealt with her broken nose, Matt began removing the skin from her index finger on the other hand. Alex screamed and struggled anew, but Matt held her down until the finger was completely skinned. He rubbed the gore on the bed and turned around to face her.

Without saying a word, he ran the vegetable peeler down her broken nose, smiling as he held her head in place. After removing most of the skin, he threw the peeler to the floor and stood up. "This is boring. Time for something new."

He reached into his bag, pulled out a thick pair of gloves and put them on. Then he pulled out a thick tree branch. On more careful inspection, Justin noticed it had thorns around the outside. He wasn't sure what Matt intended to do with it, but he had a pretty good idea. Matt also removed a box cutter from his bag.

He moved to the foot of the bed and laid the stick down next to Alex, who looked at it in horror. Using the tool, he made quick work of removing her pants and underwear and stood, staring at her exposed flesh. "I've always been a leg man, and those are some damn nice legs." The sight of Alex lying there half-naked started making Matt horny, but he suppressed his urges and picked up the stick.

He smiled and turned to show it to Justin. "Do you know what this is called?"

Justin shook his head.

"This is called a devil's walking stick. I've had it for a long time but never had the chance to use it. I'm thinking this could be fun."

Justin looked at it and smiled. It was about two feet long and two inches around, but what impressed Justin the most were the two-inch-long thorns encompassing the length of it. This was going to be nasty. He sat down at the foot of the bed and looked at Becky. He wasn't sure how, but she was still passed out, even with all the noise going on.

Matt stepped back to the foot of the bed, kneeling down and gazing at Alex's vagina. "It'd be a shame to mess up that pretty cunt of yours, but I think the blood will be worth it."

Alex tried closing her legs, but Matt held them open and put the end of the stick against her opening. "I'm sorry, sweetheart, but this might hurt a little."

He slowly pushed the stick into her vagina as she writhed and tried to scream on the bed. During those seconds where she was quiet, Matt could hear her flesh rip under the strain of the thorns. He pushed the stick in and pulled it back out, repeatedly fucking her with the thorny branch as she lay thrashing and screaming on the bed. The amount of blood coming out of her surprised Matt and Justin, but it didn't deter Matt from continuing to rape her. Alex eventually passed out and Matt threw the stick and his gloves to the floor.

Justin laughed and spoke. "Shit, man, that was fucking brutal. She's lost a lot of blood. Better make sure she's still alive."

Matt made his way to the head of the bed and felt Alex's neck for a pulse. "She's alive." He removed the tape from her mouth, making it easier for her to breathe. "What time is it?"

Justin checked his watch. “2:42. Surely you can make her last longer than that.”

“I’m nowhere near finished yet, man. Watch and learn.”

Still standing next to Alex’s head, Matt slapped her face until she woke up. “You miss all the fun when you fall asleep.”

Alex immediately realized the tape was off her mouth and began to cry. “You killed it,” she whispered.

“What’s that? I didn’t hear you. Not that I gave you permission to speak, but I’ll let you repeat yourself this one time.”

Alex spoke up as much as she could. She was losing a lot of blood and her strength was fading. “You killed it.”

“What the fuck are you talking about? I haven’t killed anything. Yet.”

Alex sobbed. “My baby. You killed it.”

Matt looked surprised. “You’re pregnant and you wanted to go out drinking with a stranger? What kind of fucked up woman are you?”

“I didn’t think I wanted it.” Alex was crying so hard she couldn’t catch her breath.

Matt looked at Justin. “Does that happen? Can you kill a baby through the pussy?”

Justin shrugged. “Fuck if I know.”

Matt smiled. “Let’s find out.”

As Matt began rooting around in his bag, Justin looked at Becky. She was awake, staring back at him. He looked back to Matt. “Better hurry, man, mine’s awake.” Since Matt wasn’t paying him any attention, he looked at Becky and winked.

***

Matt picked up the box cutter from the floor, opened it, and quickly cut away Alex’s work shirt, exposing her pink bra and bare stomach. He found himself becoming aroused again as he used the knife to cut the front of her bra, exposing her small, firm breasts, but he pushed the sensation down and asked Alex a question. “How pregnant are you?”

Alex looked away and didn't answer.

Matt grabbed her chin, twisting her head toward him. "I asked you a question. How fucking pregnant are you?"

Alex started to cry as she said, "Ten weeks."

"So two-and-a-half months. Why can't you just say that?" Matt released Alex's chin, took the roll of duct tape, tore off a four-inch piece, and placed it across her mouth. Then he knelt down next to the bed while she continued to cry.

"The question we want answered is this: Can you kill a baby by sticking something inside a woman's pussy?" Matt put his hand on Alex's stomach and pressed down, then he looked at Justin, who was rooting around in his backpack.

"I can't feel anything in here. Maybe she's lying, but I know one way to find out." He looked back to Alex and said, "Sorry, sweetheart. This may sting a little."

Using the box cutter, Matt made a deep cut into Alex's abdomen. Alex immediately passed out and blood began pooling at the incision site. Becky turned her head away and even Justin had a hard time watching. Matt pulled the box cutter out of Alex's stomach and made another pass, cutting away layers of skin and fat before stopping and staring at what he'd found.

Encased in a layer of fluid lay a baby. It was the size of a kumquat and Matt could see blood vessels through its skin.

"Fucking hell. She *is* pregnant."

Justin got up to have a closer look. "Shit." He felt for a pulse on Alex's neck and checked his watch as Matt carefully cut the sac holding the baby from her stomach. "The time is 3:32 am and your victim is dead."

"Well that didn't last as long as I wanted, but this is fucking cool. Look at this!"

Justin looked at the bag containing the fetus and felt sick. He'd never seen anything like it, and the baby resembled some kind of alien. "That's disgusting, man. Hurry up and finish what you're doing. It's my turn."

"Just wait a fucking minute. I wanna see this up close."

Matt took the sac out of Alex and watched the baby writhe around. Enthralled by the sight of it, he never noticed Justin untying Becky, or the winks the two exchanged, nor did he notice the hammer in Justin's hand. Matt cut open the sac surrounding the fetus, cursing as the amniotic fluid spilled everywhere. The fetus wriggled around for a few seconds, then lay still.

Matt dropped it back onto Alex's stomach and turned around to see Becky standing by the door and Justin coming at him with the hammer raised.

***

As Justin brought the hammer down, Matt raised his arm, shielding his face from the blow. The force of the strike cracked Matt's left arm and he hissed in pain, dropping the box cutter. Breathless, he smiled and asked Justin, "This is how you wanna play?"

Justin raised the hammer. "I told you I was gonna kill you."

"You can try." Matt raised the box cutter and, as Justin brought his arm down again, he lashed out, making a deep cut in Justin's shoulder. It didn't seem to faze him and he went after Matt again, aiming for his head. Matt ducked in time and the hammer hit empty air. When Matt stood up, he punched Justin in his stomach as hard as he could. Justin stumbled backwards, the air escaping his lungs in a huge *whoosh*. As Justin recovered, Matt thrust the box cutter at Justin's face. The big man was struggling to catch his breath and failed to move out of the way in time to avoid a huge gash across his right cheek. Justin's blood ran down his face as Matt quickly moved to the side and kicked him in the ribs. Justin lay gasping on his side and Matt stomped on his right wrist, causing it to break with a sickening crunch.

Both men were now down to one usable arm and Justin was bleeding heavily from the cut on his face. Matt stopped to catch his breath while Justin struggled to get to his feet.

Matt started laughing. "Here we are, two notorious serial killers in a battle of evil versus evil. I thought it happened by chance, the two of us running into each other, but you've had this planned all along, haven't you? Lure me somewhere and try to kill me? Clever, but it's a shame I'm better at what I do. You're gonna die and I'll add your eyeballs to my collection. I have to give you credit for trying, though. That took a lot of balls."

Justin was still catching his breath. "I've been following your movements for a while now, hoping to catch up with you and prove I'm a better killer than you are. Becky, my wife, keeps track of you when I'm out on the road and I promised her that when I found you, I'd let her come along. When she discovered you were running along Route 66, we decided to head out here and put an end to you."

By the time Justin got to his feet, Matt was coming after him again with the box cutter, but fatigue made him clumsy. This time, Justin moved out of the way and grabbed the hammer he had dropped on the floor. In one swift movement, he brought the hammer down on the back of Matt's head. The hammer went right through the bottom of Matt's skull. Justin stepped on Matt's back and pried it loose, hitting him over and over, laughing at the sound of Matt's skull cracking. By the time he finished, Matt's head was nothing more than a jumbled mash of brains, blood and bone.

Justin threw down the tool and dug through Matt's pockets, taking his money and his car keys, then looked over at Becky, who was standing in the corner by the door.

"Almost ready, babe."

He walked over to the bed and picked up his backpack. Knowing Matt had rented the room for three days meant they would be long gone before anyone discovered the bodies, and he had no worries about the police finding his DNA all over the crime scene. He had plenty of money and could exchange cars when they got out of New Mexico, having plans to head east, maybe toward Virginia or possibly even Florida.

Justin took his backpack into the bathroom and closed the door. He took a quick shower and changed out of his bloody clothes. Wearing a black t-shirt, jeans, and black sneakers, he strode out of the bathroom and grabbed Becky around the waist. The two kissed passionately before walking out the hotel room, but before the door closed, Justin took the "Do Not Disturb" sign off the back of it and hung it on the front.

Justin and Becky walked out of the hotel arm in arm, got into Matt's car, and drove off into the sunset, free to kill another day.

ROSE ABOVE

STUART KEANE

You remove the eight-inch blade from the corpse with minimal effort. You're meticulous, careful. You've done this on several occasions following precise protocol, a process of rules and regulations that protects you from the law. They'll never find you because they can't. No DNA, no evidence, and no clues.

The perfect crime.

Seven perfect crimes, in fact.

You place the dripping knife on the floor at the side of the body, gloved fingers positioning it parallel to the still-twitching arm. You push the legs of the body apart with the tip of your plastic-coated boot, and the tightly bound baggy that tickles your ankle rustles as you position your latest victim in the required pose. You look around and check the essential points: A, B, C, D, E. All done. You nod with satisfaction. Following the MO.

No one will catch you. It's impossible.

However, times have changed. Impossible is more than possible now. The laws of the new world, a world ushered in by the unthinkable, permit it.

But you still have the burning urge to quench that thirst.

The thirst for bloodshed.

New world or not, you still need to feed.

And feed you shall.

***

Rosemary Ost set a square of dark chocolate onto her tongue gently. Folding the wrapper back, creased red paper bound around crinkled golden foil, she stored the half-eaten chocolate bar in her pack. Three seconds later, she withdrew the confectionary into her mouth. Her diamond tongue stud twinkled in the daylight and clinked as it tapped against her teeth. The molten delicacy slid to the bottom of her mouth, and she smiled, curling a stray strand of ebony-coloured hair behind her ear.

Suck, not chew. Lasts longer that way.

Wise words from a wise man.

A very wise man.

Rose closed her eyes, pushed the thought from her mind, and focused on the chocolate. The rich flavour, the bitter but sweet taste of ground cocoa beans and sugar, a unique taste that always reminded her of coffee. She felt the chocolate melt and ooze beneath her tongue, felt it soften. Within a minute, it was nothing but a brown paste, a sour tasting liquid. She rolled her tongue, enjoyed the flavour for a few seconds, and swallowed.

Sliding her sleeve back, Rose clicked two buttons on her watch. It made a soft bleep as the timer started. The numbers began counting backwards. In three hours, she could afford to consume another square of chocolate.

Rationing was a new process to her, but vital and essential to staying alive.

With her mid-morning snack out of the way, she stood and walked through the damaged train carriage, her feet muffled by the plush carpet. Rose was yet to find a safer haven in the devastation she now called normality. Flicking her gaze around the shadowed interior, she realised she'd made a wise move. Small, compact, basic amenities, barricaded windows, far enough away from the main cities and protected by live rails – it was the perfect encampment for a woman on her own, left to fend for herself.

She stopped at the bottom of a bowed ladder, breathed deeply, and began to climb. Rose emerged on the roof of the beaten carriage, the sudden humid wind whipping her in the face. She held an arm out to shield her eyes against the morning sun, felt her hair caress the nape of her sodden neck, and finished the climb. The breeze eased off. The woman took a step, sighed, and stared across the landscape before her.

Nothing had changed in three weeks.

A city wracked with devastation, torn to shreds, annihilated and dangerous. In the distance, several apartment blocks stood on a steep knoll smothered in overgrown grass, battered and broken, every shard of glass blasted from their windows and doors and skylights. The faded red bricks are scorched black in places, streaked and oiled with severe heat, the results of a brutal firefight four days earlier. Two groups of people had collided and faced off, a duel to the death. Guns had blazed. Hand grenades had exploded. Limbs and heads had collapsed to nothing but visceral mulch under the immense firepower. Screaming women and children had fallen and rag-dolled in a blaze of crimson mist and bullets. No one had survived and no one had stood a chance.

She remembered thinking: *No one got up.*

She'd watched it happen in the space of seventy adrenaline-fueled seconds from the confines and safety of her carriage, undetected. Rose remembered catching her breath. Sixteen people, dead in a matter of moments.

Several questions had tapped on her mind's eye, insistent, nagging. Why was this happening? What caused it? Why was society collapsing?

She didn't know the root cause of the chaos, what had brought on the sudden change in humanity, a terrifying alteration that tore the very fabric and bodice of society apart. Civilisation was self-destructive at the best of times, but this was something completely different, ungodly, and otherworldly.

Terrified, she hadn't emerged from the carriage for twelve long hours, not until she was certain no one had survived.

No one got up.

She'd conjured a plan to go out at dark, silent and fast, to collect the guns and bring them back. But firearms caused a lot of racket. They could give away her location and attract people to it. There was also the risk of the guns backfiring if she was so inclined – or forced – to use them for self-defence. She'd never used a gun, let alone maintained one.

After much deliberation, she'd forgotten about them, changed her mind. Maybe she could sell them, maybe not. Maybe currency no longer mattered in this topsy-turvy world, and maybe guns made you a prime target. They got you dead, that was for sure.

It was less hassle to leave them.

Anyway, that was three days ago.

She hadn't seen any movement near the bodies since, no animals or even a rat. Nothing preyed on the corpses. No one came. The thought of the weapons was still present, tickling the back of her brain, tempting her. Rose shook her head with finality, putting the thought to bed.

No. Leave them.

She stared at the buildings, noting the multiple windows, cracks and fissures. No one was out there, not a living soul, not anymore. Three weeks was enough time for the human race to start relocating, to start finding an alternative home.

Was it long enough to usher in extinction?

Rose shuddered at the grisly thought.

She turned and glanced down at the rails holding the carriage: two slick, shiny strips of metal shooting off into the distance, vanishing into a small dark tunnel on the horizon. The tunnel was preceded by two platforms built of concrete, both of which were cracked and worn, their yellow safety lines faded and unmaintained – human negligence before the events, not after. The track was in excellent condition. Wooden sleepers, peppered with multi-coloured stones and debris, idled in the afternoon sun. Rose traced them with her eyes, up and down, several times. It relaxed her, soothed her. She was at home here.

For now.

So far, the live rail had been her ultimate savior, buried in overgrown grass and foliage. The carriage, shrouded by nature, stood alone on high wheels slicked with dark oil and grime. The wheels sat comfortably on the rails, adding another few inches of height to the carriage, which stood about twelve feet in all. No steps led up to the carriage doors, and the four doors – two left, two right – were solid, all tightly barricaded.

Her only means of access was the emergency roof hatch. To get to the roof, she needed to use another ladder that rappelled down the side of the train to the ground, except if she did that in the carriage's current position, it would land directly on the live rail. Instant electrocution. So Rose had modified the ladder with a hook of sorts, bending the bottom few feet upwards like a metallic letter J. When the ladder rolled down, it rested above the live rail, allowing her to climb down and scoot around the side of the carriage to safety.

She smiled, glancing at the modified folding ladder beside her.

No access. Safe as houses.

For now.

Rose knew it wouldn't last forever; the power would cease at some point and render the carriage vulnerable. Rail or no rail, ladder or no ladder, people would eventually find the carriage and become intrigued. It wouldn't take much to knock down the flimsy wire fence that separated the tracks from the knoll. No humans equaled no services or power. No laws meant scavenging. Time was against her.

Rose became aware of a fleck of shadow in her peripheral vision, off to the left. Keeping calm, she turned her head, watching carefully. She scanned the buildings, a desolate children's playground between her and the crumbling structures. A toppled striped roundabout lay on its side, the earth and rubber padding beneath cracked and buckled. Dark dirt lay strewn from its breached mooring point, the pattern of which reminded her of blood spatter from a gunshot wound. She flicked her eyes back to the devastation once more and looked at the fallen women and children. A white shirt pocked with blood flapped in the wind like a poor excuse for a surrender, the sound lost on the distance between them.

Rose ignored the crippled swing set and collapsed gazebo and returned to her vigil. A brief movement. Someone walking behind a fractured wall, the movement a result of a mere glimpse through said cracks. She followed the wall with her gaze, crouching as she did. Rose leaned on the lip of the carriage, her chin on the backs of her hands, a metal indentation obscuring her from view. Whatever it was, and whatever it was doing, it was running out of wall. Two seconds more and they would walk into the open. If they were foolish enough.

One.

Two.

A shuffling, shambling figure fell into view.

Rose felt a small pang of fear deep inside her. Frozen in two minds, she wanted to rear away and climb back inside, but found she couldn't move from the spot. She caught her breath. The figure continued on its wobbly jaunt, unbalanced, stumbling on several occasions, ignoring everything around it. Its right shoulder thrust out aggressively before the awkward legs could gather pace beneath, as if a nervous twitch was guiding the figure. Its feet poked inwards, the arms dangled inertly by its side. She didn't see the casual gait of a person walking to a destination, usually indicated by confident, swinging arms and a measured pace.

Reaching for her pocket, she slipped a small pair of binoculars from their home and placed them to her eyes. She groaned when she realised what it was.

A 'non-person.'

Non-person. Her lips moved silently, retracing the term in her head, comprehending the very word itself. Corpse, entity. She didn't know what to call it. It wasn't human; therefore, 'non-person' was appropriate.

Rose refused to use the Z word.

To her, the dreaded Z word was pure fiction, imaginary, impossible. Pure horror legend. They existed as fodder in comic books and TV shows and movies. One of her favourite genres, true, but still fictional. The genre boomed in the '80s and had lingered on the precipice of cultural folklore, producing some cracking cinema in the process.

But Rose refused to believe that the world she lived in was succumbing to the zom – the 'non-people.' There was just no way. It was preposterous!

"They aren't zombies," she uttered to herself. "They can't be."

Rose sighed, resigned to the fact that the word was entering her mature train of logical thought. She shook her head, her eyes not leaving the shambling figure in the distance. This was the first sighting of one in three weeks.

'Non-people' or zombies or rotting corpses – whatever they were called, one thing was clear: the train carriage was compromised, no longer safe.

"Shit," she uttered.

***

Rose dropped some supplies into her pack: three bars of chocolate, a pack of Kinder Eggs, two cans of soup, a box of cheese crackers, a flashlight, a Swiss Army knife, and three shirts. She also packed her beaten paperback copy of *Alice in Wonderland*, her favourite book. She'd packed light when she evacuated her home, aware of the dangers, and she'd never looked back. The grand sum of her possessions left a lot to be desired, but it guaranteed her safety. Weight leads to noise and hindrance, and those can get you killed. Pack light, easy flight.

Rose glanced at her watch and nodded, content.

Casting one final look over the carriage, and feeling her heart sink a little at leaving it all behind, she sighed and walked to the ladder. She climbed it for the final time and emerged on the roof. Rose surveyed the scene. She was clear. She picked the bent ladder up and lowered it over the side, the metal twinkling in the sunlight. Rose carefully scaled it to the ground. She stepped sideways and slid around the outside, dropping safely onto the sleepers with a crunch. Composing herself, she stepped over the rails, ambled to the fence, tossed her pack over, and climbed it. Within seconds, she flipped over the top and landed on the grassy knoll. Then she retrieved her pack, swiped her hair from her face, and starting walking with purpose, heading for the main road.

Where do I go?

The 'non-person' was gone; she'd watched it disappear around the corner of a gutted American diner, its windows missing, the red leather and stainless steel décor of the establishment shining and colourful and sleek, a stark contrast to the world around it.

Rose headed in the opposite direction, avoiding the main city. She followed the road north, turning to glance back at the diner and the silent metropolis beyond it. In the distance she could see the once dominant structure of Big Ben, its brown shell shattered and broken, the mutilated clock face a shadow of its former self. The spire on top of the tower curled at an angle, bent and mangled around a crashed airplane that sat atop it. A jagged hole gaped in the roof, displaying the bent cogs and workings of the proud landmark. It no longer chimed.

London was a death zone, a surefire way to get herself killed. She'd not been there herself, not since the world had collapsed around her, but Rose remembered watching the last-ever TV broadcasts before the signal was cut. Swarms of 'non-people' had milled around the streets in droves, invading Piccadilly Circus and Trafalgar Square, biting and eating anyone unlucky enough to stumble into their bloodthirsty paths. Within hours, the mortally vapid concrete of London had been streaked with dark crimson, captured gloriously on the most advanced High Definition cameras, which had filmed from the relevant safety of floating police and news helicopters.

Dismembered bodies had lain strewn in mangled pieces, their blood-soaked attackers walking around in a comatose daze, vermillion dripping, seeking their next meal. A red double decker bus had burned bright in the crumpled window of a Barclays bank, the passengers burnt to a black, charred heap. One woman had been carrying a baby under her arm, backing away from one of the attackers, unable to defend herself and her child from its assault. Her death had been imminent, but that's when the cameras had ceased and, Rose imagined, the TV studios had succumbed to the madness like everyone else.

Rose walked for a while, enjoying the eerie silence, the journey familiar but strange, the landscape of normal life blotted and altered by the chaos erupting around her. She recognised the road she was ambling along, familiarity tickling at the base of her brain, but her memory failed her, denied her answers.

After fifteen minutes, she paused and narrowed her eyes. The road ahead led to a small cul-de-sac consisting of six small houses. All modern, each designed identically to its neighbours, positioned acutely around a massive curved scallop of black asphalt. Each house sat behind a tired strip of faded lawn and a crazy-paved pathway. White picket fences lay in pieces on the tarmac, bent and shattered. Despite the minimal destruction, nothing moved. The stillness associated with a lack of life was heavy, obvious. Rose could feel it, sense it.

Comfortable and safe. The suburbs at work.

The familiarity tickled her brain once more. She ignored it.

Rose approached the cul-de-sac with caution, stepping through overgrown grass with light, crunching footsteps. A red Mazda sat in the nearest driveway, a black Porsche with its passenger door ajar in the driveway opposite. The other four were empty, vast expanses of smooth concrete with faded oil stains and broken leaves from the overhanging trees. Rose ducked behind a huge oak trunk and waited, watching. She sensed no movement and no threat. All six houses were silent, but she didn't intend to use a front door. Too obvious. Anyone could be waiting for her in there, or out here, hidden in a number of locations.

Rose ambled on by, feigning ignorance, walking past the most-central house with abandonment, like someone passing through. Anyone watching would think she was leaving, gone, never to be seen again.

Which was the plan.

Once behind the house, she strayed to the left and hid against a wall. She felt cold brick brush against her side, her pack scraping the coarse wall, her top riding up an inch or two to reveal bare pale skin above her beltline. She ignored it and shuffled sideways, taking in the garden before her. A cheap set of table and chairs, the former skewed with a plastic umbrella, stood before her, covered in crumbled leaves and muck. A dead pigeon, its innards splattered on the nearest seat, lay inert, its vacant eye staring at her. Rose swallowed and carried on.

She found the backdoor and tested it. Locked.

She lifted her legs over a knee-high red brick wall and found herself in the next garden. A tall fence separated the houses, providing her adequate cover to scoot to the next property. She traversed the plain concrete and stepped around the edge of a swimming pool, its plastic cover creased, the water rippling gently with the mild breeze. She approached the backdoor, stepping past some children's toys, paused, and pushed the handle down.

It opened.

Result.

Rose breathed out, a flush of heat washing through her face. Memories of being a rebel teenager, beyond curfew and sneaking home, came rushing back to her.

Pushing the access slowly, she stepped into the property. She slid through the door and closed it gently behind her. She breathed out and turned around.

A man stood there, a dead body at his feet. A knife covered in blood lay beside the corpse.

"Don't move," he uttered.

Rose didn't react, but she didn't raise her hands either. She took a gentle step backwards, putting an extra few inches between her and the mysterious man. Her feet found stiff laminate flooring, cheap and buckled, probably by damp. It squeaked beneath her.

"I said don't move!"

She knew a handbook didn't exist that explained the 101 rules of the apocalypse, but she did know one thing: Power was king. You show weakness, and you're a dead woman.

So she didn't. She just stood there.

Her eyes latched on to the man's fingers, which curled before him, held away from his body. She recognised the gesture; she did it every time she washed her hands, the conscious moments before you obtain a towel to dry yourself. One of many daily motions forgotten in the chaos. He simply stood there, holding them out like a poor excuse for a weapon. Even in the gloom of the house – the only brightness provided was by the sunlight through the kitchen window to her left – she saw they glistened and dripped with blood. She heard steady droplets hitting the floor. *Tap. Tap. Tap.*

The man wasn't armed, but he was wiry, flinching. She could see his contemplable sneer, all creases and hard lines, his bottom lip quivering, jutting towards her. His body was moving, as if a constant shiver pulsated through his torso. Wired and alert. His small frame looked harmless enough, but it was the unknown chemistry going on within that made Rose nervous.

His eyes also worried her. A blistering menace flickered behind them. No hint of sorrow or guilt or hesitation in them whatsoever. The orbs were void of softness, brimmed with a lack of empathy, and contained no morsel of humanity. The eyes looked hungry, starved, as if he was in the middle of completing a task that would quench an urge or satisfy an urgent need. The clues tied together in a little bundle. She didn't need to look at the body for a second time to realise what was happening here.

Serial killer.

Get out.

"I'm sorry to intrude," she said. "I'll be going now."

"You stay there," he said, sputum dribbling down his chin. "You move, and my dead friend here will have a new companion."

Rose said nothing.

The man turned and walked to the sink. He hesitated for a second, clearly uncomfortable with his task. He looked from his blood-soaked hands to the tap and back again. A smile crept across his lips and he nodded. "Put the bag down."

Rose did as she was instructed, placing her pack on the floor.

The man smiled. "Good. Now, get over there, by the body."

Rose remained where she was.

The man scooped a knife from his belt, held it underarm, and pointed it at her. She heard blood squelch on the handle. "Do it or I'll spill your insides all over the floor!"

Rose nodded, waited a second, and sidestepped to the body. She kept her hands by her side, her eyes on her foe, wishing she'd put her Swiss Army knife in her pocket.

The mysterious killer watched her cross the room and nodded. "Good. Now, sit in the armchair."

Rose lowered herself. The leather squeaked beneath her pert rump.

"Put your arms on the arms, palms flat."

Rose acquiesced to his demands. Her eyes remained on him.

"Excellent. You're good at obeying instructions. You wouldn't believe the people who blather and whine and end up with a fork in the fucking eye. I wish people would just do as they're *told!* Things would be so much easier."

Rose said nothing.

The man nodded. "You just earned yourself a reprieve. I won't kill you just yet. If you move, I'll hear you, I'm the fucking *zenith!* I can turn and throw this knife at you from any angle. Ask yourself: Is it worth it?" He chuckled and turned the tap on. Water splashed the metal sink. He washed his hands quickly and wiped them with a towel. Satisfied at the rush job, he bent down, zipping his bag closed. He straightened up and walked to the body, prodded it with his toe.

Rose glanced at the mutilated corpse on the floor. It was a complete mess. The face was a battered pulp – broken pink bones and severed muscle and ruptured skin. Blood still dripped from multiple, ragged open wounds, forming a dark pool around its head. Fluffy black hair lay on the carpet beside the corpse, like a discarded toupee, recently scalped. The pink flesh underneath glared at her, crinkled and creased. She noticed the jaw was hanging off, wavering on the slight, humid breeze.

The familiarity tickled her brain once more. She still couldn't place it.

The torso was slit from throat to naval, a long slim cut, perfectly executed. Precise pincers, which looked like elongated, blunt scissors, pulled back the flesh in large unequal flaps, exposing the blood-soaked ribcage. Several of the organs sat on the carpet too, in line, organised, as if the serial killer had been preparing them for something. The rest of the body seemed intact, but for the first time, Rose noticed the victim was also naked.

"Admiring the handiwork?" the man uttered, still keeping his distance.

Rose flicked her eyes to him. "Naked?"

The man nodded. "All part of the fun. For me, anyway. It's a big 'fuck you' to the police. Nothing worse than a naked man shaking and flailing, leaving skin and hair and spit and shit everywhere. And the evidence shows he suffered horribly. Nothing quite like making a police officer spill his guts. It's quite the achievement."

Rose looked around the room. *Keep him talking.* "How do you know they throw up?"

The man tapped his temple. A dull fleshy thud echoed across the room. "I'm one of them. I do my business, get out of dodge, get dressed into my uniform and turn up with the rest of them. Easy. No one suspects a thing. The police are thick as shite sometimes. Always helps to insert a little misdirection here and there." The man chuckled, closing his hand into a fist.

Rose narrowed her eyes. "There are no police. Haven't you seen outside?"

"The police will always exist, young lady. There's always a law to follow, and always a law to be broken. Even now, with the dead walking the streets and the living fearing for their very existence, that law still exists to keep us striving, keep us alive, as a race and individuals. Just because there are less of us, doesn't make it so."

Almost there, she thought. *Keep him talking.* "What about DNA?"

"DNA? Please. I have access to the crime scenes, both before and after. It's not hard to contaminate DNA and make it unusable. That's the wonder of humans relying on technology. It's come on in leaps and bounds, but when you drop some hydrogen peroxide into the mix, it royally screws it up for the chemical reaction analysis. Anything is possible if you put your mind to it."

Rose nodded. "So you leave DNA behind?"

"Yes. Why bother worrying about it when you can sabotage the tests? It's like a proverbial Get Out Of Jail Free card."

Keep him talking. "You a Monopoly fan?"

The man tilted his head. "I don't have time for games. You're beginning to test my patience. I have a job to do."

Rose clenched the arm of the chair. "Why do you do it?"

The man clapped loudly, shocking Rose. She flinched, but remained in her seat.

He laughed. "And there's the clincher. Why does everyone come around to it? People are so fucking nosy!"

Rose said nothing. She flicked her eyes to the door, then back to the man. The familiarity now burned the inside of her skull, jabbing it like a hot poker. She prepared. Tensed.

She knew. Understood.

He continued. "Someone needs to do it. I always hated the idea of hunting animals, poor defenseless bastards. Why bother when you can participate in a real sport?"

Rose nodded. "So you enjoy it? What a sad lonely life you must lead."

The man stepped forward, said nothing.

Rose continued. "It's pathetic. You should be ashamed of yourself."

She noticed a change in his posture, a tensing in his shoulders. His cheeks reddened, and the black orbs darkened, misted over.

She knew her time was up. One question too far.

He twisted the knife in his hand and held it downwards.

Rose shook her head. "I'll shut up now."

The man chuckled. "Yes. Permanently."

He walked forward, the gleaming blade aimed at Rose's heart. He stepped from the kitchen tiles to the carpet, his footfalls changing from loud to soft within half a second, and lunged towards Rose.

She leapt out of the chair and landed beside him. She heard the knife whistle on the air, inches from her neck. It sliced into the leather cushion, where her torso had been.

With all his weight now in the chair, Rose struck out, kicking the attacker in the knee. She heard the patella pop and explode, the pressure pushing the joint sideways unnaturally far. His leg buckled and bent, crunching as his entire weight slipped right and tore every ligament around the cap.

The man screamed. Rose punted him in the side, lifting him and the knife away from her. He released his grip on the weapon and dropped it onto the chair. Then he collapsed over the arm, flopping to the floor in a tangled heap. Loud moans of agony emitted from his mouth as he scrambled to regain his composure.

Not going to happen, Rose thought. *You just shattered his knee. Muscle and ligaments and cartilage and bone. He'll need crutches for the rest of his life.*

Rose scooped up the knife slowly and twirled it in the air, stalking the injured man. He rolled onto his back, dragged his body across the carpet and pulled himself up against the wall. Tears streamed down his face and pink sputum dribbled from his mouth.

Rose smiled. "My, how the tables have turned."

He said nothing, a wet whimper in his throat.

"You think you're a hot shot? Huh? You're a fraud, a nobody, a fake. You're disgusting."

The man narrowed his eyes and stared at her.

Rose smirked. "You give us all a bad name."

She stabbed the knife upwards and into his chin, hard. The blade shredded through knotted muscle and slick skin and severed his tongue down the middle. The loud punch associated with penetrated flesh filled the room. The blade scraped against the back of his teeth, creaking and groaning against the enamel, and probed the roof of his mouth. Blood squirted from the open orifice, dribbling down his chin and splattering Rose in the face. She smiled.

"You're a disgrace. No serial killer worth his or her salt ever leaves DNA at a crime scene. We follow a code, a set of rules. DNA is the one thing that can ruin our crusade, the one thing that can put an end to the justice we serve. If you have a hunger, a thirst even, you do anything and everything to ensure it remains satisfied. Even in this… this abomination of a world, where the dead walk and the pathetic rule all."

Rose twisted the knife sideways. It squeaked against his teeth like nails on a chalkboard, pushing several to the side. His gums split and blood sluiced down his throat. A wobbling tooth pinged to the floor, clattering away beneath a table. The wound in his chin opened further, sluicing a mass of crimson into his lap. The man let out a muffled howl as the blade shredded the roof of his mouth.

"My thirst for bloodshed is unlimited, but I don't cut corners or hide behind a fucking uniform to do it. And I don't claim kills that aren't rightfully mine. This body over here?" Rose pointed to the corpse. "I know you didn't do this. You don't have it in you. The right pep, the right… attitude. I see weakness in your body. When it comes to a harmless woman – because that assumption of me worked out well – you're all balls and bravado, but when it comes to a man, well, I imagine you keep quiet and hide in the corner behind your newspaper or porno magazine or a filthy keyboard. I'll give you credit; you have the eyes for it. Kudos on that. It's the toughest part, but it's nothing but empty threats. A façade, a front. Like playing a part in a movie. Am I right?"

The man stared at Rose, incredulous.

She twisted the knife more. Teeth screeched on enamel. The man howled, spraying blood onto Rose's hand.

She firmed up her grip, feeling the hot blood trickle between her fingers. "Tell me the truth. This kill wasn't you, was it?"

The man slowly shook his head. Tears rolled down his face.

Rose chuckled. "I thought not. Sure, you roughed him up a little, kicked him about like a big boy. After all, a dead body can't fight back. Then you found the knife and decided to try it out, go to work on him a little. After all, no one will stop you. The world is a different place now."

The man began to sob. "Darrrnn ssoooorrree," he uttered.

"You're sorry?" Rose asked.

He nodded.

"Unfortunately, I can't forgive you. It takes skill and practice to follow our code, to quench our bloodlust, and a competent serial killer should be able to kill a target without leaving a single trace. But a serial killer who falls at the first hurdle – a chicken-shit sociopath, basically – will never amount to anything. And taking someone else's kill? Well, you might as well fuck your brother's wife. If you kill competently, fair play. If you can't, you're a fucking amateur. And the amateurs don't get a chance to headline the main event."

Rose shoved the blade upwards, slicing through the roof of his mouth, crunching behind his eyes and into the brain. She felt the knife stop, and watched as his eyes rolled into the back of his head. His chest ceased to inflate. His body went limp.

Rose closed her eyes and smiled.

Another perfect crime. The impossible is possible.

And because of the apocalypse, it isn't changing any time soon.

Rose ran her fingers through her hair, breathing out slowly, pushing it back against her scalp. She sighed and walked over to the body, prodded it with her toe once again, like before, but there was no rustle of a plastic booty this time. The mangled face leered up at her, the bones smashed to pieces, the eyes lopsided and swaying on their twisted optic nerves.

All her hard work and hours of preparation, destroyed.

So much for the MO.

She glanced at the mysterious man behind her. His body lay slumped against the wall, the knife handle protruding from his chin.

Oh well. No one will ever know.

And you never claim another killer's kill. A wise man once said that.

She tried to force the thought from her brain. This time, it stuck. She felt a tear roll down her warm cheek. The stench of decay hung heavy in the air. She bent down and smiled. Then she addressed the wise man in question, stroking his shredded cheek.

"Hey, Dad."

TAMING THE TONGUE
CHAD LUTZKE

The sun beamed down on the ice in Tim's cup, intermittently catching his eye as the cubes shifted like misshapen disco balls in the brown, refreshing drink. He downed the rest of the tea and looked into the cup. It was stained near the bottom from 364 days of partaking in his new habit.

Before last summer, Tim had never been much of a tea drinker. It was for old folks, along with naps, bifocals, and complaining. But for the past year the drink had acted as a reminder of how sometimes things just happen that need to happen. They have a way of working themselves out.

Like two summers ago when a tremendous storm had ripped through the neighborhood, knocking the power out for days, even uprooting several trees – one of them being in Tim's front yard. The monstrous thing had crushed the roof of his front porch. Initially Tim had found himself distressed over the destruction, but within two weeks he was cashing a two thousand dollar check from his insurance company and stacking a full cord of free firewood against the garage for the following winter.

And last summer there was Mrs. Lawrence…

Things happened all in due time. Life wasn't a mistake, and neither were its happenings.

***

Mrs. Lawrence brought a unique degree of chaos with her, concealed well inside a petite, wrinkled body that was hunched far closer to the ground than it should be. At first glance the old woman gave a gentle demeanor with a face that cracked like tree bark when triggered by a smile. Eighty-five summers under a California sun had built the tanned hide she'd worn.

Her pride and joy was her garden. An abundance of flowers, herbs, and even mushrooms covered the ground in organized clusters throughout her backyard, butting up to the wooden fence dividing her property from Tim's. A gate sat oddly placed along the fence, opening to each lawn. Mr. and Mrs. Lawrence – being the original owners of both houses – in their younger years had built the gate to make room for a riding mower in order to conveniently mow both lawns. Tim had purchased the home three years ago, and the rickety gate still stood.

After Tim bought the house, he, of course, tended to the lawn himself. The outdoor maintenance had helped him get through his divorce. Energy once used on scheming ways to keep his cheating wife was then spent putting to shame even Mrs. Lawrence's colorful backyard canvas. But while the old woman's green thumb gave vibrant life to an otherwise cramped piece of land, over the years her mouth had torn down the once-strong foundation that was her World War II veteran spouse.

Mr. Lawrence often ignored his wife's verbal abuse, but Tim could tell over time the relentless belittling had softened the man from a sturdy brick wall to an absorbent castle of sand, slowly eroding. The upright walk he once held had become a slumped crawl, by no fault of his aging spine but that of his wife's venomous tongue.

The woman's nagging often played as a soundtrack to Tim's hard work in the yard. He did his best to tune out the disparaging words, but accented bits like 'useless,' 'no good,' or 'idiot' often penetrated his ears – a cringe-worthy chorus on otherwise beautiful days. At times Tim would watch from afar as Mr. Lawrence stood calmly with his broken ego, absorbing each blow from his unrelenting hag of a wife.

However, Mrs. Lawrence didn't limit her gripes and criticisms to just her husband. Through the summer months in particular, Tim often received verbal lashings himself concerning his dog and its bark seemingly directed toward Mrs. Lawrence alone.

"That hellhound of yours runs out here and scares the holy out of me," she'd complain.

It was true. Tim's German shepherd, Shadow, had no qualms about loudly declaring his opinion of Mrs. Lawrence to the rest of the neighborhood.

"I come out here to relax, not suffer a stroke because you can't keep a handle on your mutt. Either shut him up or I'll do it for you!"

Most days Tim would let Shadow out only when there was no sign of Mrs. Lawrence. But on occasion, when the old hag let loose on her unfortunate husband, Tim would allow Shadow to go and 'scare the holy out.' It helped switch her focus from the old man to the dog, who could certainly take her abuse better than any broken man.

Early last spring, Shadow had been out most of the afternoon. All was quiet, until Tim heard the most maniacal sounds the dog had ever emitted. Tim scurried to the back deck and found Shadow frantically clawing at the gate with a cacophony of intimidating growls and barks. Part of the gate was splintered, with shards of wood scattered on the ground nearby.

"Shadow! Come!" Tim yelled across his yard.

The dog obeyed and retreated to the house, his mouth covered in foam, strings of thick drool clinging to his muzzle. Tim looked over and saw Mrs. Lawrence. But instead of her usual tirade and without once looking in Tim's direction, she moved swiftly through her backyard and into her house, wearing only a housecoat and slippers, like a child up to no good.

Later that night, Tim woke to a putrid smell. He went into the dining room to find Shadow lying on the hardwood floor next to a large puddle of his own runny feces. The dog looked up shamefully at Tim and whimpered. He tried to stand but only his front legs were able to function, his back half paralyzed.

Tim cleaned up the mess and threw a blanket on the floor next to the couch in the living room. He carefully maneuvered Shadow onto it and placed a bowl of water nearby. After consoling his ill dog for several minutes, Tim stretched out on the couch and slept. He would call the veterinarian first thing in the morning.

When Tim woke, he found Shadow was awake and panting. Tim made a phone call and carried his dog to the truck. The vet took a stool sample, asked for Shadow's symptoms, and recommended the dog stay overnight. Tim agreed and went home.

The cool spring temperature had picked up that day, and by noon it was a pleasantly warm 70 degrees. Mrs. Lawrence was out and taking advantage of it. Tim noted the gate again and went to survey the damage, but there didn't seem to be much at all. Tim knelt down to pick up a splinter of the wood only to find it wasn't wood at all but bits of mushroom.

"Either shut him up or I'll do it for you!"

Normally, Tim would have thought nothing of the pieces of mushroom; perhaps they'd overgrown and squeezed through the gate. But due to the circumstances with Shadow, he contemplated other reasons. Was Mrs. Lawrence truly capable of such malevolence, to poison someone's pet? Tim considered the experiences he'd had with the woman the past three years and decided that perhaps she was, that sagging skin of hers nothing more than sheep's clothing.

He could hear Mrs. Lawrence's dry-lipped whistle through the fence. Tim sensed contentment in it. He gathered up a piece of the mushroom, headed inside and called the vet. He asked if it were possible that Shadow could have been poisoned and if so, could it have been caused by a mushroom? The vet said he would return his call the next day, hopefully with an answer to his question.

Tim then watched Mrs. Lawrence from his deck. He considered the idea of being paranoid that his elderly neighbor – nagging hag or not – was capable of such an atrocity. Mr. Lawrence was sitting on his patio, reading a book and sipping iced tea. Tim wondered if he wouldn't have gotten a divorce himself if he'd become what Mr. Lawrence had: half a man, shriveled and weak under the weight of his wife's abuse, forever stuck in a marriage too old to let go of.

Better to die alone than slowly by the tongue of an old viper.

Tim spent the remainder of the day caring for his own lawn while listening to Mrs. Lawrence's whistled tunes, at one moment looking over and catching her with a newfound spring in her step. With all day to consider it, Tim became more convinced that the woman had poisoned his dog. Eventually, as the day drew on, the whistled songs gave way to excessive yelling, Mr. Lawrence being the target.

The degrading went on and on, the crackled voice of the woman and the incessant silence from the man. Tim could no longer hold his tongue and so shouted through the fence, "Shut up already!"

Silence.

Tim squatted, his body hidden by the wooden fence where he'd been pulling weeds. Through the cracks in the fence, Tim could see the Lawrences looking in his direction. He swore he saw Mr. Lawrence give a little smile before heading inside, while Mrs. Lawrence stood surveying the fence as though attempting to make out the exact section Tim was using as a shield. Half regretting his outburst, Tim remained still until the woman's old eyes gave up and her mouth returned to whistling.

First thing the next morning, Tim received a phone call from the vet. After having something to settle his stomach and rehydrate, Shadow was alive and well, though still in need of further rest. The vet told Tim that more than likely Shadow had eaten something poisonous but he couldn't be sure it was a mushroom, and if it was, it didn't necessarily mean it was deliberate.

Later that afternoon Tim brought Shadow home and prepared a nest of blankets in the corner of the living room where the dog would get plenty of rest, per the veterinarian's orders. Shadow kept to himself most of the day and remained quiet and near the house whenever let outside.

Just before dark, Tim called for Shadow to come in after being let out for some fresh air and exercise. Mrs. Lawrence, who sat reading on her patio, looked up from her book and spotted Shadow climbing the stairs of the deck. Tim noted the look of surprise on her face.

She threw her tea at the ground, smashing the glass against the cement. "That beast'll burn in hell," she mumbled and headed inside.

For Tim, there was no longer any doubt.

Though the next few days were filled with clear blue skies and Mrs. Lawrence spent the daylight hours in her garden, the whistling and the springy step ceased – the old woman's brow furrowed heavily, the corners of her mouth pulled downward under the weight of a thousand grudges.

On the third day home, Shadow seemed himself again, running through the yard and taking chase at the occasional squirrel. The day was overcast and sprinkled off and on. Knowing Mrs. Lawrence never found herself outside on such days, Tim allowed his dog free reign of the yard, where Shadow spent most of the day without supervision.

But like earlier in the week, a vicious barking began, alerting Tim, who sprinted for the back door. The sounds were even fiercer than before, and Tim cast doubt as to whether it was Shadow at all. Upon reaching the sliding glass door, Tim could see it was indeed his dog, who had then crashed through the weakened gate and leapt onto the hunched and frail body of Mrs. Lawrence.

Shadow snapped at the old woman's throat, ripping at it with desperate ferocity, her ancient skin tearing like paper within his jaws. Tim quickly exited the house and took in a quick breath to scream at his dog but instead froze. He stood and watched as his dog mutilated its nemesis: an old, bitter woman.

Movement caught Tim's attention out the corner of his eye. Mr. Lawrence stood on his patio. He wasn't running to aid his dying wife. He wasn't yelling for help or screaming for mercy. He stood watching, sipping his iced tea.

Tim looked back at the grisly scene. Mrs. Lawrence lay twitching, a small baggie of mushrooms clutched in her hand. Her throat was gone. Her bottom dentures had broken loose and lay under her tongue, exposed through the giant hole in her neck. The top dentures fell from her palate and clapped on top of her lengthy tongue as she gurgled and gyrated, the dentures acting as a pair of wind-up chattering teeth, her tongue being bitten between them.

A little late for that now, Mrs. Lawrence. You should have learned to bite that tongue years ago.

Tim once again looked over at Mr. Lawrence, who continued to watch the mutilation. He turned to Tim and raised his glass as though presenting a toast.

***

Tim gazed out across his flourishing garden, the result of months of hard work. Shadow lifted his leg on the old gate and tagged it yellow, adding insult to an injury that was now nothing more than a memory. Tim grinned and eyed the overgrowth in the Lawrence's yard. He noted the peaceful quiet around him. Quiet enough to read. But first he'd get some more iced tea.

Yes, things happen all in due time. And they most certainly have a way of working themselves out.

A HITMAN'S DEATH

PETER OLIVER WONDER

Perched high atop the roof across the street, the shooter waited. Through the magnified scope of the high-powered rifle, he watched his unsuspecting target. He studied him. He tried to understand his movements. He always tried to learn from a kill.

The man behind the rifle made mental notes of the wind speed and direction. The changing gusts of wind would make this a tricky shot, but that's why he always had backup plans.

The biting cold of the night sank deep into his bones as he waited for the right moment to take his shot. A chill ran down his spine. No one ever said this job would be comfortable, only that it would pay well.

And pay well, it did. He would get a cool million for this hit, and he'd already received half of it in advance.

Despite the less than ideal conditions on the rooftop, he sat there, motionless, as he waited for his target to stop moving around long enough to get a clean shot. Since the shooter first spied him through the scope, the Asian man had been doing training in some form of martial art that wasn't the least bit familiar to the shooter. He reminded the shooter of Bruce Lee as he moved about the room. He'd never been given the name of his target, so he assigned him the name Bruce until the job was done and thoughts of him could leave his mind entirely.

The target had been going on with his training for over an hour already, and the shooter had been unable to draw a steady bead on him long enough to make a precise shot.

Keep on dancing, if it makes you happy, Bruce. It's the last thing you'll ever get to do, the shooter thought.

As the target jumped, twirled, and rolled around the small hotel room, the shooter observed his tattoos. Nearly his entire visible frame was covered in flames in all colors of the rainbow, swirling around his shirtless torso, and his face was covered in Chinese characters. The man behind the rifle couldn't read or speak Chinese, but was able to tell the difference between

Chinese and Japanese characters. He had, after all, traveled extensively thanks to his profession.

After nearly two hours of 'Bruce Lee' dancing around his room, he finally stopped and took a seat on the bed. Facing the window, he crossed his legs, placed his elbows on the inside of his thighs, and let his hands drop to the bed. He closed his eyes and began to meditate.

The wind gusted intensely just as the shooter began the controlled squeeze of his trigger, so he decided to let up. The wind could knock the barrel off course, and even at this short distance, the gusts of wind were great enough to change the course of the round once it was loose. There was no need to rush this job. For the pay he was getting, he would sit his ass on a roof in North Korea and freeze to death waiting to take the shot.

The shooter pulled his left hand from the rifle, balled it up into a fist, and blew some warm air into it. Never once did he pull his finger from the trigger, nor his eye from the scope.

After several minutes passed, the gusting winds slowly died off and the target remained as motionless as a corpse – as though he had been replaced with a dummy. Once satisfied with the condition of the wind, the shooter took in a deep breath, slowly let it out, and, once his lungs were nearly empty of air, repeated his steady squeeze of the trigger.

"Goodbye, motherfucker," he said to the dead man in the crosshairs.

There was nearly no recoil, and the muffled gunshot was a surprise to the shooter, as it always was. But the scene he saw unfold before him was even more of a surprise than the crack of the shot.

The target – with his eyes closed and entirely motionless on the bed – *dodged the fucking bullet.* The wind had subsided to a point where it would have had no effect on the trajectory of the round, and he was positive the barrel had remained on target throughout the shot. There was no way the target could have heard the shot, and there was obviously no way he had seen the shooter. *What the fuck is this?*

Again, he squeezed the trigger, but as the second round flew through the window, the target maneuvered backward, kicked his legs into the air to spin himself around, and fell to the floor on the other side of the bed. As soon as he landed, a thick, black smoke began to rise up and fill the room.

The motherfucker was using some sort of a smoke screen.

Such setbacks as missing your target on the first shot were an extreme annoyance, but it wasn't the end of the world. That was why there was always a contingency plan.

Taking the rifle with him, the shooter ran toward the elevator shaft. Earlier in the day, he had sabotaged the gears and left the car a useless box on the ground floor, which was home to the parking garage. While on the move, he wrapped the rifle sling over his shoulder, leaving the weapon to freely hang from his back.

With gloved hands, he grabbed onto the hand brakes attached to the elevator cable. They were a specialty item the shooter brought with him on all jobs that were to be executed from high atop a building. Dangling from the brake handles was a rope attached to a two-by-four which his feet could rest on as he fell in order to prevent them from scraping against the thick cable and opening up a nasty gash.

His descent was rapid but controlled. He applied steady pressure to the brakes so as not to gain too much speed. If that were to happen it would greatly increase the risk of not being able to come to a full stop before reaching the roof of the elevator, which would likely leave him as nothing more than a puddle of pink goo.

But that wouldn't happen. He was skilled and prepared for nearly any situation. That's why he'd been hired. That's why he could charge the ridiculous sums of money he did. That's why he'd been chosen for this very special job.

He came to a comfortable landing on the elevator car in under thirty seconds and wasted no time as he made his way through the ceiling hatch and into the car. He had already propped open the door and stuck some caution tape across the outside after he had sabotaged the gears.

Breaking through the tape, he made his way to and entered his Audi, which was parked in a handicapped spot next to the elevator. In a single, fluid motion, he removed the weapon from his back and placed it on the passenger side floor. He flipped up the passenger seat to reveal several other weapons, including a high-caliber pistol, a submachine gun, and a collapsible sword.

He withdrew the SMG from its compartment and pulled out of the parking space. The rear of the vehicle went sliding behind him as the tires spun, frictionless, beneath him and he was able to avoid contact with any other vehicle. The powerful car picked up speed in the small garage, and in no time he burst through the barrier gate, sending wood splinters flying through the air. The attendant in the booth didn't even have time to react before the car disappeared into the night.

Narrowly squeezing into rapidly moving traffic, he saw the traffic light was about to turn red. He stomped the gas pedal to the floor and careened through, making a left-hand turn toward the target's hotel. He paid no mind to the horns that sounded at him out of annoyance.

The Audi slid sideways into an open spot in front of the mark's hotel mere moments after leaving the shooting position; the shooter had strategically placed traffic cones in this particular spot earlier in the day. His jaw dropped once he saw that the tattooed man was already closing the door of his Subaru behind himself, the engine started. The tires of the silver car spat smoke up into the night sky behind it as it broke out into traffic, as though the move had been choreographed weeks in advance.

The shooter skipped the stage where he was supposed to be frustrated and went straight to being pissed off. *How did that little asshole manage to get outside and into the car so fast?*

There was no time for such thoughts so he brushed them away. He pulled his Audi into traffic, trading paint with a cab. There was no way the mark would be able to get away, no matter what the consequences were. Collateral damage meant nothing when a half million dollars – and his reputation – were on the line.

He saw the target's Subaru, which was only a few vehicles ahead of his own. With quick thinking and extreme determination, the shooter made his way onto the sidewalk in order to make up ground.

At this time of night, there were only a few people on the sidewalk, and he knew better than to honk to get them out of his way. Any extra noise would draw more attention – possibly even from the police – and would put undue strain on his job, which had already become a clusterfuck. One pedestrian wasn't able to react to the invasive vehicle in time. He bounced off to the right corner of the hood and was slammed against the building behind them. The shooter paid no mind to the inconsequential pedestrian as his one-track mind remained focused on the job at hand.

The target glanced over his shoulder in order to gain a visual on the pursuer. Not one to be outdone, he changed lanes, nearly striking the vehicle next to him, and made a tight left-hand turn.

It would take more than some sneaky maneuvering to get rid of the hitman. He bulldozed through traffic, colliding with no fewer than three other vehicles, and successfully made the turn. He was now directly behind the silver Subaru. The Audi continued to pick up speed until it rammed into the back of the target's car.

The Asian man's head struck the back of the seat before bouncing off and slamming his face into the steering wheel. A thin line of blood trickled from his left nostril. He pulled a pistol from his center console and blasted a few rounds through his rear windshield. The rounds went sailing past the pursuer's head and exited through the rear windshield of the Audi.

The rounds didn't even cause the driver to flinch. He had been shot at plenty of times and knew it took either a whole lot of skill or an inordinate amount of luck to successfully hit the driver of the vehicle behind you.

But those shots did fill the hitman with newfound rage. He pulled out the high-caliber pistol and fired a few rounds through his own windshield. Accuracy was not an issue for him, as he was not aiming to hit his target at this point. If he had, it would have been good news, but his intent was to damage the engine and bring the vehicle to a halt.

The silver vehicle began to swerve recklessly after two rounds sailed into it. The man was clearly anticipating more rounds to follow in the coming seconds. As the vehicle banged into two other cars, a thick, gray smoke began to billow up from the engine compartment.

One of the engine belts gave off a high-pitched whine, and the hitman knew that meant the target would soon have to ditch the dying car. Despite the fact that the man he was chasing was much smaller – and likely faster – this was precisely what he'd wanted. The little man could run all night and day, and he could almost certainly outrun the hitman, but he couldn't outrun a bullet.

And then he remembered that Bruce Lee had been able to dodge a bullet just a few short moments ago.

He placed the pistol back into its compartment in the passenger seat and picked up the SMG. The tools of his craft were always locked, loaded, and ready to fire; safety was child's play at this point in the game.

The lead vehicle slowed and sputtered as it crossed through lanes of oncoming traffic. Once the target felt the vehicle's tires strike the curb, he bailed out from the door. His feet struck the asphalt and, almost instantly, he was close to top speed. Like a cheetah, Bruce took off on foot down an alley.

The hitman smiled at the turn of events. The alley was plenty wide for him to continue the chase from the comfort of the Audi, and so he did.

From the first glimpse he had caught of his target, he knew he would be fast. He had seen that he had great athletic prowess. But this was something otherworldly. The man was able to maintain a steady distance between him and the vehicle while spilling every trash can, box, and any other miscellaneous item he could toss into the path of his would-be murderer.

Resigned to the fact that his windshield would require a replacement, he began to spray rounds at the ludicrously fast man. The shots were sloppy and either hit the ground or went cruising right past him.

It wasn't long before the hitman saw where the rest of the stray rounds were impacting. There was a brick wall at the end of the alley. It couldn't have turned out any more perfectly for the hitman. He eased the acceleration of the vehicle and slowed to a crawl before stopping all forward movement entirely.

At the end of the alley, Bruce searched for an escape – a fire escape, an open door, anything at all – but turned up empty-handed at every turn.

After removing his jacket, the hitman placed the SMG back into its proper spot, picked up the pistol and carefully tucked it into his waistband, and then withdrew the collapsible sword. With it in hand, he opened his door. He watched as a wisp of breath left his lungs on the cold night. He allowed a smile to escape, knowing he had the man dead to rights.

With his target standing defenseless in the glow of the headlights, the hitman took his time and admired his sword. With a quick flick of his wrist, the six inches of steel expanded into a full fifty-four-inch razor-sharp blade.

With slow, methodical steps, the hitman approached. His deliberate movements were intended to strike fear into the soul of the unarmed man, who was left with nothing but pain and despair to look forward to for the rest of his short life. This was well-deserved terror after having shot at the hitman on what should have been a quick, one-shot hit.

Inch by inch, the hitman neared the end of his job and another five hundred thousand dollars in his pocket.

However, his mark had no shortage of surprises in store. Once the hitman stepped into the light shining from the car, a smile crept over the mark's face.

"Yes, you have a beautiful smile, but this is no time for it. This is the end for you, Bruce," said the hitman.

"Wǒshìyīgèchōuyān de zhànshì. Wǒshìsǐ," the target said through a smug smile: *I am a Smoke Warrior. I am death.*

"I don't know what the fuck that was, but I sure as hell hope it was a prayer. You're about to meet your maker, son, and it's only fitting that you let him know you're coming home," the hitman said as he switched to a two-handed grip on his sword.

The target squatted down as if he were moving into a defensive posture, but then quickly spun in a circle. Smoke poured out from his hands in a spiral. The spin stopped, and as the smoke dissipated, it revealed a scythe with a long wooden shaft and an eighteen-inch curved blade.

The hitman was at a loss for words. There was nowhere for the seemingly ancient weapon to have been hidden on Bruce's body, and that trick with the smoke was nothing short of exceptional.

A little sleight of hand wasn't enough to dissuade the hitman. He rushed forward with his sword high in the air and brought down a heavy blow, directed at the target's head. The scythe was raised in a flash, and the hitman looked directly into Bruce's eyes. He was almost sure it was just the glow from the headlights of the Audi dancing in his pupils, but there appeared to be a fire burning within. This, in conjunction with the prestidigitation, made the hitman question why a hit was placed on this man.

The small frame of the target had caused the hitman to underestimate his strength. With a quick thrust, Bruce managed to send the sword, hitman attached, sailing backward several yards.

This displeased the hitman greatly as he fell to his ass in the darkness of the alley. Standing with the sword in his left hand, he reached into his waistband for the pistol. He aimed the hand cannon at the man before him. He was done playing games.

Before he was able to squeeze the trigger, the target turned toward the wall. The hitman thought it was a pointless attempt to escape and fired off his first shot. Before the round escaped the barrel of the gun, Bruce leaped toward the wall, rising nearly five feet off the ground before his feet made contact with the bricks.

The shot was far too low, but the hitman kept the weapon trained and fired off a few more rounds. Much to his chagrin, they struck nothing but the wall the scythe-wielder so effortlessly ran across, defying the laws of physics.

"What the fuck are you?" the hitman asked just loud enough for himself to hear.

Bruce came back down to solid ground with a gentle landing and let out a soft laugh. "Nǐshìhǎo yang, David, dànnǐshìbùshìzhídé," he said in a voice that projected over to his assailant and echoed off the walls of the alley: *You are good, David, but you are not worthy.*

With his ancient weapon in hand, it was now the target that approached the hitman, whose name the target somehow knew.

With his pistol emptied, David dropped it to the ground and once again gained a firm two-handed grasp on the sword. Admittedly, he hadn't had the best of training on the weapon, but he still believed strength would be on his side. All he had to do was manage to not get cut down by the scythe.

The two were separated by the glow from the headlights which still pierced the darkness of the alley. The light in between them could have been an ocean; from this distance, neither of them could strike the other. One would have to act and plunge into full illumination.

Not one to be taken by surprise, David stepped into the light, prepared to strike as soon as Bruce was within reach.

The target stood motionless. He wanted David to reach him. He wanted him to get close. He had encountered many challenges in his own line of work, and his skills had been improving due to the wonderful killers he so often encountered. He wanted to put them to the test.

David brought the sword high over his head, just as he had done before, leaving himself exposed to a quick yet deadly attack to the head, neck, and midsection. Bruce shook his head but did not make a move. He merely watched as the sword was brought down with all of the man's might.

David's face went wild with anger as he put every ounce of power he had into bringing the weapon down.

He saw the flames reappear in Bruce's eyes a second before the blade came into contact with his head. Or should have come into contact with his head. But just before the blade met the space the man's skull had recently occupied, his flesh became smoke, and the sword met no resistance during the entire strike. A shock rippled through David's bones as the weapon landed heavily upon the asphalt, sending sparks and chunks of rock flying off into the air.

All expression left David's face as he looked up from the blade to see the mass of smoke move to the side, still somehow clutching the scythe. It reformed as a person to his left.

Before David could lift the sword and prepare to engage once more, he was struck by the staff end of the scythe. Blood shot from the hitman's mouth as his head jolted to the side. He hit the ground hard and skidded to a halt in front of the car.

David considered getting into the vehicle and making an escape. Then reality set in. In his line of work, fleeing one danger meant finding himself in a new heap of trouble. Those who hired him were resourceful people with plenty of liquid funds. There was no corner on the planet in which he could call himself safe if he were to let this mark escape.

Then another thought crossed his mind. This mark had some unreal talents which he had never before encountered, but facts were facts. Bruce had been able to get out of the way of the bullets and shift form in order to avoid being struck with the blade, but he'd started off running. And why would he run? The only reason to run from something that threatens you is because it can hurt or kill you. Something inside told David there was a weakness somewhere.

There was always a weakness. He just had to feel it out.

With renewed vigor and determination, David stood and held his blade vertically before him. His eyes were locked onto those of his opponent. Inside of those eyes burned the fires of hell. Bruce stood still with the shaft of his scythe resting on the ground. For some reason, he had not a care in the world as David stared him down with murder etched in his mind.

From the peripheries of his vision, David saw little puffs of smoke materialize out of thin air. The puffs of smoke swirled as a light from within them tried to shine. It wasn't long before the patches of smoke condensed before his eyes. What David saw, once he finally broke eye contact with Bruce, were two-foot-tall imps. There were five of them surrounding him, including one standing atop the Audi.

None of the little hellions made a move as David turned in a circle to gain a visual on all of his new targets. None of them began to approach, and the first thing that came across David's mind was that Bruce must be some sort of a coward. Using some form of black magic and summoning these beasts to fight his battle for him was laughable.

Before engaging with the new threats, David gave Bruce a quick glance, shook his head disapprovingly, and said, "You've got to be fucking kidding me."

The imp to the left made its first move. The red dwarf came charging with its enormous mouth filled with bright yellow teeth. It let loose a shriek that pierced David's ears and nearly took him off his guard, but the adrenaline coursing through his veins kept him focused.

The sharp claws of the creature came within inches of his face as it flew through the air; David was narrowly able to dodge it as it passed.

As the first imp missed with its attack, David felt claws dig into his hip. He let out a pained yelp and bashed the hilt of his sword into the godforsaken red face that was getting ready to dine on one of his kidneys. The thing fell to the ground and David gave it a swift kick, sending it skidding underneath the car.

Another imp came at him, again attacking from the direction opposite of his focus. It sank its teeth into his left calf and David instinctively swung the blade down on it, slicing its head in half from ear to ear. The back of the head fell to the ground, but the side with the face remained latched onto his leg.

He had no time to pry it away, as there was already another attack coming in from behind him. At least he was able to understand their simple tactics – they wanted to maintain the element of surprise.

Before the next imp was able to manage any form of attack, David jabbed at it with his weapon, impaling it through the torso.

But this was to be a two-pronged attack; the fifth imp was right beside it, and it bit at David's hands as he attempted to shake the dead imp from the blade. The little fucker managed to get its fangs around one of his thumbs and crunched through the bone, severing the appendage and swallowing it whole.

A spurt of fresh blood sprang from the wound as David punted the beast away. The demon went sailing across the alley, into the brick wall.

David fell to the ground after putting all of his weight onto his injured leg. Focused on the battle, the hitman felt no pain. All rational thought had given way to the basic instinct to fight and win. With two imps decommissioned and the others a safe distance away, David set the sword down and used both hands to pry the dead imp jaws from his leg. As he yanked the teeth out of his flesh, fresh blood oozed out and sent warmth running down his calf.

Frustrated, he threw the large chunk of imp across the alley. As he unsuccessfully grabbed at his sword with his thumbless hand, another imp gouged its talon-like fingernails into his back, just missing his spine. He swung around with the wounded hand and jammed his fingers into the eyeballs of the foul creature. The imp dropped to the ground. David continued to press his fingers into the warm tissue until he could feel the brain, and he swirled his fingers around until he was confident that the creature was not only blind but quite dead as well.

With his good hand, he once more reached for the blade. When he had a firm grip, he stood up. The headlights shone straight into his eyes, temporarily blinding him. Something struck the back of his head. The blow caused him to fly forward and land on the damaged hood of the car; the impact caused the steel to drop from his hand.

There was an imp attached to the back of his head, clawing toward his eyes, making an attempt to cause more damage for its fallen comrades. The flesh around David's temples was gouged and torn, but his vision remained intact, aside from the blood that flowed into his eyes.

With both hands, he reached up and grabbed the unholy terror and bashed it against the windshield until the glass shattered and caved into the cab of the vehicle, raining bits of glass down from the laminated sheet. The creature's skull had given in after the first few slams, and David discarded the dead creature onto the driver's seat. As he did so, he reached down, peeled up the broken sheet of glass, and picked up the SMG that was resting peacefully in its compartment.

After quickly dropping the magazine from the weapon and inspecting it to see how many rounds were left, he slammed it back home, and then sat up on the hood of the vehicle to see the final imp on its approach. Tucking the automatic weapon into his waistband to conceal it, David rolled from the hood of the car and dropped directly onto his sword.

Woozy from blood loss, the hitman still managed to maintain his focus and rose to his feet, blade in hand. From several feet away, the red fiend bounded and took to the air on a path straight for David's face.

David took a step back and brought the sword up in a baseball stance and waited for the monster to be positioned directly in the strike zone. The wretched thing was too stupid to know it was already dead before it even reached its final destination. As it flew within striking distance, it continued to snap its jaws and swing its claws as though there was still some slight chance for victory.

Using what remained of his strength, David swung for the stands, slicing cleanly through the last of the imps, sending a shower of blood raining forth from the razor edge. Spent, David dropped the sword; he would no longer require it. With both hands, he reached up and wiped the blood from his eyes.

Holding the scythe in the crook of his elbow, Bruce began a slow clap for the spectacle he had just witnessed. He snatched up the bladed weapon and approached the hitman, speaking – now in English – as he did.

"I was right about you," he began with a heavy Chinese accent. "You are truly a great warrior. You possess the foresight and intelligence to understand the necessity for secondary and even tertiary plans. You have trained your body to be in near-peak physical condition. Your determination shows that you truly are unable to give up and you lack the capability to accept defeat even when it is looking you directly in the face. You have managed to fight creatures that are not of this world. Broken and battered though you may be, your skills and weapon selection have allowed you to achieve victory in what was a battle that even the most imaginative warrior could not have anticipated.

"However," he continued, "despite all of the talent you possess, you were unable to kill me. As I send you into the afterlife, I want you to take no shame in this defeat. I have hired many men to try to take my place, and there have been but few who have come as far as you have on this night. It is with the highest regard that I must now put an end to your life."

David fell onto his knees beside the sword; blood dripped to the ground from every open wound as he made impact. He had no idea what the hell the target was talking about, but he assumed Bruce was high as hell on some new street drug and had perhaps slipped something to him as well. Maybe it was even the lack of blood that was causing him to hallucinate.

Bruce walked over and kicked the sword away before taking a few steps back to observe his beaten foe.

Soaking in the fact that his enemy had seemingly accepted defeat, Bruce once more set the shaft of his scythe on the ground. He shut his eyes and began what seemed to be some sort of a prayer in Chinese.

An opportunity like this is something to be seized at once.

Doing his best to not make a peep, to not even alter the course of his breathing, David reached into his waistband and withdrew the SMG. Using both hands and all of his remaining strength, he lifted the weapon and took careful aim. Once he had the shot lined up, he squeezed the trigger and held it down until the weapon ran dry. As the rounds spewed forth from the weapon, David clenched his eyes shut. He had no desire to see some crazy bullshit like he had when he had initially attempted to strike Bruce with the sword and the man had transubstantiated into smoke.

Once the weapon was empty, David opened his eyes, half expecting to see the mark had jumped on top of him despite the barrage of rounds, with great big devil horns jutting from his head.

But that was not the case.

The shocked look on Bruce's face was cause enough for a joyful smile to slither across David's blood-covered lips.

"Now it is you who surprises me," said the man that had been riddled with holes.

Though a normal man would have fallen over dead after incurring so much damage, Bruce took the last steps over to David and knelt beside him. "You have killed me. But I still must tell you what the purpose behind my death is. For over one thousand years, I have helped souls cross from the mortal world into the afterlife. I am what is known most commonly as a Smoke Warrior, though there are many names for us. There are tales of Death, or the Grim Reaper, and while they may have some facts correct, they are not entirely accurate. There is a legion of us who work to maintain the balance between life and death in this world.

"Occasionally, we will seek a challenge – someone that may rise to our ranks. We seek out the top killers and hire them to attempt to kill us. Those who accept and fight to the death with honor are rewarded with great status in the afterlife. Those who accept only to turn their tails and flee in cowardice are punished with an eternity of servitude. And then there are those such as you – those who fight and win. Be it through skill or trickery – there are no rules in the field of battle other than to win – those who prove themselves a worthy adversary and take the life of a Smoke Warrior are to carry on the scythe.

"You are to become part of both worlds. You now belong to the mortal world, as well as the world of the afterlife."

Once the Smoke Warrior finished speaking, the flame disappeared from his eyes. The colorful flame tattoos that covered his skin began to swirl as though they too had become living smoke that was contained within his flesh. The black, swirling patches made their way up his body, toward his arms, and out toward his hands. Once the curious patches began to accumulate there, his hands began to glow. They glowed brighter and brighter until they gleamed as if they contained pure starlight. The light began to transfer from his hands to the weapon, which then began to glow and float of its own accord.

The dying man's hands dropped from the shaft and, endowed with some mysterious power, the scythe floated toward its new owner, David. The hitman dropped the empty SMG and reached out toward the scythe, but hesitated to grasp it.

"You must accept it," said the dying Smoke Warrior. All of his tattoos were now gone, leaving his flesh clean, aside from the bullet wounds and trickling blood. "It is the only way to keep you from dying a true death."

David looked down at his own wounds. Blood freely flowed from many wounds that would surely lead to his death were he not given the proper medical attention in the near future. His vision blurred, yet the scythe still shone brightly before him. With the headlights behind him, he still wasn't entirely sure this wasn't some optical illusion. Even in his weakened condition, he couldn't fully accept this as reality.

And so, with his outstretched hands, he grasped the shaft of the Smoke Warrior's weapon. The glow from the wooden handle warmed his hand. Its warmth radiated through his hands, up his arms, and filled the rest of his body.

The light that entered him filled him with strength, but there was something more. It filled him with life. It filled him with death. The mysterious light healed his wounds and made him into something else – something better than the mere man he had been when he woke up that morning.

David looked down at his arms once the light had finished its transfer from the scythe into his body. The tattoos he had noticed on the shadow warrior from high atop the hotel roof were now on his own arms.

Then he noticed that his entire thumb had grown back. The pain in his face, back, hip, and leg had also not only lessened but had gone away entirely.

Near the end of his life, the Shadow Warrior felt the need to give what little advice he could while there was still time. He spoke as blood trickled from his nose and mouth. "You have proven yourself. Fall not victim to my ways. For too long, I have suffered the sin of pride. No matter how certain you are of the fate of one you seek to send to the other side, never let your guard down."

Once the last word left his mouth, the Smoke Warrior slumped over, dead. David took a step toward him, but before he could attempt to rouse him, the body slowly dissipated into a whirl of smoke.

David could feel the light from above shining within, now that he was a Smoke Warrior. The hellfire danced in his eyes as he took off into the night, nothing more than a wisp of smoke.

WHERE THE MONSTERS LIVE
DUNCAN RALSTON

It was raining the day I brought my daughter's CD player back to the sex offenders under the bridge, and everyone was in a crummy mood. Miami's weather is a blessing when you're living on the street, where you can sleep on a sofa for months at a time. The exception is the rainy season, those summer months when you've got to get a roof over your head that isn't just a doorway alcove or the underside of a bridge, or you'll be soaked to the skin in seconds. By the day I went home for the first time in months, it had already been raining three days, and most of us were sure the sun would never come out again.

I left camp early that morning, walking a little over three hours to the house where I used to live. My feet hurt and my clothes ran with a hundred rivers of dirt, but I hoped it would be worth the trek. There was a method to the madness, as they say. Or so I'd thought then.

Marnie was just pulling out of the drive when I arrived, our little girl Nola in the backseat playing with a doll I didn't recognize, making it dance. Neither of my girls saw me hiding behind the sprawling gumbo limbo in the Garrisons' front yard as they drove past, the two of them smiling and singing. Tears clawed out from my eyes, seeing the both of them looking forward instead of back, the way I thought they ought to be looking, toward a life when all three of us were still together. Toward the past I'd left behind in pursuit of my singular goal, this burning obsession. I'd been gone a little over four months by then, and it wasn't as though I'd expected life to stay in a sort of freeze-frame with me out of the picture. Still, seeing them singing along to one of Nola's CDs, seemingly as happy as you please... it was a blow.

Once the car disappeared around the corner, I did what I could to smother the pain. I drew the hoodie up over my head and crossed to the house, looking both ways, skirting the garbage cans which lined both sides of the street, glad the municipality hadn't changed trash pickup to another day while I was gone. If Marnie had re-keyed the locks, God forbid, I figured I could wait around and break a window when the truck came rumbling up the street. But I didn't need to wait. My key slid in effortlessly. Twisting it in the lock, I let out a sigh of relief.

The house was as I remembered it, if a little messier. It smelled nice, like the lilac shampoo both Marnie and Nola apparently still used. It smelled *clean*. Even the hints of last night's dinner in the garbage – a spaghetti sauce starting to turn – smelled terrific. Smelled like *home*. Stink permeates homelessness: the smell of trash, the smell of dirty streets, of fire bins and piss and other people's body odor, the wet dog smell that saturates your clothes and bedding, the smell of rust and dirt and decay. It felt good being back here. Felt right. I wanted to strip off my clothes and climb into the shower, wash off the layers of grime the rain hadn't been able to make a dent on, wash off all the hell and scum I'd had to wade through to get to where I was now, with the Rabbit Man almost within my reach, and stretch out on the fresh clean sheets. To wait for Marnie to come home and tell her I'd been stupid, that I'd give it all up if only she'd let me stay.

Our bedroom was exactly the way it was the day I left. If she'd taken down the pictures of the two of us together, the trips we'd taken before we had Nola, our engagement and wedding and honeymoon photos, I might have paused to reflect on its meaning. That they were still right where they'd been when I left made me think I could still come back if I wanted, if I could just summon the courage to quit. To give up on death and allow life and love back into my heart.

Anger rushed into my veins, and I pushed these thoughts away. Useless speculation. The thoughts of a coward. I had to protect my family, and the only way I knew how to do it was by leaving them behind.

I headed for the closet.

The night before I left home, Marnie had been off at a parent-teacher conference, listening to 'suggestions' from parents who believed their fourth-grade children weren't receiving an adequate learning experience. And so Nola and I were home alone, which happened every so often. While Nola read her favorite book for the hundredth time, listening to her little CD player, I watched the Yankees get their asses fed to them with the sound turned off. After a while I headed out to the garage, fed up with the lousy game and Nola's repetitive pop music. I remembered she'd always been curious about the music Marnie and I used to listen to when we were young, and so I hunted down a handful of mixed CDs I'd made in college, most of them for when we'd turned the overhead lights off and the Christmas lights strung up around her dorm room twinkled over the bed like stars. I came back to the living room with the box and hunkered down in front of Nola. She scowled when I turned off her music, but when I showed her the words I'd written on that first CD, her eyes lit up and she tented her fingers in a devious manner reminiscent of her mother hamming it up over some cunning plan she'd devised to rope me into something I didn't want to do.

The first song was *Sweet Child O' Mine*. Nola seemed to enjoy it, even though she said Axl Rose's voice was funny. After that were a couple of songs I don't recall – one-hit wonders, most likely. Then came *Sympathy for the Devil*, and it wasn't long before Nola and I got to howling along with Mick Jagger – "Hoo hoooo! Hoo hoooo!" I skipped the Chili Peppers' *Under the Bridge* since it's about suicide or heroin – or both – and even though Nola had already been through more than most kids had by sixteen, she was still only six. (I'd missed her seventh birthday while I was gone, something I imagine every parent with a deadbeat dad like mine promises themselves never to do. I sent a card procured from money I'd panhandled, but I can't be sure it arrived in time. And even if it had, Marnie might not have passed it along. By then she was probably sick of hearing Nola ask what had happened to her daddy. It's a question I often ask myself: What happened to me? It's a question I'm afraid to answer.)

Near the end of the CD, Nola and I had nestled down on the rug with the ball game flickering unwatched on the TV. I'd been staring up at the ceiling with my arms behind my head while Nola talked about what she liked and disliked about each song, a running commentary that was amusing at first but then sort of droned on as I began to daydream about grabbing the Rabbit Man by the throat and feeling his trachea splinter between my fingers. The image made me smile.

The cops still hadn't caught him, the man who'd assaulted my child, my little Nola, and I'd been spending most of my waking hours daydreaming about choking a man in a bunny suit to death as if the whole thing was a joke when the truth was far more sinister. Even then, I'm sure some dark part of me knew I could never move beyond the blind hatred, beyond thoughts of bloody revenge. That the wound he'd opened in me would turn gangrenous. Deadly.

I'd found myself sympathizing with those hovering parents Marnie and I used to berate. I heard the truth in meaningless catchphrases like 'stranger danger.' Buffer zones like Ron Book's sex offender ordinances, barring perverts and pedophiles from living within a short distance of any place children gather, seemed to make some kind of logical sense to me. I was deluding myself, because I couldn't live with the truth: that I would never feel Nola was safe again without my constant supervision.

When I snapped out of it, a song I hadn't heard since Marnie and I were in grade school had come on, and I realized Nola had grown silent. I rolled over onto my stomach to see she sat frozen, her face, framed under the little brown bangs Marnie cut with scissors on a kitchen stool, twisted into a rictus of fear.

"Nola," I said. She didn't respond, didn't take her eyes off the CD player we'd gotten for her fourth birthday, the little pink one with *Dora the Explorer* stickers plastered all over it. I snapped my fingers in front of her face and she didn't flinch. A runner of drool spilled from her lip and pattered on the carpet.

Was she having a seizure?

The chorus kicked in then, the choir singing of tiny hands in larger ones, of a love that could be seen as a crime. The words struck me like a hammer in the chest. Wanting to be her daddy. Her preacher. Suddenly the love song seemed sinister. When I reached to turn it off, an odd creeping sensation like when you're about to crush a particularly large and wriggly insect crawled up my spine.

The song stopped. Nola snapped out of her trance.

"Nola," I said. "Sweetheart, have you heard that song before?"

Nola shook her head violently, wide blue eyes obscured by her bangs as she looked down in curiosity at the drool spots on the floor. Though she'd never spoken a word about the monster who'd assaulted her, the trauma still far too pervasive, I felt certain he would have told her never to tell, that if she told on him he'd come to her house and murder her family or something equally abhorrent. I understood that fear, but rage overcame me, and I grabbed her arm, much rougher than I'd meant. "Nola, don't lie to Daddy."

I didn't realize Marnie had come home until I looked up in that awful moment to find her standing in the doorway. My hand fell away from Nola's tiny arm, the skin red in the shape of my fingers. Tears stood in Nola's eyes, though the look on her face was not pain but surprise. I'd never laid a finger on her for discipline until just then. Quite frankly, the look on my face in that moment probably mirrored hers.

There was no argument that night or ever. Marnie simply looked at me, straight into my heart where the poison had been festering. She took Nola by the hand, who'd run to her crying as the shock of what had happened finally struck her, and the two of them went upstairs to bed. I spent a few sleepless hours twisting back and forth on the couch under a small throw blanket. Eventually, I crept upstairs to my office and picked up the journal the family therapist had suggested I use to jot down what she'd called "irrational thoughts and/or behavior." I'd had neither the time nor inclination to use it, just left it on my desk to gather dust. What good would writing about it do? I needed *action*, not *words.*

When I opened it that night, I realized I'd been wrong about that. Marnie had been filling in the journal for me, and her words were exactly what I needed in that moment. Reading it made me sick, looking at my transformation through Marnie's eyes. In her words, it was like I'd been holding the family underwater, drowning us in my grief, determined to make Nola relive what that monster did to her over and over so she'd remember something, *anything*, about him: a smell, his voice, something about the place he took her, something about the rabbits. Dr. Ambrose might have held similar suspicions, but Marnie had known in her bones I would never get past it, that I'd never wanted to. She'd known before I fully understood myself just how badly I'd wanted to hurt him, even *kill* him – to make the Rabbit Man suffer for what he'd done to our little girl. Our sweet Nola.

The next day I told Marnie my plan. All she did was sigh. As if it had been inevitable, like she'd been waiting for me to admit it. Finally she'd asked me, "Do you really think it's going to help her? Nola needs a father, not a vigilante." She'd told me if I went through with it to never come back.

That was a third of a year ago. This rain-soaked morning was the first time I'd been home since.

***

I found the little pink CD player right where I'd hidden it that night, under the musty old sleeping bag we'd used at the Grand Canyon the summer before Nola was born. I took that, too, and returned to Bookville shortly after one, dog-tired but eager to share my "find" with the others. The battery had died in Walker's RV a few weeks back, and our little area of the camp hadn't had music since. I was sure they would be pleased.

As I trudged down the concrete shoulder toward camp, I was reminded of a phrase from one of Nola's favorite picture books: *Under the bridge, where the Monsters live…* A story about a family of nice, cuddly monsters. *Here is that fabled place*, I thought. Only the monsters down here were most definitely not nice, and trying to cuddle one would be dangerous, like kissing a piranha.

By then I'd narrowed the Rabbit Man's identity down to three suspects: Tony Walker, Alejandro Gonzalez, and Orville "Popcorn" Perry. These were the convicted pedophiles I'd been living among for the last three months. Not everyone in Bookville had committed the sort of vile crimes these men had. Some were rapists, others were molesters, but most had been stuck there for petty sexual assaults, hadn't even spent a day in jail but had been forced to register anyhow. Forced out of their homes, into the shadows, and under the bridge. Statutory cases, groping, sodomy. Some drunk guy caught pissing in public near a school yard. You could almost laugh at a creep who exposed himself to old ladies, so long as one of them wasn't your relative. It's sick, sure, but it doesn't *hurt* anyone. But regardless of their crime's severity, lobbyist Ron Book's ordinance forced these men and women to live 2,500 feet from any school, park, or bus stop. Without violating parole or removing their ankle monitor and skipping town, the Causeway and the Everglades were the only places left for a sex offender to live. Ron Book's folly had pushed them underground and off the grid. Instead of making Miami safer he'd made the city a thousand times more dangerous.

Walker, Gonzalez, and Popcorn Perry – these guys had done hard time. Gonzalez liked little girls. Popcorn preferred boys, but he'd gotten arrested for trying to diddle one of the girls on his school bus route. He told us she had a short haircut and had yet to hit puberty, so it was easy enough to imagine her as a boy despite not having the parts. From my understanding, Walker was a pinch hitter. None of these men had ever killed anyone as far as I knew, but together they'd strangled the souls of at least half a dozen children. What had sent me rushing home that morning was Gonzalez had told a story a few days prior about the rabbit he'd had as a boy, reminiscing about how soft its fur had been. I could easily imagine it reminding him of the silken hair of his victims, which I thought was probably why he'd liked it.

"Look what I found," I said, holding up Nola's CD player.

The three of them looked up from their game of Rummy on a table made of plywood and wooden cable spools. Gonzalez's eyes lit up like a kid who'd just found the bra of his best friend's mom on their shower rod (though I suppose that wouldn't have interested him much even as a child). I plastered on a smile to cover for the sneer I felt trying to creep its way onto my face, having placed all bets on him.

He was my Rabbit Man. I was sure of it.

"Got batteries?" Walker asked.

"These ones still work," I said, and put it on the table by the discards.

"What's all this pink shit?" Popcorn wondered, eyeing me with suspicion. "You break your parole, or what?"

I pretended to be shocked. Early on, I'd made up a story to ingratiate myself with these three, telling them I'd done two years in Alamosa County for assaulting my niece. Popcorn and Walker had wanted details, and so I fed them details: said I'd been grooming her for years before I actually got up the courage to go through with it. That I'd babysat for my brother and his wife – I have no siblings, only in-laws – for months just working up the nerve to touch her. Popcorn had wanted to know about her underwear, if it had 'decals,' which I took to mean prints. Walker hadn't even tried to conceal the erection in his frayed jeans. But Gonzalez had just stared, open-mouthed. Afterward, I'd excused myself for a piss and ended up being sick in the shadows behind one of the big pillars, my guts churning the whole time I'd concocted the story.

"Nah," I answered Popcorn. "Just found it. It's amazing what people will throw out on the street these days." I popped the top open, revealing the mixed CD. The words *FOR MARNIE* had long faded, printed in block letters eleven or twelve years ago, the same words that had made Nola's eyes light up the night before I left her and her mother to live under the bridge with these animals.

"Still got a disc," Walker said. "Wonder who the fuck Marnie is?"

Again, I held back an unconscious sneer.

"That's the kind of question could get your ass in a whole lot of trouble," Popcorn said, before turning to me. "A'ight. Play that fuckin' music, white boy."

I sat down beside Gonzalez, who continued to eyeball the CD player the way Nola had that night in the living room, albeit somehow managing not to drool. One of the benefits of camping out close to the Bay, we could rinse our clothes out regularly or use laundry soap when we could find some. Hell, we could even give ourselves a good wash once in a while. Gonzalez wasn't most of us. He reeked of cigarettes and an omnipresent aroma of unwashed asshole. He hadn't brushed his teeth in months, maybe years. Sitting next to him you could imagine stink lines rising from his body, like that kid from *Peanuts*. It was difficult to sit so close to him, but I wanted him close when it happened.

This mound of dirt and repurposed trash under the Julia Tuttle Causeway was our living room. Graffiti on the pillars was the art on our walls. I pushed PLAY.

Sympathy for the Devil came on, over the shouts and laughter and music from the other encampments. Popcorn bit his lower lip and began to bob his head to the music.

Walker – who fucked girls, boys, adult women and once, according to his own account, a sedated gator – grew a sick smile. "I used to fuck to this song," he said, and stood up from the broken sofa to demonstrate, gyrating his hips with one hand at his side and the other holding down his imagined victim, be it human or animal.

"Sit your ass down," Popcorn said.

"You want some a this?" Walker said, thrusting his crotch toward the larger man.

"You best be gettin' your skinny dick outta my face." Popcorn picked up the discard pile from their Rummy game and threw the cards at Walker, who giggled and flopped back down on the couch.

"Man, you're pickin' those up!"

"Bull*shit.*"

Popcorn and Walker left the cards scattered on the ground and the ratty old sofa. I let the song play out, then skipped the next two. Still couldn't remember them, even if I tried.

"Hey, I like that song," Walker groaned about the second, but the next song had already started: the haunting chords on a keyboard, the *tss-tss-tss* of a hi-hat.

When George Michael began to sing in his raspy whisper, Gonzalez turned to me. He met my eyes for only a moment, but the shock was palpable, the guilt evident. He returned his gaze to the CD player, and as the song played out my eyes never left him. I felt them tearing up, thinking about what he must have done to my Nola, but I blinked it away. I couldn't let my grief, my anger, and a sudden disturbing rush of exhilaration from being so close after searching for so long come between me and my revenge. I studied Gonzalez with glistening eyes: this bland monster, this mild-mannered beast. I watched him and pictured my knife slipping into the hot meat between his ribs.

"*The fuck is that shit?*" someone called over, tearing me from my fantasy. I allowed my gaze to move beyond Gonzalez to the '80s Chevy Impala resting beside a spray-painted entreaty that had once made the papers: *WE ARE NOT MONSTERS*. A guy I'd seen around a few times sat hanging out the driver door. He had a little mustache and silky blond hair like a man on a box of hair dye, except the circles under his eyes were so dark they could have been bruises.

"It's called music," Popcorn shouted back. "The fuck you think it is?"

The blond dude got out of his car and approached. "Why you listenin' to that faggot, huh?"

"Actually, he's bisexual," Walker answered. "Not that it makes any goddamn difference."

"You listen to that shit, you're no better'n a faggot yourself." Blondie came right up to the table and reached for the CD player.

Popcorn swatted his hand away.

"Don't you fuckin touch me, nigger."

Popcorn's eyes narrowed. He grabbed the blond guy's arm and jerked it up behind his back, the kind of move a cop or someone who'd been trained in military might use, and I found myself suddenly glad to be up against Gonzalez instead of Popcorn.

"That's uncalled for," a woman I knew only as Pip shouted.

Others crowded around. A man with a lisp and cargo shorts cinched high on his waist by a frayed piece of rope asked why we couldn't all just get along.

In the fracas, the blond dude stomped down on Popcorn's foot. The heels of his cowboy boots sounded hard, and Popcorn's sneakers had seen better days. They were bound together by duct tape and falling apart at the seams, his tube socks so dirty they were black in places visible at the sides. Popcorn's howl of pain just about matched Mick Jagger's, and he let go of the blond dude's arm.

Blondie shook his hair as if Popcorn had just ruffled it instead of nearly breaking his arm, and then locked eyes with Gonzalez. The wretched little smelly man looked behind himself, shrinking from the cold gaze. Blondie had found his prey, a victim to reclaim his dominance. Before Gonzalez could scramble over the back of the couch, Blondie had yanked him back by his filthy jeans and began raining down on his back with balled-up fists, calling him *queer* and *runt* and *pussy*.

Whatever he was, Gonzalez was *mine*.

A surge of frenetic energy ran through me as I grabbed a fistful of Blondie's hair and yanked him away from Gonzalez, who used the distraction to squirm away. I threw a punch before Blondie could swing at me, clipping him in the jaw. Having never been in a fight before, only ever using my fists against inanimate objects, it stunned me how much of a rush I got from the feel of his jaw against my knuckles. The feeling was short-lived as Blondie slugged me hard in the gut. I staggered back, the breath knocked out of me, while Popcorn and Walker jumped in to pull Blondie back from doing me some real damage.

In all the commotion, Gonzalez had gotten up and was slinking off. I gathered up my strength and followed him. The ruckus of the other three men struggling and the crowd either egging them on or jeering them grew quieter the further Gonzalez and I ran.

This is it, I thought, feeling stronger and almost hyperaware the closer I got to my quarry. I didn't think about going back home. I didn't think about Nola. All I could think of was *blood* and *blood* and *blood…*

***

I suppose I should tell you about the rabbits.

The day Nola ran away, Marnie and I had been fighting. Silly argument. She'd caught me smoking, something I hadn't done since she was pregnant – as far as she knew – and we'd gotten into it. She accused me of not caring to live long enough to see Nola graduate from college, and I accused her of not letting me relieve my stress the way I wanted. Nola heard us. She'd packed up some things in her knapsack: her stuffed lion Julio, which she spelled with a W-H-O, her favorite book about the elephant king, a bag of marshmallows (*mushmellows*, she called them), and a flashlight. I suspect she was going to camp out and roast her mushmellows over a fire, but how she'd planned to light one, I don't know. I suppose the thought might never have crossed a six-year-old's mind.

Whatever she'd gotten in her head, Nola sneaked out the back door while Marnie and I argued in raised whispers, knowing full well she could hear us despite the closed bedroom door. Somewhere after the corner of Day and Matilda, where a crossing guard told police she'd scolded Nola about crossing the street without looking both ways, our little girl disappeared.

Marnie noticed she'd slipped away just when we'd gotten to the root of the argument. At first, we thought she'd been playing. Nola had always loved hide and seek. So we looked in all the usual spots we might find her: behind the curtains, crouched behind the big ficus in my office, in the basement shower, or in her closet, under a pile of stuffed animals.

Nowhere. Anxiety grew to full-blown fear. She knew enough not to run away, but if she'd heard us arguing…

We searched outside, in the front and back yards, Marnie running out into the street and calling out her name. We phoned her friends, spoke to baffled, concerned parents. Finally, we called the police. Fifteen minutes later, officers showed up at our door. Marnie kept tugging at her shirt sleeves, pacing the room while the two officers took down what we had to tell them: what she was wearing, how old, hair color, about how tall, could she have gone to a relative's? I'd been watching Marnie unravel the whole time until she finally exploded, screaming at the officers, "Somebody's taken my baby and you're wasting our *fucking time*!" They'd looked at each other, offered their apologies, and then put out an AMBER alert.

While Marnie waited at the house for Nola to return, the both of us sick with the absolute certainty that at any moment they would call back to tell us they'd found her body in a ditch somewhere, I drove up and down the neighborhood, scouring the grounds at Liz Virrick Park, where we often took her when neither of us were busy on the weekend. I'd even gone to her school (where Marnie still taught the fourth grade), filled with the dreadful certainty Nola would never have her mother as a teacher because some monster had taken her life.

Lost. Gone. Dead. My little girl is dead. These thoughts circled my mind as I drove through the neighborhood, once, twice, three times, certain I'd missed somewhere, hoping to return home to find her eating peanut butter out of the jar with her fingers, laughing at cartoons with her mother. But each time I returned, Marnie had been pacing the porch, or sitting, tugging at her shirt sleeves, and the house had been empty. I feared – *we* feared – there would never be laughter in that house again. So, back into the car, driving down the same streets, shouting her name as the neighborhood darkened.

It was just after 8 p.m. when the police called. My sweaty hand shook so badly the phone slipped into my lap. I pulled the car over and listened to the officer speak, holding the cell in a trembling hand as my heart pounded in my throat.

Imagination can be a terrible curse. I never saw it with my own eyes, but the image still haunts every waking moment of my life. It drove me to live among the sex offenders. It compelled me to find the monster who'd done it, the Rabbit Man, and to put him six feet in the fucking ground.

The sick fuck had left Nola naked beside a trash bin on the bare asphalt in an alley in Little Haiti. Eventually a busboy from a nearby restaurant had come out to dump his mop bucket and saw her shivering there. He'd called the police without going to her – worried, perhaps, that even attempting to help a naked child might be misconstrued as sexual abuse.

When Officer Samuel Higgins arrived, he found a feral child huddled with her arms around her bruised knees, matted hair tangled in her face. Bleeding not just from the places she'd been violated, but from dozens of raised marks forensics later determined to be tiny scratches. Higgins wrapped the emergency blanket from his trunk around Nola, told her everything was going to be okay, that he was going to bring her to her mom and dad. At these words she leapt into his arms, latching around his neck, smearing his uniform with her blood.

The police were taking photographs of her injuries when I burst through the door, demanding to see her. Officer Higgins got in the way. Three officers had to hold me back from punching him, and if not for Sam's interference, I might have been charged with assaulting an officer. Sam and I hashed it out later; with two daughters himself, he keenly understood my rage. The Special Victims Bureau had taken over the case, but he'd promised to update me personally.

Marnie, Nola, and I went to the family therapist together. Dr. Ambrose had us explore our emotions in excruciating detail. She wanted us to open up, to work through our feelings, but each Thursday at 2 p.m. I begrudgingly entered her office and sat on that plush sofa entirely numb while Marnie droned and Nola played with toys in the corner. I saw no point to those visits; we were picking at scabs. While their meaningless words filled the terrifying silence, I sat alongside my wife, brewing hatred. My most violent fantasies were born in that room: gruesome acts I suspected I'd never be able to stomach even if the opportunity arose – thoughts which belonged to the monster growing inside me.

Eventually Dr. Ambrose accused me of stalling progress. I questioned her methods, her motives, called her a sadist. She asked me to leave. I apologized and she'd allowed me to return to the room. I'd lose myself in fantasy again. Several sessions passed this way, until our time was up.

Detective Rosario called a few weeks into this routine to inform us the lab had analyzed the white hairs they'd found on Nola's skin. Turned out to be animal fur, not human hair. They suspected the rapist kept rabbits, which kicked off a wide search for rabbit hutches in backyards and on rooftops.

Rosario didn't seem hopeful. By then, most registered sex offenders were living under the Tuttle Causeway, many of them already wearing ankle monitors.

I found myself driving several miles out of my way after work, slowing down over the water, catching a look at their tents and vehicles before driving ponderously back home. I'd seen them gathered down there, huddled from the rain, sharing food they'd scrounged, arguing, laughing. It all seemed normal and yet so alien to me. I wondered how they lived.

I wondered how they'd *bleed*.

Since I couldn't deal with the injuries to Nola's privates, I'd saddled Marnie with the unenviable task of applying ointment for several weeks before they healed. We spoke to each other less and less. We ate in front of the TV. I spent hours each night in the garage, pretending to work on the car. Mostly I would read my dad's old hunting magazines, fantasizing.

Late one night, Marnie entered the garage where I'd been sitting on a stool reading an old magazine, not even bothering to cover for the work I wasn't doing, and handed me the portable phone with no discernable expression in her gaze. I took it, listened to Sam Higgins apologize while feeling the floor drop out from beneath me, and mechanically thanked him for his help. Special Victims had made no progress in their search, and Nola had been unable to remember any details despite my coaching and our increasingly acrimonious sessions with Dr. Ambrose. Barring anything new, the case had effectively fizzled out. Went cold, like the darkened corners of my heart. After that, we never heard from him again. The Rabbit Man had gotten away.

That night I aimed to make sure it never happened again.

***

Breathing heavily, I caught up to Gonzalez near the fence at the base of the bridge and jerked him around roughly to face me.

"Hey! What gives?"

My vision was on a dimmer, timed to the unsteady beat of my heart. After being sucker punched by the blond dude and then chasing after Gonzalez, I was on the verge of blacking out. But I would make sure he looked me in the eyes as the life drained out of him. I would make sure he knew what he'd done.

"*Nola*," I said. I shook him by his lumberjack jacket, raising a cloud of dust. "Nola, Nola," I blubbered, "my fucking *daughter*, you sick *fuck*!"

Mortified, Gonzalez threw his filthy hands in the air, a gesture of innocence. "Hey, no wait, man, I haven't – *done that* – for ten years! I slipped up *once*. I would never – I've *never* – I…"

I saw it dawn on him: first disgust, then fear, shock… and then confusion, suspicion. He looked over my shoulder, where the altercation had died down and Blondie was walking backwards to his car, shouting curses and kicking the dirt. "You have a *daughter*?"

My grip on him lessened. I grabbed him harder, attempting to embolden myself. "Bullshit!"

"I swear, I haven't – " Gonzalez couldn't say the words, as if his own crime disgusted him. "Not since, you know, back then. I served my time. She's *forgiven* me. I swear to Jesus, man, I haven't done it again since!"

I felt the monster inside me step back from its cage. Gradually, I let Gonzalez go. He brushed his jacket off as if I was the one who'd made him dirty. "I'm sorry," I said as a cloud of dust rose around us.

"It's okay. I'm fine." With another look over my shoulder his eyes narrowed, and he returned his gaze to me. "You know, I knew there was something not right about you when you first came down here. Something about the way you moved. Not quite Walker's swagger, more like you were looking down your nose at us." He shook his head. "And that story about your niece? The things you said you did to her…" Gonzalez trailed off, swallowing hard, avoiding the unpleasant terminology.

I'd noticed him wincing as we listened to Walker describe his escapades in nasty detail. All this time I thought Gonzalez had just been putting on a show, the way some of the most vile politicians and religious figures act sanctimonious when inside they were repugnant.

"I didn't buy that for a second," he finished.

"You didn't?"

Gonzalez shook his head.

"Why not?"

"It's like there was nothing there," Gonzalez said, and gestured toward his own face. "In your eyes. No regret. No pride. No *lusting*, like the way how Walker talks about his…" Another hard swallow. "Just this blank look. A *dead* look."

I regarded him silently.

"So you think somebody here – what? They – *did something* – to your little girl?"

I nodded, feeling like a fool. All this time it had been so plain to Gonzalez I was a fraud, it must have been obvious to the others. Fear crept into my nerves, setting the monster back on edge. I would have to be more careful.

"Why did you think it was me?"

It took a moment for me to realize what he was asking. "The song," I told him. "The way you reacted to it, I just figured…" I didn't need to mention the rabbit. It didn't seem smart to reveal such evidence.

"Which song? That '80s one?"

I'd nearly blown it all because of that song. Again, I nodded.

"It wasn't the song," Gonzalez said. "It's the tape player. It's the exact same…" He shook his head, his eyes downcast, and with that look I understood. His own victim must have had the same CD player. He hadn't been reacting to the song at all. "Anyway," he said, "I wasn't the one acting strange. Popcorn and Telly, those guys started a fight over it."

"Telly? He the blond guy?"

Gonzalez was about to speak when the blip of a siren startled us both. We turned to look as a police cruiser crawled into the center of camp, parting the crowd. Miami P.D. swinging by for a routine check, although just as often they came through to harass the residents. Some of these men and women had parole terms stating no alcohol or illicit drugs. Others weren't allowed to be within a certain distance of other offenders, which didn't make much sense under the bridge, where everyone was here for the same basic reason. Most of the cops who came through here were just looking for a reason to use unacceptable force. For the most part, I wouldn't say I could blame them.

Gonzalez shifted nervously in the dirt. The cop got out of the car and headed over to a huddled group of sex offenders. As he turned in the direction of the scuffle, fear struck me and I hid my face, muttering, "Shit!"

Officer Sam Higgins' bald head gleamed as he patted a woman in boxer shorts and galoshes on the shoulder and passed a bottle of water to an elderly man I didn't recognize. New people wandered in here every day, as more and more were forced to sign the registry, many for petty offences. Higgins checked on a guy's ankle monitor. The guy – Dolph, I think – offered his hand, and Higgins shook it without hesitation.

It amazed me to see how humanely he treated these people, knowing his own children could easily have been victimized by some of them. It was clear he believed in basic human decency, though if he'd caught these same people in a crime I was certain he wouldn't hesitate to tackle the prick and put him in the back of his cruiser, maybe put a little more elbow into the bust than was necessary. He was a cop after all, not Gandhi. But the fact that a man who dealt with the absolute worst of humanity every single day could still find a moment to be charitable gave me a glimmer of hope.

As I watched him smile and shake hands, I felt like I could forget about the Rabbit Man. I could leave here and never come back. I could return to my long-suffering wife, to my courageous little girl who had somehow managed to put her assault in the past while her father continued to grieve.

Sam laughed at something one of the men said and got back in his cruiser. I watched him drive back to the topside of the Tuttle, watched everyone return to whatever they'd been doing. I felt myself relax.

"You know, if it's anyone here, I'd put money on Telly," Gonzalez said, dragging me right back down.

"Why him?" I snapped.

"I just overheard him bragging once, about all the stuff he'd gotten away with. He said he – "

It was clear he couldn't repeat the actual words Telly had used. "You don't have to say it."

Gonzalez gave a brief smile. "Thanks. He did it to a little girl, and all they got him on was trying to lure some cop posing as an eight-year-old."

Down there among the others, the blond guy, Telly, chucked a stone in the direction the cop car had gone, having since recaptured his bravado. I watched him swagger back to his own car and climb in, slamming the squeaky door behind himself.

"You're gonna kill him, aren't you?"

I thought about the scratches, the rabbits. My mind ran through all the gruesome scenarios I'd dreamed up during our sessions with Dr. Ambrose. "What if I said yes?"

Gonzalez followed my gaze. Telly's dirty work boots rested on the driver's window. Behind the windshield, the orange ember of his cigarette burned.

"I won't tell," Gonzalez said. "He'll just do it again, the second he gets a chance. You can tell just by looking at him. Heck, I wouldn't be surprised if that's what he does at night, driving off all by himself."

I considered this in silence, knowing the decision had already been made for me.

***

Except for those times he left camp well after sundown, I didn't let Telly leave my sight again for over a week. He'd recline the driver's seat and nod off as the sun began to sink beyond the skyline, well before anyone else had even considered sleep. Later, when most of us had been out for a few hours, I'd watch him light up a smoke in the dark behind the windshield. Then he'd creep out with the running lights off. A few hours later, he'd pull back into his spot. I'd watch him fire up a butt with his Zippo, lighting a dark smile on his face. The little orange ember of his cigarette would wax and wane. After a few minutes, he'd flick it out the window in a shower of sparks, put his booted feet out the window, and go back to sleep. Once, he'd gone directly to the water and washed his hands. To wash off what, I don't know.

But I can guess.

About a week into this routine, Telly left the car to go down to the water to fish. (We caught a fair bit down in that part of Biscayne Bay. Going hungry was never a worry, though I lost the taste for fish quickly.) I wandered over to the car, curiosity getting the best of me, and peeked in the dusty window. The passenger seat was covered in cassette tapes, mostly metal and hard rock bands: AC/DC, Iron Maiden, Metallica, Slayer. With a collection like that, it wasn't likely he'd have ever listened to George Michael, but I considered it might be a part of his pathology, like maybe he'd been abused to it when he was younger. Or maybe it reminded him of a junior school crush. Parking tickets were scattered on the floor like the bottom of a birdcage.

I spotted what I'd been hoping to find hanging from the rearview mirror. Due to the fine layer of dust on the windshield, I hadn't been able to see it before. A little white rabbit's foot swayed gently on a bathtub chain, a few spots of something dark on its fur. I shaded my eyes against the glass for a closer look, thinking it might just be blood.

"Lookin' for somethin', asshole?"

I stepped away, caught. Telly sauntered back with the fishing pole over his shoulder and no fish. I stammered something about looking for cigarettes, and Telly narrowed his eyes.

"You want a smoke, you coulda just ast." He reached into the back pocket of his jeans and pulled out a pack of Camels, shifting the pole to his other shoulder. He shook one out and flicked it at me. I caught it, fumbled it into the dirt. I picked it up and blew on it, then nestled it between my lips. The sweet smell of tobacco filled my nostrils. Marnie and I had quit when we found out she was pregnant. I'd sneaked a few puffs here and there after Nola was born, but after Marnie caught me lighting up the day of the argument, the day Nola ran away, I hadn't smoked since.

"Got a light?"

He threw that, too, but I caught it deftly. Lit the smoke. Inhaled. The first drag felt like pins jabbing my lungs. After that, the drags were smoother. "Thanks," I said, holding the cigarette between my teeth as I handed the Rabbit Man his lighter.

"No problem." He squinted at me. "No hard feelings about that love tap last week. I woulda hit me, too, if they'da been my buddies you was messin' with."

"They're not my buddies. Thanks again for the smoke," I added, walking away.

"Any time, amigo. Just stay the fuck away from my car next time."

I lied and said I would.

***

It was two nights later when I dared approach his car again. He was asleep inside, his boots on the dash. I crept up to the driver door and listened to his slow, deep breathing for a while, maybe too long. I needed to be sure he was sleeping. I wanted to catch him off guard. He looked at peace. Like he slept well. It enraged me to see that, when my own sleep was so fitful because of him.

I wondered how many other children he might have abused since the police sent him down here, how many childhoods he'd taken away. How many families he'd destroyed. How many fathers he'd poisoned, the way he poisoned me. I still knew nothing about him, but none of that mattered. I could have called in with Officer Higgins' badge number, got them to run Telly's plates. I could have found a previous address. I could have rented a car – unless Marnie had cancelled my credit cards, which was possible – and followed him the next time he left camp. I didn't do any of these things. I didn't want to know about his life. All I wanted was for it to be him, and for it to end *tonight*.

I rounded the dirty front of the car to the passenger side. Ever so gently, I pulled up the handle. The door came open an inch with a click that seemed to rebound off the cement pillars and the underside of the bridge. Telly snored and shifted in his sleep. I froze, blood hammering. We were mere feet from each other, but his car was far enough away from the rest of Bookville, a pariah among pariahs, that I thought I'd be safe from potential witnesses. Despite the distance, if he woke up and saw me looming over him, no doubt he'd shout, and my whole stupid reckless plan, the months of research and preparation and time away from the girls – all of it would have been for nothing.

I held my breath.

He didn't wake.

Slowly, I pulled the door open. The amount of times I'd watched him open it to get one thing or another, I knew it wouldn't creak, not like the driver door. I knew the dome light wouldn't come on, either; it had burned out or didn't work. I slipped in cautiously beside him and pulled the door closed.

Telly slept with his seat reclined, his knees curled up to his chest. He breathed deeply, a sure sign he was either asleep or faking it, ready to gut me like he gutted fish with the jagged hunting knife attached to his belt.

His eyes suddenly snapped open and he scrambled up against the door, sucking in a breath with childlike terror before squinting at me coolly.

"What the fuck do you want?"

"Roll up your window."

"Why the fuck should I?" He looked in the direction I indicated: the tip of my father's old buck knife aimed at the faded crotch of his tight jeans. "*Jesus*, man," he said on exhale and rolled up the window, not taking his eyes off me. "You mind tellin' me what the fuck you're doin' in my car? And don't say you're lookin' for a cigarette, amigo, 'cause I know you ain't a smoker."

For a long while, I said nothing. All the time I'd spent dreaming about this moment, it felt like he should know why I was here before I took his life away. It felt like I should make him aware, for Nola's sake if not mine. But everything I started to say seemed wrong. Like I'd be offering him an explanation he surely didn't deserve. Like I'd be allowing him the opportunity for forgiveness when forgiveness had never been an option.

"Take out the tape," I said finally.

"What?"

"*The tape. Take out the fucking tape.*"

"All right, man. *Shit.*" Eyeing me the whole time, Telly reached for the cassette player in the dash. His dirty fingers found the eject button and he pushed it. The tape popped out with a satisfying clunk. Telly fumbled it into his hand, then held it up for me to see. "All right?"

"All right," I said, and thrust the knife at his crotch.

Telly's eyes opened wider than I'd thought humanly possible, like something you'd see on a Saturday morning cartoon. He made to cry out, but I pressed a hand over his mouth, his mustache prickling against my palm, his tongue flicking out, probably involuntarily, as I mashed his head against the doorjamb.

Relishing the agonized terror in his eyes, I missed the sight of his hand scrabbling for the knife at his hip. He had it pulled out and pain tore up my chest before I could react. Smashing his head back against the door, I thrust my elbow against his wrist, pushing it back. I shoved my knee down hard against his legs, yanking on the knife in his groin. It came free with a jet of blood that splashed my wrist, his jeans already dark with it.

The wet blade gleamed in the arc lights as I pulled it back to strike again, and I shoved it straight into his throat, to the hilt. The monster's tongue flicked against my palm as his life spurted out from the hole in his neck, soaking my shirt. His legs kicked weakly, like a dying insect's. A gout of blood poured from the hole as he gagged. His fingers relaxed, dropping his knife. The life left his eyes.

I sat there a moment longer, watching his body leak blood, listening for his breath. I couldn't believe he was dead, that it was finally over and I could leave this godforsaken place and return to my family. Telly slid another few inches toward the floor. In the dim light beyond the space he'd left, I spotted Gonzalez huddled against a pillar, watching us with wide eyes. I wondered how long he'd been standing there. Long enough, I guessed.

His eyes met mine, and he nodded. Somehow, I managed to nod back.

The rabbit's foot jingled on its chain from the mirror as I pushed on the door. In all the commotion, I'd forgotten about it. I tore it down then to get a better look. The dark stains were no doubt blood. Whether it was fresh or not I couldn't tell, not when I'd just smeared Telly's blood onto its dirty off-white fur.

I tucked the totem into my pocket and tumbled out of the car. Gonzalez had turned away from me, heading back toward the others, though I knew he wouldn't tell, and I doubted he would be able to sleep. I felt like I could sleep for days, weeks. I stumbled headlong for the embankment, falling to my knees in the dirt and gravel. Clawing my way up the steep concrete grade, my father's knife left scrapes and drops of blood, black in the moonlight, I left the Rabbit Man behind me.

Or so I thought.

Because murder has a cost. That's something I've come to learn in the time since. Life doesn't just evaporate with the expiration of the body. The Rabbit Man is still alive, running through those dark, cold recesses in my heart. I carry his death with me like a haunting. It eats at me like cancer.

If I'd known then what I know now, I would have stuck with Dr. Ambrose and her words.

Lord knows it would have been cheaper.

***

I showered and shaved at my old 24-hour gym. It was late, and the attendant gave me a funny look. When I got to the showers, I understood why. I hadn't been into the city for a week, hadn't shaved, hadn't slept. My shirt was gouged open at the chest, matted to my skin with blood. I looked like a man who'd gotten lost in the jungle, fought a wild animal, and narrowly escaped with his life. I left, clean and shaven, my wound – Telly's blade had cut my left nipple in half – washed and dressed with paper towels, surprised that the kid wiping down the equipment hadn't called the cops. Far enough away from the mess I'd left under the Tuttle, I had no worries they would finger me for the crime even if the kid called in my appearance and had them pull the security video. For all they knew, I'd taken time off work to deal with the aftermath of what had happened to Nola. If they'd ever come around to check on us, I doubted Marnie would cover for me, but I was certain she wouldn't turn me in. Likely she would have told them we'd separated. That I'd gone back home to New Jersey to stay with my mother for a while.

I could picture her tenting her fingers deviously later on the way she sometimes did when she lied, and it broke my heart to know it would never be the same between us, no matter how hard I tried. Even if she'd have me back, our time apart would always be between us. And the Rabbit Man's death would seep into every seemingly pleasant conversation, every social engagement, every one of Nola's milestones. In the back of my mind and hers, the Rabbit Man would still be running.

Back at the house in Coral Gables, I used my key in the door, pleased for a second time to find it still worked. I crept up to our bedroom, saw Marnie sleeping with legs stretched over my side of the bed. It had been four months since we'd slept in that bed together, and she still slept mostly on her side.

I slipped by into Nola's room. The moon illuminated her head against the pillow. Nola had a thumb in her mouth, a habit she'd grown out of at age four but had taken up again in the wake of her experience with the Rabbit Man.

My sweet little girl's eyes opened wide as she drew the covers up to her chin, and for a terrible moment I flashed back to the eerily similar look Telly had given me when I woke him with the knife. Nola relaxed, seeing it was me. "I thought you were a monster," she said.

I wondered, *Am I a monster?*

Could I tell her there was nothing to be afraid of, that there was one less monster in the world because of me? I flashed on the tape in Telly's hand, completely unreadable in the dark. It could have been a polka album for all I'd cared. That splotch on the rabbit's foot could have been dirt or paint or just about anything.

I *wanted* it to be him. I *needed* it. I needed to be home with my wife. Our daughter.

Standing over her, it struck me with almost comical suddenness that Marnie had been right: Nola didn't need a vigilante… but I'd needed to *be* one. I'd fooled myself into believing that killing the Rabbit Man was about seeking justice for my little girl, but it had never been for her. I'd needed to take him out of the world to feel strong again. I needed to erase him from our family history because of my own shame. So I wouldn't feel like a coward anymore. So *I* would feel safe. It had never been about justice. And the fear, the shame… it would never end.

"No, honey," I told her, faking a reassuring smile. "It's me. Daddy's home."

THE KILLING FLOOR
ALICE J BLACK

All of his life, Nigel had never fit in. Not with his parents, not at school, not in any relationship, and for a long time he couldn't figure out why. Until he met her.

She smiled at him across the café, her lips a little lopsided and her blonde hair pulled back into pigtails. He met her eyes and looked away. Nobody normally looked at him and when they did, it wasn't with the fervour she watched him with. He ordered his coffee, picked up the tray and stepped tentatively among the tables.

"Hello," she greeted him in a small, sweet voice.

Their meeting was like an awakening in his mundane world and though he normally stayed away from human interaction for fear of making a fool of himself, something drew him in. "Hi." He smiled back, heat rushing across his cheeks.

"Want to join me?" She pointed to the chair opposite, palm facing the ceiling in an open gesture.

His natural reaction would be to turn away but the place was busy. Most of the tables were taken and usually he would have refused such an offer through lack of confidence in his own social skills, but if he wanted to stay and enjoy the coffee he had no choice.

"Thanks." Nigel sat across from the small woman and placed his cup on the table. When he looked up, he realised she was staring. Clearing his throat, he glanced away and then back only to find her still staring, a smile on her face.

"I'm sorry for staring." Her grin widened. "But there's something about you."

"Wh–what do you mean?" he stuttered. Had he been recognised from some geeky school photo or was he being called out on his nefarious gamer tags?

"I mean, I sense something about you. What's your name?"

"Nigel."

"I'm Phoebe."

He nodded once. "Nice to meet you."

She sat back in her chair, still observing. Her hands were clasped across her stomach and one leg was curled beneath her. Her eyes were blue and keener than anything he had ever seen.

"Nigel," she began, voice quiet, "have you ever heard of the Guild?"

He shook his head. He knew *of* guilds. He knew clubs and clans and guilds but none in real life. They were all in his gaming life.

"I suspect it is something that would interest you."

"You do?"

Nodding, she leaned forward again and he got a whiff of her perfume. Soft, subtle and feminine. "Come with me."

When she stood up it was like she held an invisible leash that led to his throat. He sprang to his feet, coffee long forgotten, and followed her out of the Basement Café. He felt like a puppy, eager to please and happy for some contact, and the truth was she was the first person to show him attention for a long time.

They walked down streets, across the town and down alleyways. He was lost before he knew it but, under the watchful eye of Phoebe, he didn't care. Nigel didn't even stop to consider what the Guild could be. He didn't care. The moment the woman had told him there was something special, he'd been caught up.

Finally, after they seemed to walk for miles, Phoebe stopped dead in front of him. Nigel stopped short and almost toppled but managed to catch his balance. He watched as the small woman knocked on a door. He realised there was a pattern and it was committed to memory within seconds.

A minute later, a small hatch was drawn back and a pair of steel-grey eyes stared out. They glanced over Phoebe then flicked to him. He bit his lip. What did it mean? Were they going to be granted admission or did his face spark controversy? He didn't have to wonder for long as the door opened seconds later.

"Come on." Phoebe winked at him and stepped inside.

Nigel followed her. As the door shut behind him, he found himself face to face with a man who had the stature of a giant.

He must have been over six and a half feet tall and his shoulders were wider than anything Nigel had ever seen.

"Who's this?" the man asked, looking Nigel up and down.

Nigel shuddered under his gaze. There was no way he wanted to get on the wrong side of this guy.

"This is Nigel."

Phoebe grasped his arm and a tingle ran down his skin. He stared at her fingers where they glanced his arm and realised he didn't remember the last time he had been touched. It had been months, years even.

"I met him in the coffee shop."

"Basement?"

"Yes."

"Why's he here?" the man boomed, his voice deep. He crossed his arms over his chest and continued to stare at Nigel.

"Relax, Dave. The guy's fine."

"That's what you think." Dave shook his head. "You better go see the Boss."

"Sure thing." She winked again and skipped towards another door.

Nigel was quick to follow, his footsteps heavy compared to hers. They made it to the door and she pushed it open with ease. Nigel followed her inside and his jaw dropped.

He had never seen anything like it. The room was huge, the ceilings high and supported by thick beams. The walls were made of stone, with stained glass windows dotted around the room, some mottled with dirt and others just dulled with age. Ahead of him, two long tables stretched the length of the room, with simple benches for sitting on either side. They were crammed full of food, drink and people.

At their entry, all heads turned their way. Nigel kept close to Phoebe as she made her way to the top table. He heard whispers – no doubt at his presence – and calls to his host as she skipped further up the hall. Finally, she stopped in front of a table that overlooked the entire room. Behind it sat a man with a dark goatee and sharp eyes, and beside him was a woman with long, fair locks and a wry smile on her face. Nigel knew without a doubt that he was the Boss.

"Who is this?" the Boss asked. His voice was soft with a hint of authority. Beside him, the woman curled on his arm, her stare unwavering.

"This is Nigel," Phoebe announced, pushing him forward.

"And he is here why?" The Boss eyed Nigel with hawk eyes and a twist in his lip.

"Nigel would like to join the Guild."

"Is that right?"

Nigel nodded as the eyes of the man bore down on him. He wanted it more than he had ever wanted anything. Instant belonging had been his the moment he'd set foot in the room, and although anxiety rolled in his gut and fear prevented him from speaking, he knew, in time, this would come to be his second home.

It seemed the stare and the silence lasted a lifetime. He was being weighed up, thought out and set into a pile. He just hoped it was the right one.

The Boss nodded. "Very well. Nigel, you must go through the trials."

Nigel's heart thumped. He was accepted into their folds. All he had to do was go through a few trials and then he would be a part of something. Part of a team. Wanted. Accepted. "Yes," he managed to say.

The Boss' mouth curved into a half smile. "Phoebe will mentor you. Induction begins today."

Beside him, Phoebe hopped up and down, her arm grazing his. "Come on, Nigel. We have a lot of work to do."

Her fingers wrapped around his arm and dragged him away from the top table. As he turned, he caught sight of the benches and his new family. They all eyed him silently. Some wore grim smiles, others grimaces, but he didn't falter. He was willing to take the bad with the good.

He followed Phoebe down a set of stone steps and into a dark basement, where he found himself in a long corridor. There was a copper tang to the air and the chill licked his skin. He shuddered but continued to follow.

Phoebe stopped in front of a door, unlocked it and kicked it open with her boot. She flicked a light and it burst to life, illuminating a square chamber. The ground beneath his feet was sandy and the walls emanated a deep cold that permeated his skin, but the thing that drew his attention was the woman sitting in the chair in front of him. Her ankles were bound with rope, her arms drawn behind the chair and presumably tied. A gag covered her mouth but he could not mistake the fear in her wide eyes, the tear tracks on her face.

"What is this?" he addressed Phoebe, his voice a whisper.

"This is your first trial."

Nigel looked from the woman to Phoebe. "What do you mean?"

Phoebe sighed. "Nigel, the Guild is expecting you to do this. The Boss doesn't accept just anybody into the fold. He rarely offers the chance of the trials. He saw the same thing in you that I did."

"What did you see?"

"That you have a flare for killing, just like the rest of us."

Nigel's jaw dropped. His hands hung limply at his sides. He dared to look at the woman who strained against her bonds, a muffled plea coming through the filthy cloth covering her mouth, and it all clicked into place. The Guild was a group of killers. They lived together, ate together and probably killed together. His first trial, as it were, was to kill the woman in front of him.

He swallowed hard. Never before had he considered the possibility that he could be a killer. Sure, he had moments much like any other human alive where he was so frustrated he thought he could, but the idea to actually go ahead with it had never crossed his mind. He wasn't that sort of person.

"There are instruments on the table to the right. You can use any one of them," Phoebe said, directing him to an old wooden table.

He saw them all laid out neatly: knives, hammers, nails, pliers, guns, tasers, power tools and other things he had never seen in his life. Instruments hung on the walls above the table and all of them looked as dangerous as the last. All of them put there for one purpose: to maim and kill this woman.

"Phoebe," he said, shaking his head. "I can't do this."

"Yes, you can." She nodded once, her eyes hard. "You have to. Already you know too much. Should you not complete the trial, you must face the punishment."

"Punishment?"

"Death."

The word hung between them like a balloon waiting to pop. He almost didn't dare take a breath. The simplicity was genius: kill or be killed. It was a moral choice, one he never thought he would have to make for himself. He glanced at the captive woman who pleaded with wide, red-rimmed eyes. His jaw dropped and then closed again. Words failed him. What she was asking – what *they* were asking – was murder. Sure, he wasn't the best person in the world, but was he a murderer?

"Nigel, you need to decide."

Phoebe's voice was flat, harsh, and as he looked at her in the severe light of the basement, he realised she wasn't the entirely cute, cheerful personality he had met at the café. This woman was one with secrets, one who lured him in with promises of happier times. Her bubbles and cuteness were masks she wore to snare people, perhaps as a way to cope with life. What did she know about him anyway? She'd brought him to this place thinking he was a killer. Why would she think that? He had given her no reason yet he was there.

He shook his head. "I can't."

"Nigel," she said in a low growl. Gone was the gorgeous smile, replaced with something so dark he almost looked away.

He swallowed. There was no way out of this. Kill or be killed.

He glanced at the bound woman and then at the tools on display. He would do it. He would kill the woman and he would leave and go to the police, tell them he was forced to murder. He couldn't forfeit his own life. He knew he didn't have much of an existence to begin with, but he was a coward. There was no way he could give in and let someone kill him, and he suspected it wouldn't be a quick death. At least with this woman – his trial – he would make it quick.

He took a step toward the bench. The woman in the chair bucked, eyes bulging. He forced his gaze away. He took four more quick steps, eyes on his feet and the way the thin layer of sand shifted beneath them. He reached the table. The tools were lined up with the precision of someone with OCD. His hand grazed the handles and a chill ran through his fingers.

He didn't want to do this and figured he would blow chunks as soon as he hurt the girl, but he had to do it. There was no way around it. So the least he could do was make it as quick as possible and not let the woman suffer. He grabbed a knife, wrapped it in his palm and faced the woman. From behind he saw her hair hung limp and greasy. He wondered how long she had been there.

He swallowed and took a step forward. He was doing her a favour. The woman would die down there no matter what. His killing would be merciful. He pictured the band of murderers upstairs and wondered how long they would take, what sort of torture they would put her through.

He took a step closer and saw her body quiver. He glanced up and saw Phoebe's eyes trained on him, the briefest of smiles on her thin lips. Inhaling, he looked down at the woman. It helped not being able to see her face, to hear her scream or know her name. That would have been the defining boundary.

Lifting the knife in his hand, he watched his shadow throw across the wall and the way the woman's head snapped towards it. She knew it was coming. She bucked and thrashed but her bonds were too tight. Closing his eyes, he muttered something close to a prayer under his breath and, without allowing himself to think anymore, brought the blade down.

He'd intended it to go over her shoulder and pierce her heart, but she wrenched to the side and the knife sliced through her neck instead. Blood spurted from the wound and he skittered back, heart pounding. It wasn't a deep cut but she would slowly bleed out. That wouldn't do.

He made another attempt. This time, the knife sunk into her chest but he hadn't thrust hard enough. When it slid back out, goose bumps rose on his flesh. He went a third time, aiming to kill. It felt good to rip her skin, to be the one in power for once.

Something in his stomach flipped and a smile curled his lips.

His hand became a frenzied tool as the knife hacked at her flesh. He moved around, his feet carrying him to face her. Tears streamed down her cheeks and her eyes perpetually bulged from their sockets. The woman was terrified, in pain, and he loved it. He realised with a sick relish that sliding that knife into the woman's flesh was home. He was finally home. This is what he had been missing all these years. This is who he had been hiding.

He chopped and slashed, the knife opening wounds on her face and neck until she looked like something from a nightmare. She was cut and bleeding and her spirit was ebbing. Her head lolled on her shoulders and fell forward. She was on the verge of death. He knew it wouldn't be long. He had to see it, had to see the life leak from her eyes.

Crouching, he pushed her forehead back. Her eyes came to rest on him and instead of the terror he'd seen moments ago, he saw relief. Then her eyes glazed over and she was gone.

He took a deep breath and dropped her head. She sat still, lifeless in the chair she was bound to. Blood snaked down her body and dripped to the floor. He realised he was panting. His body was exerted, and for the first time in his life he felt good. He felt like he had just done something he was meant to carry on doing for the rest of his life. He had found his calling.

Then a hand was on his shoulder. It was soft and warm. Nigel pushed himself up, toying with the knife in his hand. Emotions rushed through his body. Adrenaline, heat, lust. Turning to face Phoebe, he pulled her slender body close and pressed his lips to hers. She tasted sweet and soft and opened her mouth to slide her tongue into his mouth. He shuddered. She felt soft and womanly, yet there was a killer hidden inside. Just like there was a killer inside of him.

When he pulled away, his arm still holding her close, she leaned back and giggled. "You did it, Nigel. She was your first."

They both looked at the woman. Her clothes were redder than their natural colour and the sandy floor around them was soaking up the blood.

"What now?" he asked. The room was a mess. He was a mess.

"I'll show you." Skipping around the body, Phoebe hit a switch. Beneath the chair a trapdoor opened and everything – wooden chair, body and blood – disappeared through it. He heard a dull thump.

"Where does it go?" he asked.

"You'll see soon." She grinned. "Oh, and Nigel, welcome to the killing floor."

***

He knew from that moment, his life was going to change forever. He was finally at one with himself, at peace with the world and eager for more. "What's next?" he asked as Phoebe showed him to a room. It was kitted out with everything he could need from a bed to a walk-in shower.

"Take a shower. You're disgusting."

Her face melted into a smile and he couldn't help but smile back. He understood her demeanour now. She was a cold-hearted killer just like him, but with her kin, she was herself. Just like he would be.

She left the room, pulling the door shut behind her, and Nigel was left alone. His heart still thumped and his fingers clenched and unclenched like they longed to hold the knife again. He wondered what the next trial would be, when it would be, and when he would be officially inducted into the folds of the Guild.

Nigel took a shower. The water was hot and strong, washing away the blood and gore. He watched as the red liquid swirled down the drain. When he got out, he pulled a plush towel from the rail and dried off. A fresh set of clothes waited on the bed. Phoebe must have snuck in while he was showering. He tingled at the thought. It seemed his thirst for blood had awakened something else too.

He dressed and sat on the bed. His feet danced and his fingers intertwined with one another. He wanted to move, to act, to kill. Instead it seemed he was destined to sit there for a long time.

A few hours later, there was a rap on his door. Nigel jumped up and rushed across the room, still wired from the kill. He opened the door to find Phoebe. She looked glamorous in a black mini, her hair cascading over her shoulders.

"Wow."

She giggled. "You like?"

He could only nod.

"Come on. It's time for dinner, and to meet the rest of the crew."

He stepped from the room and pulled the door shut behind him, eager to meet the family he would spend his life with. As they walked down corridors and descended stairs, he made a mental note of the direction. With his photographic memory, he knew he would find his way back to his room later.

They entered the same room as earlier but this time Nigel was greeted with candles lining the tables, a darker atmosphere and lots of well-dressed people.

"Welcome!" The Boss' voice boomed across the room and everyone stood to look at him. "Phoebe tells us you have completed the first task. Therefore, we are able to induct you into the Guild. While you still have two trials ahead of you, I am confident you will become a permanent fixture in the halls of this building."

A roar went up around him as people stamped feet, banged tables and hollered. People grinned at him, and as he made his way to a space on the bench beside Phoebe, he knew it was all for him. Nigel the destroyer. Nigel the defiler.

He grinned like an idiot as he took a seat and tucked in. The meal was delicious. Hot chicken smothered in barbecue sauce, roasted peppers and plenty of homemade bread to go around. He was in heaven. He couldn't remember the last time he'd eaten so well – or so much.

"So Nigel, I'm Glenn," the man beside him said, striking up a conversation.

"Hello." Nigel nodded towards him, swallowing his mouthful of food.

"I'm known for the power-tool murders around here."

"He gets very defensive about it," Phoebe whispered.

"Do not!"

"Uh-huh!"

"So what's your forte?" he asked Nigel.

It was the first time Nigel had considered the possibility that he might need to have a *thing*. He looked around the hall at the sea of faces and knew they all had something special. They all had a way about them, a certain style, and that's what he was missing. He needed an MO. He shrugged. "I don't know yet."

"Well, if you want help to work on it, let me know." Glenn bit a hunk of chicken off the bone.

Nigel nodded. Now this was something. He had to make his identity. Each move from now on would be monitored, criticised and reviewed. He needed to focus, and quick.

"Hey." Phoebe nudged him. "Don't look so worried. It's in there."

He bit his lip. Perhaps it was, but his mind was blank at that moment and it was like he was pre-Guild Nigel again. He wouldn't go back to that now, couldn't. "What's yours?"

"Hammer."

Nigel looked about the room at the ruthless killers he was breaking bread with.

As if she sensed his anxiety, Phoebe leaned in. "We have a strict pact here in the Guild. No killing the other members. It's the only rule we have beyond the trials."

He breathed a sigh of relief. It felt good to know he was both safe and protected here in the Guild, though it didn't stop the worry flowing through him. The next trials were tomorrow and he had to work on it, to find something that portrayed him as a person, his style and flair. What could that be? He glanced around the room. Everybody there had an MO, a unique style, and he would have to find something that would fit him and prevent him from treading on toes.

He sighed. It was going to be a long night.

"Listen up." The Boss thumped the table and instant silence ensued. "Tomorrow night, the annual kill fest begins."

A round of cheers coursed through the room.

The Boss held up his hand and peace reigned once more. "The story this year is that a gang of convicts has escaped from the nearby facility and are wreaking havoc."

Phoebe smiled and whispered, "He comes up with a great cover story every year."

"We have a leader board in the common room. With each kill you make you are expected to keep a tally. At the end of the night the person with the most wins the grand prize."

"What's the grand prize?" Nigel asked Phoebe.

"No idea." She shrugged. "It's top secret."

"Nigel, are you in?" the Boss asked him directly.

Suddenly all eyes were on him. He stammered and fell silent.

"I know you are still completing your trials but I have every faith in you. Yes or no?"

The word came out without a thought. "Yes."

The Boss' face erupted into that wry grin. "Good. That's what I like to hear. The challenge starts at midnight tomorrow, after which you have twelve hours, my lambs. Good night."

The room erupted in a series of mutters and excited giggles.

This killing spree was it. This was Nigel's chance to prove himself once and for all. He would show them all he could do this. He was meant for this life. It was what he had been waiting for.

"Who won last year?" Nigel asked.

"The Prickler." Phoebe nodded to a man across the room. He sat in a corner, eyes closed and arms held in a pose above his legs as if he was meditating. "But I came close. This year I'm going to nail it."

Nigel took a breath as he glanced at Phoebe. The woman was clearly well-respected and if he had anything to go by, the crazy faraway look in her eye told him all he needed to know. She would certainly put up a good fight. He wondered if he would even come close to top on the leader board. He sure had to try.

"So it starts at midnight. I'm guessing there won't be a lot of sleeping going on."

Phoebe shook her head. "We prepare for this event over the year and when it comes, we go wild. The whole point is to show the world that there is more to death than just killing. It's an art, and we need people to understand that."

Nigel nodded. He understood that, all right. He remembered the way the knife had slid into the woman's flesh and the way hot blood spurted on his hand, the thump in his chest. He bit his lip. "I can't wait to do it again."

"Hold your horses, cowboy. Get some sleep. You have a big day ahead of you."

She slapped his arm playfully and Nigel took it as his cue to leave. Besides, she was right. He wanted to rest, to sleep and prepare for the big day ahead.

***

"So where are we going this time?" he asked as he followed Phoebe the next day. It was close to midday and despite not having slept well, he felt fresh. The woman could have been leading him into the very depths of hell but he inherently trusted her.

Phoebe, his mentor, his friend. Without her he would have found none of this. He would still be living his same dull life, moving from café to work to home and repeating the process. He had been stuck on a spin cycle and now that he was finally out of it, he felt invigorated. His whole body tingled with anticipation as he wondered what would be coming next. Whatever it was, he would do it, hands down.

"Back to the killing floor."

He grinned. The killing floor. The place where he'd made his first kill. Something swooped in his stomach and his grin widened. "What is my trial?"

"You'll see."

It wasn't long before they reached the floor. Phoebe led him down a dark corridor with doors on either side and stopped in the middle. Nigel took in the scenery. Hell, if he had been on the other side of this, he would have been terrified. The place was dark beyond belief, the air colder than ice and the décor less than tasteful. The doors were made of metal, the studs either side depicting nail heads in a coffin. Overhead, only one bare bulb lit the entire corridor and he shuddered. The place was a nightmare.

"There are ten doors in this corridor. Behind each door awaits a surprise," Phoebe announced.

Nigel looked up and down the corridor once more and saw numbers painted in red above each one of the doors. "I go through all ten?" he asked. He didn't know whether that made him eager or worried.

Phoebe shook her head. "You get to pick one. Whatever you come across in that room, you have to deal with it."

Nigel nodded. He got the concept but he had no idea what he faced. And everything was a game of luck. He could pick something awful or he could pick something nice. He glanced up and down the room.

"You ready?" she asked, her voice light and bubbly.

Nigel nodded. "Number seven."

They walked to the door, their footsteps echoing across the stone. Phoebe lifted a key and inserted it into the lock. She turned it and he heard it click. When she tried the handle it moved with ease.

She turned to grin at Nigel. "What's behind door number seven?"

He smiled back and pushed the door, stepping into the darkness beyond.

As if sensing movement, a light came on. It was bright enough to illuminate his prey but not so bright as to make him shy away. He realised something in that moment: people like him dwelled in the dark. It covered them and hid them. Darkness was a friend, an ally, and he would come to use it to his advantage.

Inside he found a man strung up from the ceiling. His wrists were bound by chains and a piece of silver duct tape covered his mouth. The man's eyes flicked open and bulged as he saw Nigel standing there in the doorway. He writhed against the chains but they held fast, his feet swaying and his big toe trailing across the ground where Nigel saw a thin sliver of blood.

He wondered how long the man had been chained up, awaiting his end. Ignoring the man, Nigel's eyes moved across to a table at the side of the room. He strode to it and took in his array of tools. Then something else caught his attention. A note. He picked it up, unfolded the paper, and read the few lines there:

This man is a rapist.
He has hurt and tortured women for much of his life.
He gets away with it because he's a cop.
Do what you will.

Anger boiled through him as he crushed the paper in his fist. There was nothing worse than a cop abusing their position of power. The man swinging in the room was a scumbag. He tortured women for his own needs, held them against their will and then told them nobody would believe them.

He dropped the note back on the table and picked up a small knife. Running it across his finger, he felt the blade slice through his skin and smiled. Small and sharp. Good. He could have fun with this.

Strolling back to the man, Nigel circled him. He took in the pale white skin, the hairy ass, the sweat pooling at the base of his back. Then in a swift motion, he darted forward and felt the knife penetrate skin. The man bucked and when his legs dropped, Nigel saw a thin line of blood streaming from his side.

He continued to circle, coming to face the man. Nigel stood inches from him and watched as the man's eyes filled with tears. Tears that would do him no good in a place like this. Crocodile tears. After all, how many women had he hurt? How many women had he made cry? Fucking sick pig.

Nigel slashed again. This time the blade crossed the chest and a small gash appeared, blood instantly seeping through the skin. They were shallow cuts but the sight of blood had Nigel wanting more. His little knife was like a razor and he knew it could do a lot of damage.

Lifting his hand, he pressed the flat side of the blade to the man's cheek. The man thrashed, his legs coming to fall back against Nigel, but he didn't move and the knife came back to place.

"You think I'm going to spare your life?"

The man nodded, eyes wide and tears running down his face. Nigel wondered how he would plead his case, if he could.

"Did you think of all those women you hurt? The women you raped?"

More tears.

Nigel snarled. "You are the worst kind of sick fuck there is and you are going to pay." Spittle flew from his mouth and hit the man. He flinched for a second but then went back to pleading with his eyes.

Nigel turned the knife until the blade touched the man's skin. Putting some pressure on the handle, he pulled the knife down the man's cheek, watching as the flesh opened. Beneath he caught a glimpse of pink muscle and, as he pressed deeper, the maw of the mouth. He grinned, taking the blade away. The man's face trickled blood and his mouth hung open. Nigel wondered whether it was pain or disbelief. Probably both. He didn't care. What he cared about was revenge.

The rapist's most important tool was below the belt, so Nigel decided he would take that away. His eyes travelled down the man's sweaty, bloody body and came to rest at his groin. The man bucked as he watched Nigel reach forward, but his swing only took him so far away before he was thrown right back into place and his cock came to rest in Nigel's hand. Nigel squeezed hard and watched the man's face ball up, his eyes screwed tight, lines cutting across his temples.

"You'll never hurt anyone again."

Nigel stabbed the knife down into the base of the man's groin and grinned as a feral growl came from behind the gag. He hacked and sawed, laughing as blood spurted from the member. It covered him, dripped on the floor, and then, finally, it was detached. He held it up in his hand, high enough for the man to see, and dangled it there for a second. Then he ripped the tape from the man's mouth, releasing his squeal of pain. Taking the opportunity, he rammed the dislodged member into the man's mouth and watched as he gagged and choked. Blood kept on spurting and it wasn't long before his body began to slow.

Nigel stepped forward and grabbed the man either side of the face. "You deserve this."

The light left the man's eyes and his body fell limp against his shackles. Nigel stood there breathing hard, heart pounding in his chest.

Just then the door opened behind him and Phoebe bounced in. Her feet splashed through the blood on the concrete floor. Her hand reached up and grabbed Nigel's arm, fingers stroking. Spinning, he mashed his lips against hers. She pressed her body into his and they stood in the gore of the killing, enjoying each other.

When she finally pulled away, she had a huge grin on her face. "Wow, Nigel. I didn't think you had it in you."

"I thought that's why you recruited me," he said, panting.

"Oh, the killing, yes." She nodded. "I meant a kiss like that." She giggled.

"What now?"

"Want to do the honours?" She nodded towards the switch.

Nigel strode across the room to the bench and hit the button. Beneath the man, a hatch opened up and the chains that bound him released. Nigel smiled as he heard the body slam on the floor beneath before the hatch closed.

"Now go clean up and get ready for the next trial. I know you can do it."

Nodding, Nigel left the room. He made his way back through twisting corridors and upstairs until he reached his room. He took a shower and watched as blood and gore pooled down the drain. He smiled. That was his work. His doing. He had done the world a favour and they didn't even know about it. Well, maybe one day they would. They would know his name all over town, all over the world. He would be hailed as the most horrific killer of their time, a fable told to children to make sure they stayed in bed at night. All he had to do was perfect his MO.

When he was done showering, a pile of clothes lay on the bed for him. His groin twitched at the thought of Phoebe creeping into his room. Man, he wanted that woman so bad. She was clearly a force to be reckoned with and he would have a lot of competition when it came to the killing spree, but he was determined to beat her and then fuck her.

He dressed and then stepped out into the corridor. Phoebe waited for him there, leaning against a banister, hair wrapped around her fingers.

"Ready, soldier?"

"What's next?"

"Something a little bit different. Come on."

She skipped down the hallway and he followed. This time they avoided the killing floor, instead making their way along a corridor that looked relatively normal if not a little bland. Strip lights flickered overhead and windows showed him scenes of empty rooms. Then they stopped. Phoebe opened a door and motioned for him to step inside.

As soon as he did the door was closed and locked. He was stuck in there. Sudden panic crept up his throat but he swallowed it down. He wasn't in any danger. He knew he was safe. He just had to figure it out.

In front of him was a square room. The walls were white and in the centre was a metal table. Three chairs were seated around the table and he knew instinctively he had to take the single. He did so, planting his ass and leaning on the table. This couldn't be any worse than anything he had already faced. He just had to suck it up and deal with whatever came through the door.

It wasn't long before the door opened. His back straightened and he watched as two men dressed in suits entered the room. They each took a seat opposite him, elbows resting on the table, stern looks firing his way, and he instantly knew what this was. An interrogation.

"Mr. Nigel Somersby?" the one on the left said. "I am Detective Allinson and this is Detective May. We're here to ask you some questions."

Nigel nodded and tried to hide the smile on his face. Though he knew what it was, he had to take it seriously. This was his last trial. All he had to do was work through this and pass the test and he would be a part of the Guild.

"One of our colleagues, Sergeant Wills, has been reported missing. He has not been seen for three days and we have reason to believe you know of his whereabouts."

Nigel shook his head. "I don't believe I've ever met the man." He pictured the man hanging in the room, his foot trailing the floor, his body covered in welts.

"Come on, Nigel," May added. "We know you know something."

"What makes you think that?" Nigel asked, chin coming to rest on his hands.

"Traces of your DNA were found at his home."

"That's impossible. I don't even know who he is." He shook his head. He might have killed the fucker but he wouldn't know his apartment.

"Where were you on the night of the 3rd?" Allinson asked.

Nigel rubbed his chin, pretending to think, and then finally answered, "Oh, I was in the café."

"Which café is that?"

"Basement, in town."

"I know the place," May told Allinson.

"We will make moves to corroborate your story, Nigel," Allinson warned him.

"That's fine." Nigel smiled. This was going well.

"Can you explain the newspaper clippings found in your flat that all pertain to a series of sexual assaults?" May asked.

Nigel's mouth turned down. He certainly hadn't collected anything of the sort but he had to keep cool. This was a trial. He chanted the words in his head. "I was getting ready to move, Detectives. I was collecting newspaper in order to wrap some of my precious belongings."

They remained quiet. He could tell they didn't believe him but there was no proof otherwise. He swallowed a smile. This was no time to gloat.

"Very well. That's all for now," Allinson announced. "But we will be in touch, Nigel."

The two officers stood and left the room, slamming the door behind them.

Seconds later, Phoebe burst into the room and rushed forward. She dived across the table, her arms looping around Nigel's neck as she kissed him. "You did it!" she screeched. "I knew you could do it." She planted kiss after kiss on his lips.

Nigel pulled her onto his lap and pressed his lips to hers. He was on fire. He was untouchable. Standing, he cradled the small woman in his arms and sat her on the table. He pressed his groin into the groove of her legs and moaned. He had completed his trials. It was time to take what he wanted.

He took her right there on the table in the interrogation room, her screams filled with the pleasure he'd always dreamed he could elicit.

He had made it. He was finally the person he was born to be and he couldn't wait for the next stage.

***

"I'm two ahead of you already," Nigel said as Phoebe pulled her clothes on, hiding the flesh that had become his to taste.

She turned and winked. "Don't worry, I'll catch up."

Something knotted in his chest. No matter who she was, no matter how much he liked the woman, she couldn't beat him. Nobody could.

"Does everyone have a patch?" he asked. He didn't want to step on toes though he already knew what lengths he was willing to go to, to prove his worth.

"Not really." She shrugged. "If you get there first it's your kill. Don't get caught and don't spill the beans."

"Never." He shook his head. Now that he'd found his home, the one place he could be himself, there was no way he would give it up.

"Good luck, soldier." Reaching up, she kissed him on the cheek and skipped from the room.

***

As he stepped into the corridor, Nigel found himself converging in a long line of people making their way into a room. It looked like the kill fest was about to begin. The line trickled incessantly and he danced on his feet, peering over the tops of heads and craning his neck forward. It wasn't long before he got there and he soon realised why the line had moved fast. The weapons room was huge. Its ceilings were cavernous and it stretched on as far as he could see. Shelving lined the walls with an array of weaponry beyond his comprehension.

He stood in the doorway and looked around the room. This was his moment, the time he would pick his MO. It had been on his mind for some time now, since he'd completed his first trial. The knife. A simple blade but one that he would make his. He would be the Slasher. He would make his victims hurt, cutting open their skin before he killed them. There lay his art, his style, himself.

He headed over to the right, where knives of all shapes and sizes lined a shelf. His fingers ran across the blades and a tingle coursed down his spine. Yes, this was right for him. He would be the Slasher.

He finally settled on a blade of eight inches in length, the steel sharp. As he picked it up, he caught a glimpse of his reflection in the steel. The person staring back at him was a different man. He had changed. Nigel grinned and sheathed the blade in his jacket.

The room quieted and as he spun, Nigel saw the Boss standing in the doorway. His woman hung on his arm, the blonde wearing a painted smile on her face. He wondered why they did not take part in the revelry, why the couple didn't want to enjoy the night as the others did.

"Ladies and gentleman," the Boss addressed them. "Now is the time to perform your art. Now is the time to cull the population of the town and make them see just what we do." His eyes scanned the room and came to rest on Nigel. "I expect complete honestly from all of you. I have eyes and ears everywhere. Come the morning, we will have our new champion. Good luck to you all."

A chorus of cheers rocked the room, hitting the ceiling and echoing back. Nigel's chest swelled as he sucked it all in. This was heaven, his home, and he would take the title of champion. He knew it.

The horde set out from the Guild as an army readies for battle. Silently they leaked from the doorway, parting ways and becoming individual in the night. As Nigel set foot into the alley outside, he took a deep breath. This was his town and he knew most of it like the back of his hand.

"Good luck," Phoebe whispered, nudging him with her arm as she passed.

Nigel watched her leave. The woman of his dreams, off to compete against him. He gritted his teeth and turned the opposite way.

He made his way down alleys, across streets, skirting around houses. He heard laughter and watched the merriment inside as he passed them, but that wasn't his forte. He wasn't the type to break into houses.

He kept moving. This side of the neighbourhood was rough. It wouldn't be a problem for him but it meant plenty of people around, plenty of victims. He slipped down the next dark lane and his heart sped up as he spotted a lone figure near the bottom. The person walked upright, albeit wobbling side to side. This was not one of his clan. He grinned. This would be his first.

Nigel crept forward, hand sliding into his jacket and pulling out the knife. It glinted in the dark and he held it close. On and on he moved, keeping his steps as quiet as possible while making his way towards his prey. He was gaining on her, a small brunette woman on her way home, he guessed. Not anymore.

He was feet away from her and caught the scent of cherries and smoke. He breathed it all in. He wanted to remember this.

Then he lunged. He caught the girl by her throat and slammed her against the wall, her yelp like music to his ears. Her eyes were huge and though fear lingered in them, he realised she was too far gone to understand the enormity of what she was going through. Lifting the knife, he pressed it to her face. She flinched and tried to back away but he held her firm. This little weasel wasn't going to pop anymore.

Twisting the blade, he sliced it down her cheek, watching as the flesh opened. She strained against his hand, trying to move her face away from the weapon as small shrieks escaped her mouth, and it wasn't until the knife completed its journey that the real panic set in. Her eyes were wide, tears dripping down her cheeks as she pressed a palm to the wound on her face and glimpsed her own blood in the dim light of the alley. Realisation was dawning. She knew she wouldn't make it home.

He slashed at her skin again and again. Angry red welts ripped up her flesh, her bare arms, her neck and face. With each mark she lost a little of herself. She began to sag and he knew she was willing the end to come. He would give it to her. Nigel would make this woman his first official kill and she would be forever remembered in his mind.

Lifting the knife one final time, he pressed it to her throat. Then he leaned forward and pressed his lips to her forehead. "I will always remember you," he whispered as he drew the knife across her throat.

She drew her last breath and gurgled as her air supply was cut off. Then she slid down the wall, her body lifeless.

Nigel didn't know how long he stood there watching her, looking at his first. He wanted to remember the moment forever. He wanted to recall the way her hand slumped on the ground and the way her head lolled to one side. She was a beauty and he had only just begun to perfect his art.

Finally he left the scene. It was time to find his next. Tonight was not only about new things and defying the world, but proving he could be a champion. He had to get as many kills as he could.

On and on he stalked, moving down alleyways and streets. Everything was dim but every now and again he caught a glimpse of a shadow moving across the darkness and he smiled as he recognised one of his own. As he came across his next victim he continued on his spree.

It wasn't until the sky woke in a purple haze that he realised the time. He had to get back to the Guild and chalk his kills on the board. He gritted his teeth and ignored the bubble in his stomach as he hurried back to his new home. He had no idea how he had done compared to anyone else. There was no way of knowing how many kills could have been totted up.

He finally made it, stepping into the old building and striding straight to the staff room. It was already full of people squashing their way to the board, clamouring for attention and pens. Once they cleared out, he made his way forward and made seven strikes underneath his name. Seven kills, including the two trials earlier that day. A quick glance at the board showed he was top.

His heart skipped as he moved away. He was top. He had done it. His kills outranked everyone else. He hid his grin. He couldn't gloat, not yet.

A few minutes later the Boss arrived. He stepped towards the chart and tallied up the counts. He nodded and murmured under his breath, and then Nigel heard a sharp intake. This was it, his moment. He would be crowned Champion and he would forever be remembered as both the newcomer and the herald of the Guild.

The Boss spun on his heel and eyed his subjects.

"Well, it seems that this year you have all done me proud. These numbers show your dedication to our course, and as the sun rises and their bodies are found, our art will be known across the world. Of that I have no doubt."

A polite round of applause ensued. Nigel knew everyone waited for that moment. They wanted to know who was being crowned the victor. He squared his shoulders and crossed his arms over his chest.

"It seems that this year, something has happened that has never happened before," the Boss continued.

Nigel's shoulders sagged. That didn't sound good.

"We have a tie. Congratulations to our two highest kill streaks tonight, Nigel and Phoebe."

His heart stopped. He had done so well. He had taken it all on board, had accepted his personality and stalked like a hunter, and still he had not done well enough to beat her. His eyes found her in the crowd and he saw the same venom staring straight back at him. He caught sight of blood spatters on her face, on her clothes. The woman was a monster. Just like him.

"I simply cannot have two champions. It is not the done thing." The Boss shook his head.

"We fight," Phoebe hissed.

"To the death," Nigel threatened.

All eyes in the room moved between the two. There was no sound. Nigel's hands tightened into fists as he stared her down. He would win. He would take the title and he would be their king.

"You want me to forsake the one rule of the Guild?" the Boss asked. His gaze moved from Phoebe to Nigel.

"Yes," Nigel replied. There was no question about it. It would happen whether the Boss allowed it or not.

"Very well. To the chamber."

A huge roar went up and Nigel was swept along with the crowd. He had no idea what the chamber was or where he would find it but none of that mattered. What mattered was preserving his name and being crowned champion of the Guild. He moved with the crowd, at one with his people, but he saw none of them, felt none of the pats on his back or shouts of encouragement. All he saw was red.

They made it to a huge doorway and as it was pushed open, both he and Phoebe were ushered inside. Then it closed and he heard it lock. Thundering feet continued outside, and when he looked around the room he caught glimpses of faces above him. They were in an arena.

"Ready to die?" Phoebe asked.

"Are you?" he threw back. There was no way she was beating him. He pulled the knife out from his jacket and watched as the hammer came out of her belt. It was covered in hair and gore.

"Only one of you will walk out of this room," the Boss' voice came over a Tannoy, thick and metallic. "Good luck."

Nigel hunkered down as Phoebe began to circle. He had to be ready. He had to watch. If she struck him with the hammer he would go down, and she knew it. His knife, compared to her weapon of choice, looked like a flimsy alternative. He would have to outwit her.

She lunged, her face twisting into a ferocious snarl. Nigel spun out of the way. The movement of air swished behind him and he knew the hammer had missed him by inches. He took a deep breath as he came back to face her. He held the knife out in front of him but he felt defenceless. He wanted a shield – something – to protect himself.

Pushing forward, his reach meant the knife entered her circle of defence and it slashed her arm. She hissed. Above, the crowd sucked in a breath. As he saw blood seeping from her arm, Nigel smiled. His first blow had hit home. It was just a matter of time.

"Think you can beat me?" she taunted him. "I've been doing this for as long as I can remember, newbie."

Nigel grinned. "That's what you think." Until entering the Guild, he had never killed, but as soon as that knife had been in his hand it became an extension of his arm. He was finally at one with himself and peace with the world, and he knew that gave him the advantage.

She circled, arms wide. Nigel thrust again and caught her right arm this time, the flesh opening up in a red welt. She hissed again.

Two hits against none. He was on top of the world.

Just then the hammer came crashing down on his shoulder. Growling in pain, he backed away. He knew something was broken, or at least dislocated. His left arm throbbed with a dull ache but he knew he had to stay focused. Focus or die.

With a snarl, he made to dodge left, but as she spun he moved right. This time he caught her in the neck. Blood spurted from her pale skin and dripped down her cape. With wide eyes she pressed her hand to the wound. It could be fatal if she kept bleeding out but he knew what she was thinking. She planned to kill him, get it over with now, and then get patched up. He couldn't let that happen.

While she was still stunned, he made another move, this time ducking beneath her arms and coming up under her stomach. He rammed the knife home. It went through ribs and lungs and up into her heart.

Her jaw dropped as a feral moan escaped her lips, spittle dangling from her mouth. The hammer fell from her hand and she became limp in his arms. Cradling her body, he eased her onto the floor, where she stared up at him.

"I knew you had it in you," she whispered. The light faded from her eyes and she became still.

Suddenly, his heart dropped. He had killed her. The woman who had rescued him from the mundane. The woman who had walked by him through the trials and the one he'd taken as his own. She was dead.

A roar went up in the crowd as the Boss named him Champion and promised him the ultimate prize, but all he could thing about was the loss of the best thing in his life.

REVENGE EXACTLY
TAMARA FEY TURNER

Her fingernails caught skin and blood under them as she raked the tender neck of her assailant. His hot breath brushed her face and her breasts. His large hands pressed on her throat, crushing her beneath him, stopping her screams and tears. She did not feel him penetrate her skin, peeling it back, spraying her blood, and putting his face inside her to take a bite of her heart.

***

The waiting room is shiny and smells bleachy. The middle-aged woman sits. *The doctor will be with me shortly,* she repeats in her head. Three times. Six. Nine. Multiples of three keep her calm. The phrase is suddenly purged as her mind is riveted to another thought, a flash of memory causing physical jolts, as if she is being struck by lightning. Or perhaps something worse.

The memory takes her back more than 15 years to her life as a younger woman. *"Malachi, please tell me what happened! Tell me now, so I can help you."*

"You will help me, Mother. You will."

"I need to at least try to understand."

"You understand enough."

The police had questioned her then. And Malachi.

"Mrs. Andersen…"

"Ms. Jacoby, officer."

"Uh, sorry. Ms. Jacoby, when was the last time you saw your son?"

"I'm not sure, officer. I must have been distracted somehow."

"May I speak with your other son?"

"I'm right here, Officer Jordan, sir!"

The high-spirited voice had seemed to catch the officer off guard. *"Son, were you out with your brother today?"*

"No, sir. Michael has a bad habit of wandering off on his own. I always tell him something's bound to kill you out there if you don't watch out."

Clearing his throat, the policeman had looked at her. *"Well, ma'am, thank you. We'll do everything we can, and keep you posted, of course."* Tipping his hat, Officer Sam Jordan had then exited the tiny wooden shotgun home without looking back.

In the years that followed, in the states and towns that changed all too frequently, the police would knock on her door often. Always questions without answers.

Karla Hughes. Jolene Perry. Laura Minks. There were others. Many others. The police did not believe she had no knowledge of the girls, or of Malachi's involvement with them.

For years, Ruth had kept newspaper clippings of all local deaths in her area, whether she thought Malachi was involved or not. Just in case. In case of what? That, she was unsure of.

In truth, she knew very little; she had no more proof than the authorities. But she had her feelings. Her gut. Her instincts about her only remaining child. She knew he must be the serial killer he was accused of being. Although, no one ever put it together quite like that. One suspicious circumstance after another seemed to be connected by no one except her.

At four years old, Malachi had killed the family cat and concealed it in his room. She'd tried to talk to the boys' father, Sean, but he left soon thereafter, thinking she was crazy in the way she felt about the boys: one dangerous, the other in danger. He'd accused Ruth because her mother was a self-proclaimed witch, but Constance was also mentally ill. Could one or both of their children be as well? Sean had said it was she who was mentally ill, but left the boys with her anyway.

The police inquiries, though, were never official. If they had found some evidence, taken him away from her, perhaps things would have been made right with the universe. It was the police's job to help her! After all, she had no choice but to protect him. They should have been able to see the monster he was… is.

Girls missing. Murdered. Not only girls. But in Malachi's teens, she could see his lust growing, and there was no denying the number of missing young girls wherever they lived. His appetite was strong then. Out of control. Although he never caused her physical harm, Ruth was terrified.

"Remember, I love you, Mother. And you must love me too. I am your only son now."

These words echo in her head today. Reverberate. Crash. Consume her. Three times. Six.

A tear gravitates toward Ruth's chin. She does not wipe it.

Across the hall, a nasally voice mumbles over a static-filled intercom. Ruth cannot understand it, but she already knows what it says. 6pm. "Visiting hours for the B wing of Shepherd Psychiatric Hospital are now over." She has no visitors. She has never had a visit. The announcement means nothing to her.

Ruth sits up in the straight-back chair and adjusts the buttons on the front of her blouse. She glances at the calendar on the wall across the room. December 2011.

She has felt safer in this place. Lonely and still frightened, but not like before. Life on the outside seems overwhelming. The thought of it sends a cold spinal-tap chill down her back.

In those days, she'd remained fearful. Of the police, of her son, *for* her son. And for herself. But the real horror fell upon the residents, especially young women, of Valley Village. Surely, Malachi was their tormentor.

"*... three, four, five... caught a hare alive...*" These words in the voice of a young child taunt her, filling the room. She glances around the small square that seems to move in on her. There is a sudden rip through her hair at the base of her neck, hard enough to pull her head into the back of the chair. No one looks at her; her tiny yelp doesn't seem to draw any attention. Gripping the chair with both hands and pulling herself up again, she looks for the culprit, slowly, so she is not caught off-guard. She knows what she is looking for. Perhaps not exactly, but she knows.

When it seemed the killings had stopped, the dreams had begun. Not simple night terrors, no. That would be too generous to the mother who'd created a monster and released him upon the world.

Ruth is visited by these women in the least-expected daylight hours. Their presences are what had brought her here, to this hospital, in the hope she was simply crazy and had been wrong about her son. But now she knows she is not insane.

These tortured women live in the world of darkness and enjoy opportunities to sneak out of it. They appear to her, accusing, blaming her, hating her for birthing such a creature into the world of light.

Disfigured, discolored, bloody, dirty are these once-beautiful women. Destroyed and condemned by Malachi.

A pleasant woman's voice speaks to her. "Ruth, Doctor Eli will see you now."

Smiling, Ruth shakily stands.

"This way. Room number three."

The attractive nurse, probably in her early thirties, with long dark hair and green eyes, leaves Ruth alone.

A moment later, before any further thoughts can ravage her mind, the doctor is in front of her, putting his hand on her shoulder.

"Ruth, how are you feeling today?" His tone is thoughtful, perhaps overly so. It seems forced, yet his face is kind.

"I feel fine, doctor. Thank you."

"Any nightmares or visions since we last spoke? Any contact from your son, or anyone else not actually present?"

"Of course not, doctor. I'm not crazy." A weak smile crosses her thin lips.

"I've never thought that, Ruth. I just want to be certain you are feeling as you should."

"Normal?"

"There is no such thing as normal, Ruth. You know we don't use that word here."

"Maybe you should."

The woman finds her mind somewhere else. A damp sugar cane field. She is surrounded by it. Suddenly, only inches from her face, Stephanie Sheets appears. Ruth knows the young lady's features from the newspaper and from past experiences with her. Sometimes the women speak to her. They speak with their minds, giving her their thoughts directly from their brains to hers. Stephanie, however, does not speak.

Stephanie is horrific: blackened eyes, green veins at the surface of her skin, jaw slightly askew. She hovers close enough for Ruth to whiff her putrid odor. A swollen, blackened tongue thrusts itself in Ruth's direction, and Stephanie hisses something inaudible. This is the sound Stephanie makes when she visits: angry hissing.

These women disturb Ruth, but they no longer frighten her. She accepts that this is their revenge. They deserve it. It is her reckoning; she deserves it. At various times she has thought of them as heinous gifts from her son, because of her close bond with Malachi and her inability to break it.

She knows these women will never let her go. They know she has a conscience. It is unlikely that Malachi can conceive of the existence of a conscience. It is therefore unlikely they will ever be able to exact their revenge directly upon him. Ruth wonders if she truly deserves this punishment, but she accepts it.

"So, Ruth, how do you feel about the prospect of leaving our facility in a few weeks?"

"I'm sure I feel fine about it, doctor."

Ruth suddenly jerks her hands up from her lap. One of the women, or someone, has pulled on two fingernails so hard there is a thin line of blood at their nailbeds. She conceals her bloody hands and looks at the doctor.

"Sorry, got a chill."

"You seem to be looking and feeling well, Ruth. We'll talk again next week."

Ruth nods and glances around for the one who pulled at her nails. She searches her brain, trying to recall a victim whose nails were ripped away. She cannot. Perhaps it is simply a premonition and has not yet occurred?

She and the dead Stephanie Sheets exit, cross through the waiting area, and enter the corridor to return to her room. Room 33, with its white sheets, white walls, and bright lights, which are turned off at 8pm. Then, there is only darkness.

***

In the year 2002, the local newspaper of Mt. Vernon, Texas ran an article on its front page. The headline read: *Missing Twin Found*

Dead. Further details read: *'Michael Andersen was found in a wooded area not far from the home he shared with his mother and twin brother. It seemed apparent he had slipped on wet plant debris and hit his head on the root of a large oak tree. Tragic."*

Then the decision. A choice.

Ruth had known she must return home for help. It wouldn't be easy. Malachi couldn't know, couldn't suspect, couldn't sense. And he hadn't.

In a small room in the back of an antique store in Algiers, Louisiana, Ruth nervously pulled back the flimsy curtain.

"You've considered me dead, Annie Ruth, ever since you birthed those mongrels. But I smelled you coming." The old lady eyed Ruth. A pink paisley scarf lay knotted on her head, and long fingers with jagged nails the color of blood wrapped around a large deck of dragon cards.

Ruth did not stutter, did not hesitate. She straightened her body, held her head high, and spoke in a solid voice. "I've come for the address."

***

"Malachi, do you remember when we first saw each other again, on Kauai?"

"Of course. You took my breath away. You still do."

Pursing her lips together to redirect her smile, she recalls a humid day three years ago.

'Wow! What a small world! I can't believe you live here! It must be amazing. What fortune that you would be my dive master."

'It's been good seeing you, Mari. High school seems like a long time ago."

'I couldn't agree more."

'I wish you weren't leaving out so soon."

'Maybe you'll come to Colorado to visit."

'I hope we'll at least stay in touch now."

"Thank you. For all of this," she whispers, smiling up at him.

He kisses her forehead and leans back in bed, with Mari on his chest. His mind wanders back to that time of which she spoke.

Malachi had made quite a life for himself scuba diving in the Hawaiian Islands. And hunting. Mostly women, but not always. From time to time, he liked the workout, the challenge of a man. Regardless of the sex of the game, the end result of taking a life always brought the same sexual gratification. Female tourists, though, were the most inviting targets, of course.

After meeting Mari, a would-be victim, Malachi had decided to perform a field test of sorts, to see if he could handle a relationship. Mari is sweet and kind. She seems to handle his sarcastic tendencies well, and they have some history, since they had both participated in theater in one of the many stateside high schools he'd attended. His mother had moved around a great number of times to keep him in school, until finally she had forced him to take his GED. Mari seems accepting of his troubled high school days and of what he tells her of his mother's mental illness. He blames the moves on his mother's three divorces, but always remembers to extend the loving son act, accepting and understanding of his mother. Mari is supportive and humble, and seems like a prime candidate for the experiment. She is lovely in every way, both body and mind. She is family-oriented and makes him feel warm.

Could she really help him change? Can he go straight?

Surely Mari suspects nothing of his past. Hasn't smelled a hint of it. Malachi sometimes wonders if he leaves any clues Mari may home in on.

He has distanced himself from Mother, speaking to her less and less frequently, as Mari thinks Malachi's relationship with his mother is quite odd. She has never met or spoken to Ruth directly. She only knows what Malachi has told her.

While visiting Mari in Colorado, he had decided to make an effort to abandon his natural hunting tendencies. After two weeks of Mari and her family, Malachi joined the Army. With surprising ease, Mari's family accepted him. So did the Army.

The military seemed to be another good place to experiment. Eighteen months after boot camp, engrossed in his new language proficiencies, it seems the Army isn't a bad place to channel a psychological disorder. Especially with a magnificent brain like his, testing off the charts. Of course, his physical condition and marksman skills are also in the top 2% of his class.

When Malachi was stationed in Monterey, Mari did not hesitate to rush out to California to be closer to him. A quaint town in the center of the state, Monterey is home to an all-branches base and many high-ranking foreign officers. Although the base is occasionally a terrorist target, Mari doesn't seem worried about Malachi.

Malachi is thriving in this environment. Career. Girl. Life is good.

"Sure you're comfortable with the transition out of the country?" he speaks flatly into the air straight ahead.

Mari doesn't move from her safe position with him. "Of course. This has been the goal. I can wait a little longer for us to be together full-time. Besides, I'll be with my parents."

He is speaking three languages already. Russian is the language in demand for interrogators right now. His assignment will move him out of the States soon. She is willing to wait. She's already waited, living off base while he was on it most of the time.

Both agree she deserves a fairytale wedding and a life with a husband who will spend time by her side. A couple of years will make this happen.

"I'm excited about the trip home, Malachi. Not only Christmas with my folks, but spending time with Kylie too, now that she has moved back home."

"Your sister is strong, and your dad seems more than happy with her returning home."

"Both my parents are totally jazzed she is moving back and leaving Leon."

"Good."

"You know Daddy is also looking forward to your company at the range."

"I'm eager to spend some time with Charles as well. The only civilian I know who can sometimes outshoot me." Malachi smirks.

So does Mari. She knows her father is more than the average Colorado gun enthusiast. He is a trained marksman, though in the private sector. A hunter in his own right, more than most people realize. Mari is hopeful Malachi intends to ask her if they can become engaged before he ships out.

Mari loves her family and is the light of her parents' eyes. She has already spoken to them about returning home while Malachi is away. They are eager to all be together again as a family.

***

Running. Panting. No breath left with which to scream, she collapses. He is teasing her. She knows she cannot escape. She wants to give up, but she cannot. Her fear fuels her to get up and run again. She can't help but continue to look behind her. She knows it's slowing her down, but she prays she will no longer see the thing following her.

Looking back over her shoulder, her prayers are answered. Perhaps she will make her high school graduation next week. The ends of her lips curl upward.

The smile never leaves her face as her head is removed from her body.

He finds her spasming body orgasmic.

***

Powder on the windshield. Malachi turns on the wipers. Although not a fan of driving in the snow, he wants to please Mari and makes great effort to fulfill her every whim. She wants to drive from California to Colorado in spite of the time of year and weather. They are prepared with blankets, water, snacks, and chains.

"The Rockies are always an amazing sight."

"I'm so glad we are able to make this trip together before you leave."

"Thank you for talking me into driving to take in the scen–"

The back tire of the small sedan finds ice, concealed by freshly fallen snow and the setting sun.

Several minutes later, falling into hypothermia, Mari groans. Upside-down a quarter mile down an embankment, blood drips on her chest from somewhere on her body. She sees no movement from Malachi. Her years of volunteer work at the Red Cross kick in and keep her calm.

Her purse is gone. Did Malachi have his cell phone charging inside the center compartment? She is freezing. Becoming frantic, she finds his phone and dials 9-1-1 before passing out again.

It is five hours before Charles and Nina rush into the hospital. Nina's tears have evidently been staining her face for some time.

Malachi's greatest fear is quashed when he knows Mari is well and safe. His second greatest fear is also not realized when Charles does not blame him for the accident. Still, it nags at him, Charles' calmness.

Malachi is convinced Charles feels secure that Malachi is always looking out for Mari, doing his best. This pumps Malachi's ego, and he walks with a bounce in his step even though his head is pounding and his groin is, for some reason, aroused. Could he be this excited from the accident? Had the sight of all the blood done this to him?

Sexual tension cannot be ignored forever. It must be fed, drained, depleted, or it never leaves and is always there, tapping at our shoulders. Given the opportunity to freely lap at blood and organs, strip clothing, rip flesh – would anyone turn it down? Surely we all have the same demons; I am not alone. Others must be driven as well. They must feel consumed by lust, at least sometimes. I do not think it is a bad thing that I act upon it.

These thoughts have justified more than one frenzy in Malachi's past. Irony blood spikes his arousal even further, as he finds its warmth and life nurturing, the only thing able to quench him.

***

He and Mari are warm now, even though banged up from the car's rolling. Mari's arm and Malachi's head received the worst of it. With each of them tightly bandaged, relief and exhaustion set in as Charles drives them back to the luxury cabin in Bailey, where Kylie is excited for their return.

The next afternoon brings blessings to the door of the sprawling cabin, as everyone sits around the fireplace in the sparsely populated area of the Rockies. There is talk of more snow. The prediction is up to 36 inches, but only one inch has fallen thus far. Snow is always unpredictable here, and sometimes this area can get snowed in for days at a time. They are prepared for the worst.

Malachi has six days before he must be back on base. Although the totaled car presents an issue, it can be worked out. He may need to call his mother, though.

A hard rap at the downstairs door causes Nina and Kylie to yelp, encouraging the tiny terrier, Harley, at Kylie's feet to do the same. Charles disappears downstairs and reappears quickly. He approaches Malachi and places two items in his hands. Then he says something in a low voice, clapping the young man on his shoulder.

Malachi is grinning and staring at Mari. Slipping his wallet into the back pocket of his jeans, and looking up toward the ceiling, Malachi feels more emotion than he can ever remember.

He takes three steps across the room with the small box in his hand and stops in front of Mari. Bending down to one knee, he opens the box. She is flushed and smiling. Her eyes flood.

"Please, Mari Frances Christianson, make me the happiest man on this planet."

Nodding, she wraps her arms around his neck, and he stands up to hold her. A brief kiss, and everyone is right there with them, hugging them both, filling the room with happiness and positivity.

"I feel like the luckiest man alive today," he whispers to Mari, holding her gaze. "Thank you."

She shyly puts her head down.

***

Sometimes her ways provoke him. He wonders why he did not kill her, rape her, or eat her in Kauai. It's at these times that he looks around to see if anyone is watching him, if anyone can possibly see his hunger or read his thoughts. These times are not sweet and warm but aching and needful.

Sometimes he wants to literally hold her heart.

***

"Dinner was great. Thank you, Nina."

"You're welcome, son. Have you spoken with your mother since the accident?"

Before Malachi can answer, Charles speaks.

"What a miracle that your wallet and the ring were found in all this snow. And with the vehicle flipping twice, and you two safe and sound. Definitely an act of God, Malachi. Wouldn't you say?"

Malachi nods, always refraining from 'God talk' whenever possible, especially in this situation when it can only be counterproductive. Although he doesn't believe in God, he is feeling like the luckiest bastard in the world to have his wallet and the ring. And to now be engaged to Mari.

The feelings of family course through his body like never before. He accepts this. It should be satisfying.

Still, he needs something more.

***

Sex with Mari is not their usual love-making. It is dark, rough, as he takes her and selfishly satisfies himself with her like never before. She doesn't complain, doesn't question. He hopes this will get him through the last days in Colorado. Then he can leave Mari with her folks. He knows he will have to hunt upon his return to California, if he can last that long. His appetite has been kept at bay too long. It is growing and will soon be beyond his control.

***

The next morning brings little additional snow and bright sunshine. Malachi is relieved that nothing will delay his return to base.

He picks up his cell, dials, and waits for her voice. "Mother, I need you to purchase a plane ticket for me. From DIA into Monterey Regional."

"Of course, Malachi. Merry Christmas. How are you? Is everything going well for you? It's been a long time."

He rolls his eyes. He has told his mother nothing of Mari or his enlistment, not while she's in that place. "Everything is fine, Mother. I waited a long time for you to answer the phone."

"I would love to see you, you know."

"Yes. Have the ticket confirmation sent to my e-mail. I have to leave Denver no later than Tuesday."

"Sure, son. How are – "

Click.

***

Illegally on a plane out of uniform, he scans it for a potential target. Almost anyone will do, but he wants to home in on someone he can keep his eye on. He hopes people traveling during the holidays are traveling to see family, not with them. His hopes are dashed as couples and families join their parties and sit together. His window seat offers no comfort as he stares through it.

Soon, a young man, perhaps 17, sits in the aisle seat next to him. The seat between them is empty, and they begin a conversation about skateboarding and heavy metal bands. The young man is making a connection in Monterey and has a four-hour layover. Malachi believes he can create an opportunity with this young man. His name is unimportant.

Malachi is no better with names than with faces, especially those of his prey.

***

The young man from the plane had a sweet taste, and Malachi had abused him and ravished him in every way, leaving little more than mush in the corner bathroom stall. He licks his lips when he thinks about the brutality of it. The empowerment he'd felt. The strength. Release.

Hailing a cab toward base, Malachi checks himself for blood and bone fragments. He directs the cab to Denny's, where he changes into his uniform, then walks the last three-quarters of a mile to the base.

***

At-home terrorism keeps Malachi in the continental states. He turns down an invitation to Ft. Benning, Georgia, and opts to stay in central California. He is a valuable asset, considering his knowledge of Russian, German, and Arabic. For Malachi, this is comfort. Peace. Excitement.

Mari is eager to move closer to Malachi again and stay off base near him. He will stay on base during the week but is able to be with her most weekends. When he was initially given the assignment to stay on base yet was allowed to bring Mari for off-site housing even though they were not yet married, he'd yelped with excitement.

Immediately, the old arousal was upon him, overpowering his every thought and sense.

His head and body stir and stiffen. He feels like King Kong, with an erection to match. This is his nature.

His first kill had been at age 12. Then, it was long overdue. He wondered why he hadn't done it sooner. The release, the overwhelming calmness and happiness that it brought, to watch life drain from another. To take it. To use the strength of his body to weaken, corrupt, overpower another. To be God!

He does not remember the faces of his victims. None of them. (Except perhaps his third. That one was more difficult to forget.) He did not care about them. Not any of them. They were insignificant. Meaningless. Useless. Nothing. They were there for his pleasure, for his release.

Murder is like sex. The more creative, the better. The more practice, the better. Take a natural skill, add experience, create a God! That's how Malachi had felt since his first kill, which had not been his brother. Michael had been his third.

Did Michael ever suspect? Fear? Irrelevant. The last in the practice series, that's all Michael was – another act building Malachi's confidence. By 15, he had gotten creative. He'd known how to cause enough trouble at school to get expelled and force his mother to move. New cities and towns smelled fresh and made him want to hunt that much more.

Malachi not killing Mari was an exercise in extreme patience. Not being able to hunt or feed was self-torture, and not something to which he was accustomed. She should at least be a good mother, do a good job with some pups.

He knows he's made his way into the perfect career. Soon he'll be able to feed his soul on the lives of others regularly again. Legitimately. Who wouldn't smile about that?

His smile broadens as he thinks about starting his assignment as an official intelligence interrogator.

***

Third time is the charm for making things right. Malachi's thoughts wander to his brother. He can see the boy's face sometimes, if he tries really hard. Of course, Michael would probably look like him now. But then, what did he look like?

The third girl. That was exciting, yet Malachi cannot recall the specific girl or feeling. Hunting and feeding arouse him and satisfy him, and that is all that matters.

This is his third legal murder. Torture. Hmmm. Exhilarating, to pull out the fingernails of another human while others watch. Blood, beating, eventual death. Not as sexually gratifying as if inflicted alone, but thrilling nonetheless.

***

Ruth exits the hospital with one small suitcase and four floating corpses that no one else can see. Making her way to a small room previously obtained for her with the help of the Shepherd staff, she settles in for a long evening with her daytime companions, until the night will take them away.

***

Three months later, Malachi feels his practice of legal murder is well behind him. He is an expert in his own eyes. He is God again. Let the experimentation begin. And that is all he can process, all he can think about: experimentation. Concentrating on anything else is a chore.

In his military life of legitimate secrecy and permission to kill, he can legally harm, terrorize, and murder others. It is the perfect outlet that strings together the surreal with the real, the insane with the sane.

Malachi is flourishing.

He is content. But something slightly unsettling keeps tickling him in an unused portion of his brain, a faint itch he doesn't know how to reach. He's unsure what it means, and scoffs it away.

Malachi encourages Mari to start making wedding plans. He thinks she is becoming more independent, self-assured. She is leaning on him less, allowing him more freedom. This makes him even more content with the totality of his glorious circumstances.

Mari has definitely softened him up, opened his heart to some degree. He is seriously thinking of the possibility of having children with her. She seems eager for a large family. A litter.

He can speak little about his job, and although she feels he is pulling further away from her, she consoles herself with wine and the understanding that this is his career. She knows there are things about which he cannot speak, things she can never know.

Malachi is beginning to feel a greedy excitement. Terrorist torture is not completely fulfilling, especially since it is often under the watch of another. He is cautious and makes the experiences as gratifying as possible, but he wants more.

***

As Ruth marks the days on her calendar – March 2012 – she wonders why she has had no more word from either Malachi or the 4Cs. She would like to believe she's made a mistake, that her worries could somehow be disproven. Even the dead women could, somehow, be wrong.

She knows better, but mothers always hold hope regarding their children.

When the apparitions come, she sometimes feels a connection with them and tries to communicate. They do not want to hear her words. They only want her to suffer and pay and make things right. She does not know what else she can do to appease their lost souls.

They visit her daily now. She weeps for them.

And for herself.

***

For the first time in his life, Malachi is jolted out of a dead sleep.

Bolting upright, covered in sweat, Mari awakens at his side. "Baby, what's wrong? Did you have a nightmare?"

"I must have."

"Can you recall what it was about?"

Staring at her with a confused expression, he shakes his head and leans back against the headboard. She is looking at him, smiling as always. She is perfect. Like a best friend or a favorite wind-up doll that he created. She is always kind and supportive, and lovely.

He remembers the nightmarish vision perfectly. A redhead. She was filthy, covered in grime, with sunken eyes and pale blue skin covered in black and yellow splotches, hovering above him. Slugs squirmed in her hair, and she was missing something. More than one something: her jaw and her left arm. And there were bite marks on her stomach, visible through the thin, tattered cloth strips running over her small frame. She had looked down on him in bed, her face moving closer and closer to his, a slimy, blackened tongue outstretched in his direction. He could smell her. She smelled of earth and death.

Malachi jumps up and hurries to the bathroom. What the hell is wrong with him? He's never had a nightmare and never gets sick, not even while scuba diving or eating human flesh. He turns on the cold water and stands under the shower. He is startled when he steps out to find Mari standing there with a towel in her hand, waiting for him. He shakes his head and laughs off his jitteriness.

"Malachi, perhaps you are coming down with something. Can you see a doctor in the morning?"

"I have so much to do tomorrow, honey. We'll see how I feel then." Finishing with the towel, he drops it on the floor. "Let's go back to bed."

The dead woman remains in Malachi's head all night, even after he drifts back to sleep.

In the morning, he feels bruised with the memory but refreshed enough to tell Mari he's fine and heading to the base. "You probably won't see me until Friday," he says as he kisses her cheek.

She rolls over in bed and smiles at him, then snuggles back under the covers. Mari is content, proud even, that she has warmed Malachi's heart. She can see the changes in him, and she is satisfied that all is going according to plan.

***

Things are slow at the base office. Paperwork is complete, and there are no assignments, no terrorists, nothing to do but work out or drink. Malachi knows he should go home, but he doesn't need to see Mari again so soon, and he doesn't want to sleep in the bed in which his nightmare had originated. That bed had come with the off-base apartment. Perhaps a new one is in order.

A workout is his decision. Hopping on the bus that runs from his barracks to the gym, Malachi hears an old song in his head:

...Don't fear the reaper...
...La la la la la...

He steps off the bus and it drives away, but the gym is nowhere in sight. In front of him is a warehouse-style interrogation room. There is a single chair in the middle of it. A light hangs above the chair. He sees no one. Besides the light and the surreal room, there is only darkness, all around.

A chilling breeze blows around him, strong enough to push him toward the room. He squints toward the light and the chair, and takes a small step in their direction. The wind swirls and moans. His senses are open. He raises his chin to the sky and sniffs the air. It smells like a winter night some place colder than central California. He peers into the darkness, searching for movement, light, anything. He shakes his head and briefly entertains the idea that he is dreaming. There is a cold steel pipe of fear deep inside him, deep in his stomach, and he knows this is not a dream.

Suddenly he is surrounded and pushed into the room. The roller door is pulled down fast and hard. Several hands remain on him, seating him firmly in the chair. He cannot see his captors. They are blurs. Nothing more.

Handcuffs bind his hands and ankles to the legs of the chair. Bungee cords are wrapped around his waist, shoulders, and thighs. Gorilla tape confines his upper arms and calves. Then the hands are gone, and he is alone. He can wiggle the tips of his fingers, his feet, and his head. His mouth is not restricted in any way.

He turns his head in all directions, trying to better see his captors that he knows must still be nearby. They do not speak to him, and he has not uttered a word. From the shadows all around him, they appear again. He cannot tell for sure how many there are. A hundred perhaps. Is the room really that large? In the darkness, depth is difficult to judge.

What is wrong with these people? Don't they know who he is? Are they not Americans? He squints to try to see them. At first glance, they appear to be American, although somewhat disheveled and unkempt. But it is difficult to tell.

They draw closer to him. They seem to be suspended above the ground, floating, not walking, reaching out for him, hissing and grabbing. Fingernails claw into him and putrid breath assails his senses. Then, nothing. Quiet. It seems they have all disappeared.

He looks around. Not disappeared, just receded. But why?

Then he sees what must have scared them away from him.

"Charles." Malachi gasps. Not only Charles, but Nina, Kylie, and Mari as well, standing inside the door of his torture chamber. They all smile at him, big toothy smiles.

Malachi's eyes are wide and confused. "Mari!"

She cocks her head to the right and looks at him quizzically. "Yes, mongrel?"

"Mongrel?"

"Not even a real werewolf. Some mixed breed throwback," Nina speaks through gritted teeth.

"Yeah, but he's still kinda cute." Kylie winks at Mari. Mari slaps her sister's arm.

"Help me, Mari. Please!" pleads Malachi.

"We are not here to help you," Charles' voice booms. "This room is the equivalent of a hologram, built with a special energy similar to electricity. It will contain you for the rest of eternity."

"What the fuck are you talking about?"

"I can see you are terrified, my love." Mari approaches her lover and traces his neck with a single index finger. "You should be."

He snarls at her.

"Your mother contacted us some years back, Malachi, but we were unable to hunt you legally until after your twenty-first birthday," Nina says to the young man bound in the chair.

"Yes, hunters of all kinds have rules, and these rules dictate the outcome of the game. You see, you could not be legitimately captured until adulthood, and it seemed unfair to so many victims to simply kill you without offering them revenge." Charles says. "Their hold on you could only be obtained through tormenting your mother. She may or may not deserve this; regardless, it is time for you to pay the piper. These souls will release Ruth once they have access to you, which is what we offer them here and now."

"But I'm done. I quit! I love Mari. Mari… tell him…"

"No. Lies. Just how big a fool do you believe me to be? You have not stopped. You have no idea of love. Selfishness and dark desires are all you know."

"Mari, no!"

"Your mother really did all she could. She tried to love you and accept you and cover for you, but the loss of Michael was too much for her." Nina may have had a tear in her eye, but it was difficult for Malachi to know for sure.

"Don't cry for the loss of my inferior, weak brother. He was nothing!"

The 4Cs turn away from Malachi, walking straight through the closed roll-down door in front of them and into the darkness beyond.

As they do, Malachi's victims once again appear to him, in various states of decomposition. They move into the light, and he can see and smell how grotesque they are. He can hear them, in his head. They accuse and blame him for their murders, all sparring for space inside his brain. The vibrations are agonizing. His mind is unable to block them out, unable to evict their voices from his head

They are close to him now, fighting for his body as well. Reaching, grabbing, clawing, biting, feeding upon him, tearing him open and apart. He feels every pain they deliver. He sees blood spurting from his body, feels the flesh being ripped from his bones, but there are no wounds. They will be able to feast upon him for all eternity. He will suffer pain everlasting.

His screams do not stop the voices in his mind or ward off the constant physical attack. It seems they too enjoy the power and life of blood.

He continues to scream.

***

Constance catches her breath and smiles. She senses the savage Malachi is finally paying his dues. She feels justified and continues to shuffle the dragon cards.

UNDER CURSED MOONLIGHT
JONATHAN MOON

Jethro Sapp wakes up, rolls away from the pale dead girl in his bed, and staggers to the bathroom. He makes little effort to aim and winces at the burning sensation accompanying his urination. He doesn't curse the discomfort, however, because it's well worth it for the fun he has had with his bedmate over the past few days. Jethro shakes the last few drops of liquid fire from his pecker and the smell hits him. A ripe mix of dried blood, semen and decay stabs up his nostrils with enough force to make him gag.

"I guess that means it's time for a new girlfriend," Jethro admits aloud while walking out of the bathroom without flushing the toilet.

He walks to the kitchen and retrieves a box of cereal (SUGAR SQUIDS) from atop the pale yellow refrigerator. He reaches into another cupboard, shoves aside several plastic cups and bowls to find a human skull with the top missing. Jethro pours the cereal into the skull, tops it with milk and sits down on his battered and stained couch to enjoy his breakfast. As he eats the sugary multi-colored puffs, he remembers the feisty young runaway whose skull his spoon is scraping. She had fought with all she was worth, but since Jethro had picked her up in an alley where she had been trading blow-jobs for baggies of crystal, he had figured her worth to society was minimal.

Jethro smiles as he finishes and drops his bowl into the sink, where it disappears amongst all manner of soiled dinnerware. He goes back to his bedroom and grabs his stiff girlfriend. He spares a drawn-out breakup speech and instead hefts her out to the small shack outside, where he hangs her on a hook so he can come back and skin the rotten meat from her bones later. If he hadn't waited so long and let her skin get so greasy and grey, he could have stretched and tanned her skinned hide. He isn't much of a tailor, but he has been steadily replacing the battered old lampshades around the trailer one by one with the skin of meth-head hitchhikers and runaways. No time to do it now – he had a new girlfriend to find, and they had all night to have some fun under the swollen moon. His ex would just have to wait until morning to be rid of all that reeking skin and meat.

Jethro padlocks the shed shut and gives a long suspicious glance around despite the trailer's remote location high in the Hoo-Doo County hills. Jethro was born in the trailer and has lived in it all his life. The last six years he has been on his own, after his parents drove their beat-up Chevy to town for a night of drinking and fighting. They had drunk at a bar without brawling, but on the drive home, they had a fist-fight while going almost sixty miles an hour on treacherous mountain roads. With his mom and dad gone, there wasn't anyone to talk Jethro out of his urges, which had started with hurting things and progressed to bodies stacking up.

Jethro doesn't remember his father bestowing great wisdom upon him, but he does recall his old man explaining once in a slurred tone, "Ya don't shit where ya eat, boy." Jethro could never be completely sure what his dad meant, but he chooses to apply it as 'don't torture and kill the meth-head hookers where ya live'. So he thinks himself a good son when he drags his prey out to an old abandoned farmhouse known as the Old Harker Place to have some fun on its sprawling acres. He spends hours hurting them in fun and exciting ways, and often makes love to them several times over the course of the night.

Of course, Jethro has some attachment issues and after having so much fun with his 'girlfriends', he always ends up bringing them home anyways. Hence the dead girl hanging in the shed. Still, he is a creature of habit, and so he lumbers across the yard to his Dodge Aries to cruise town and find a new plaything.

He may be a beast of instinct, brutal and simple rather than cold and calculating, but still he has his rituals. Jethro likes them skinny, but it doesn't matter much beyond that because, in his head, she's one of the many girls who scorned and scoffed at him during his difficult high school years. He felt those specific girls had turned him into what he was today, and if he could ever find one he wouldn't need to make another lampshade again. But he had heard they had all moved away, and so he couldn't stop acting out his fantasies with random victims.

If his new victim is a brunette, he sees her as Arlene Gracias, the foreign beauty; if she has sun-kissed blond hair, she's Dolly Dingo, the cheerleader; if she has hair as dark as the shadows, she's Lilian Poe, the rich girl, and if she is a ginger she'll be Sarah Anne McGee, the pale tease. First he chooses a girl, likens her unto one of the four. Then, on the way out to the Harker Place, Jethro tells her where he is taking her and what happened there once upon a time, under cursed moonlight.

Jethro cruises away from his trailer and into town. It doesn't take him long to find someone walking the side of the road. The woman is slender and twitchy, kicking up dust as she stomps. Her hair has streaks of pink and black, with blond teasing at her roots – a mix of Lilian Poe and some exotic punk-rock girl, he supposes. Jethro can see from her heavy steps she is upset, and as he pulls up behind her, she turns and faces him, her mascara running down her cheeks like tears of oil. She rolls her eyes at Jethro's car, and then looks down the road in the direction she is heading as if to weigh accepting a ride or not.

Jethro leans out his window to holler at her. "Hey, lady, you need a ride?"

She turns back to him still half-scowling, obviously expecting the worst from Jethro but still considering his offer. She scratches at scabs on her face, which Jethro imagines was at one time beautiful, and takes a small step in his direction. "Depends. Where are you going?"

"I was headed over to Stillwater, doing some shopping and shit."

She bites her lip; her destination is Stillwater as well. Most likely she is headed to the Randy Goat – Stillwater's premier low-budget strip joint, one of Jethro's favorite places to find temporary playthings.

"Okay, sure, I'll take a ride. But no creepy stuff, mister, I know the deputy around here real good."

"Sure, sure." Jethro waves away her worries as he steps out to open the door for her. When he stands up straight to his full height of over six feet tall, she cowers slightly and looks back down the road again as if already regretting her decision. He opens her door and stands aside in his best demonstration of gentlemanly behavior. She smiles nervously at him, a feeble smile hidden under scabs and acne, and steps into his car. Jethro closes the door for her, then walks back around and slides into his seat with a malicious smile on his face.

"You can fiddle with the radio stations if you want to," Jethro tells her while giving the old stock stereo unit a stab with one meaty finger.

She nods her appreciation and starts flipping through the frequency dial. She bounces over an oldies song, two top-40 pop stations, and static-clouded hip-hop before settling on a signal from the country music station out of Stillwater. She sings along under her breath while Jethro watches the road. Just as the song ends, Jethro spots the street sign he has been waiting for: Whittleback Road.

"Oh, damn, lady. I do got to make one stop real quick," Jethro announces as he cranks the wheel hard and guides his Aries onto the gravel road.

"Mister, I don't got time! I have to be to work. If I'm late again I'm gonna get fired! Please, mister, just drop me back off here."

Jethro steps on the gas pedal rather than the brake and tells her, "Oh, I wouldn't go worrying about any of that now."

"Okay, look mister, I should have just said it up front, but I'll blow you for the ride. But only if you turn around right now."

"Well…" Jethro says as he rubs at his swollen crotch.

Her hand is on the door handle as she speaks, and Jethro knows she plans to dive out rather than suck his corpse-reeking manhood – hell, it has happened before. She proves Jethro correct as she leans against the door and wiggles the handle frantically. The handle is disabled, however, and she instead repeatedly slams herself against the door while Jethro fills the car with hateful laughter. Her fear turns to fury and she lunges at him, fingernails clawing at his face. She hisses and spits as she attempts to scrape his eyes from his skull. Jethro laughs through it all.

He finally gets sick of her attack, reaches up, and grabs her by the side of the head. She screams once before he smashes her head into the dashboard twice and tosses her back against her door. She moans, hurt but conscious.

"You might as well save some of that feistiness. I like you, Lilian, and I am glad you are my girlfriend now, but if you're already this spunky I'll have to put you in the trunk until we get where we're going."

He pauses, hoping she asks him where he is taking her, but she merely moans in answer. He pretends she asked anyways.

"Oh, out to the Old Harker Place, baby. Yeah, *that* place. They was a Devil-worshipping clan, all right. Ain't nobody going to bother us out there. Haha! Ain't nobody but me even still go out there since old Elijah Harker went devil on his family all them years ago. The big old bastard killed all his kin before the sheriff showed up, and when he did Elijah done set himself on fire in front of the lawman. All kinds of sheds and shacks them Harkers had, and they used them proper, so I like to honor them old devil-hollers and use them proper too. You can run and scream and I can chase you down and make you bleed, just like the Harkers used ta. See, them old devil-worshipers cursed the moon out here, so no one can see the sins happening under it.

"We are gonna have some fun tonight, sweetheart. Ha, at least I am."

He pulls over and she lunges at him again, but he punches her in the middle of her face and she slumps back as she was. Feeling her nose crush against his knuckles really gets Jethro's blood flowing. His throbbing erection makes tugging her out of the car and carrying her to the trunk more difficult. And that proves the first surprise of Jethro's day.

The second is mere minutes later when he notices a moving van parked in front of his favorite place to rape and murder and rape again.

***

Jethro left the meth-head runaway in the trunk of his Dodge Aries to investigate further, and hadn't thought of her since then, not after seeing the family. He has been stalking around the 12-acre Harker property since arriving, watching the new family as they settle into the sprawling two-story farmhouse. He stands in the hip-deep grass, one hand shielding his eyes from the overpowering glare of the full moon above as he watches the teenage girl remove her faded blue sweatshirt. And sure, his other hand is gripped halfheartedly around his manhood, but he is no simple 'Peeping Tom.' He considers himself a predator of higher order than that.

Jethro had kept a safe distance, creeping around the decrepit sheds and shacks dotting the property, careful to remain in the long shadows cast by the willows and aspens while he watched the family unload the van. They'd laughed and joked all the while, calling each other by pet names as they worked. The boy was called Junior, but Jethro didn't know if that was his real name or if he shared his daddy's name and preferred answering to 'Jr.'. The teenage girl was named Alison, but she answered to 'Sweetheart', 'Sis', and 'Al.'

Mom and Alison are prime pieces of sex meat in Jethro's eyes; with hair so blond it is almost white, they are a pair of Dolly Dingos if Jethro has ever seen one.

Jethro's simple mind is a train wreck of twisted perversion, fantasies, and ill-fated kidnapping plots as he watches Alison through her second story bedroom window. She tugs her sweatshirt over her head and tosses it aside, then stands in front of a vanity mirror in her lacy black bra supporting her pert breasts – b cups by Jethro's best guess. Jethro squeezes his prick as she grabs both breasts, jiggles one up and one down, and then both of them together, as if she is still getting used to the weight and dimensions of her pubescent developments. She scrunches up her pretty face, contorting it into exaggerated expressions as she socializes with imaginary people while still bouncing her breasts with her hands.

Jethro's grip tightens. His stroke gains speed and rhythm.

From his short distance from the house Jethro hears Mom shouting, "Dinnertime!"

His eyes dart back and forth between Alison's second story window and the window on the opposite end of the first floor. Mom and Dad bustle about the kitchen, moving plates and platters of food from counters to table. Dad gently sets a casserole dish down and then gives Mom a playful slap on her fabulous ass. Jethro isn't the only one to catch the heavy-handed flirtation; Junior walks into the kitchen and covers his eyes while exclaiming in disgust with words Jethro can't quite hear.

His eyes go back to Alison's window. Her facial expressions change again, softer, sexier, as she makes immature kissy faces at her mirror. She holds one finger to her lips, shushing her imaginary lover, as her other hand reaches behind her to undo her bra.

Downstairs, Junior runs from the kitchen, through the living room and up the stairs to his sister's room.

"Damn it, Junior!" Jethro complains under his breath as he quickens and tightens his strokes. "I think I am going to kill you first just for ruining my fun."

Upstairs, Alison slips the thin bra straps off one shoulder and then the other while cupping her breasts in her hands, effectively denying Jethro a look at the nipples he pictures standing firm between her fingers. Suddenly her bedroom door swings open, and Junior pops his head in. Her brother's sudden appearance shocks Alison. She lets go of her tits to scream in her brother's face. Junior flushes red and backs up, apologizing. He sneaks several more glances at his sister's bouncing breasts as she tries in vain to cover them with flailing arms. She chases him out, screaming at him before slamming the door behind him. Junior slinks back downstairs, shaking his head and absentmindedly rubbing his crotch.

Up in her room Alison throws her back against the door in order to prevent any more unexpected guests, finally giving Jethro the unobstructed view he has been hoping for. She takes a few deep breaths, her bosom rising and falling with the action, and unbuttons her jeans. She shimmies them, shifting one leg and then the other to slide them down, revealing a pair of lacy black boy-short panties which match her discarded bra.

The muscles in his forearm burn with frantic effort, and drool slips from the corners of his mouth as Jethro furiously masturbates to the sight of the mostly nude teenager. His stomach tightens, his toes curl within his boots, and his breath grows raspier as his climax nears.

"Oh, we are going to have some fun tonight, sweetheart. Oh, yeah. Maybe I'll keep the rest of your family alive just so they can watch us fool around. Yeah, yeah, yeah, you nasty little slut..."

As his dick swells in final preparation of blasting his spoiled spunk all over the ground, he hears something heavy crunching gravel behind him. Jethro curses as headlights bounce at the edges of his vision. He turns towards the intrusion and sees Sheriff Rourke's rusted Jeep Cherokee bouncing up the long driveway to the Old Harker Place. Jethro keeps his eyes on the Sheriff's Jeep as it pulls up between the gray sport utility vehicle and the large moving van. As Sheriff Rourke exits the driver's side, his top Deputy, a trigger-happy son of the Klan named Bobby Dingo, steps out of the passenger side.

Jethro knows both men well, having attended the first two years of high school with Bobby Dingo before dropping out, and on account of Sheriff Rourke breaking his nose with an elbow that would have done Dusty Rhodes proud for lifting a Penthouse from the old Dino Co. gas station. But as he watches the men, Jethro wants nothing more than to scream at them for interrupting his masturbation session. He stalks through the shadows closer to the porch, but still hidden from sight. Sheriff Rourke knocks on the front door with zero respect for the hour, or the fact the family inside have spent the day moving into their new home. Jethro has heard that same knock, and he manages a small subconscious flinch at the thudding sound. He can see into the kitchen, and watches Mom and Dad exchange a nervous look before Dad drops his napkin next to his plate, scoots his chair away from the dinner table, and excuses himself.

A moment later, Dad opens the front door to the two police officers standing on his porch. Jethro is close enough to hear the conversation.

"Uh, hello. Can I help you officers?"

"Good evening, sir. My name is Sheriff Rourke and this is Deputy Dingo. I apologize for showing up all unannounced…"

"Yeah, I'm afraid you've shown up as we're eating dinner after a long day of moving."

"We'll be quick enough," Deputy Dingo snaps with a lazy yet threatening drawl.

Sheriff Rourke nods his thanks to his deputy and turns back to Dad. "I am here for your safety and your family's safety, sir, not just making social calls."

"Well, then, is everything okay, officers?" Concern tints Dad's voice.

"Sheriff," Rourke corrects, and then says, "Well, I'm not rightfully sure."

Sheriff Rourke rubs the back of his neck, an old nervous habit, and looks at Deputy Dingo as if for advice on what to say next. Bobby Dingo is too busy looking like a tough guy to notice his boss looking at him. Rourke scowls at his deputy and turns back to Dad.

Mom walks from the kitchen to stand behind her husband. Sheriff Rourke sees her approach and takes off his wide-brimmed hat to greet her. An elbow to his ribs later, Deputy Dingo does the same.

"Evening, ma'am," Sheriff Rourke says.

"Good evening, Sheriff." Mom nods a greeting at both he and his deputy, then turns to her husband. "Everything okay?"

"Actually, ma'am," Sheriff Rourke begins, "I was just about to tell your husband we found a car parked about a mile away, and it don't belong to the Haskills down the road from ya."

"Like an accident?" Dad clears his throat and asks.

"Nah, nothing like that. Just pulled over to the side of the road by a copse of willows with its trunk wide open. We know who owns it, a local dirtbag named Jethro Sapp, but we don't know where said dirtbag is at the moment," Deputy Dingo informs them in a tone of sheer self-important shitheel.

Jethro feels his face flush red with a flood of emotions. That's him and his car and his meth-head hitchhiker they are talking about. His thoughts twist and constrict on his sanity until he forces his attention back to the men on the porch.

"Should we be worried?" Mom asks with her hands over her heart.

"Aw, naw, ma'am," Sheriff Rourke assures her. "I'd lock your doors when y'all call it a night just to be safe, but I don't think Jethro is much of a risk to you folks."

"He's just a dirtbag," Deputy Dingo reaffirms.

"Yeah, I already called Big Roger, and he'll be out here with his tow truck to drag his heap of junk off the road. If'n y'all need anything, just call at the station."

Sheriff Rourke tips his hat and leads Deputy Dingo down the porch steps. Mom waves and steps from the door, heading back to the kitchen. Dad remains at the threshold watching their retreat, obviously unnerved.

Sheriff Rourke and Deputy Dingo slide into the Jeep. The highlights turn on, illuminating the west end of the two story house.

Dad goes back inside, mumbling under his breath. Jethro can't make out any of what he is saying except "fucking with me."

The next instant Jethro spins around and rushes over the grounds. He can't let them take away his fun – the hitchhiker is his to do with as he pleases! Darkened scenery flashes by as he charges towards the dirt road. A minute later, low hanging branches scrape at Jethro's cheeks as he forces his way through thick growth of old trees and waits for the lawmen. He just needs to stay hidden long enough for them to pass so he can get back to his car.

Unfortunately, he would have to shit where he ate for once – the Harker Place had been compromised for the night.

The Jeep finally turns out of the driveway and onto Whittleback Road. Its headlights bounce momentarily over

Jethro peeking, blinding him. Gravel crunches under the wheels as the sheriff slams on the brakes. The headlights come to rest on Jethro, brighter than the light of the cursed moon above. Rourke clicks on his high-beams, and Jethro's eyes sparkle in the dark.

Shit. He thought he'd been hidden well enough…

"Jethro! Jethro Sapp! Stay right there!" Sheriff Rourke barks as he exits the Jeep and draws his sidearm, a handsome .454 Smith & Wesson. Behind him, .357 already drawn before he jumps out from his passenger seat, is Deputy Dingo.

"Don't you move, you motherfucker, or I'll blow your brains out!"

Jethro has no choice but to comply – there is nowhere else to hide. He doesn't want to end up in a jail cell, but he can see no way around it now.

The men approach, each step they take either illuminating them in the warm glow of the headlights, casting them as walking shadows twitching in the dimness at the edge, or blocking the light out completely. They stop several feet away, Deputy Dingo silhouetted smack in the middle of the light and Sheriff Rourke just at its edge, but illuminated slightly by the light of the moon.

"We done saw ya, shithead! Don't even try to run!" Deputy Dingo snarls at his former classmate.

"Jethro," Sheriff Rourke says. "Now, come on over here and talk with us. I don't want ya sneaking around this property and bothering that nice family. They got enough to be weary of, goddamn it."

"Hey! Dirtbag! He said git' over here!"

Jethro fails to hear a branch snap somewhere behind him, and he inhales deep the pungent tandem odors of petrol and decay emanating at his back. His mind, already stretched and torn, loses all sense as he moves to leave his concealment, too scared to turn and see what could be emitting such powerful, outright rank smells so near to him.

The next instant, hands clamp tight around Jethro's head, hands so large the palms slap over his ears and the fingers – charred black and reeking of gasoline – press forcefully against his cheeks. The hands squeeze, vise-like and merciless, and Jethro feels several of his facial bones crack under the impossible pressure. The hands lift as they squeeze. The ground disappears beneath him, and he desperately kicks his feet as he is hoisted into the air. He feels his neck break; excruciating pain shoots down his spine to his limbs and extremities. He hears the sound of his vertebrae snapping, the huge palms pressed against his ears forcing the sound back into his panicking brain. The flaring pain throbs to nothingness as he is heaved through the cool evening air at Deputy Dingo.

As Jethro is flung forward he hears a thudding to his left, and the sheriff shouts something angry and muffled. Jethro sees the look of frightened shock on the deputy's face a split second before their craniums collide, and Jethro's limp body crashes down on the much smaller man. Deputy Dingo flails his extremities, which only serves to tangle them together. When the two hit the gravel, he not only takes Jethro's full weight onto his chest, but gets two more head-butts from the momentum. The back of his head smacks against the gravel each time, ensuring a state of unconsciousness.

Jethro gets blasted in the face by Deputy Dingo's cigarette breath as his crushing weight forces all the air from the unconscious cop. He then slips off the deputy until his head comes to rest on his chest like a pair of relaxed lovers cuddling at the edge of the desolate road.

Jethro tries to move, but his nerves have been so badly damaged he cannot even close his eyelids or alter the awestruck grimace frozen on his face, much less wiggle a finger or toe. He smells his bowels and bladder empty into his overalls, but their combined stenches are the only sensation he experiences. Fear consumes him, nibbling on his remaining sanity. He was no small man and he hadn't met a meth-head hitchhiker yet that could fight him off, but something had just lifted him up by his head and snapped his neck like a goddamned twig. That something stood above him now, its shadow falling across his face and cooling his reddened cheeks. Its reek drifts down on him like a wet blanket of gas-soaked rot.

Despite never having left the forested mountains of Hoo-Doo County, Jethro senses a malevolence – ancient and evil – in its looming presence.

The shadow shuffles off. Jethro sees Sheriff Rourke just out of the glow of the headlights and illuminated only by the light of the cursed moon above, slapping at the hulking shadow attacking him. Jethro can see the look of absolute terror etched on the old lawman's face. Sheriff Rourke jerks his hand away from the attacker and pulls the hammer back on his .454. However, before he can either aim or fire his weapon, a giant hand – charred black except for where strange symbols have been carved and appear as angry pink scars – wraps around his forearm and snaps it as easily as it had Jethro's neck.

The attacker leans into the light, allowing Jethro to finally see what had broken his neck. And in all of his hellish and malevolent glory, standing there as real as the fact Jethro couldn't feel his feet, is the monstrous Elijah Harker, freshly risen from the dead. The big man wears tattered, scorched jean overalls, and a filthy red flannel stained black-brown from its years under the earth, melted into his burnt flesh in several locations. Elijah is charred crispy black over ninety percent of his body, and is equally covered in the pink scarred symbols. A few long greasy strands of tar-black hair hang over a face melted beyond recognition, a face with uneven yellowed eyes sunk deep in lumpy oozing flesh covered with deep red cracks and dripping jaundiced pus.

Sheriff Rourke bellows a scream of confused agony, but the shadowed hulk reaches one hand down and rips the Sheriff's lower jaw away in a nonchalant fashion. Then Elijah tucks the severed jaw bone, with wet scraps of flesh dangling from it, into the back pocket of his overalls while Sheriff Rourke slaps his remaining hand uselessly at the sudden crater gushing bright red blood from the bottom of his face.

With the stolen jaw secured, Elijah presses his huge hands against the Sheriff's chest as if he's about to attempt some sort of crude CPR. Instead, Elijah shoves down with all his supernatural strength. Jethro hears a symphony of the Sheriff's sternum and rib bones cracking and splintering. A flood of deep red and brown spurts from Rourke's ruined face as he twitches and dies before Jethro's aching eyes.

The monster stands. Its shoeless feet are charred black and covered in pink symbol scars like the rest of him. They stomp in Jethro's direction.

Elijah grabs both men by their ankles, though Jethro doesn't realize it until he's tugged from in front of the Jeep. With Jethro still tangled and on top of Deputy Dingo, both men are dragged next to Rourke. The way his head is resting on Bobby Dingo's chest, Jethro's view rises and falls with each of Dingo's shallow breaths, and his involuntary focus is purely on the dead sheriff's eyes, which are solid red with every blood vessel within them burst.

Elijah smashes the head and taillights with his fists, and then shoves the sport utility vehicle off the road and into the dry ditch on the opposite side as if it were made of balsa wood. As the Jeep rolls away, Jethro's view is cast back into near darkness, lit only by the cursed moon above.

In the dimness of the evening, Jethro sees no defined edges or shapes, only darker patches of shadows. He hears Elijah's big bare feet crunching the gravel as he re-approaches. Then Elijah hefts the Sheriff onto his shoulders. Jethro doesn't feel Elijah's grip, but senses sudden, steady movement as he and the unconscious Deputy Dingo are dragged back in the direction of the house.

As he is tugged roughly through the overgrown yard, Jethro tries in vain to close his eyes. When that proves fruitless, he then tries to gauge which direction he is being taken. It proves useless as well, until he is suddenly jerked back up into the air and hefted against a slab of stone sticking up out of the ground. Since the only nerves still sending signals to Jethro's turpentine-soaked brain are in his cranium, he is swallowed in sharp, resounding pain as his skull cracks against the stone monolith. His vision blurs and doubles, and Jethro more senses than sees Deputy Dingo slumped against a second monolith a few feet to his left.

Elijah bumps Jethro while moving the Sheriff's corpse and Jethro's view is momentarily only of the moon-splashed ground rapidly approaching, and then he feels the sensation of his face crashing into it.

***

Jethro awakens and tries to turn his head, then remembers he's been broken. He remembers Elijah as well and panics, heart thudding in his chest. The monster is nowhere in sight.

The Sheriff is slumped forward at a nearby monolith, his cowboy hat resting in his lap. The crater at the bottom of his face has slowed its flow of gore down onto his blood-soaked khaki uniform. Several of his ribs jut through his flesh as if he has sprouted crimson thorns, and have ripped through the filthy fabric of his uniform like too many thumb tacks in a gunny sack. Only one of his eyes is open, and it stares back at Jethro.

Jethro now has a better view of three more monoliths as well, each placed in a wide circle and fashioned from an odd green and gray stone covered in the same strange symbols embedded into Elijah Harker's burnt flesh. The meth-head hitchhiker Jethro had been planning on having some fun with tonight is propped one slab over from the Sheriff. Both of her arms have been ripped off and her face is lumpen and misshapen, not near the trailer park beauty she had been a few hours ago.

Beyond the Sheriff, Jethro's stolen victim, and the monolithic circle is a peeping tom's dream view into the Old Harker farmhouse. Mom hasn't had time to put up any drapes or blinds so all the rooms on both floors are visible. Unable to move or speak, Jethro looks into each lit room, observing the family as they settle in for the evening, though any sense of malice, menace, or perversion has left him along with the control of his extremities and sensation in his genitalia.

Jethro looks into Junior's room as the teenager tacks up posters of buxom beauties in skimpy thong bikinis. Jethro feels something akin to worry for the poor unsuspecting boy as Elijah Harker steps out of a shadow into the first floor living room, two windows over. Every light in the house flickers with each of the monster's steps.

Alison doesn't notice because she is washing her face in the upstairs bathroom, leaning over the sink so her muscled rump flexes beneath her cotton panties. Mom and Dad fail to see the lights flickering because, the instant before Elijah takes his first step, Dad wraps his arms around Mom's waist and tugs her into the darkened walk-in closet in the master bedroom.

Junior is the only one to take notice of the lights as they spasm. He yanks his headphones off his head and throws them at the pillows on his bed as if they had screeched in his ears, flinching visibly from the flickering bulbs above.

Jethro doesn't witness the monster take an actual step – he seems to just move several feet at a time in some jerky supernatural fashion. In two of these long strides, somehow convulsing and motionless at the same time, Elijah stands just outside the door to Junior's bedroom. Inside the room, Junior dashes towards his door, but the lights cease blinking and he stands there with his hands trembling mere inches from the doorknob. The boy sniffs the air and whimpers. Jethro can tell Junior is frightened, can see the fear etched on the kid's face, but he can also see the brash teenage attitude fighting it full force.

Jethro screams inside his head. This wasn't supposed to happen like this. He should be the one in there making them shake in fear, not Elijah – not some risen ghoul!

He hears sounds to the right of him. Groans, unintelligible curses, and soft scraping, shifting noises emanate from the direction of Deputy Dingo.

"Wha..wha..wh, whu…where the hell am I? Jethro? Jethro! What the hell did you do, you motherless fuck!"

Jethro can't turn to face his accuser, can't take his eyes off the monster he sees through the living room window.

"Jethro, you hear me? Jethro, hey, you okay? What the fuck is going on here? Sheriff? Oh, my God…Sheriff!"

Seeing his best friend and idol in his current cold and mutilated state breaks something deep inside poor Bobby Dingo. He screeches non-coherent words as he scrambles across the patch of land and into Jethro's line of sight. Deputy Dingo cradles the jawless face of Sheriff Rourke, rubbing his ruddy cheeks and attempting to smooth his blood-sticky hair while blubbering uncontrollably. Strings of snot and drool dangle off his face, sparkling under the cursed moonlight.

While in the thrall of confusion and sorrow, Deputy Dingo finally sees the third body, Jethro's would-be victim, leaning against another monolith. He catches it first out of the corner of his eye, and Jethro figures it frightens him pretty bad because he reaches for the gun on his hip. But, due to his crouched position so low next to the Sheriff, his weight shifts backwards quicker than his balance and he falls flat on his ass. His flailing hand slaps Jethro across the face as he falls and his cowboy boots kick up into the air as he comes to a stop. He spins on his ass like a breakdancing bumpkin, and comes up with his weapon pointed at the arm-less corpse. The scowl melts off his face and his lips pout, his bottom lip specifically quivering pathetically.

"Dolly? Holy Jesus above, what happened to you? You scared the hell right out of me, girl. Get your skinny ass over here right now."

Despite the concern and authority in his whispered command, the dead girl doesn't comply in the least.

If Jethro had any control of his useless body he would point and laugh at Deputy Dingo right now. For he hadn't recognized her at the time of picking her up from the side of the road and smashing her head against his dashboard (or at seeing her with her arms yanked off for that matter), but the meth-head hitchhiker Jethro had been planning on having his rowdy fun with tonight was, in fact, sweet little Dolly Dingo, Deputy Bobby Dingo's little sister.

It was common knowledge that the years since high school have been hard on little Dolly. Jethro had heard she dropped out of college when she figured she wouldn't be able to blow her way to a degree. She left the big city and came crawling back to Hoo-Doo County, but not before picking up a ravenous appetite for methamphetamines. After that she found some minor fame over in the city of Stillwater with a stripper routine which included her old high school cheerleading outfit and pom-poms, a show Jethro had heard much about and had long promised himself he would one day witness with his own eyes.

Jethro's breath catches in his throat. Had he known who she was, he would never have had the urge to watch Mom and Dad and Alison and Junior. He would have run deep into the Harker acreage, away from prying eyes, and had his way with her. His need for revenge against those high school girls would have been sated, he thinks, and none of this would be happening now.

Jethro sobs internally as Deputy Bobby Dingo totally loses his shit over the great personal losses he is suddenly confronted with. Jethro has never heard anything like the bellowing, screeching wails of agony and longing which Bobby Dingo begins to emit at the top of his goddamned lungs.

Inside the house, Elijah turns his disfigured face and looks out the back window, in the direction of Deputy Dingo's mournful wailing. Even from the distance between them Jethro can see pure hateful evil glowing in Elijah's eyes, especially the one slipped down his melted cheek next to the crater where his nose had been. If Jethro still had control over his facilities he would have pissed himself in fear.

Junior's hand, trembling uncontrollably, remains floating in the air inches from his doorknob. Despite not knowing why he is so frightened, the teenager is suddenly fighting back tears (Jethro recognizes the grimace which accompanies them) and his knees threaten to give way when he too hears Deputy Dingo's wails.

In fact, everyone inside the house hears the caterwauling; Mom and Dad hustle out of the closet, Mom adjusting her sundress and Dad struggling to do his pants back up, and Alison rushes from the bathroom and out of Jethro's view. Mom and Dad exit their room seconds after her and disappear from view as well.

Downstairs, Elijah takes one of his jerky, teleporting steps, causing the lights in the house to flicker as he moves towards the back door. Inside his room, Junior freaks out when the lights in his twin Star Wars lamps explode in unison. As he is showered with shards of shattered bulb, Junior opens the door to his room and dashes through it only to see the terrifying form of Elijah Harker standing across from him in the living room. At the same precise moment, the rest of the family re-emerges into Jethro's view, scampering down the stairs.

At the base of the staircase they find Junior, pale-faced and weeping. A few feet away from him stands the seven-foot monster, its flesh charred and covered in unnerving scars. They scream at the unbelievable abomination, and Junior's prepubescent voice climbs an octave higher than his mother and sister. Elijah reacts with fury and reaches down to fling their couch out the window.

The window shatters and the heavy couch is smashed to shards of wood, metal, and navy blue fabric in the middle of the back yard.

The commotion pulls the Deputy's attention from his slaughtered sister and the Sheriff. He turns his bloodshot eyes towards the destroyed window, and sees the family screaming in terror and Elijah Harker in all his hellborne glory. The monster sees him as well, recognition twitching in his jaundiced, uneven eyes. It bawls a noise that sounds as if it's truly emitting from the throats of a thousand demons, which forces the family to cover their ears and crowd in the direction of the back door.

Still on his knees in the dirt, Deputy Dingo fires a shot into the air. His brash tactic works, gaining everyone's attention before the family bursts through the back door to the old farmhouse. The spring-loaded screen door slams back into place, but the sound is muffled under everyone's screams. As they scramble past the scattered remnants of their broken couch, Elijah Harker takes one of his unnatural steps across the living room in pursuit. With the monster's second step, it is at the back door. Rather than open it, Elijah slaps it off its hinges.

It soars through the air until it clips Dad's shoulders and knocks him into Mom, and both of them go down. Alison and Junior stop and help their parents up so they can continue their escape. Dad requires more assistance; he seems dazed, and blood trickles from a fresh wound at the back of his head. Alison and

Mom support Dad's weight and Junior leads them through the back yard towards Deputy Dingo. The lawman stands, spits a mouthful of blood like it was tobacco juice, and waves them in his direction.

The family crowd behind Deputy Dingo. Bolstered by their presence, he swaggers towards Elijah Harker with his .357 leading the way. The enormous atrocity opens a wide slouched mouth and wails like a cave of dying rabbits. The mouth is lined with rows of jagged, broken teeth, and spits slimy black spittle as it shrieks. The family reacts to the hellish sound as they had before and cowers with their hands slapped over their ears. Deputy Dingo reacts by compressing the trigger several times.

The .357 in Deputy Dingo's grip barks and spits; six bullets bite into Elijah. As the bullets hit the monster, small scraps of burnt flesh and tattered flannel fall from wounds in his stomach to chest, but not a single one explodes out his back as Deputy Dingo expects them to. Also, despite piercing his pancreas, liver, lungs and heart, Elijah Harker doesn't slow his steps. Before Deputy Dingo has a chance to ponder why his marksmanship has failed him, Elijah is upon him, wrapping one giant fist around his throat and squeezing.

Deputy Dingo doesn't die easy, and even as his life is choked away, he presses the muzzle of his .357 to the monster's head. Elijah constricts his grip and lifts, tugging the Deputy into the air by his neck like a one-man gallows. As his world erupts into dozens of brilliant colors, Dingo compresses the trigger. Warm chunks of bone and bits of brain spackle the lawman's face and he hears the family behind him wail at the horrific spectacle. Bobby manages to blink a few times, working enough of the gore from his eyes to see that his bullet blew away almost a fifth of Elijah's malformed head, but the monster's yellow eyes are glowing with hateful malevolence and still staring deep into his dying soul.

Even with the fresh gash across the back of his cranium, Dad knows the Deputy isn't in a fight he can win, and he needs to get his family to safety. His family continues screaming, but he shoves them all away from the dying Deputy and inadvertently into the circle of monoliths, dead folk, and the once-menacing Jethro, now paralyzed and bearing witness to it all. Dad knows he can't fight the monster, and he doesn't know for sure if they can even outrun it for long, and his eyes, darting between the murder happening in front of them and the dirt road somewhere off in the darkness, tell Jethro so.

Headlights bounce at the edge of Jethro's vison and he remembers the tow truck Sheriff Rourke had promised would be out to drag away his car. Dad and the rest of the family miss them because, at the same moment, Elijah Harker decides he is done toying with his prey. The charred abomination begins pulling the stuffing out of the lawman as if he was a ragdoll, jamming its massive fists into Bobby's stomach and yanking out handfuls of internal organs. He squeezes them between his meaty fingers before throwing them at the ground and going back for more.

One by one, the gruesome scene becomes too much for them. They turn from it and see instead the disfigured corpses surrounding them. More screams from the family, screams until their voices crack and sanities splinter. Dad looks at the corpses in turn, starting with the armless and pummeled Dolly Dingo, then on to the jawless Sheriff Rourke with his ribs poking through his crushed torso, and, finally, on to Jethro. By some miraculous stroke of luck, Dad makes eye contact with Jethro and sees his eyes twitch.

For the briefest of moments Jethro thinks Dad might toss him over his shoulder and carry him to safety, maybe even to a goddamned doctor who could fix his busted neck. As Jethro's thoughts race, his eyes twitch a second time, and this time Dad – panicked beyond comprehension – looks in the direction Jethro's eyes seem to be signaling, and he sees the headlights bouncing up the road. Jethro figures Dad sees the glow of some merciful god dancing through the trees in those lights, because once he sees them he is dragging Mom, Alison, and Junior in their direction, out of Jethro's sight.

Jethro is left alone as Elijah Harker drops a thoroughly gutted Deputy Dingo against the slab between Dolly Dingo and Sheriff

Rourke, and then turns to him. Jethro prays his eyes don't twitch involuntarily again, and then a single tear slips down his cheek, warm salty damnation. He begins to mentally unload his sins, confessing to a god who has never listened, while Elijah reaches back and removes the Sheriff's severed jawbone from his pocket. Elijah takes one strange twitchy teleporting step and Jethro smells petrol, decay, and blood.

Elijah draws his arm back and slams it forward.

The second before the severed jawbone is driven through his face and into his brain, Jethro thinks Elijah Harker will catch the family and complete his foul ritual. And he worries with his dying thought that no one will see the evil committed here tonight because it has all been hidden under the cursed moonlight.

SOMETHING OLD, SOMETHING NEW, SOMETHING CURSED, SOMETHING BLUE

SARAH DALE

Mary wasn't sure when the blue sun-bird in the picture had first spoken. Royal had gotten the print for her as a gift after he'd given her that first black eye, when they were still newlyweds. She'd been less than two months pregnant at the time, and the morning sickness had been awful. Late one morning, she'd been busily ironing when she'd had to stop suddenly and run for the bathroom. He'd stepped in and seen one of his pristine white dress shirts crumpled on the floor and had flown into a rage.

It was a beautiful picture. It was just a framed print, of course, but the original was painted by Prymachenko, an artist from Ukraine, Mary's home. The creature was bright blue, in flight over a red-orange field of flowers. The sun-bird's voice was low and strong in Mary's mind. She was sure the bird had spoken first. It was only later the motanka doll had joined the conversations.

They sat together on the shelf above her vanity in her dressing room. It was the only room in the house Royal didn't often come into. It was technically a walk-in closet. He had his own. With so many clothes, he needed the larger of the two, and hers was decidedly smaller. She would retreat there late at night after Royal and the baby had gone to sleep, or sometimes during the day when he was at work. The bird and doll didn't always speak early on, but recently it seemed they spoke nearly every time she was nearby. She thought it might have something to do with the time between Royal's rages getting shorter and shorter.

She sat there now, staring vacantly at her reflection in the vanity mirror. Royal was in the living room, eating his dinner and watching basketball. Baby Leo was asleep. She'd come into the master bathroom to care for her hand. The fingers were terribly swollen. She'd soaked them in cold water for as long as she could stand and had then carefully wrapped both the wrist and the two smallest fingers with ace bandages.

You need a doctor, the sun-bird intoned sadly.

Mary shook her head and whispered, "No, maybe tomorrow. He's settled for the night and the baby is asleep. It can wait."

You should go tonight, the sun-bird insisted. *The ribs are broken too. You could puncture a lung.*

The motanka doll chimed in then. *She needs to be careful. She can't be caught. She should stay until he leaves tomorrow. It isn't safe tonight.*

The motanka doll didn't have a face, just blank white fabric under dark braids. She wore a bright red dress Mary's mama had sent her as a wedding gift. Her parents hadn't been able to attend the ceremony on such short notice, but they'd sent lovely things from home.

Home. Northern Ukraine. It had felt so stifling there, no place for a beautiful, bright, vivacious girl. Coming here had seemed like a dream come true. Some of the girls had called it being a mail-order bride, but Mary had thought of it as an adventure. Royal was handsome and charismatic. He had a successful business and a beautiful home.

At first, she'd been grateful for his rules and instructions. Everything had seemed difficult to navigate, once she'd arrived in the States. She'd believed herself fluent in English, but she'd never heard anything that sounded like the accent in New Orleans. She'd set herself the task of listening and learning as quickly as possible. She had always been a fast learner; it had seemed like a wonderful way to prove she was the right girl for him.

Then she'd gotten pregnant and everything had happened so quickly.

What was it for tonight? The bird directed her question at the motanka doll. *Five broken bones for olives? He's escalating and you know it. She has to get out of here.*

The doll sighed. *Tak…yes, but it's so dangerous when he's at home!*

Even when he's at work he comes home to check on her. No time is safe, the sun-bird responded angrily.

The argument went on and Mary's attention faded from the present. She slipped back to earlier in the evening when she'd been making his dinner. When had he told her about the olives? She tried to remember. She always tried to remember, but it was hard. There were so many things, and sometimes they changed. She thought she'd done everything perfectly tonight. The chicken was roasted beautifully with just the right amount of rosemary. The potatoes were thinly and uniformly sliced. What was it about the olives?

***

She stared blurrily at the olives. The cutting board was inches from her nose, her cheek pressed hard against the cold marble counter. She'd remembered checking them all for pits, cutting them each carefully across…

A sunburst of agony flashed through Mary's brain. Her vision blazed with color and she thought she heard something crack. She stayed perfectly silent. That was best, she'd learned. Cries of pain just inspired him, and scared the baby. She could hear little Leo in the next room, playing with his big plastic blocks. He was sitting up now, almost ready to crawl.

Royal had her face pinned against the countertop, her left arm twisted up behind her back.

"What did I tell you about putting olives in the salad?"

His voice held that tone: patient, amused, but with the undercurrent of cruelty she knew too well. He leaned harder into her back, pressing her ribs into the corner of the countertop. For a second the pain in her ribs distracted her from the pain in her wrist. Her shoulder was on fire, her cheek throbbed. She could feel his erection pressing into her hip.

"No pits," she whispered, mostly into the counter, "no pits and…" Oh, that was it. Her brain clicked at last. "And slice them the long way?" Black stars arced in front of her eyes. She fought to stay conscious. "I'm sorry," she said, voice barely audible. "I forgot to slice them the long way."

Royal let her arm down and turned her to face him, keeping hold of her wrist. She would have staggered, but he still had her pinned against the countertop. His beautiful face looked pleased, like a teacher with a difficult student who had finally produced a correct answer. "See?" He smiled, revealing perfectly white teeth behind sensual lips. "That's my good girl." He laid his cheek against hers, his lips brushing her skin. She struggled to stay still, to not recoil.

He slid his hand up from her wrist to her fingers and whispered in her ear, "So you don't forget again." With one quick movement, he bent the fingers of her left hand backwards.

The cracks of her finger bones breaking sounded loud in the quiet kitchen.

***

She flashed back to the present and found herself in Leo's room. Mary shook her head. It was getting harder to keep track of when and where she was anymore. She wondered, and not for the first time, if one of Royal's beatings had damaged something in her head.

She had evidently gone in to retrieve the diaper bag, as it was now slung over her right shoulder. It was such a nice bag. She remembered picking it out of the catalog. They hadn't known yet if they were having a boy or a girl, so she'd chosen purple. There were compartments for everything, so many that sometimes she'd forget what was in each one. She adjusted it so it wasn't squashing the motanka doll which was tucked securely into the pocket of her cardigan.

Come, the doll whispered.

Mary left Leo sleeping in his crib and returned to her dressing room. She set the bag down and sat on the bench next to the basket of clean baby clothes she'd brought in before dinner. It was a good thing she had done it earlier. She wasn't sure she would've been able to manage a full laundry basket with broken fingers.

She folded one-handed as well as she could, and laid the onesies and pants sets out on the bench next to her in preparation for going back in the bag. She stroked his little Simba jammies meditatively. He grew so fast, it seemed that each time she repacked his bag it was with the next size up in little clothes.

Her mind drifted on the soothing scent of Leo's clean laundry. She used a special detergent for the baby's clothes so they smelled different from Royal's. Leo didn't care if she misplaced a sock here or there, but Royal…

Mary…

A lost sock. Where did they go? It didn't make sense. You put a pair of socks in the washer, by the time they came out of the dryer, one was gone. It was ominous, like so many things seemed to be in Royal's big house.

He got so angry if things weren't just right. There was a particular way he wanted the rugs vacuumed, so all the lines went the same way and the fringe didn't tangle. There was a certain way he wanted the bedspread on the bed, and the screens on the many electronics in the house had to be perfectly dust free.

Mary!

The anxiety built in her, the constant, gnawing fear of knowing he was watching, the way in which he was always just around the corner, lurking…

"Mary!"

She jumped. Royal was standing in the doorway. He looked drunk. And angry.

"What's the matter? Can I get you something?" she said, trying not to stutter.

"Damn refs. Can't call a fucking game to save themselves. Fucking rat bastards." That was one of Royal's insults of choice, for men at least. Women he didn't like were sluts or whores. She laid the last of Leo's little jackets into the open bag and waited silently.

He stared at her.

She was still wearing her cardigan. Most of the blouses Royal picked out for her to wear were thin, silky things, but she was always cold. He didn't like it when she put the bulky sweater on, so she tried to only wear it when he was occupied with something else. He was eyeing it now with displeasure. She must have set the motanka doll back on the shelf, because it no longer occupied her sweater pocket. She didn't remember doing it. She tried to slip it off but the sleeve snagged on her bandaged hand.

He beckoned her over. She rose reluctantly and went to him.

***

An hour later, Royal was asleep. Mary staggered from the edge of the bed to the bathroom. Her good hand shook so badly she could hardly turn on the shower. The blood ran down her legs and swirled around the drain. She stayed there until the water ran cold.

She walked unsteadily from the shower to her closet, a towel loosely draped around her chest. She was so cold. She couldn't even muster up the energy to shiver. Blood continued to run down her legs, and she instinctively dropped the towel so it wouldn't soil the rug.

Do it now, came the voice of the sun-bird. *You have to do it now.*

Yes, came the doll's agreement. *Do it now.*

She carefully slid the business card from its hiding place behind the picture frame. Standing naked on the towel, she switched her phone on and texted the number on the card. She typed in the one word the woman had printed there: "PHARMACY"

***

"She's made the call, my lady."

"Good, do you have everything you need to find her?"

"Yes. She gave me the address the last time we spoke."

"Excellent, Brielle. We have a place made ready for her. Go now."

"Yes, my lady."

Laelia eased back onto her pillows. The house was quiet for once. With so many sheltering here now, there was often activity at all hours. Laelia loved her girls, and she believed in their mission here, but it was lovely to have a moment to herself. If what she suspected was true, if this girl's husband was the kind of monster she believed him to be, it may be some time before she had any peace and quiet again.

She turned and inhaled the fragrance of the bouquet one of the children had picked for her that morning.

The time was right. They were ready for this challenge.

***

Brielle had befriended Mary at the local library where Mary took Leo for storytime. The librarian who did the baby storytimes, Miss Diane, was wildly popular and her sessions were always packed full. Brielle volunteered along with another young woman, who helped manage the crowds.

Brielle hadn't been fooled for a moment by Mary's attempts to explain away her burns and bruises, but she hadn't pushed. She'd played this role enough times to know how best to approach women in bad situations, and this time she'd had some unexpected help.

On one particular morning, the motanka doll had ridden along in the diaper bag to the library, faceless head poking out of the top of a purple Velcroed pocket. It had recognized Brielle at once, or rather, had recognized her as bearing Laelia's mark. Brielle had been surprised to see one of the ancient ones from back home. It had only happened once before that she could recall in the last ninety or so years. Once she put everything together with Mary's story, though, it all made sense.

You! Mavka! Come here now, the doll had hissed urgently from around the corner of the picture bookshelf.

Brielle went.

"Yes, mother?" she'd whispered, kneeling in front of the shelf, ostensibly straightening the books.

Is your mistress nearby? Can she help this girl?

"She can, but the girl must choose her own path. You know the rules, mother."

Tak, tak. But this girl, she needs the help. This cholovik, this husband, the doll spat. *He is no man. He is monster.*

"Yes, mother. I will talk to her. There are things she needs to do, to prepare."

Tell me these things.

"Yes, mother."

Brielle did her best to explain green cards and ATMs and text messages to the centuries-old goddess spirit within the doll. It went about as well as one would expect.

***

The text response came back immediately, as though it wasn't past midnight, and as if it was anticipated. It was coded as Mary had been told to expect, in case the wrong eyes were to see it.

"Your prescription will be ready for pickup in 45 minutes. Please come to the east door."

An icy finger of fear touched Mary's heart. An hour from now, she would either be free, or dead.

***

She dressed, slowly. She had to put in a pad. She wasn't sure exactly what all was bleeding because everything hurt, but whatever it was wasn't stopping. She couldn't manage buttons or zippers, or even socks, she discovered. She frowned at that. It was cold outside.

Use these, the sun-bird said. Its voice didn't seem muffled despite its being rolled up and stuck into a side pocket of the diaper bag.

Next to her feet appeared a pair of the shearling boots that had been popular for a while. They were slip-on; she could manage that. Sweat pants, a big t-shirt, and her coat. She stood shakily and looked around the room.

Don't dawdle, child, the motanka doll whispered from her usual pocket of the diaper bag, her head sticking out, eyelessly watching. *Go, child. Quietly. Get the baby. You need to go, now!*

Listening closely to their instructions, she put the bag over her right shoulder. She wasn't sure how she was going to carry both it and the baby, but it was important. She knew that. She crept silently across the thick carpet of the master bedroom suite and out into the hallway, then slipped through the double doors that led to the second floor landing.

Mary tiptoed down the carpeted hallway to the baby's room. She gathered him in his blanket and strained to lift him from his crib. An explosion rocked her ribcage and she gasped for breath, then immediately wished she hadn't.

Damn that rib, the sun-bird muttered. *Mary, take shallow breaths. You just have to get to the door. Help is coming.*

The new pain sent a shot of adrenaline through Mary's system. She wobbled, hanging on to Leo's crib for support. Every cell in her body screamed at her to just stop, just collapse. Sink down and die. She staggered, her vision fading in and out.

Then Leo opened his sleepy eyes and reached up his arms. Strength flooded her and she gathered him up again in his blanket. She boosted him up over her shoulder, trying to avoid touching her sore ribs and inhaled his baby sweetness. He nuzzled his little face into her neck and fell back asleep.

Mary took a shallow breath, turned, and walked out the door. She used the back stairway to the kitchen. It was farther from the master bedroom and closer to the east door. She navigated the stairs carefully, leaning against the wall and taking one careful step at a time. When she reached the kitchen she was seeing black spots again. She took a moment and gathered herself. The east door was off the kitchen, through the laundry room. From there it was just a few steps through the back gate out to the driveway. She desperately hoped she wouldn't have to go much farther than that. She wasn't sure she could.

The diaper bag thumped noisily against the dryer as she unlocked the door. She froze, listening, heart pounding.

Don't stop. Keep going, child.

Mary slipped out the door, closing it softly behind her, and stepped out into the night. She got to the gate and it was opened from the other side. Strong arms took the heavy bag from her shoulder and led her to a waiting car without lights. There was an infant seat already strapped into the back.

Brielle opened the passenger door for Mary and took Leo. She secured him in the seat as if she did it every day. She slid the bag onto the floor of the back seat and swiftly came around to the driver's side.

They backed out quickly. The car was new, a hybrid, so it made almost no sound. Even so, Brielle waited until they were well away before she turned on the headlights.

***

Royal awoke with a raging hard-on, as usual. He reached across the big bed in search of Mary and encountered empty space. He sighed and looked at the clock. It was early, before six. She'd be downstairs making coffee by now. Maybe she'd be wearing that little housedress he'd bought her. If he went downstairs now, he'd probably have time for a quickie in the kitchen before work. He knew she didn't like it when he fucked her in front of the baby. She'd try not to resist him, but he knew she hated it and that made it all the sweeter.

He headed for the bathroom. Something seemed off. Mary usually showered first thing in the morning, but there were no damp towels. In fact, her towel was missing altogether. Royal frowned and turned, the feeling of wrongness mounting. He walked to her closet, where she had her makeup table.

He stood in the doorway and stared. Her towel lay on the floor, tacky with blood. He puzzled for a moment before he saw what was off. The picture he'd gotten for her, that weird blue bird – the frame lay on the bench, face down. He stepped inside, avoiding the towel, and turned the frame over. The picture was gone.

He spun and sprinted out of the master suite to the baby's room. Empty crib. His son. The fucking whore had gone and taken his son.

His howl of rage rattled the windows in their frames.

***

It hadn't taken Brielle long to figure out that Mary needed a doctor, fast. Fortunately, the organization she worked for was well connected. By the time they got a safe distance outside the city, she'd been able get an emergency clinic opened and had a doctor waiting. Between her and the motanka, they'd been able to keep Mary conscious, despite her continued blood loss. The doctor later said that had probably saved her life.

As anxious as Brielle was to get Mary and Leo to their destination, the doctor refused to let them go for at least twenty-four hours.

"You were incredibly lucky getting her this far, but she's still at risk of hemorrhaging. She could have bled out in a matter of minutes."

Brielle sighed her acceptance and handed baby Leo off to the nurse to be checked over and cuddled. Before turning over his diaper bag, she carefully removed the picture of the bird and the motanka doll from their pockets. She gave Leo a kiss on the nose and his nurse a smile and a nod before she turned to the hall table where she'd set the picture.

Brielle gasped. The doll she had laid on its back was now standing near the edge of the table, allowing plenty of room for what transpired next. The print of the bird had been rolled up and fitted as carefully as possible into the bag. It was unrolling now, under its own power. As Brielle watched, fascinated, a blue wing stretched from the roll and shook its feathers out. As the wing took shape and form, the paper shrank back with a crinkling sound and unrolled further. The sun-bird's head emerged, its painted crown falling back and down, becoming a design on the feathers of its neck and back. It shook one final time as the last of the paper fell away, leaving the brilliant blue sun-bird perched on the table next to the motanka doll.

Greetings, sister, the bird said, nodding to Brielle. *You've done well and we thank you, but mother must speak to Laelia before any further plans can be made. We are in possession of information she will need for the battle at hand.*

"Yes, of course. I'll call her now." Brielle dialed, deciding that speaker-phone was probably the best way to facilitate communication between the two ancient spirits, particularly given the one on her end didn't appear to have working arms, or, for that matter, a mouth. She squeezed her eyes shut and ran with it.

"Laelia, we're at the clinic now. I'll let you know the minute I hear anything from the doctor. Yes. With your permission, I'm going to put you on speaker now so you can speak to Mary's friends." She set the phone down on the table between the bird and the doll and stepped aside, courteously listening to the ensuing conversation.

The news was not good. The spirit residing inside the Luger was every bit the old, powerful demon Laelia suspected, and from the stories the old mother and the sun-bird shared, it seemed to have fashioned the consummate disciple out of Royal. That kind of power was going to be exceedingly difficult to combat, let alone defeat. It was decided there was no choice but to allow them to discover the shelter, but a plan must be laid to not only protect Mary and Leo, but all the other women who had sought refuge there as well.

Once the elders had decided their strategy, she disconnected the call and found the two on her end a suitable place to monitor the baby and wait for Mary. Brielle had her instructions. She retrieved her valise from the car and laid out her tools: salt, candles, sage, and one or two other ingredients. It was a simple spell, but cast in a complicated pattern. Once constructed, she would need to monitor the spell to be sure it stayed intact. That said, it was going to be a long night… and day.

Brielle sighed and began creating the circles.

***

"ROYAL!" the voice roared loud enough to be heard over his fury.

Royal looked up. He knew the voice as well as he knew his own. He'd heard it nearly every day since his father had died.

"ROYAL! *Schluss, damit*! Enough! Mizerable *weichei*, komm heir, NOW!"

Royal scrubbed his fists across his eyes and looked around. The room he stood in was demolished. Curtains were ripped down, lamps smashed, furniture in pieces. The door looked like it had been kicked in. For a moment, he didn't even register on what room he was in. Nothing looked familiar. It finally clicked, and his fragmented mind wondered, *Why am I in the guest room*?

Royal staggered to his feet and lurched out onto the open second floor hallway and looked around. More disaster. In his rage, he had gone from room to room, searching for Mary and Leo, even knowing they were gone. There was a path of destruction throughout the second floor. He caught sight of broken glass on the stairs and glanced down at his hands. They were cut and bleeding.

He felt nothing. No pain. Just an agonizing emptiness where the rage had been.

"ROYAL!"

The voice came from his room. Head bowed, he shuffled that way. Zigging and zagging between torn bedding and shards of broken wood and glass that littered the floor, he made for his closet. It was his sanctuary. His den.

When the desire first came to him to find a bride, to actually cohabitate with someone, he'd panicked, thinking he might have to share his most intimate space. The house he'd been in back then had only had one walk-in closet. That simply wouldn't do. The first thing he'd designed with the architect when he'd commissioned this house was the master suite.

He'd designed his room meticulously. It housed his most precious belongings. He had always been terribly vain about his appearance, even during his brief Army service. There was space for his suits, ties, and shoes, of course. There was a full length mirror and a garment steamer. There were shelves, cubbies, and drawers everywhere, and he knew the contents of each one like the back of his hand. Teaching Mary where everything belonged had been a long and sometimes painful process.

Royal pushed down a flare of anger and grabbed the handle of the drawer he needed. He pulled it all the way out and tossed it aside, pristinely ironed handkerchiefs tumbling to the floor. He was after the biometric safe concealed behind it. He carefully positioned his fingertip on the scanner and pressed the button. Seconds later he was rewarded with a beep and the door opened.

He reached in and removed the Luger. His great grandfather had taken the gun as a trophy from an SS officer he'd killed during an attack on an Austrian castle near the end of World War II.

Royal felt the mix of relief and nervous excitement he felt any time he handled the Luger. It was a family treasure, handed down from father to son for four generations, but it was far more than that.

The Luger was alive.

"Yes, sir?" Royal addressed the old weapon respectfully.

"Dat whore you insisted on keeping has betrayed us," the Luger snarled at Royal, its Old High German warring with its more recently acquired English. "I warned you, too much spirit, that one, but you must have die extrawurst – the… special favors."

His head fell. Royal cradled the weapon. "Yes, sir. You were right, sir."

The Luger made a harumphing sound. "What is important now is the boy. We must get him back."

"Yes, sir."

"You listen now!"

"Yes, sir."

Royal paid strict attention as the Luger spelled out its plan. Within a few minutes, he had a bag stuffed with supplies and was headed for his car. Preoccupied as he was, listening to the archaic German creature's instructions, he failed to notice that in his rampage, curtains from the kitchen window had been torn down and had landed dangerously close to the gas stove.

The slight breeze he caused pulling the garage door open was enough to ignite a corner of one curtain. By the time he reached his car, they were blazing merrily and inviting some tea towels to join the party. Royal was passing the golf course for which the neighborhood had been named when he felt a *WOOMPF* and heard a deep boom. He ignored it and drove on, golden lights flickering in his rearview mirror.

The neighbors called 911. By the time they arrived, the house was a complete loss.

***

Royal had been driving with the Luger stowed next to him on the passenger seat for several hours. He was following orders and had little recall of where they had been, but he felt in some dim way that they'd been circling a specific point.

The Luger, which had seemed so sure of itself, was beginning to get edgy. Royal pulled off the main road. They were at the eastern boundary of whatever parish they'd just driven through. There were hotels and restaurants here and there amid the tangle of frontage roads and parking lots. Royal waited and listened.

The Luger muttered and swore in German. Royal had learned some of the language in school. His father and great grandfather had encouraged it, although he hadn't known why at the time. When his father died and the Luger came to him, it had made sense. Granted, the Luger often spoke a much older form of the language, but it helped.

Now it was spitting out words Royal thought he remembered reading in some fairy tale his senior year. *Der zauber, hexe…magic?* Witches? He waited patiently to be told what to do.

Royal didn't try to defy the Luger any more. He had once, when he'd first started feeling that he was losing himself. That night had nearly ended badly. He wondered, and not for the first time, if his father had tried something similar. His father had died from a bullet to the brain. It hadn't been the Luger – it had been another handgun, the one his father kept handy in his office drawer – but the circumstances made Royal wonder.

The last time Royal had seen his father alive was when he and his mother had come to see him graduate from basic training. Royal was, if not liked, at least admired, and his intelligence and physical prowess were a promising combination in the view of his superiors. Offers for special schools were forthcoming; he was being eyed for officer potential. Then he'd gotten the call about his father's suicide. It was scandalous, and his mother was preoccupied with the attorneys, keeping the truth of the matter out of the papers and away from the boardroom. The family business didn't need that kind of publicity.

He'd gotten a two-day leave to go to the funeral and help his mother settle the paperwork. After the services, he'd been summoned to the law offices. His mother's presence wasn't required, Mr. Hofmann had told him quietly in the lobby of the funeral parlor. So he'd gone alone.

Mr. Hofmann had handed him the box, along with an envelope. He had seemed focused and determined, but also loathe to touch the box containing the old gun. "Our offices have been with your family for many generations, Royal," he began, seriously. "We began our relationship with your great grandfather in 1946, shortly after he returned from Europe and opened his first business. He always held this artifact in great regard and one of his first instructions to our firm was with regard to its protection and to make sure it was passed down each generation to the eldest son."

Royal had touched the box without opening it. He'd seen the Luger before; his father had shown it to him on a couple of notable occasions, carefully unlocking it from the gun safe in his office, lecturing him on its irreplaceable value. Royal had always hated being called in there. It had been the setting for many a beating he'd received at the hand of his father, and many a hand-job as well.

He was never sure which he'd hated more.

He'd taken the gun from the lawyer's office with the promise and full intent of returning it to the safe in his father's office for safekeeping, but on the way home it had spoken to him from inside its polished rosewood box.

The Luger had returned with Royal to Fort Jackson. In the weeks that followed, Royal changed. He'd always been strong, competitive, and athletic. He'd played every contact sport available in school, and the Army training had awakened an interest in all sorts of new combat skills, but it had all stayed within some sorts of acceptable boundaries.

The Luger changed that.

Minor annoyances became major catastrophes. Casual friendships that had been competitive became adversarial. Royal had never had any trouble finding women to date, but he began to eschew the easy targets, aiming instead for women who were more of a challenge: married or above him in rank. These changes in Royal's behavior inevitably led to conflicts, which he savored. Fort Jackson became his training ground, and, in short order, his hunting ground.

Some bad behavior gets ignored, particularly when it is perpetrated by a young, good-looking, clever white man. But Royal, driven by the bloodthirsty nature of the Luger, pushed the boundaries too far. An affair with a Major who was married to a Senator proved his undoing, and nearly ended in the beheading of the Senator when he arrived home unexpectedly one afternoon.

Due to the depraved nature of the events that had unfolded in the Major's bedroom that day, and the proximity of her husband's next political campaign, both she and the Senator were interested in keeping things quiet. Royal spent less than a month in lockup on the base before receiving a Bad Conduct Discharge. No civil or criminal charges were ever filed. And then he was set free.

Royal spent the next year or so honing his skills. Blessed with more than adequate funds from the family business, of which he was now entirely in charge, Royal thoroughly enjoyed the process of becoming a monster under the tutelage of a demon who had created many. The SS officer had been a joy to the old imp, but in Royal he found not only an apt pupil, but a human being with a true gift for atrocity.

Acquiring a mother for Royal's son had been a challenge for the pair. Royal wouldn't be satisfied with someone who was completely pliable like his mother and grandmother had been. He wanted a woman with looks, some smarts, and spirit. He wanted a challenge, and someone who would provide him with a son who had spirit as well. He wanted a son who would be worthy of the Luger, and a wife who would be worthy of breaking.

There was no ecstasy, he had learned, without blood.

The Luger spoke, and Royal snapped out of his daze.

Your damned hure *has found herself some helpers, it seems, or perhaps brought them with her. Vee may haf more of a challenge on our hands than we thought,* bengel.

Bengel was what the Luger called him when it was interested in something new. It meant 'scoundrel' or 'troublemaker'. Whenever he used it, Royal had learned, he was wise to anticipate some new, often inspired wickedness.

He smiled. "What is it, sir? Who does she have?"

I believe our little Ukrainian princess has taken up with a brood of Mavkas.

"Mavkas?"

Waldnymphen, nymphs. From the wood, the forest. Demon women. Loud, ungrateful whores. It is said they died violent deaths so they return to avenge themselves. HA! They should think to protect her. All they have is some gypsy spells and weak magic. HA! I say such whores need to STAY DEAD.

"How do we find them, sir?"

You leave that to me, Bengel. Find us some place where we can have our way. We shall need some nourishment for this search.

"Ecstasy, sir?"

Ja, ja. Yes, Bengel. We must have blood.

***

Royal followed a playbook they'd used many times in the past. He booked a room in the nicest hotel in the area where he showered and changed. Leaving the Luger locked in the hotel safe, he set out to find the seedier part of the city. It wasn't difficult; it was a relatively small city. He found a pocket of rough bars and rougher convenience stores located near the old downtown and followed his instincts to the working girls.

The deed itself was completed outdoors. He and the Luger had participated in this ceremony so many times over the past years that it was no longer necessary for the old gun to be physically present. The creature's hold on Royal was strong enough that, with the proper elements in place, it could be there, within Royal, taking part of and adding power to the ritual.

No ecstasy without blood.

There was plenty of blood. The girl, a runaway of perhaps 15, provided for that need admirably. This ceremony, Royal knew, did more than provide the Luger's spirit with the power it needed to find their prey; it cemented anew its hold on him. It was a bizarre and horrible marriage, and he loved it, welcomed it. Every stroke, every slice, every blow bound them together with chains of depravity. The shreds of Royal's soul ornamented the Luger's demon like ribbons on a bride's bouquet. For a time, they were one, and Royal was complete.

And then, it was over. The demon was sated for the moment, and Royal was left wanting more. Always wanting more.

He dragged the remains of the girl's body to the edge of the lake and rolled it in. He felt no fear at the thought of being discovered. The old Luger's magic was strong enough to protect them in more trying circumstances than this one, and the shoreline was swampy. Odds were some of the local critters would recycle this chunk of meat before anyone was the wiser. These backwater parishes were handy that way.

Royal stripped off the scrubs and latex gloves he always wore. He would still need to bathe vigorously to remove the rest of the mess from his skin, but he'd learned to minimize it. He bundled the shower cap into a ball with the rest of the items he'd used and walked back to the small fire he'd lit. He waited while the items burned completely, allowing the last drops of the girl's blood to smolder away into the dark air.

Royal returned to his five-star suite, showered until his skin was tender, put on the thick comfortable robe provided by the fine establishment, and fell to on the room service he'd ordered before the kitchen closed. He checked to see that the Luger had everything it needed to complete its next magical workings, and relieved, flung himself onto the king-sized bed and slept, drenched in glorious dreams of blood and ecstasy.

***

It was late in the night when Brielle first felt the pulsating energy pushing against her protection spell. She knew instantly who it was and was relieved that Laelia had anticipated this and given her time to augment her spells. Forewarned was forearmed.

As Brielle walked the intricate series of concentric circles interlaid with runes and sigils with which she had surrounded the entire clinic, she allowed herself to wonder how Laelia knew so much about this particular demon. A sudden tear, a rip in one of her lines interrupted her musings. Leaping and spinning through the glowing bands of force, she identified the exact place, mended the tear, and then re-routed the lines around it to avoid the tender spot. She finished in time to feel another line rip.

For the rest of that long night, Brielle had no time for thought, only action. All the while, as she danced and stitched and drew and gathered her lines of power into an ever more protective web, Mary and Leo slept peacefully for the first night in a countless stretch of nights.

From her nest near the girls' hidden sanctuary in the woods, Laelia watched, and was satisfied.

From his box inside the hotel safe, the Luger cursed and growled, aiming increasingly calculated and vicious attacks at Brielle's spell.

***

Sunrise finally came, boosting Brielle's magic and weakening the Luger's. Exhausted, Brielle lay on the floor underneath intersecting ribbons of glowing magic fading into the sunbeams. Dust motes flickered down, blissfully unaware of the battle that had so recently raged. Brielle knew a few of the demon's thrusts had made it through for more than a quick instant, and she feared what he may have learned about their location or, worse yet, their plans.

Brielle pulled herself to her feet. She had to get Mary and the baby out of there, now.

***

Royal awoke to find the Luger in a foul but pensive mood. A road map from the car lay on the table near the sandalwood box. It looked like it had been hit with a round of buckshot. However, amid the scattering of holes, a faint pattern emerged. A path.

"Looks like we're headed northeast, Kemosabe," Royal said, packing up his few things.

Hmmmph. Do not waste time. Move now. There is a chance we can catch up with them before they enter the Mavkas' den.

Royal was intrigued. The Luger was talking strategy, not just force. He took a risk and pushed for details. "Tell me more about these Mavkas. Who are these bitches that have my boy?"

You drive the auto. I will tell you what you need to know. Schnell!

Royal did as he was bid.

***

Brielle was wondering how in the world she was going to have the energy to drive another eight or ten hours when her phone buzzed. It was Anna, with excellent news. Reinforcements had arrived. A car was waiting. It was time to go.

She knocked and entered to find Mary sitting up, ribs bandaged, carefully feeding Leo. She was smiling. Brielle paused and let the peace of that moment wash over her. Heavens knew it may be a while before there was more peace to be had.

"I'm glad to see you're feeling better. Laelia has sent us a vehicle and some additional help. Unfortunately, we know Royal is on our trail, and he has help too. We need to get moving."

A look of fearful concern crossed Mary's face and her embrace tightened around the baby. "It's that gun, isn't it? The German one?"

Brielle sighed. "Yes. It is. But it's an enemy Laelia is familiar with. She has experience with his kind and I promise, we will get you to safety and we can protect you," she said, praying that she was right.

Mary, jaw firm, baby at her breast, looked Brielle in the eye. "Either I fight back or he will kill me. I am ready. Let us go and do this."

Brielle grinned. Leo let go his hold on his mother's breast, turned to look at her face, and a peal of joyful baby laughter emerged from him, the kind that makes the sun shine brighter and the hardest hearts melt. It was as if he were cheering them on. Brielle and Mary looked at one another, eyebrows raised.

Leo gave one last giggle, then filled his diaper and fell promptly to sleep.

***

Royal checked out of the hotel and threw his things in the trunk. He stopped for gas and breakfast at the same place, a practice that guaranteed heartburn later in the morning, and hit the road. The path the Luger had determined would lead them north and east across Mississippi and Alabama, toward Georgia.

He had no idea why they were headed that way. Mary knew nobody in any of those places. In fact, Royal believed he'd made sure she hadn't made any significant friendships since she'd been in the States.

Where had he gone wrong? His mind raced back and forth over the events of the last two years. Everything had been so good, so perfect… so according to plan. Royal loved nothing more than having things fall into line, especially difficult and spirited things. The more Mary had struggled, the more he'd loved putting her back into her place. Recently, however, it had seemed she'd given up some of her fight. He'd had to work harder to get the responses out of her that he wanted.

Well, you know what they say. You have to work on relationships to keep them fresh. This little jaunt may just prove to be the thing needed to spice up their relationship. Of course, the likelihood that Mary would survive the reunion celebration was pretty low, but that was all right too. There was nothing more romantically appealing to a young woman on her own than a handsome wealthy widow with a baby to raise.

Royal drove on, his thoughts alternating between fantasies of showing Mary the error of her ways and the challenge of breaking in someone new. Once, he might have been appalled at his own thinking. Once, he may have tried to escape the hell he was trapped in. But not now. Royal's mind didn't even go there any more. Not after the last time. This was his life now.

His hands played over his crotch in concert with the smile on his handsome face.

***

Brielle and Mary stepped outside the clinic, laden with medicines and instructions. Brielle carried the motanka doll and the baby paraphernalia, and Mary had Leo. The sun-bird perched on Mary's shoulder, keeping a sharp eye on her charges.

Waiting outside the door was a hulking black SUV driven by a petite, dark-haired woman wearing a bright green jacket emblazoned with the number 10. The other woman appeared to be finishing up casting a spell that encompassed the SUV and the clinic itself. She motioned them over to stand next to the passenger doors.

They did as instructed and waited while she loaded each of them quickly and efficiently with magic so thick, even Mary could see it hanging in the air. Leo looked like he was surrounded by fireflies before she was done. And then, with one final movement of the woman's hands, the sparkling lights were gone – absorbed by each of them. The motanka doll sneezed, Mary giggled, and Leo farted.

The women exchanged another amused look as they loaded in. Mary, Leo and Anna, the spellcaster, took the large, roomy back seat. Anna instructed Mary how to adjust the seat so she could stretch out and rest per the doctor's instructions. She reminded Brielle in the passenger seat that Laelia expected her to rest as well, and they set off.

In truth, they hurtled off, as though someone had waved some otherworldly checkered flag. Mary's eyes widened as she peered out the tinted window at the trees and buildings and other cars flying by. It was as if they were slipping along in some jet stream just outside everyone else's reality. Despite the fact that they were traveling well over the speed limit, and defying all sorts of laws of physics, nobody raised an eyebrow or honked a horn.

She looked across Leo to Anna, eyebrows raised. "Have we engaged the warp engines, Captain?" Mary asked, pleased to remember the phrase from the old American TV show she used to watch back home.

"Ha! In a manner of speaking, yes. One thing is for sure, we will reach our destination long before *he* does."

"That is a good thing," Mary murmured, stroking Leo's hair. She felt a glimmer of renewed hope. "A very good thing."

***

Royal was tired. He'd stopped only once in nine hours. He wasn't even sure where they were at the moment. Somewhere north of

Atlanta. The land had become increasingly hilly and he'd seen some signs mentioning the Appalachian Trail. Royal wasn't much of an outdoorsman, and the extent of his knowledge of Appalachia was that sick movie with Burt Reynolds and Angelina Jolie's dad. Chuckling to himself, he hummed snatches of *Dueling Banjos* as he drove along.

The Luger had been muttering to itself for the last hour or so, only occasionally directing Royal to turn. They'd gotten off the interstate some time ago and were creeping along twisty state highways at an infuriating 55 mph.

It is close, I can feel it. I can feel their hexenwerk… majick. Dummen huren. The place, it is close. There! Leave the auto there. We must walk.

Royal pulled over as instructed. The sun was going down off to the left somewhere, behind the hills. It was going to be a dark walk. He popped the trunk. The Luger may not have instructed him to pack much in the way of toiletries, but it seemed to have thought ahead to a hike in the woods. Royal pulled out his hiking boots and utility jacket. They were items made more for style than practicality, but they'd have to do.

More important was some of the other equipment; the lantern, axe, and rifle would all come in handy. He shoved smaller items into a backpack, holstered the Luger, and stepped away from the parking area onto a clearly defined path. He caught a glimpse of the sign by the entrance, telling him that in just over 2,000 miles he'd be in Maine.

The Luger's muttering got louder and more excited once they were out of the car. They were close. Royal could feel the demon's excitement enter his consciousness. It lifted his exhaustion and filled him with electric energy. Royal welcomed it. When they were together like this, primed for a fight, he felt immense, powerful, and driven. Anticipation of the ecstasy he knew was coming grew in him like a ravening hunger.

It got dark fast. There was no moon this night. Royal hiked at a steady pace while they stayed on the path. His senses, augmented by the demon's presence, were alert to the smallest sounds, the tiniest movements. He intuitively altered his pace so his footsteps made little sound on the trail. It was early spring yet, so many of the trees were still bare. The air was cold and damp.

After about forty-five minutes, the Luger directed him off the main path. Royal tried to keep on the direction the demon pointed him, but it was hard. The wood defied straight lines. He stumbled and struggled through undergrowth, over fallen logs, through stickers that tore at his hands and face, but he hardly noticed.

He could sense them now, as well. They weren't far. It was a small house, more like a hut, really, in the wood. He could sense their presence – women, all of them, except for Leo. He could sense the lines of magic surrounding the house, snaking out into the wood.

They had to know he was coming. They'd be fools not to know, not to have taken precautions. He strained to sense hidden lines of magic, booby traps, spies. He doused the lantern and continued on by the faint starlight, hunting knife drawn.

Royal and the old demon were so preoccupied with the terrain, they failed to look up.

***

Mary, Brielle, and the others had arrived hours before. Mary knew a little of the Mavka from fairy stories when she was young. She wasn't surprised when they came out of warp, or however they'd been traveling, in a fairly dense wood. She was a little surprised at the sheer number of women who came out to greet them, given the relatively tiny size of the house they'd emerged from. Once she was ushered inside, it became clear that magic was at work here as well.

The inside of the tiny shack was far, far larger than the outside. Room opened onto room inside, the floor soft underfoot with layers of rugs, flowers everywhere, in vases, in pots on windowsills, crackling fires in tiny fireplaces in nearly every room. There must have been thirty or forty women staying there, and each seemed to have her own cozy bedroom with space enough for a little table and chairs. Mary was shown to a room with a bassinet snugged up against a bed piled high with pillows and quilts.

Once she'd settled her few belongings, she was ushered down another set of twisty hallways to a large, open space that was a combination kitchen and eating area. There was an enormous table surrounded by chairs of every description, and a fireplace equipped with metal shelves and hooks at different heights, obviously designed to cook for a crowd.

Standing at the kitchen counter slicing bread and issuing instructions was one of the most beautiful creatures Mary had ever seen. She was tall, well over six feet. Her bare arms were exquisitely muscled and her smile was wide. Her dress was a wonder. It was a simple shift, utilitarian in design, but the fabric was breathtaking, some kind of shimmery silver grey, with a pattern reminiscent of scales. Mary stared at it, but only until she met Laclia's eyes. They were not human eyes. The pupils were long and narrow like a cat's, but ever so much wilder and more dangerous.

Mary bowed awkwardly. Laelia strode over and embraced her. She held her arms out for Leo. He eyed her seriously for a moment and reached for her and wriggled to be free. Laelia took him and looked him over carefully. Leo returned the scrutiny in kind. At last they each seemed satisfied, and everyone in the room let go a collective breath they hardly realized they'd been holding. Laelia nodded at Leo decisively, as though something had been silently settled between the two.

Laelia exchanged the barest of respectful nods with the doll and then held out her arm. The sun-bird flew to her. The bird seemed fluttery, almost starstruck. Laelia stroked the brilliant blue head and back and whispered, just loud enough for Mary to hear, "Welcome, little sister. I welcome your light." The sun-bird made a happy sort of cooing sound and settled back into her normal easy demeanor.

"You are welcome, each of you. Come and sit at our table." She addressed Mary directly. "You, child, are pursued by an old and dangerous enemy. After making the risks known to all here, those you see gathered are the souls who have accepted your enemy as our own."

Mary's face reflected her surprise and gratitude at this revelation.

"Now we must prepare." Laelia turned and addressed everyone in the room. "Come, all. Break bread with our sisters, and let us make ready for battle."

From her perch in Anna's overalls pocket, the motanka doll muttered, *Hmmmpf! Drakons.*

***

Royal's first indication that something was nearby was a soft downdraft that fluttered his hair. He froze and stared upwards at the enormous form of a dragon that flew directly over his head. It was huge, far larger than the little four-seater aircraft in which he'd learned basic aviation at a camp when he was sixteen. He couldn't say for sure in the low light, but its scales appeared to be a silvery grey color, and its talons were enormous, sharp and terrifying.

Royal hissed at the Luger. "You didn't say anything about dragons."

The Luger's demon laughed. *Why do you think we brought the verdammt dinosaur gun?*

Royal, teeth bared, eyes fierce, had already unslung the .577 T-Rex rifle he was carrying on his back. He'd purchased it the year before for a safari he'd taken to Africa, just before Mary had fallen pregnant. That had been a strange trip, he vaguely recalled. Their guide had been about half unhinged that whole week. There had been some lion attacks in the area and all the locals were spewing some old wives' tale about ghost lions. The only lion they'd seen the entire time was one grizzled and scarred male, too old to be any sort of a challenge.

They'd been after elephants that week, and he'd taken down a big male.

In point of fact, it hadn't been Royal's shot that had brought down the bull elephant. The guide had done that after Royal had shot once with the .577 and had gotten knocked back so hard by its recoil he'd dislocated a shoulder. Royal's memory of that part of the adventure was vague. The thrill of the hunt, and afterward the enjoyment of the local girl who had tended his shoulder, were much more present in his mind.

The .577 held three rounds. By the time he brought the gun to bear, the dragon had disappeared off to their right. Royal shouldered the huge weapon and turned slowly, willing the dragon to reappear.

It came from behind, flying silently on enormous scaled wings, breathing a swath of fire twenty feet wide. Royal spun and fired. The report was deafening. The recoil knocked him clean off his feet, dislocated his shoulder and sent him rolling ass-over-teakettle down the hill. The shot went wide, missing the dragon's body but grazing one wing. She roared, still flaming, and veered away. Royal's fall downhill resulted in a badly sprained ankle, but it saved him from being completely incinerated.

Get up, dammit. I see someone.

Royal rose to his knees and elbows, singed but still in the game. He knew from experience when this was all over he was going to feel the pain, but for now he was good. The demon's energy was flowing freely and he felt strong. He looked in the direction the Luger indicated, eyes hard, anticipating some fresh warrior or beast.

It was a girl.

Pay attention, dumme. That is no girl.

Royal scowled. The Luger had told him about the Mavkas, how they were the spirits of girls who had died violent deaths. It had told him they preyed on men, luring them out into the woods like this to get revenge. Frankly, Royal had anticipated something more terrifying than a scantily clad girl sitting in the grass. The dragon had been an exciting start, but this? It was just a fucking girl.

She stood and walked toward him. It was early spring and still chilly, especially with the sun going down, and she wasn't wearing much, just a little slip of a dress. Royal pushed himself up to his full height and watched her approach, one hand on his knife.

She looked young, but she moved enticingly. There was a swing to her hips and a look in her eyes that Royal was finding increasingly difficult to ignore. The Luger's spluttering and swearing seemed to fade the closer she got to him. Her eyes were a deep blue, and her hair fell free, just covering her breasts. He could smell her sweetness; his head buzzed with it. Flowers. She had a flower tucked behind one ear.

He had to touch her, *needed* to touch her. Every inch of him quivered. The scent of her was electric in his brain. He reached out, fingertips brushing her cheek. Royal could barely hear the Luger shouting. It sounded like bees buzzing somewhere in the distance.

The girl curled one hand around the back of his neck and drew his face toward hers. In her other hand she held a handful of freshly picked flowers, delicate things, columbines or something. She held the bouquet between them, inhaled their scent, and looked at him invitingly from behind the petals.

Royal tilted his head toward her, breathed in, and screamed.

It was as if he'd inhaled white-hot barbed wire. His face, his sinuses – everything was on fire. Blood erupted from his eyes and nose. He shoved the girl away with as much strength as he could muster and scrambled away from her, gasping and coughing.

The girl fell back laughing in the grass, and from behind her came another girl, and another. Royal regained his feet. The girls approached him from three sides. Royal had never imagined anything like it. His eyes and nose were still on fire and gushing blood, but he *WANTED*. He wanted those girls, needed to have them. His cock was rock hard, his hands reaching for them, his shambling steps taking him toward them instead of away.

ROYAL! the Luger screamed.

A burst of light exploded behind his eyes, momentarily clearing his thoughts.

ROYAL! Go! Now! Go toward the lake, there!

Royal turned and through blood-hazed eyes saw where the Luger wanted him to go. He also saw why.

About a hundred yards away, in front of a small, almost perfectly round lake, he saw Mary. His Mary. She was wearing that little house dress he liked, the red one. In her arms was Leo. She had him bundled against the chill, wrapped in some sort of fur-lined wrap.

One of the girls reached him from behind, flowers in hand, and touched his shoulder. He shuddered. Her touch was electric, sensual, intensely arousing, and then the pain slammed into him again, radiating down his shoulder, exploding through his back. He felt like he was being stabbed from the inside with rusty wire.

Royal screamed again and fled away from the girls toward the lake. From the corners of his eyes he could see more and more girls appearing from the trees on either side and behind him. They seemed to be funneling him down toward Mary. They drew close as he ran past. He cringed away from their hands, their flowers, their eyes.

Terrifying, insensible pain stabbed at Royal, overriding even the demon's ability to block it out. But there was one thing keeping pace with the agony: anger. He was dead furious. These were fucking *girls.* They had some sort of magic the Luger hadn't *fucking* prepared him for and that was *fucked up* and *fucking wrong* and it *hurt* and this was *all Mary's fucking fault that things were Not Going According To Plan.*

The Luger's low voice cut through his panic briefly. *Use the gas.*

Royal's hand clutched at his jacket pocket, fumbling for the canister. There was a light wind at his face – at least that one thing was in his favor. He ripped the tab from the tear gas grenade and tossed it over his shoulder. He ran on, and delighted at the sound of screaming and crying coming from the girls behind him.

The girls up ahead on either side saw the gas and hesitated. Royal let fly one more canister, ran unimpeded the last twenty yards of the gauntlet, and gained the clearing where he had first sighted Mary and Leo. During his wild run, Mary had been busy. She'd placed Leo in some sort of contraption that looked like a floating nest, and had pushed him out into the lake. He was sitting up, still bundled in the furry blanket, contentedly watching his mother on the shoreline. Now Mary stood between them as if guarding the baby from his raging approach.

He raced toward her, knife arm upraised, meaning to tackle her and crush her skull into the rocks that surrounded the lake. Mary stood motionless as he raced toward her, snarling. His fingertips were inches from her throat when he was jerked off his feet and heaved upward.

Huge, sharp claws held of him from shoulders to knees. The dragon. It was back. His rifle shot had torn a ragged hole in one of the beast's wings, but it hadn't taken it out.

The dragon landed, balancing on its hind legs and holding Royal firmly in its front talons. It angled downward until Royal's feet brushed the ground, but did not let him go.

Mary approached with slow but firm steps. Under one arm was tucked the motanka doll. On her shoulder was perched a blue bird that looked remarkably like the one from the painting. Royal wasn't sure why, amid all the other bizarre and magical things that had populated his world recently, the bird seemed so damned unlikely, but there it was. He stared at it, dazed.

Mary stopped less than a foot away from him. The dragon held his arms tightly pinned, and the shoulder he'd dislocated was starting to become a torment. He'd hardly noticed it before, but now it was throbbing like mad. The big rifle, still on its sling, was pressed into his armpit, the barrel pinned between his back and the beast's claws. Royal struggled to get his other hand closer to the trigger.

Mary looked at him coldly, piercingly. Royal gathered up the embers of his fury, fueled by the demon still inside him, and sneered at her.

She spat in his face. "You are an evil beast," she hissed at him. "You sold your soul to a demon. You lied to me, to my mama and papa. You said you would care for me, love me and cherish me, and what did you do? You beat me with tools when your fists grew tired, you blacked my eyes and broke my bones, burned me and raped me and tried to kill my spirit. And what would you do to our son? You created him to be evil, just like you. You brought him into this world so he too could be a tool for your perverted evil games.

"I say to you, no more. I will not allow your evil to destroy me or my son. This is the end, Royal. It is time for you to pay the price for all you have done."

Royal laughed. "What will you do to me, cunt? Let your pet dragon here have at me? Coward! Bitch! You were a fine fuck for a little while, but I'm done with you. You were – "

The dragon, Laelia, squeezed. There was an audible crack, and suddenly Royal found it difficult to breathe. He cast about in his mind, listening for the Luger, waiting to be told what to do.

All he heard was silence.

Then a light brightened around Mary. It seemed to be coming from the doll in her arms. It grew bright and then brighter, and surrounded her with a shine that almost looked like armor. Cloaked in the brightness, Mary reached in between Laelia's talons and plucked the Luger from its holster at Royal's hip.

She held it up for a moment, staring at it as if trying to understand. Her skin, shielded by the doll's power, never touched the gun's metal; instead, the gun too was encased by it, surrounded by a casket of light.

Royal felt a strange draining sensation and then a familiar emptiness. The demon was gone from him, and like it always did when it left him, the pain reinstated itself. All the cuts and burns and broken bones screamed to life in the primal lizard part of Royal's brain. If he'd been able to scream, he would have.

Mary held the Luger up, and then the bird launched itself from her shoulder. It swooped over her hands and gingerly took the gun in its claws. It hovered there for a second, and Mary looked into the dragon's huge catlike eyes. "Are you sure?"

Laelia's voice rumbled from the depths of her dragon form. "Yes. He has bidden it be so, and I trust him."

"But he's just a baby!"

"This is how it must be," replied the dragon sternly.

The drakon speaks truth, said the motanka doll soothingly. *Fear not, child.*

Mary wrapped her arms around the doll. "Very well. Let us finish this."

Just then, Royal managed to get his thumb hooked on the trigger of the dinosaur gun. Using every last ounce of strength he could force from his hands, he squeezed. The bullet ripped up the dragon's chest and shoulder. A spray of thick greenish blood spattered upward. The recoil from the weapon forced Royal's body downwards, and the dragon let him loose to tumble to the ground.

He half fell, half lunged at Mary. His knife, which had been clutched in his other hand the whole time, was propelled toward Mary's belly. The sun-bird screeched and flapped madly to clear herself of the falling bodies and spraying blood.

Still cloaked in the motanka's armor, Mary never moved, never wavered. The knife glanced away and fell harmlessly to the ground. The dragon, bleeding, eyes alight with pain, heaved her body closer to Royal and impaled him with a claw. Royal gasped as the curved talon entered through his lower back and exited through his thigh.

There was so much blood. His brain stuttered and tried to connect. Why? There was supposed to be ecstasy… but this time, there was only blood.

The sun-bird flew up and over the lake until it hovered over Leo in his floating nest, Luger still clutched in her claws. Leo reached up and grasped at the gun. The sun-bird dropped it into his hands. Everyone froze in place near the shore and watched, not breathing.

For a moment, the golden light continued to shield the gun, but then a dark mist pressed outward from around the Luger, pushing, stabbing against the light. Leo continued to hold his little hands out, observing as the demon's magic battled against that of the old goddess within the doll, the Luger floating a few inches above his baby fingers. The baby watched with bright eyes at the play of light and darkness, and then with a sudden swatting movement of his hands, he dismissed the light, and let the dark mist free.

Mary gasped. Royal stared. The light was fading from his eyes, but he fought it. He had to see.

Leo's face became serene as he watched the darkness dart around him, sniffing at his eyes, his mouth, as if it were looking for a way in. He watched it tolerantly, the way a big old lion will allow a cub to pester it for a little while. The light shifted. The glow of the old goddess's magic had faded, yet Leo was still surrounded by a golden radiance. It lit his fluff of brown hair, making it look lighter and more golden. It illuminated his eyes, making them seem both tranquil and wise.

The Luger's spirit gathered itself for one final attack. It dove at the baby's mouth, intent on possessing him, this child it had manipulated into being.

Leo threw back his little head, took a deep breath, and roared. The sound was as deep as the bedrock and louder than the report from Royal's preposterous dinosaur gun. It vibrated the water and the stone and the trees.

The waves of sound blasted through the demon's dark form, pulsing, reverberating, tearing it apart.

The old demon tried desperately to hold itself together, but it was no use. The fog shook and shuddered and spun, and finally it was gone.

Leo allowed the roar to subside, and sat quietly, looking at the now-empty Luger hanging in the air in front of him. After a moment, he gave it a little swat with his baby paw and it shattered into a million darkly shining metal fragments. They dropped, harmless, into the water around his nest.

Mary collapsed, weeping with relief, and Anna and several of the others waded out to grasp Leo's floating nest and pull it back to shore. Once there, Mary gathered Leo into her arms and held him tightly, stroking his hair and whispering in his ear.

Laelia pulled her talon out of Royal's lifeless body. She flipped it onto a large stone, away from the women crowding around Mary and Leo. She aimed a blast of fiery breath at his body, and before anyone had time to suggest S'mores, Royal's body was reduced to ash.

Leo watched contentedly from the safety of his mother's arms, making what sounded like an unnervingly large purring noise with each exhale.

QUEEN B
ROSE GARNETT

The young man screamed as the pointed end of the stake was driven up his rectum, a coloratura performance that reached heights Morgana hadn't believed possible for any mere human.

Leaning into the bloodied face, she stared into his remaining eye and said, "All this fuss over such a little prick."

A susurration, like the first spark of a forest fire, swept through the assembled vampires. Morgana motioned to the pair restraining the victim. They loosened their grip, features warped and distorted like wax facsimiles held too close to the fire.

Some of the dull-eyed human hangers-on tried to turn their faces away, only to have them yanked back by their chittering vampire hosts. Morgana had never understood why humans were so fascinated with her kind, squandering their freedom for the mere promise of illicit thrills which in reality meant being used as blood bags and then death.

This particular specimen hadn't stood a chance from the moment he'd stepped over the bin-bag strewn threshold in search of adventure and a name for himself. He hadn't been the first, and the huge basement of the house bore testament to that, carpeted wall to wall with their bones, skulls stacked to the ceiling.

"So you wanted to play the big vampire hunter, did you?" Morgana crooned, trailing a sharp fingernail down the side of his face and parting skin from bone. "Something to brag about to your friends, perhaps? True, you ended up on the – I almost hate to say – shitty end of the stick, but on the plus side your disappearance will be a hot topic of conversation, for a little while at least. And let's not beat about anyone's bush – it is what you were planning to do to me, isn't it?"

He gurgled; blood flooded his mouth and sprayed onto the stained wall. This one was done and she felt that old familiar disappointment. He'd been filled with bravado at first as they all were, but he hadn't even lasted the hour and now he was broken, a dumb, useless slab of meat not even fit for her to eat.

It had started well enough when they caught him, boasting and blustering about how he was going to annihilate the nest and Morgana with it. But that ended as it always did after Morgana had prised his teeth out with pliers, scattering them on the floor to be crunched underfoot by the milling crowd along with any spirit he might have had. Early promise had yet again faded to the same old routine, and somewhere along that familiar continuum she had lost all interest.

Blood and urine dripped in long lines from the filthy kitchen table where he was pinned, pooling together on the rubbish-strewn floor. The smell of excrement hung thick and sickly sweet in the air, almost but not quite disguising the rank, reptilian odour of vampire.

Home, sweet home.

The young man convulsed as though an electric current had passed through his body, reminding her of an old game. Easing the stake from the meat with a delicacy belied by the shrieks, she motioned to the crowd to back off. They obeyed like a well-drilled army and withdrew as one from the table.

She paused to glare at her assembled nest for a brief moment and then, without a backward glance, hurried into the hallway towards the lounge, drawing them and their blood-bags with her as though she was the moon to their tide. It made no difference where she was in the house; her senses were so acute she was aware of everything from the scratching of mice deep within the walls to the scent of old blood and fresh corpses in the basement. To the victim, however, it made all the difference in the world, bringing as it did the possibility of escape. Did he have it in him to try?

Listening from her new perch in the bay window of the vast, dilapidated lounge, the wheeze of his breathing in the kitchen complemented the howling gale outside and the intermittent buzzing of dying blue-bottles against the newspaper-covered windows. Was he already in his death-throes? No; a desperate scrabbling followed by a loud crash told a different story. Small, animal sounds of pain ensued – he had fallen onto his own extracted teeth. She cast her mind back to when they'd taken his eye, gouging it out with a rusty nail, and then left it sitting on his cheekbone, optic nerve and all, asking him if he could see into his own head.

This had proved to be too much for one of the vampires, who had made a grab for the eye, stuffing it into her mouth and chewing with greedy relish until Morgana raised an admonitory eye-brow. Spitting the jellied mass onto the floor as though it was molten, the vampire stamped it under a high-heeled boot for good measure.

Morgana pictured the French windows at the far end of the kitchen. They led out onto the back garden and were the obvious escape point. Obvious, that is, if he still had his wits about him, but he'd struck her as a dim-witted sort and she wasn't confident his wits stretched very far at the best of times, never mind now in extremis.

Sounds of stumbling and then sobs, full-throated, piteous, erupted from the kitchen.

"Is there no end to the tedium?" Morgana muttered. She swept back into the room to find him collapsed against the French windows, forehead pressed against the glass, a bloody trail of handprints charting his journey from the table. He really should have known better than to think she'd let him escape. She was Baobhan Sith, after all, the most savage of vampire breeds. If he'd really done his research he'd have known that the Sith were no mere blood-suckers. True carnivores, they shredded meat and crunched bone, only pausing to suck the marrow dry. The blood-bags, toyed with as cats did mice, would suffer the same fate. They just didn't know it yet.

"Pleassh," he wheezed against the glass covered in blood and snot.

Morgana gazed into the arctic night, oblivious to the snow flurries covering the unkempt back garden, waiting for the prey to realise there was no way out. Even if he did manage to break the door open and flee into the dark beyond, no one would hear his screams.

This was Ann Street, after all, one of the most exclusive areas in the city where multi-millionaires laid their well-groomed heads and houses were separated by too many acres of lush lawn for the sounds of murder and mayhem to travel. She had wanted him to try, though. Nothing flavoured the meat like the death of hope just before the death of the flesh. It wasn't good enough for her, but the nest would accept it with relish and be grateful, for now anyway.

"Take him, children," she commanded.

And they did, ripping the limbs off first like children with a fly, keen to keep him alive until the very last, carried away with bloodlust. One of her brood pierced the man's lower intestine and the stench become overpowering, even for Morgana.

"Don't wait up," she whispered, slipping out into the night and the hard, dark heart of a Scottish winter.

***

She wandered down Ann Street, unheeding of the worsening storm. She was coatless but felt no cold. The thin cotton shift she wore was covered in no time with big, fat flakes, but she did not increase her pace, merely brushed her fingertips along bushes and fences as though on a lazy, dawdling summer stroll.

She headed up to Queen Street, past the gated gardens that only the wealthy residents could access. She'd had more than a few wild nights of sport inside and was familiar with its secret spaces guarded by mature trees and shrubs. She was an outdoor girl at heart, and, just as she had planned tonight, liked the prey to think they had escaped after a mad headlong dash, a few moments of fevered delirium, before she swooped in for the kill to put them right. Or at least she used to. Tonight had been a perfunctory attempt to recreate that thrill and she had failed. Again.

She walked up the steep hill to Princes Street, the city's main thoroughfare, sodium lights the colour of old blood visible through the icy sheets descending from a black sky, gravid with more of the same. Princes Street was also where the New Town confronted the Old. The New Town was the playground of the wealthy, leaving the poor to rot in Old Town, where the world's first sky-scrapers had not so long ago overflowed with contagion, death and the soured milk of human misery.

The storm was so bad that even with her more than human sight, she struggled to see that ultimate symbol of the Old Town: Edinburgh Castle, a gothic monstrosity perched atop a chunk of volcanic rock. If the extinct volcano had erupted at that moment she would have laughed as she plunged into the boiling lava, glad to at least have felt something, however fleeting, before death took her.

She was headed for the Snake-Pit, a club in the Old Town's Grassmarket where no questions were asked and no quarter given. It had been owned by a black warlock called Mortimer Crowe, a devil worshipper of the lowest order, until he had been killed by one of those he had professed to worship: the demon Lukastor.

Lukastor was the ultimate predator in an increasingly long chain but she was not many rungs below. Even in her current state of ennui, she was more than a match for anything. Lukastor himself had no taste for clubs and nightlife so there was nothing to fear; he was too busy playing hide and bleed with his own victims to spare any thoughts for her.

As she walked, a babble of voices competed in her head. Some were victims long gone; some occupied that shadow land between the real and dreamed. She was usually comforted by their presence, reliving her favourite kills even as she planned more. Tonight, however, they were no match for the growing rage, the appetite for carnage that threatened to burst its banks and jeopardise her survival.

Which was probably why she walked without a care into the oldest trap in the book.

***

She entered the hot, steamy foyer of the club, listening without interest to the pounding beat of the Cramps' *The Way I Walk*. A small, dark-haired man put a hand on her chest.

"Esther says you're not allowed back in," he said.

Before he could say more, she broke his neck, flung the body behind the cashier's desk and stalked into the club. Esther was a voodoo priestess of no insignificant power, but she wouldn't try anything here and now. True, she'd have to keep watch for a while for whatever slithering thing Esther decided to send her way, but there was no danger of an immediate confrontation. For most people that was worse, but Morgana welcomed it. Anything to fill the bottomless pit of boredom that consumed all.

The Deftones' *Change In The House of Flies* erupted from the speakers as she walked across the dance floor toward the glittering horseshoe-shaped bar. People parted to make way for her as though they knew what she was and what was good for them. It was busy tonight, and most of the crowd were under twenty-five and as high as their expectations. This was where you could get all tastes and drugs of choice catered for without comment or so much as a second glance.

"A double vodka," she said to the barmaid, a cherubic blonde girl stuffed into a short dress two sizes too small.

The girl glanced at her, a nervous flick of the eyes, and did as she was told without bothering to ask for money. And with good reason: a fine rage was on Morgana tonight, her veil of humanity thinning as it grew.

Her vampires were imperfect copies of her own cool blonde beauty and not one of them could pass for human. She, however, was able to not only pass but also attract the humans of her choice. Of course, she had to do it before they noticed the vacuity in her pale blue eyes and lack of empathy in her conversation, but she was more than equal to the job when she put her mind to it. She raked sodden hair back from her face and downed the drink in one, slamming the glass on the bar.

"Another," she ordered the barmaid, not needing to raise her voice to be heard.

The drink appeared. As she was about to pick it up, a warm brown hand covered hers. Unable to believe such a gross violation, she whipped round to be confronted by a tall man with eyes like chips of polished obsidian and long black hair. He was shirtless, smooth brown chest toned and broad. He laughed, and Morgana's lip curled as she fought the urge to rip his throat out.

"Well, hello there, gorgeous," he said, Glaswegian accent thick enough to carve out and eat. "To what does my humble club owe the honour?"

"You," she said. "You own this?" She gestured at the room.

"I certainly do. So maybe there's something I can help you with…" It wasn't a question and his meaning was plain as his hot brown eyes travelled the length of her body in the soaked shift.

Morgana smiled. How long would this one last on her kitchen table? He clearly thought he was a player, and this was the type that cracked first, giving it all up in a hot, screaming rush. He was also lying because she had an up close and personal knowledge of the real owner.

"Liars tend to get set on fire where I come from," she said, running a sharp fingernail down his breastbone hard enough to draw a little blood but not enough to hurt. Not yet.

He shivered as though someone had walked over his grave, easy manner slipping. "Okay, okay, maybe I don't. I was only having a laugh. What the hell's your problem anyway?"

She gave him a look that silenced whatever else he had been going to say. "What's your name?" she asked. Names had power – of a simple elemental sort, perhaps, but power nonetheless.

"Noah," he told her, frowning.

"Noah," she repeated. "What is it with the modern fad for Biblical names? A desire for Armageddon, perhaps? Still, at least it isn't Obadiah, so it could be worse." She had mastered a semblance of what passed for conversation, even humour, on a good day. It drew the food in. After all, who would suspect the pretty girl with the long honey-blonde hair?

His pupils contracted, a movement so minute she might have missed it had she been human. This was not just a chance encounter with someone who fancied the look of her. There was something else going on here. What that was, she had no idea. It didn't matter, though, because it was a welcome reprieve from the hollow echo-chamber of her thoughts and maybe, just maybe, it would lead to something more interesting.

"Have a drink," she said, motioning for more of the same to the little barmaid, "and tell me all about yourself." She patted the seat next to her and grinned.

He seemed to relax, but something about him was off. At first glance, there was no hint that he was anything other than human, but there was a glow and a draw to his dark eyes that gave the lie to that. Why hadn't she noticed it before?

"Don't mind if I do," he said at last, smirking. "Here, let me," he continued, getting his wallet out and raising an eyebrow. "Why don't you grab a table and I'll bring these over? You look like you could do with a real drink."

"I don't think you could handle my idea of a real drink," she said drumming her long nails on the marble bar. "But hey, have it your way."

Some of the shine came off his bravado but he did as he was bid. He was handsome, too. Handsome in that obvious way some of them had: a lustre that faded with age and left the once proud possessor bereft of any other selling point.

Morgana's appetites were red in tooth and claw, and sex did not figure high on that particular totem pole. Vampire reproduction was functional and without pleasure: every hundred years or so she selected a male drone from another nest, and the fruit of their brief – and, for him, fatal – union was a new nest, useful not least because the old one had usually expired. Vampire society, nominally matriarchal, had precious little in the way of nurturing for its young.

She shrugged and wandered to the nearest table. Four young men sat around it and the crowded assortment of pints and shots told the story of their night so far.

"Move," she told them, smoothing down her dress.

"Go fuck yourself," one of them said, ignoring her and rolling up a pound note to snort a line on the table.

She cleared the table with a sweep of her arm. The rain of glass and alcohol finally got the table's occupants' full attention, if not the entire club's. Snake-Pit or not, she would normally have made more of an effort to blend in, but not tonight. They could take her or leave her; this was as good as it was going to get.

"What the fuck?" a bull-necked youth roared, jumping up, face bloodied by glass shards.

She leaned over the table and raked its now empty glass surface with her nails, leaving furrows in their wake. The four froze, mouths agape. She snarled and they fled in a clatter of falling chairs and tinkling glass. There were a couple of beats of silence, and then it was business as usual as *Highway to Hell* blasted from the speakers and the revellers turned their attention to more important matters.

"I suppose that's one way to get a table," said Noah, putting her drink in front of her.

He was charming enough, she supposed, although the way he kept flipping his hair over his shoulder had a practised air about it, as though he had spent quality time in front of the mirror checking what worked best.

She downed the drink in one.

"You don't mess about, do you? Wait here," he said, downing his own. "I'll get us another." He grinned and ambled off to the bar, looking back at her with a sidelong glance he clearly thought was seductive.

The world seemed to have softened around the edges and the screaming rage that sang through her veins softened with it. What was going on? Booze never usually affected her much.

"Here," he said, appearing as though out of nowhere, almost startling her. "Bottoms up and all that."

"More," she said slinging it back.

"Always happy to oblige a lady," he said, winking.

"Quite the Casanova, aren't you?" she said with the faintest slur of words.

"Casa what now?" He laughed, showing too many teeth and the tip of a sinuous pink tongue.

She decided he looked good enough to eat after all and waved him off to the bar to fetch her another.

And that was the last thing she remembered before slumping forward and sliding out of her seat in a boneless heap.

***

She woke to a ringing pain in her head and a coughing fit. Something had been shoved in her mouth and she was almost totally submerged in stinking sewage that washed to and fro. A hand grasped her arm, stopping her from going under.

"Keep your mouth shut, dear," a cheery voice advised. "Or the water'll give you a iffy tummy."

With a growl, she wrenched herself free from the grasp of the woman who had spoken and sank under the surface without touching the bottom. She emerged seconds later, choking on effluent, and banged her head on the top of the cage inches above the surface. If the water got any higher they'd all drown.

"Shush, you'll attract their attention," another voice said. "It's not been fed yet and they're bound to be looking for someone."

The speaker was a skeletal male of indeterminate age. They all looked like that if you held them captive long enough – Morgana's dungeons were full of them.

The woman who had first spoken did so again. "Best take that rag out of her mouth, poppet, or she'll choke."

"We're all dead anyway," said a second, younger female voice.

Morgana almost pulled her tongue out by the root in her haste to get the offending wad of material out of her mouth. Her stomach growled, the need for blood overpowering all other imperatives. "What are you talking about?" she croaked, eyeing some glistening detritus bobbing near her head.

"*He's* got us, hasn't he?" the younger female voice said. A pair of large blue eyes dominated a filthy little face partially submerged in the rank waters.

They were trapped in the confines of a large metal cage six feet by six and almost totally underwater. Visibility beneath them was limited because of the water's viscosity. The top of the cage was covered and three sides of it were flush against a wall or some other barrier. On the remaining side, a continuous line of cages could be seen, rammed against each other and containing gaunt and subdued captives. Except that wasn't quite right. There weren't multiple cages, just one separated into different sections by a single set of iron bars on each side. The cage next to them was much bigger and bereft of occupants. The *slap, slap* of the water and the slide of hands seeking better purchase on the bars punctuated the silence.

Morgana clung to the bars of the cage like the other residents. How deep was this water?

The clatter of booted feet roused her.

"Right, pull together now. One, two, three," said a woman's voice.

A small hatch in the roof opened and fell back with a screech of metal on metal. A square of light appeared, followed by a grinning hooded face and then a metal pole which plunged into the depths of the cage, forcing the occupants to fling themselves against the sides.

Morgana pressed against the bars, ready to lunge out of the water and leap for the open hatch, but her traitorous body would not obey and she managed only a derisory splash of her arms in the water, like a baby bird fallen from its nest. The drug was still in her system and there was no way of knowing when that would change. Thanks to the new arrivals, however, she now knew that one of the so-called walls had to be a platform of some sort and, hence, the way out – if she ever figured out a way to escape.

The pole flailed around in the cage like a living thing, knocking the skinny male from his perch into the effluent and pushing him under. Bubbles popped to the surface, accompanied by a muffled gurgling.

A coarse laugh rang out above their heads. The hooded one's yellow-toothed grin grew wider. "Aw, look at 'im go. This one's a fighter, this. I should've put money on 'im."

Two other hooded figures joined the first. Together they pulled on the pole which had the skinny captive thrashing on the end of it. He emerged from the sewage gasping like a mutated fish, attached to the pole by a collar. One of the other fisher's of men threw a grappling hook, which pierced the captive's chest, lodging in one of his ribs.

Laughing and joking, the trio pulled him from the water, his blood turning it a dark crimson. Morgana salivated at the scent . The smell of sewage was only marginally worse than the perfumed rot in her own nest.

The skinny male fought on, feet kicking at the hatch, blood spattering down into the water and onto his erstwhile roommates, his only reward raucous jeers and a reign of blows to the head. His right foot quivered as he was pulled free of the cage, leaving only an oblong of grey ceiling once more.

"Right, take these rags off, clean it up in the pool and leave it for the Lord," said one of the fishermen.

"Who died and put you in charge then?" whined a second male voice.

"You'll be the one dying if you don't belt up," said the first.

"Just 'cause you think you're the favourite."

"I'm the one that feeds Him, all right? Or maybe you'd like to take over, is that it, eh? Go on then, you stupid inbred little fucker, be my guest." A slap, like a gunshot, rang out.

There was a pause.

"You didn't need to do that, Silas! 'Sides" – the man sniggered as though nothing had happened – "I'd rather tenderise the meat anyway. He likes it better like that."

The renewed thud of booted feet against flesh could be heard, followed by a long drawn out howl of, "Please, no." The skinny male was still alive.

"Come on, we don't have time for this. We're screwed if we don't give Him the offerings while they're fresh." The third voice was girlish and educated. "Hurry up and take him through, Murdo. Don't bother with the pool, we'll be through in a bit."

The hatch was replaced with a heavy *thunk* and then locked. Sounds of dragging were overlaid with a refrain of "ohgodohgodohgod" before receding into the distance. Someone started to climb onto the roof of the next cage with a jingling of keys.

"No, don't lock that one, Silas," the girl ordered. "We're getting a new batch later. C'mon, we need to check Murdo isn't fucking it up again."

Footsteps; a door was opened and slammed. The captors had business elsewhere. The fact that they called each other by name spoke volumes about the likely chances of survival.

"Where are we?" asked Morgana.

"Shush. They'll hear you and come back for someone else. It's what they do," whispered the younger woman with the large eyes.

"Fine, if you won't tell me… Hey there!" Morgana called.

"Oh, for goodness sake – what a fuss!" said the first woman. "All right, I'll tell you what I know. Just try not to make any noise. Not exactly sure where to start though…," she said, trailing off.

"Jesus," the younger girl spat in disgust, "you're such a useless cow. Guess it's all down to me then, as per usual. Okay," she said in a bright voice as though explaining something to a small and confused child, "my name is Jade and this is Claire. The guy who was just 'selected' for food duty is Robert, but I'm guessing he'll be an ex-Robert any minute now."

"Please, dear," Claire protested, "you mustn't talk like that."

"Shut it. I'll kill you myself if you don't, I swear to God. Christ, as if it's not bad enough being the next meal in some monster's cupboard, I have to be locked up with flamin' Mary Poppins here. You'll be telling me next that if life hands you some lemons, you can use them to clean up this shitey cage." She slammed her palm on the rancid water, forgetting her own injunction to silence.

"What do you mean, 'monster'?" Morgana asked.

"We don't exactly know, dear," said Claire, wiping waste from her forehead. "We hear it sometimes. It screams and its, er, helpers, the ones you've just seen, attend to it."

"Attend how?"

"How do you think?" Jade sneered. "They feed it and we're the dish du jour."

Morgana knew from her own extensive experience of imprisoning and torturing victims that most of them passed through a series of stages, starting with angry disbelief and ending with cowed acceptance. If she had to guess, she'd have said this pair had been stashed here for a couple of days at most. Victims didn't generally make for the most coherent of companions.

There was a low hubbub now from the other cages, as though the occupants felt safer after dinner had been selected and served.

She tried again, reduced to reason because she didn't have the strength for rage. "How did you end up here?" she asked Jade.

"Well, now that you ask, I won first prize in a competition and it's everything I could have hoped for and more," said Jade. "What the actual fuck, you nosy cow?"

"It's okay. You need to relax and focus your energy into your chakras," Claire said, reaching out a hand to the younger woman, a gesture that was rebuffed with an angry shrug.

"I'll go first, shall I? Alrighty then, although I don't want you to think I'm hogging the lime-light!" Claire said as though nothing had happened. "I was going to get some shopping for my elderly neighbour. She's a real sweetie actually," Claire continued, warming to her story.

"Of course you were," Jade muttered.

"Pardon? What's wrong with that?"

"Nothing. Just get the fuck on with it before we die of old age. Never mind, I'll go first because I'll top myself if I have to listen to any more of this."

Morgana was still drained of energy – had she died and gone to Hell after all? It was all she could do to grip the bars to keep her head above the rancid water.

"Any chance of hurrying this along?" she asked. Once she had her strength back and the information she needed to get out of this literal shit-hole, dining on this pair would be her number one priority. But no, that was wrong – someone else topped that particular shit list.

"Jesus, you're so fucking impatient," said Jade with no apparent irony. "All I know is that I was out clubbing and met this guy. He was hot and hetero, which should have been my first clue that it was too good to be true. But before I could work that out he gave me a spiked drink. Everything went all woozy and I must have passed out. Next thing, I'm here, in this cage, World-of-Shit, with the pair of you."

"And as you can see, there are others like us," said Claire as though imparting an invaluable nugget of wisdom. "Not as many as when we were put in here, though, judging by the drop in the noise level." She sniffed and something fell from her nose. The water was a little below body temperature so the two women were shivering.

Morgana nodded at Claire. "What happened to you?"

A man started screaming a woman's name until the sound was cut off. Only Morgana had heard the slap of a palm on the man's face a split second before a voice whispered, "Shut up. It knows."

"As I said, I was on an errand and cut through the local park, which I don't normally do. It wasn't late – around two – and the day was quite mild, but already getting dark like it does at this time of the year. I decided to sit on a bench for a bit and gather my thoughts because my husband and I have been having some problems. We've been in separate bedrooms for a while now, which actually *is* a big part of the problem. Anyway," she said a little louder as if anticipating an interruption, "this strange wee woman sat next to me and asked me if I knew how to get to Pumpherston.

'That was weird in itself considering we were in Edinburgh, and before I knew it we were deep in conversation and she was telling me about the problems in her own marriage. You know, in the bedroom department, as it were. Quite interesting it was, too. Well, she offered me a drink of tea from a flask, which I accepted and then… then I don't remember much else," she said.

"Okay, we've all been drugged and brought here," Morgana cut in. "And according to you it's to feed some creature you've not seen. Do the keepers feed you or is there some other routine?"

"Keepers?" Jade scoffed. "Well, that's one word for them. And no, they don't feed us – are you insane?" Her voice rose. "Didn't you see the state of Robert? He'd been here longer than Claire and I and would've starved if he hadn't been… took. And yeah, there is a routine. You know, the one where they appear out the blue to haul one of us out to feed that thing. Why the fuck didn't I just go home to Kev, like I'd planned? Oh God, Kev." Her voice broke and she started to sob.

A wave of nausea passed over Morgana, almost causing her to slip back under the surface. She strengthened her grip on the bars. She never did very well in close proximity to so much iron, albeit iron that had been converted into steel. The old ones all had that reaction to the metal. Garlic and crosses and the rest were just fanciful bullshit, but iron had its own raw magic that weakened most of the supernaturals she could name. That, combined with the residual effects of the unaccustomed drug, and she was as helpless as any human – a novel and unwelcome first.

She would have to manipulate this idiotic pair to do her bidding using nothing but her wits. The old myth about vampires being able to overcome an individual's will was exactly that. She took what she wanted by extreme force once she had trapped her human victims with the aid of strong sexual attraction and stronger drink. That was why she scoured the city's pubs and clubs: they were the victim pools of choice and they had never failed her… until now, when the tables had been turned.

Noah was in for a surprise when she got hold of him.

"There were four of us in here originally," said Claire, as though she was a guide giving the grand tour of a stately home. "An older lady called Marsha was brought in just after me. Really nice she was, too. Taken, though, just like that. So the guards, for want of a better word, have visited us three times, including the time they brought you. I have no idea when they'll next appear, either. I don't even know how long I've been here – it's hard to say with no sunlight, no real way to tell the passage of time. I was the second in this cage, after Robert, but for whatever reason I haven't been chosen.'

"Story of your life, that, isn't it? Don't worry though. I'm sure it'll be your turn soon," said Jade.

"If I were them, I'd pick you first," said Morgana to Jade, a small smile tugging the corners of her mouth.

"Wh-what?"

"You heard."

"Yeah? And why's that then?" Jade's voice threatened tears.

"Because you're young. And juicy. I'd also pick you first just to stop your incessant whining. You shouldn't be too pleased, though, because you don't exactly have much competition. Claire here is a bit long in the tooth and stringy with it," she said, making a chewing sound. "Although to be fair, she does give you a run for your money in the irritating bitch stakes."

Morgana grinned, then cursed as Jade resumed her godawful sobbing. She was meant to be getting them onside, not indulging in casual sadism just for the hell of it.

"That's a terrible thing to say," said Claire, genuine shock in her voice. "I demand that you apologise."

"Oh, all right, if you insist. I would pick you but you'd have to keep talk, talk, talking like you do," said Morgana, the monster peeking out before she shoved it back down hard into its oubliette. "All better now?" She couldn't kill them yet, but the urge was growing at an exponential rate.

An idea struck her. She took a deep breath and dived down, channelling the overwhelming rage to counteract her body's lassitude. She anticipated the bottom to be a few feet or so under them, but her expectations were confounded. This sewage pit had to have a bottom, it was just a matter of how far down. Muffled voices shouted to her to come back, unaware that it was better for them if she did not.

The matter in the water was thicker down here and she saw nothing. Her gut – her very core – burned with proximity to the iron of the cage as though she had been set alight. Lungs bursting, she thought she would have to admit defeat and return to the surface – until her hands struck the brick floor.

She swam along the bottom, feeling her way over bricks and old bone shards. Had some people just let go, preferring to drown rather than to feed the beast, whatever it was? There were barriers beyond three sides of the cage, making the weakest point the bars shared with the next one along. The girl had said one was to be left unlocked, hadn't she? Morgana began kicking at them without success until, moving along, her feet failed to connect to anything but water. It took her oxygen-starved brain vital seconds to work out she'd found a hole, one which on further investigation was big enough for her to slip through and into the next cage. Thank the gods she didn't believe in there was only one set of iron bars.

Whoever had built this particular prison clearly hadn't considered that the prisoners would be able to swim down this far, hadn't dreamed one of them might be a vampire. She wriggled through the hole, catching her hair on a protruding bar. She jerked her head, desperate to get back to the surface, leaving a clump of it behind for her pains. She thrashed up, up, up, making slow progress through the slurry and breaking the surface in the adjacent cage. Her former cage-mates looked on, mouths open, speechless for once. The occupants of the next cage over were so far gone they didn't react at all. Being in the shit affected most like that.

Resisting the urge to head-butt the spot where the hatch was, she stayed put, fighting for breath. This had to be the unlocked cage the girl had been talking about, otherwise she would die here. Vampires lived long lives but they could die just like everything else. Bracing her feet on the bars, she launched herself at the metal hatch, again and again, hands and forearms bearing the brunt of the impact as her footing slipped and slid. It wouldn't budge. Was it the wrong cage? There was only one way to find out: she punched upwards with all her strength. There, it had shifted, hadn't it? Scrabbling, she pressed herself against the hatch. And then she saw it: a chink of light. Tiny, but enough to tell her this was indeed the right one, the cage that was hungry for new occupants.

"If you stopped and thought for a second you'd realise how selfish you're being," said Claire.

"Move it, you stupid cow," said Jade. "And get us the fuck out of here."

"Yeah," shouted a bald, tattooed man from another cage. "Get us out!"

Others took up the cry, some even banging on the bars as though they were in a position to make such demands.

Morgana turned to them, staring for a few seconds before she threw back her head and snarled, enraged, bestial, letting them see what she was, what she could do.

The room fell silent. She braced her feet against the bars of the cage and grunted as she tried to push the hatch past the tipping point and force it open – it had, after all, taken three of the keepers to open it. A loud reverberating crash sounded and it fell back at last on its hinge.

She climbed out and hauled herself onto a ledge three feet above the top of the cage. Except it wasn't a ledge; it was part of a curved concrete walkway that filled most of a vast, windowless room. Why the cages had to be crammed into a slurry pit was a mystery. Perhaps it flavoured the meat as she herself was wont to do. The captives began to shout again, finally shocked out of their torpor, aware something out of the ordinary was happening.

"Shh," she said, echoing her former cage-mates' words. "Or they'll come."

"Hello," called a man's voice. "Did you just break out?"

"Help," many voices clamoured. "Get us out of here."

"I'll come back for you," said Morgana. She laughed as she passed the cages and headed for the closed door at the far end of the room.

***

The door was unlocked – another bad sign. Maybe someone was toying with her as they had done to others. She opened it a crack and saw a long winding corridor with nobody in it. She was stronger now that she was out of the cage. Not full strength, not even close, but it was an improvement.

A tuneless whistle and the tip tap of footsteps sounded, faint but getting louder. She flattened herself against the wall. The steps and whistling paused. Did they know she was here? Time passed and she forgot to breathe.

The footsteps resumed and the door opened. Morgana flung herself on the hooded whistler, snapping the neck with a sharp crack. The body fell supine to the floor and the hood fell back, revealing the face of a young man barely clear of his teens. His glassy eyes bulged and his mouth hung open, showing the yellowed donkey teeth of the first keeper she'd seen. No time to feed from the man, however; stripping him of his clothing would have to do for now.

The keepers had mentioned a pool and, sure enough, there it was just a few feet away, sunk into the walkway. Slipping off her dress, she lowered herself into the clean water and washed off the worst of the fecal matter. Even with the keeper's robes on, the smell of shit would give her away to anyone with half a nose. The threat of discovery spurred her on, but silence reigned unchallenged, punctuated by sobbing from one of the cages and an odd high-pitched sound she had been hearing since she'd arrived. Were they playing with her?

She tugged on the keeper's stiff hemp robes, which had an odour of stale sweat and tobacco. The high-pitched sound came again, accompanied by a babble of voices. She could make out what they were saying, indicating a distance of at least a hundred yards.

"Our Lord needs more. Go get Murdo and see to it," said the girl.

"Aw, c'mon, he's a big boy now. Why can't he do it on his own?"

"You know fine and well he can't open the bloody hatch on his own. You also know," she said, her voice louder, "you can't leave him unsupervised. He's completely unreliable. Last week I found him trying to talk to one of the sacrifices as though he was on a date. We can't risk any of them escaping and all it will take is for some bloody girl to persuade him to let her go and then we'll have to up sticks and relocate. Again."

"I've told you I'm handling it. And I am."

"Well, handle it quicker, for Christ's sake."

He was coming down the corridor. No whistling, just the clatter of boots and the *scratch, scratch* of his robe on the floor.

Morgana licked cracked lips and resumed her position against the wall, waiting. She was starving. She had resisted the first keeper but the food just kept flinging itself in her path. The door opened and a burly, bearded man appeared, stopping short when he saw his dead charge lying on the floor. Before he had time to react, Morgana struck. Fangs bared, she ripped his throat out and guzzled the quivering chunks of flesh. Blood frenzy took over as she dug talons deep into his chest and snapped the ribcage to have at his still-beating heart. She ripped it out and bit into it, blood streaming down her chin and robes.

"They do say the only way to a man's heart is through his ribs," said the girl, stepping into the room. "And I have to say, I agree." She was slight, her thin mousy hair scraped back from a sharp little face, but her appearance was belied by an air of assured confidence that spoke of experience and an ability to handle herself.

Morgana roared, enraged at the distraction.

"Please don't speak with your mouth full. It's not polite."

And with that, the keeper lashed out with one of the pole collars, trapping Morgana's neck and wrenching it tight. The collar burned, forcing her to let go of the heart. With a sour smile, the keeper tightened the collar further by pulling on the pole as though it was a dog leash, choking Morgana and forcing her to her knees.

"Ah, yes. Should've said that's a specially made collar. It's got a very high iron content, y'know. Higher than the bars of the cages." She smiled, a sly, sliding affair. "We don't see many like you, your majesty, but when we do, we know just how to treat you with the proper respect." She wrenched the pole again.

Morgana collapsed onto the floor. She clawed at her neck, drawing blood, the world reduced to pulsing bands of white-hot agony.

"You are going to make an extra special treat for our Lord. We didn't realise what you were at first. But we've got hidden cameras to help us keep an eye on things. Nothing human could have escaped from the holding pens. You really are a remarkable specimen, you know."

She hauled Morgana, stumbling, to her feet. "But you're not so strong and special with this little baby round your neck, are you?" She grinned, the cynical expression ill at ease with her obvious youth. Her dark eyes burned a zealot's fire. "What's that? Oh, that's right, you can't talk, can you? Did you think you'd steal my Lord from me? Did you? Well, you'll serve him soon enough, just not the way you'd planned."

Did the stupid bitch think she'd come to date whatever was haunting this seventh circle of hell?

"Come, my Queen," sniggered the girl, jerking on the leash. "Destiny waits."

Morgana's newfound strength had dissipated as fast as deserters from a losing side, and she was dragged along a series of ill-lit, grey corridors until they arrived at a huge steel door upon which was a deadbolt set in a key pad. Whatever was inside clearly couldn't be allowed to roam free. Water dripped from somewhere overhead and the lights buzzed and dimmed as though the electricity was going to cut out.

"We have a backup if the 'lecy goes tits up," said the keeper as though reading Morgana's mind before forcing her to her knees. Fumbling in her capacious robes, she fished out a bunch of keys and set about unlocking the assortment of bolts on the door.

Despite the pain, Morgana growled. The contemptuousness of this human, holding her at bay as though she was nothing more than a stray dog!

"Which reminds me, we're going to need reinforcements," the girl continued, producing a pager and pressing a button while keeping her eyes on the vampire.

Morgana motioned to the collar.

"What's that, sweetheart? You want me to tighten this?" She pulled on the pole, causing Morgana to fall forward onto her front.

Struggling to her knees, Morgana considered her options. She put out a placatory hand, knowing the girl wouldn't come any nearer to her than the extent of the pole's reach. "Wait," she said, gasping. "What's in there?"

"What? Don't you mean 'who'? I know what you're doing, by the way. Your desperation to rip my throat is only equaled by your need to play for time and get some information that might help you. Well, I've seen you're kind before, Sith bitch. Don't think I haven't. And in the end you all just plead and bleed like the rest of us. Did you know I was the one who killed Lilith?"

Morgana averted her face to mask her reaction. She hadn't known that, but she had known Lilith, a powerful Baobhan Sith who had just vanished, leaving her nest to fend for itself. Most assumed she'd just upped sticks because the idea that something or someone had been powerful enough to kill her was nothing less than inconceivable.

"Well, I say 'I', but I really mean my Lord," she said, giggling like a schoolgirl and loosening the collar a little. "I just popped her in there" – she indicated the door – "and the rest, as they say, is history. Not a well-known history, of course, but the best ones aren't."

Morgana found her voice. "Don't… don't you think you should give your Lord a little appetiser? He might even reward you." She stopped as a coughing fit wracked her.

The girl loosened the collar more. "Reward?" she said, frowning. "Serving Him is reward enough. We are his loyal servants."

The door moved, just a little. It was open.

"And what do you mean, 'an appetiser'?"

"I was in a cage with two other women. You could give them to your god before me."

"Nice try. I'm not going back to the cages trailing you with me. And you're going to be with Him before my backup buddies arrive. Anyway, don't sell yourself short: you're a tasty wee snack all on your own. After Lilith, our Lord displayed new powers I hadn't seen before."

"How did you know I was Sith?"

"You wouldn't have been able to escape – you've been the only one. Lilith didn't get a chance, by the way. She put up such a struggle when we tried to get her in the cage – killed four of our order – before we realised she wasn't human. That's why we keep these handy." She tugged the pole, grinning.

In a blur of motion the door crashed open, and both keeper and vampire were hauled inside by invisible hands.

The girl gasped. "My Lord, I didn't realise the door was unlocked – I hadn't undone the last dead bolt. Please forgive me."

The windowless room was cavernous and covered in droppings, white like guano. The girl was still, eyes downcast, not daring to move or even breathe.

A low rumble started up: a vent blowing hot air into the room and violating the silence. Man-sized deposits littered the floor. One of the deposits twitched and a low moaning started up: "Ohgodohgodohgod." Robert was still alive. A white femur poked out, the head shiny and picked clean, the rest of it wreathed in scarlet and black shreds of flesh.

"Where is it?" Morgana asked.

"Shh. It'll hear," whispered the girl.

An interesting switch from divine reverence to the impersonal pronoun – humans were so bloody fickle. But there wasn't time for anything else because the mound moved, a swishing like a parting of curtains, a whirr through the air. The girl screamed in agony, a long drawn out shriek that became more frenzied.

And there it was, its flexing wings resplendent with soft, downy feathers. It towered above Morgana at over six feet, neon orange eyes blazing out from a feathered head above a short curved beak. Below the beak a red glistening maw opened and shut, drool running in ropes to the down-covered, male human chest. The mouth was human too, the lips well-shaped, the teeth tiny and razor sharp. The creature plunged the beak into the girl's eye and the human mouth tore great chunks of flesh from the keeper's cheek. Her screaming changed in pitch when her flesh was ripped open, becoming a hopeless gurgle when the monster took her tongue.

It held its victim still with a great taloned foot, with the foremost claw plunged into the girl's neck. From the lack of movement from the neck down, it looked like her spinal cord had been severed. The beast's eyes held Morgana as it tracked her slow, sidling movements by turning its head as it feasted on her former captor. Then it started the serious business of crunching bone and snapping sinew. The maw widened like a snake as it swallowed the girl's head, widening further for the shoulders and then on down the trunk of the body, pausing only to spit out the keys, which landed at Morgana's feet.

Its eyes and beak proclaimed an unmistakable owl heritage and yet it was human too. Precisely what that made it or where the divine fit in was anyone's guess.

"I've got something tastier than me if you let me go. I'll bring you a shape-shifter."

The air rippled as though something was speaking in a frequency she couldn't hear. It could take her before she reached the door, there was no question about it.

"I promise," she said. Promises, like names, had their own power, and woe betide the breaker. Its eyes flickered and the creature turned its back and resumed its feast in earnest.

She didn't need to be told twice. Ripping the collar off with bloodied hands, she bent down to grab the keys and then sprinted back the way she'd come. She looked back, doorknob in hand, ready to slam it shut, but the Bird Man was as good as his unheard words. He eyed her with an incurious fiery gaze as he finished off the dead girl's legs.

"I won't be long."

A sound filled the room, so low and prolonged that vibrations threatened to burst her chest. She slammed the door and bolted it. This thing could never be allowed to get out. It would spoil everything for predators like her because it didn't care about the rules, number one of which was: thou shalt not draw attention to thyself. She was careless and had a lot to answer for, but nothing like this.

She sped through the ill-lit corridors, guided by the shouts and screams of her fellow captives. She would need them as a distraction if more keepers were going to show. Damn. Her hunger flared and she opened her mouth in a soundless growl. Time enough for that.

Running into the room with the cages, she was greeted by shouts, howls and desperate sobbing.

"About bloody time," said a voice she knew only too well. Jade clung to the bars, teeth bared, eyes rolling in her head.

Morgana knelt down on the walkway and hand the keys to Claire. "Pass them on."

"There's an empty cage next to ours," said Claire. "What if the keys fall into the water?"

"Then you'll have a lot on your conscience. Reinforcements are on the way. For the keepers, I mean."

And with that she walked toward the distant sound of car engines and slamming doors, eager for the slaughter to come.

***

Back home on Ann Street, Morgana gazed past the fly-blown body parts in the kitchen sink. There was unfinished business and she was damned if it was going to stay that way. Of late her lack of control had been such that the nest was now avoiding all contact with her. Five dead children bore silent witness to just why that was.

It was dark and the sky was clear. An infinity of twinkling stars gazed down with alien indifference. The first few flakes of a coming snowstorm crisscrossed their way to an unwelcoming earth. She left the house and made her way to the Snake-Pit, slipping in a backdoor she had bribed one of her human acolytes to keep open and clear. Bumping into Esther, voodoo queen extraordinaire, was not part of her plan for tonight.

She spotted him at the bar, shirtless, sipping a drink and checking out the room, black hair unbound. She sashayed over, smiling at the expression of naked fear on his face.

"Hey there, good lookin'. I would say I have an idea about what we could get cooking later on, but something tells me you taste better raw."

He turned to run, but she grabbed a handful of his thick, shiny mane and slammed his face onto the marble-topped bar.

His nose broke with a sickening crunch, blood cascading onto the floor as though in tribute to her.

Noah was going to be a very busy boy tonight. He had a date with God, and Morgana was going to make sure he kept it.

THOSE BORROWED FACES

CRAIG SAUNDERS

A man sits facing another man. Both have worn many different guises throughout the centuries, and not just clothing. No matter the attire, they would have looked like different people. They had *been* different people. And, as fashions changed from laced leggings and long socks, or tunics, long gloves or short, cloaks or coats, the faces humanity wore changed, too. They've worn smiles just as easily as frowns, and sideburns or sideboards, grey whiskers and the soft down of young faces, mutton chops and shitkicker cowboy moustaches and heavy beards in the wild snows of Canada's Yukon, trapping, and further afield, too – Alaska, and to Siberia, and once in 1642 with a ship captained by Abel Tasman all the way to New Zealand, long, long ago, when the Maori danced unfettered and Captain Cook had yet to be born.

Long centuries and cold years on blank-white land or sea, though no matter how frozen a man gets, he might still know heat. Perhaps because of that constant chill, a moment's warmth is a bright, lurid spot on an otherwise blank landscape. One knows the painful bite of the Arctic seas and the delight of hot whale blood splashing on chill-bit skin that wasn't his own. He knows blood well and wears pale faces, most often, that seem well suited to snow and ice, enlivened only when splashed with blood or scorched with gunpowder, or, like during the Crimean War, cannon and bloodfire both.

The other, the man in the chair who is bound and waiting, has known warmth and light, the friendship of men and women and the things that bring humanity back to the hearth away from the bitterest cruelties they inflict upon themselves. He tends toward darker faces, and lands bleached by sun, not ice. He has lived in hot lands with sweat running down whatever face he wears, that face only borrowed for a time.

Both have worn humanity all those centuries, a cloak or a mask to hide what is within.

The unbound man, he is the kind who leans into that peculiarly human coldness and smiles as it blisters his skin.

The man in the chair longs for the warmth, and only warm. That longing, though, will not help. Not here. This is a cold place, once again. The chair is cold, the wires that bite into the dark-skinned man's flesh are cold, and the landscape outside is white and hard bright as a winter day in South America's mountains.

Though they wear human faces neither are human, and the cold will not – cannot – kill them. They have known far harsher ills than these: fire, gunshot and gutshot, blown asunder, limbs severed from body with ancient claymores in the Highland uprisings and newer claymores in the heart of Vietnamese and Cambodian jungles. They survive, they abide, they live on.

Sometimes, eternity grows tiresome.

They still feel it, though – not the weather, but the cold inside. It's a hard thing to bear, sometimes, and the knowledge that they can never die, never love, never live a life in the span of the people they live within, can be a heavy, uneven weight across their shoulders.

In the Boxer rebellion, the coldest of these two – the one who likes the ice inside men which makes them war upon each other – once wore a Chinese man's face. The man had been old when he'd taken that face, and the Chinese man had a long wisp of a moustache people called Fu Man Chu at some time or another. In China, he spoke Chinese and he knew of dragons and heard their stories as heroin burned in his pipe and sweet, thick smoke swirled around his head. It was shortly after China that he, the pale, unbound man, hunted the greatest beasts of the sea with a harpoon and a snarl on his face.

They saw each other perhaps every century or more. Once was in Africa before the British shod the continent in iron, and later in a civil war. They saw and fought the Spanish as marauders along the coasts of the South Americas where they knew immense wealth, yet at other times these two men had not a coin to their name. They knew of Cibola, but such things as fables and truth or poverty and wealth never, ever mattered. What wealth is there in gold when you are undying?

They're kin because they are of a kind, and no more than that. They wear borrowed faces until those faces wear thin or grow tired or slew from the creatures that hide underneath. Face-shedders, changelings, or perhaps the elf-kin: They don't know what they are any more than man does. They know, at least, that they are among us, apart from us, above us. Perhaps once, long ago, they'd been the mythical Aes Sidhe, left behind before their kind travelled below the earth to live out their lives in barrows away from the people above.

Seithe, thinks the dark-skinned man. It's a better word. It's similar, the Irish, or at least it is to a man who has seen the evolution of many, many languages.

'Seithe' means skin and hide, both.

It's a good word.

While those skins and hides they wear change, their teeth do not. The paler changeling has only two long, needle-sharp teeth, white and young (it's the face outside that changes, not the beast within).

One feeds on blood; the other, flesh.

Kin. Never brothers. Just two things who recognise each other and feel nothing. Not love, not hate.

Nothing.

"Eternity drags, though, doesn't it?" says the pale man with the long needle teeth to the man in the chair.

The man in the chair nods. "I understand." His words are slurred a little, because his long teeth are for rending flesh, as are all canids' teeth.

Canids: Dogs, jackals, foxes, wolves.

***

The man in the white-skinned face has blue eyes so bright they're nearly white. The black-skinned man has one tan eye – a brown bordering on yellow – and one of a heavy, deep-sea blue. They can change the colour of their eyes just as easily as the faces they wear, then wear out.

Life is different now, with cameras and computers which are able to read men's faces and sort them like the index cards they used to have in libraries. Once, a man could walk the breadth of a country or continent as he pleased, or board a ship and travel far over clean seas to distant lands where people were almost alien, not all joined-up and shared like they are now. Now, everyone is tied together with technology and travel is harder. Faster for most, but slower for these two creatures because they cannot board planes or pass x-rays or scanners or be searched or held in a jail. Once, the black-skinned man was in a jail, but the walls were thin and the people had slow guns that didn't matter. Now, humans have scalpels and bunkers underground where fey things disappear.

Times change. Travel in 1759, or 1459? Slow, but better, in ways humans might not understand. Then, it meant something. *Now,* thinks the man with too many teeth for a man, *is it any different to the way they send their shit along a pipe?*

The man in the black face – he with the teeth like a wolf – misses the things that came before. Both hunt, of course, but one likes his prey close, in the cities and the houses. A short walk. A lazy kind of hunter. The wolf, with his odd eyes and perfect teeth, likes to run. Plains and fields, forests and mountains, long soft beaches beneath hard grey cliffs with sea mist on his skin and in his lungs. If these changelings were human at all, he would be the one to camp, to boil water from a stream, to keep away from the cities. The long-toothed pale man would take a hotel and order room service, feed in dark corners away from streetlights and never know the phase of the moon, or the season, because those things don't touch him as they do the other.

Three years, they'd sought each other.

They are not bound by mobile phones with their invisible wires, or the Internet and social media and televisions and mortgages and commutes. Those are the bonds of humanity. It is a skein of history which holds these two.

Now?

Now the black-skinned man is held down, wire wound all around him and a heavy chair beneath him. Through his mismatched eyes he watches the other. The other is not tied to his chair, but that skein is there for both men, heavier than a rope that might be seen. Some bonds are for life, severed only by death.

***

The pale one nods. "You call yourself something now?"

"Carlos," says the darker man. He's not afraid. What can a man do to another man, or a changeling do to another changeling? For some reason, human lives, short as they are, seem to matter more.

Carlos does not care. He is not immortal, perhaps. Just… longer.

"It's a good name. You were in Brazil?"

Carlos nods. Now, they're in Argentina, inside an old wooden house not far from the disused Transandine railway near Puente del Inca, and miles and miles from anywhere else. The owners of that house are dead and propped against the wooden wall outside. They won't stink when the time comes that bodies usually start to smell. It's high in the Andes, this place; it's never warm. It's the kind of place where wet bodies just dry out and stick where they fall.

Carlos had been hunting through mountains and arid, endless dull plains and steppes.

The pale man smiles. "I was in Russia for a long time. I heard tales of you… I took a boat to the USA, then I walked. 1992? USA, Mexico, Guatemala, Honduras… you know. Long time, long walk, but it's better here. Like back when. More people," says the pale man. "But less eyes."

Carlos nods. His arms, chest, and legs are bound, not his head. He can nod and talk just fine and his face is expressive.

"I am called Michael, now. Biblical, I think. There, Mihael; here, Miguel. It's a good name. Travels well," says the pale man, who calls himself Mihael and Miguel and Michael.

"How long," asks Carlos, "since we last spoke? How long do you think?"

"French Indian war? 1760? '61?"

"Thought it was longer," says Carlos. "Saw you in Africa… maybe we didn't speak."

Michael laughs, smiles. "I remember you, what, a thousand years ago? Ninth, tenth century, was it? You bathed in blood. Ireland!"

"Yes," said Carlos, and smiles despite himself. "Better then, in a way. More… alive? I liked the Norsemen. The fighters."

"Better?" says Michael. "Mad bastards and swinging balls, wasn't it?"

Carlos smiles, a shallow thing, but he guesses Michael's right.

Michael shrugs, kind of see-saws his hands before he lays those pale thin fingers back on his knees. "More honest, perhaps. It is the same now, but with their guns. Their guns." Michael shakes his head and spits to one side. A tidy man, and somehow the gesture's obscene.

Wear whatever face he might, the man's just as much a barbarian as those who sacked Rome.

But Carlos is watching. He misses the open skies already, tied in this house and away from the night. But he can't fidget, and probably wouldn't even if he could.

He is long-lived, possibly immortal, and patient.

"You ever get tired?" asks Carlos.

"Of the faces?"

"Of *us*."

Michael thinks about it. "No," he says. "I don't think so. We are us, they are not." He shrugs. "Does it matter?"

Carlos nods. He nods often, but he is tired, and talking to this pale man is tiring. Carlos finds most of the things people do, they do to an unnecessary degree: talking, feeding, killing.

Carlos does the things he does and nods more than he talks. He's wolven, a predator, but, like the wolf, he feels he is just a thing which hunts to feed. Carlos knows he's a changeling, a face-shedder, but whatever he might be called by men, Carlos' nature is set.

Michael is not the same. His teeth *need* the blood. Perhaps something of humanity bled into him, through his throat, over so many long years. Michael's apart, sure, like Carlos. But Carlos thinks Michael's closer to human than he.

"Why did you hunt, bring me here? You could have just..."

Michael understands Carlos' meaning well enough. He nods, this time. "Why? What? Why are you doing this?" Michael mocks softly, and smiles. Those two needle-sharp teeth hang over his bottom lip nearly all the time. "You sound like them. I do it because I can. I hunt... and *I kill everything*, Carlos. *Everything*. You ask if I tire. I say I do not. But sometimes I grow..." Michael pauses, searches for the right word in a vocabulary made of many languages both old and new. "Bored. Not quite bored. Restless?"

"I understand," says Carlos. He does. He and Michael have plenty in common; some days, nights, months, years, maybe as long as decades here and there, he's grown tired and restless and unsettled. It's a long life. Like a human might have a bad night with nightmares and tossing and turning, such endless creatures have nightmares that span generations.

They sit, watching each other for a time, until Michael slaps his knees and smiles. "Shall we?"

"How's it to be?" asks Carlos. "You going to drink me, taste me, like food?"

Michael laughs. "Really? Thousands of years between us and we should just stab and bite, like those Vikings, the Moors? We shall swing swords and see whose arm is strongest?" Michael laughs again, genuinely amused. "No."

Carlos smiles too, but his smile is guarded. "You want to know who is better, stronger, though? Like, we compete? What for? We are who we are. Stronger, faster – does not matter. You mock, but you wish to fight that which cannot be fought because you are bored? Like a child? Shall we keep score with medals, or stickers?"

"No," agrees Michael. "You're right, of course. But wrong, too, Carlos. Nothing *matters*. But I tire, yes. I bore. We see who is strongest, but like we do with them."

This time Carlos does laugh, and though the bonds of thin wire round his chest cut his borrowed skin, he can't stop his body from shaking.

"You want a contest of our will?"

Carlos laughs again, and Michael joins in until, with those long fingers of his, he reaches forward and dips into the blood running from the place at Carlos' wrist where his changeling blood leaks. Then Michael puts the bloody finger into his mouth. He sighs, like Carlos is a rare treat.

"Yes," says Michael, abrupt and full of business. "We ask. I ask, you ask. Then, we take… the losing face."

"But what end?"

"A game. You play games? I like games," says Michael. "They pass long hours."

Carlos stares back at the pale-faced man, his mismatched eyes narrowed and bright. "I don't like games."

***

The changeling's power is not in brawn, but knowledge, perhaps, or just in their gaze. A glamour, a spell, a kind of cunning bred in creatures of such immeasurable age. To a human, their gaze is stronger than any charismatic man's ever was, more powerful than a grandparent watching a young child and waiting for the truth that follows a lie. Undeniable, to something mortal.

To each other, something else entirely.

Great armies across a plain. Immense, heavy bodies waiting to move, the Sumo of Japan, or celestial bodies waiting for the right moment – an eclipse – when a winning stroke can slide unseen in the one dark moment in decades, or centuries.

"You want to give me your face," says Michael.

Outside, those bodies he left leaning against the wall of the farmhouse are desiccated, mummies, their moisture frozen and then evaporated.

Moments, for an immortal. Seasons for the corpses left staring at the high, cold plateau where the changelings battle.

Carlos doesn't want to lose.

He thinks, slowly, eyes narrow and hard and cold as the ice that covers the Andes outside, that Michael is right.

Nothing matters.

Perhaps nothing ever mattered.

Nothing matters.

Is that my thought, he wonders, *or Michael's?*

Carlos knows how this works. The Norsemen knew. The Celts, they knew. But then time sprawls so long and wide that people forget those old things which came before man. They disbelieve, they move on in their minds to thinking about the next thing, not the last thing. They watch planets that revolve around the sun, and they think in angles, and Pythagorean theorems and Doppler effects and CPUs.

The Norsemen knew.

Science is real, the world is real, the things people can see and feel: all real.

The things people forget, though – they're real, too. Thin, perhaps, or shallow now. But the old ones live long lives and while they are not seen, it does not mean they are not real or cannot come back. A door closes, but it can open again. A myth can return through a door just as it can leave, and those kinds of doors never lock, never warp, never rot and turn to dust.

Such doors are eternal.

Changelings do not *take*. They never did.

Myths are flexible. The elf-kin steal children in the night. The Romany, they do the same. The vampire. The wolf.

Blood and moon, people think.

But they're all old ones, and they never take. They ask, and they're beguiling, aren't they? Those creatures that come unwanted in the night and ask for a husband or wife or child. And you give them because you want to, don't you? Or you give yourself when asked. You take your face off and give it away, and after so many borrowed faces how can a man or creature know who or what it is any longer?

No, thinks Carlos, *I don't want to give you this face. This is my face.*

"Is it, Carlos? Is it yours any more than this is mine?"

Though they stare, unblinking, through the stretch of seasons such as they are in the high mountains, and though they stare in bright sun and black, moonless nights, Carlos' eyes do not tire.

Michael doesn't believe that at all.

If he did, then what would it matter if he took my face? Or what would it matter if I just gave it to him?

But Michael is strong. *He's strong,* Carlos thinks, *because he does this more than I.*

"Of course it doesn't matter, and you can give it to me. It doesn't matter at all, Carlos. Nothing does."

Michael takes what he does not need because he *wants* it. Something of humanity has seeped in, and along with it came greed.

"I do," says Carlos. He doesn't want to give his face to Michael, but his words are just as strong as the pale man's imprecations.

"I do," says Michael.

It's glamour, but only as seen in a mirror.

***

The face in the mirror won't ever be the same, thinks Carlos, staring back just as hard as Michael.

Won't be the same. Won't be human, will it?

It's just a reflection. It's just an image. Flat, unthinking. No more than a copy of a man.

Changelings ask for a face and sometimes they're given it. Maybe three, four times in more than a thousand years has a man said no. And in saying no, that man walked on to live in his own face. Those men are rare indeed. Men who never wanted to be elsewhere, or be anyone or anything else. Truly content, perhaps. Men who don't look for someone else in a mirror at all.

Are you content, Michael?

Are you who you want to be? Or is there a man in a mirror that you can never, ever reach?

Men who live eons and change with generations – are they truly content with who they *are* when they can simply *wear* whomever they want to be?

"Clever, Carlos," says Michael. "You? Are you who you want to be, Carlos?"

As they speak their voices are preternaturally persuasive, and their thoughts are as loud as a shout.

They remember Stalingrad and St. Petersburg. They remember Mao and Cambodia under Pot. Time and memory and blood skips around. Earlier, monks writing the false words of prophets in a cold monastery with coloured, laboured scripts. The first printing of the Gutenberg bible, the earnest Protestants on distant shores of an old, old America. Pizarro, Cortez. Incans, Aztecs, and, earlier still, Olmecs. Boats and ships that sailed before men thought to write about their voyages to new worlds. Viking boats on Iceland and an Ottoman empire and Roman, first, second, and the many falls of great nations. Alexander, the Macedonians. Things before Christ and in the years since.

Such a long time, thinks Carlos.

"Just give me your face, brother. Rest now. It has been *so* long. *So* long."

"You do not wish your face, Michael. You do not wish the face you wear nor mine. You wish to see what lies beneath, don't you? The thing within, to *know* what you are…"

And on, through centuries and millennia.

Changelings tire. Humanity tires. Same thing, just longer.

Rhodesia. British empire. The Indies. A mercenary bathed in blood diamonds, a soldier in the depths of the Congo. But small times, too, that somehow seemed just as important when men and changelings were there, living inside them.

One minute, hard-rock African lands with names that changed through centuries; the next, Carlos remembers hunting a bear for three days with a flintlock pistol in heavy rain and just an oiled pouch to keep the powder dry.

Small times, important times, big things, small things. The things that make a life, no matter how long or short.

Life does not have to be long, thinks Carlos. But that isn't his thought.

Or perhaps it is.

Outside the farmhouse where they sit, Carlos bound and Michael free to leave, the summer comes around again. At such a lofty altitude the air remains cold and the family propped against the house walls now grin like their teeth have become longer, though it is just that their flesh is receding. Their faces wear away as time moves on.

"Rest," says Michael.

"I won't," says Carlos.

Outside, the dead stand watch and will until they crumble, but such things as seasons and centuries are just a blinking eye to the eternal.

***

Something of humanity in him, thinks Carlos. *Greed, but hubris, too.*

Michael thinks he is strong. He is strong. He's strong because he wants to be.

I am stronger, Michael thinks.

I am.

Michael looks down and sees the bonds are not around Carlos, but around his chest and his arms and thighs and ankles.

Under the face he once wore, his flesh is tender and it's still cold enough that the bodies against the wall of the house don't smell no matter how long dead they are. Carlos rises and moves briskly from the chair, free, then pauses at the door. That dark-skinned face of his that is so expressive seems sad.

"Funny," Carlos says. "Seeing what's inside us."

Michael struggles to answer. Lips form many words. Some slithering and lisping sound is all that comes out.

Carlos shrugs. It doesn't matter what Michael says.

"I told you I don't like games," says Carlos. "I don't enjoy them. You do, because you *know* you will always win. I do not like games for exactly the same reason."

Carlos doesn't feel the need to say anything else, and Michael is hard to look at now that his face is wiped clean, leaving just the thing below.

The wolven man steps out into a day waiting for snow, higher than the sea someplace on the border between countries in a continent where places can sometimes remind him of an old world long gone by. He shrugs inside his skin.

For a moment, he wonders who he is, *why* he is. He wonders if he's the same inside as Michael.

Or Carlos?

He's not sure, walking into the snow, whose face it is he wears. After so many borrowed faces, how can a thing even know what it is anymore?

Maybe, he thinks, *I'm just human and the creature I left behind is what we all look like inside.*

The family against the wall of the house stare with blood frozen on faces skinned and switched. None quite fit right.

They never do quite fit, thinks Carlos. Maybe he hopes he'll find one that'll fit just right and he can settle. Maybe not. He's not human, but only because he takes what he needs, not what he wants. A predator, and…

Carlos pauses for a moment, hunched against the rising cold on the plateau. He frowns, confused. He runs his tongue over his teeth before he's sure, and though the face on his flesh has yet to settle, he can smile just fine.

Everyone's wearing a borrowed face, he thinks. *What does it matter which one I wear?*

KNACKERED

SKIP NOVAK

Rob downshifted into eighth gear. He reached over, turned off the repeat of the 'Paul Harvey Podcast' on his iPod. Country music from the late 1970s and early 1980s filled the cab of his White Freightliner. He braked and downshifted again. He looked into his passenger side mirror and saw the hitchhiker picking up his bags. "This night just got a whole lot better," he commented to the empty cab as he opened the armrest console, pulled out a bunch of porno magazines and tossed them into the passenger seat.

The hitchhiker, a young male with a back pack and a duffel bag, caused him to slow his rig down in the middle of the Arizona desert. The hitchhiker was already jogging towards where Rob was pulling the eighteen wheeler over. The young man's gait and the way he held his head straight forward made Rob think of his family back in Wisconsin.

Rob's wife, a vice president of a furniture company, was a youthful thirty-six. Mary didn't mind that Rob was twenty years her senior. She had three kids from a previous marriage, all of whom were in high school. Rob met Mary not three years after her divorce from her first husband, a deadbeat who never paid his alimony and had, according to the government, only paid into the tax base for three quarters. Meaning, he'd been working under the table for cash since he'd gotten out of the Army in 1972.

When Rob met Mary, her twin girls, Lucy and Matilda, were just going into high school and the boy, Jordan, was in middle school. Rob had tried not to think too much about the kids and what stage of development they were in. Besides, Mary was one repressed and horny woman. She was more than willing to try anything he suggested.

If he wanted to get laid while they were watching a movie, she was game. If he wanted a blow job after a night out at a fancy restaurant, she complied. Hell, she was a real wildcat when it came to adult relations and exploration. It was a great relationship. That is, until she had started getting serious.

Rob had explained to Mary that his first wife, Sheila, was in a vegetative state caused by a car accident that had damaged her brain. Sheila had been in a coma for five years and Rob had seen each of his three kids through their high school years by himself. He had two daughters – Wendy, the oldest, and Anna, the middle child – as well as a son, Larry. Larry had joined the Navy and had been accepted into the SEAL teams, but never seemed to be able or willing to communicate with his family. Wendy had developed Alzheimer's at the age of thirty-eight. Anna had moved to Seattle and had not communicated with him in ten years.

Mary hadn't cared about his previous life or why his children almost never kept in touch with their father. All she'd seen was an opportunity to improve not just her life, but the lives of her children as well.

Their wedding had been held in a mutual friend's back yard. It was a great day. The sun shined and the stress of life was held at bay by the happiness of the attendees. Rob's urges that insinuated themselves into his life seemed to be at bay that day too. Of course, a pre-marital romp in their friend's master bedroom had helped alleviate the tension.

Yet it wasn't long before his more obscure tastes started to betray him. Urges he'd learned to enjoy while he was in Southeast Asia in the 1970s. Hedonistic tastes unacceptable in America but readily fulfilled in third world countries. He'd been lucky enough at the time of the wedding to be a sales representative for a large car manufacturer.

They would send him on week-long trips overseas where he could immerse himself in any and all strange fantasies that popped into his twisted and perverse mind. Trips that he came back from feeling extremely sated physically and only a bit guilty.

Though Rob had woke up every morning to his beautiful newlywed wife lying next to him, all he'd been able to think about was his newly betrothed wife's offspring: two daughters, both of whom were in the budding stages of their pubescence, and a young boy who was just then starting to experience the uncontrollable nocturnal emissions of youth. What were they doing? Were any of them sexually active? Did any of them ever step out of line and need a stern hand to punish them?

Such thoughts had made Rob anxious, which hadn't helped him and his condition at all.

Soon after the wedding, he'd had closed circuit television cameras installed in the new house he had moved Mary and her kids into. The monitors had been built inside a secret panel behind his suits in his large walk-in closet. He'd often found himself there, watching, even after having had his way with Mary. He'd hoped to catch the kids masturbating or dressing and going about their daily grooming rituals, but more often than not both girls were sleeping, and the boy was jumping up and down spastically in the middle of his room.

He'd wondered if any of the kids would appreciate his advances when the time came. Would they shun his bald, pink scalp and the stark white hairs covering his chest, which reminded him of a small polar bear? What of his toes? Ugh, they looked awful. The nails were an ugly yellow-and-green color. He'd picked up a fungus during his army career – something he couldn't shake no matter what sort of anti-fungal treatment the podiatrist prescribed him. His feet smelled like rotten eggs, and yet the nails always grew like little daggers.

He'd known, though, there'd eventually be an opportunity to test their reactions. And if an opportunity didn't present itself, he'd always be watching. That was what digital recording was for.

Over the course of the next three years of marriage, he'd had plenty of opportunity to take advantage of his new wards. It had started simple enough: give them a few drinks at dinner, and when they got silly, he'd carry them to bed, accidently brushing against their privates. This activity soon escalated, and Mary was none the wiser.

The cab door opened, interrupting his reverie. A young man with long dark hair and a ratty old army coat started climbing in. "Man, thanks for stopping. I've been trying to get a ride for hours."

"Not a problem. Everyone needs help now and again. I'm Rob."

"Joey. I've been trying to get to California. You going there?"

"I am, actually. Got a load of tires in the trailer headed for San Diego."

"Awesome," Joey said as he placed his bags on the floor of the cab. Which was when he noticed all the porn magazines on the seat. He started to push them aside and then said, "Man, you like porn."

"Need something to pass the time besides music when I'm stuck on the side of the road."

Joey closed the door to the cab, fastened his seat belt and started to stack the magazines next to him. The kid seemed completely uninterested in paging through the stacks of naked women and men doing all sorts of bedroom activities with each other. "So, you pick up hitchhikers often?"

"Once in a while, when I'm feeling generous. Say, you want a drink? There are some Pepsis and beer in the cooler in the sleeper."

"Thanks, man," Joey said, unbuckling his seat belt. He crawled into the sleeper compartment and emerged with two cold Budweisers. "Grabbed one for you."

"Thanks. Not supposed to drink and drive but I ain't stopped this rig in almost eight hours," Rob said. He popped the top of the beer, took a sip and then set it in the cup holder. He shifted the rig into gear and started back down the interstate.

An hour later, Rob pulled the rig onto a siding to get some sleep. He'd only taken one sip of the beer his passenger had given him. The young boy had drank three of the cold beverages and had fallen asleep with his head resting against the window.

Rob unbuckled his seat belt, nudged Joey a bit and got no response. He then crawled into the sleeper and stripped out of his clothes, took a syringe and leaned back into the cab of the truck. Which was when the lights went out.

***

Rob's head lolled to the left and right. He opened his eyes and was greeted with blackness. His head throbbed like ten jackhammers were inside his skull trying to break out. He tasted dust and grime in his mouth.

He tried to gain his bearings. He was seated with his back against a wall and he was naked. His hands were bound behind his back, but not with rope or metal. It was plastic. Zip ties, he thought. He tried moving his feet; they were bound at the ankles with the same tight plastic. After a few moments, his eyes adjusted to the blackness and he saw a sliver of light to his left. The light was thin, tall, and didn't cast enough light into his cage for him to see any of his surroundings.

There was a low rumble coursing through the floor of his cage, which told him where he was, locked in the back of a tractor. Presumably the one he'd been escorting to San Diego before he'd been taken captive by his hitchhiker. Within a few minutes he realized the truck was moving and, by the feel of it, traveling at high pace.

He bent his legs, placed his feet flat on the ground, and scooted forward. As he did so he lost his balance and tumbled to his right, causing him to fall into something hard and wrapped in plastic. This was when the smell of the trailer became apparent.

It was earthy, with a chemical overtone. Almost damp, like a newly opened can of oil. Rob smiled a bit. He was in the back of his own truck. New tires always had the same smell.

He tried to right himself, but he was canted over at such an awkward angle that he wasn't able to find any traction. Well, that, and the years of eating greasy fried food at truck stops had not been kind to his waistline, or his muscle mass. He tried to use the leverage of his head on the edge of the shrink-wrapped tires, but all he managed to do was slip further down on his right side.

Once he was fully on his side, he tried to push himself back toward the wall where he'd woken up. Within a few minutes, he found himself in a worse situation. The top of his head was resting against the side of the truck, his face pressed up against an old wooden pallet, and he had several splinters stuck in his cheek and nose. He wasn't sure but he felt a wetness and stinging in his right hip. He could feel blood dripping off his face and the coppery scent of his own fluid filled his nose.

With no logical means of escape, Rob did the only thing he could do: he fell asleep.

***

In the cab of the rig, Joey drove east toward the rising sun. He knew of a place in Illinois where he could get rid of the load of tires in the trailer. Before he did that, he'd have to find a quiet, secluded place to get his captive back inside the sleeper. He didn't look forward to transferring the son-of-a-bitch again.

With great care, Joey took his left hand and reached under his right shoulder to pull a small medical hose out of his sleeve. He removed the bulb of the makeshift siphon and the large water bag that held the contents of the beer he had supposedly drunk. He then rolled the window down and tossed the contents out into the night air.

He reached down, picked up his back-pack, unzipped it, and rooted around until his hand felt a piece of hard plastic about the size of a satellite phone. He pulled it out and held it in front of his lap near the steering wheel. Two metal probes on the end of it glimmered in the morning light. He depressed the trigger on the side and bright blue and white sparks danced between the poles of metal. Joey smiled.

His Taser had helped him out of more jams than any gun or knife could. Not that he didn't know how to use those tools, he just found it much easier to stun and knock out his target before the real work began. If it had been up to him, he'd sooner have just taken care of this asshole in the desert and left different parts of him buried over a hundred square miles. But, his contractor had been very specific about not killing the guy and where to deliver him.

Oh well, no biggie, he thought. Easy payday for him. The hardest part had been tracking the guy all over the southwest and pinpointing exactly which route he would be taking to San Diego.

Joey had tracked him through three states before an opportunity had presented itself. Rob had gotten arrogant or sloppy; either way, when Rob had pulled into a truck stop in Western Texas with a parking lot full of trucks and cars, he'd been forced to park his rig near the back of the lot.

Joey had known that was his chance.

Of course, he'd had to wait because Rob had taken advantage of two of the lot lizards' night time offerings. It took forty-five minutes before he'd left his cab with the two hookers. His teeth had gleamed in the bright lights of the parking lot as his two temporary concubines, who had suddenly developed slight limps and grimaced with each step, tried to hurry away from the man they had spent some very painful time with.

When the coast was clear, Joey had walked around to the front of the truck stop, stood next to an SUV, and scanned the patrons on the other side of the glass. He'd soon spotted his prey. He'd been sitting at the counter, slowly sipping out of a coffee cup while a grey-haired waitress stood in front of him patiently holding a pen in one hand and a pad of paper in the other.

Joey had quickly moved back to the man's truck, tested the door locks and was surprised to find out it was unlocked. Too fucking easy, he'd thought. He had climbed into the cab and was greeted with the sour, stale scent of sex. He'd grimaced at the thought of what had happened inside that metal beast.

He had pulled out a pocket flashlight and looked around the cab. Within a few minutes he found what he was looking for: a Garmin GPS navigator. He'd pushed a few buttons, and the driver's route appeared. Not trusting his memory, he'd written down all the directions on a note pad. When he was done, he placed everything back where he had found it, exited the cab, and went back to his car, where he placed a copy of the driver's route in his own GPS unit. He'd spent the next fifteen minutes searching for the right place to get picked up as a hitchhiker.

Four hours later, just east of Concho, Arizona, Joey had ditched his car, put on a stringy black wig made of real human hair, a false nose, and colored eye contacts, dirtied his face up with some dust which clung to the spirit gum on his face, and changed his clothes. He'd gotten the clothes from a thrift store, and before he had put them on, he kicked them around in the desert sand so they didn't look so clean.

Then he'd started walking. He'd walked about five miles before his target spotted him and pulled to the side of the road. "Let the fun begin," he'd said to the empty landscape as he trotted toward the rig.

It had been almost too easy.

***

Just north of the Illinois border and south of Marion, Illinois, Joey pulled the rig off the highway and went down an old road that led to an abandoned factory. It was a place he'd discovered years ago and used only a few times. He knew routines were an easy way to get caught; however, it'd been over a year since he had been there, and the probability of any law enforcement agency having anyone on stake-out there was almost zero. This, to him, was the best he could hope for.

The factory hadn't really changed, except that the undergrowth had spread around the empty parking lot and up against the brick buildings. It seemed additional glass from the industrial windows had been broken since the last time he'd been there. Also, new graffiti graced the walls.

Joey wheeled the rig in behind one of the buildings and slowly drove through the compound to make sure there were no stray cars or trespassers around. He was in luck. The place was completely abandoned. He parked near the side of the main building so he could see the entrance road.

Before he got out of the cab, he retrieved his Smith and Wesson .45 caliber gun, checked the magazine, chambered a round, and tucked the gun into his pants. He then took out his Bowie knife and placed it on his belt. As he got out of the truck he pulled his Taser out of his pocket and checked to make sure it was energized.

The raspy clicking noise was like music to his ears and he smiled. Time to get the show on the road. He walked to the back of the trailer and opened the doors.

***

Rob knew he was in trouble. He didn't know where he was, but he knew by the way the truck had slowed down and the bumps and ruts had caused him to bounce around the floor of the trailer that they were nowhere near civilization. He tried to maneuver himself near the door. When he felt his feet against the cool solid metal door he wiggled closer to it, until his knees rested firmly against his overextended stomach. He swore to himself that if he survived this mess he was going to go on a diet and lose some weight.

He didn't have to wait long. Soon he heard the all too familiar sound of the metal hasp being flipped and the heavy steel handle of the door being lifted out of its cradle. Just another few seconds, Rob thought. Just a few more seconds.

His ears filled with the squeal of the metal locking claws of the door handles as they were pried loose from their secure fittings. As the door creaked open, Rob kicked with all two-hundred and seventy pounds of his gluttonous frame. He heard a grunt of surprise as the door bounced into the body opening it. "Fuck you, asshole!" Rob screamed as the heavy door bounced back against his feet, sending dull but searing pain throughout his body. He let out his own cry of pain and kicked the door again.

This time the door swung wide open and light flooded Rob's eyes, causing him more pain. He knew he didn't have much time and tried to ignore it as he squirmed his way toward freedom, feet first.

The three-foot drop to the ground was quick and not as painful as he'd expected. Of course he'd landed partially on his captor. He quickly rolled over until he was lying almost completely on top of the young man. Rob's face was only inches from Joey's. He noticed something was very wrong with the young man. His nose was askew and looked as if it had been torn away from the rest of the skin, but there was no blood. Also, the boy's hair was all crooked, as if his entire scalp had been twisted in such a way as to make the skin below it twist like a screw-top beer.

Rob had no time to study the facts. Joey started to groan and move so Rob head-butted him as hard as he could. His forehead crashed into the boy's fleshy and torn nose. Joey stopped groaning and moving. Rob rolled off of him and looked for something, anything, to help him escape the binds on his wrists and ankles.

He saw a gun handle sticking out of Joey's pants, and, better yet, a large Bowie knife sitting in its sheath on his hip. Rob quickly maneuvered his way around the unconscious man until his bound hands felt the knife handle. He quickly unsnapped the leather strap holding the blade in place and pulled it free.

"Please, oh please, let this damn thing be sharp," he said to any and all gods or demons that might be listening.

***

Mike hated working daytime security. Nothing ever happened in the daytime, especially on his route. He'd been assigned the eight-to-six shift because his lieutenant had received several anonymous complaints about Mike abusing his authority. Abuse, hell. All Mike had done was stop some graffiti kids from tagging the abandoned houses and factories. Well, at least that was what the complaint was about. No one said anything about his penchant for sneaking up on young lovers in their cars and watching them fuck, and right before they reached their release point he'd turn on his mag-light and rap loudly on the window.

He always got a kick out of seeing the fear in their faces; it was extremely amusing to watch them try to cover up their private parts in some sense of modesty. Once in a while he would know the kids' parents and tell them if they wanted him to keep his mouth shut, they'd have to pay him hush money. Which usually amounted to forty or fifty bucks extra in his wallet.

Once, he'd caught the city's mayor getting a blowjob from one of the well-known hookers in town. They'd been parked behind the high school gymnasium, and he'd been able to extort five hundred bucks from the man. Boy, that had been a great night. 'Course, at the time, he hadn't realized by taking the money he'd basically destroyed any chance he'd had at getting hired as a patrol officer. But, since he hadn't known this fact, he'd just assumed the city was prejudiced against him because his family didn't belong to the good-ol'-boy network.

So, as he approached his fourth stop of the day – an abandoned fender factory from the 1920s – he was surprised to see the sun glint off of clean glass. He was extremely familiar with this factory. Hell, it was the best spot to catch people fucking, drinking and breaking the frosted glass of the old brick buildings. Not to mention he'd taken a few of his dates out here and told them to either "put out or get out." They always put out; after all, it was a twelve-mile walk back to town on an unlit abandoned road that hadn't been paved in years.

"Jackpot," Mike said aloud as he reached for his car radio. He was about to call in the trespass, but then thought, Maybe it's some high school kids playing hooky, coming out here to fuck. He put the microphone back on the dashboard clip and slowed down so his car would not kick up too much dust and draw attention to his arrival.

He looked in his rearview mirror. The street behind him was empty, the sun glimmering in the west. He knew there was almost no way for the trespassers to spot him. After all, they had parked on the north side of the main factory, a place that would be shaded soon.

When he entered the main parking lot he turned right. No sense in driving right up on them; he would take the long way to where they were parked. Like a border collie, he thought. His mind was immediately filled with thoughts of his own dog he'd had as a boy.

Fluffy, he'd called her. She was a mixed mutt, part border collie, part German shepherd and part Labrador retriever. Or so his dad had said. He remembered that every time he'd thrown a ball or stick for a game of fetch, Fluffy would watch where the ball was going and then head ninety degrees off from that direction. Fluffy would then run along the nearest obstacle she could find until she'd run almost twice the straight distance any normal dog would have taken, and then she would sprint at full speed and fetch the trophy.

Fluffy did the same action in returning the object, never coming straight at Mike. No, she'd always take the long way. When Mike had asked his dad about this behavior, his father explained to him that border collies' minds worked in different ways. They didn't want to be seen. They tried to stay hidden until the last minute so their prey wouldn't get a sense of their attack. Or so his dad had always said.

His father had gone on to explain that all dogs descended from wolves and different traits were bred into or out of the domesticated animals so they could be used for specific purposes. That information had struck a chord in young Mike. Over the course of his middle school years and the first half of his high school years, all he'd cared about was reading about dogs and their different traits. Why they acted the way they did and what they were bred for.

He'd even written several reports on different breeds for school and his 4-H club. When he was a junior he got a job working for a vet and learned all about how to handle the different types of animals that came into the office. By his senior year he'd become fascinated with service, military, and police dogs. His dream was to become either a bomb dog handler in the army or K-9 officer in law enforcement.

Those dreams had all gone to hell the night of his graduation. He'd been at a house party with some of his friends when his buddy told him they had a purebred German shepherd that was always barking and was mean to the family.

Mike had remembered how to calm aggressive dogs down. "You have to mount him," he'd said in front of sixteen of his drunken classmates.

"What do you mean, mount him?" his pal had questioned.

"Simple. Just get behind him, place your hands on the back of his neck, and act as if you are about to fuck him," Mike had said without thinking.

Fifteen minutes later, with everyone in the party watching, Mike had approached the aggressive dog, which was chained up in the back yard. He tossed the dog some bologna and moved around the dog's backside. With a swift movement he was behind the shepherd, his hands arounds the dog's neck. He then thrusted his hips in a mocking gesture as if he were fucking the animal.

It had worked. The dog immediately became docile and stopped growling and snapping. Mike had proven his point.

What Mike hadn't known was that no less than three of his classmates had recorded the scene on their phones and then quickly uploaded it to the internet.

By the end of the next day no one in town would talk to him aside from calling him 'dog-fucker.' And his hopes of joining the military had been quashed. He'd also been fired from his job at the vet's clinic. Hell, they hadn't even done it to his face; instead, they'd just called and left a message on his answering machine.

It had taken him almost three years to get hired on to a private security company. Three long and lonely years. He'd sworn to himself he'd never be taken advantage of again. He'd become the 'alpha-male' in whatever job he landed. No one was going to make a fool of him again. He'd always get the upper hand on everyone he came into contact with. This had served him well over the years, yet it seemed his tactics had led him into a life of loneliness, a fact he hadn't quite been able to put together. He'd just thought everyone had hated him for the long-forgotten video, not because he'd become a complete and utter asshole.

He pulled his car up to the side of the building. He tried to avoid the broken glass on the pavement and all the fallen bricks, but he heard the crunch of the material under his tires and hoped the trespassers were too involved with each other to notice the sounds.

He got out of his car, leaving the door open so as not to alert the perpetrators to his presence, and drew his revolver.

"Mike, where are you?" came the sultry voice of the dispatcher over the radio. That was the only thing sultry about Glenda. She was an over-the-hill, overweight, grey-haired woman who ate sweets all day. She'd eaten so much candy over the years that they'd removed all her rotten, blackened teeth and fit her with dentures. Dentures she didn't like to wear. Most of the time she'd just sit in the dispatch office and suck on tootsie rolls or sugar daddies and talk to him in innuendo.

He reached in the car, grabbed the microphone, and said, "Dispatch, this is Mike, I'm at the abandoned fender factory. I'm going out on foot. One of the doors is open."

"Okilee dokilee, Mikey," Glenda said in her best impersonation of Marilyn Monroe.

Mike dropped the microphone, reached in, and turned the radio off. "Can't have you fucking up my fun," he whispered into the empty car.

He inched his way across the front of the building, trying to make as little sound as possible. As he got closer to a large tractor trailer, he heard moaning and groaning coming from the rear of the rig. Jackpot, he thought. I'm gonna get a free show and an extra payday out of this.

The cab of the rig was parked just forward of the building and the rest of the rig was parked too close for him to squeeze his body between it and the factory wall. He quickly crossed in front of the cab and made his way down the side of the trailer. When he got to the back of the trailer, the noises of what he believed to be fucking filled the air.

"C'mon… Hurry up… Get it over already… Shit… Ouch. Goddammit…"

Mike took the opportunity to jump out from the side of the trailer with his gun pointed at what he thought was two people fucking. Instead, he was greeted by a naked, hairy, dirty and bleeding man sitting on the ground with his arms behind his back, pumping them up and down feverishly against another man's groin. As if he were giving the man some sort of backwards hand-job.

"What the..."

The naked man looked up and all color drained from his face. "Thank God, officer! You're here! Help me! This man has kidnapped me!"

Mike moved his gun from the naked man to the man lying on the ground, then back to the naked man. He'd read about this sort of freaky shit on the internet but he'd never thought he'd see it. "What the hell is going on here? You're trespassing," was all he could mutter

"I told you. I've been kidnapped. This man is trying to hurt me. I've done nothing wrong!" the naked man said as he continued to piston his arms up and down.

"Wha..." was all Mike could get out.

Then, the naked man's arms were in the air, his right hand wielding a large knife.

Mike fired, the shot went wide, and the air around all the men became filled with smoke and noise.

***

Joey opened his eyes. His ears and face were filled with explosive pain. He looked to his left and saw Rob standing up as some man in a uniform was falling down. Joey's Bowie knife was buried in the uniformed man's neck. Blood poured out at an alarming rate. Like when he'd worked on a hog farm and had to slit the squealing throats of mature sows as they hung upside-down by their hind legs. It hadn't been Joey's first taste of death, but it was the first time he'd seen the light of life slowly spill out of the eyes of a living creature.

He knew then and there that the cop or security guard was a goner.

He quickly forgot about the man. He had other problems; his target was up and moving. From where Joey lay, he could see Rob still had the tie wraps around his feet but his hands and arms were free to do whatever damage they could. Proof of that was slowly bleeding out not ten feet from them.

Joey looked around and saw his Taser lying on the ground a few feet from him, but he knew if he tried to get it he would be heard. So he lay there and played possum. When he saw Rob start to turn around he closed his eyes and didn't move. When he heard Rob move, he opened them again.

He saw Rob trying to hop his way toward the dead man. He waited, and watched as Rob bent his knees and began another lame attempt at a hop forward. Joey flipped over. When Rob tried to jump again, Joey lunged for the Taser.

Rob heard him the second time and turned toward him.

Joey saw fear in Rob's eyes and hoped his own eyes didn't betray him.

Rob lunged for the dead man's neck as Joey felt the familiar coolness of the Taser in his left hand. He leapt to his feet and charged his target. The air was filled with burnt ozone and the sound of electrical clicking.

Joey stood over Rob's unconscious body. The man's hairy belly was still quivering like a bowl of Jell-O in the early afternoon sun. "Fucker," he said and kicked the man in his side. "Try that shit again and you won't make it to your final destination."

Joey then flipped the dead man over and noticed a private security patch on his arm. "Good, ain't no one gonna miss you for a while," he said. He found the man's handcuffs and quickly secured Rob's wrists behind his back. "Fucker. You're almost too damn heavy to get back into the cab."

Twenty sweaty minutes later, Joey found the car the security officer had driven and drove around to where the dead man was slowly drying out in the sun. He hoisted the dead meat into the trunk of the car and drove around to the loading docks. When he found a loose door, he opened it and parked the car inside.

Hopefully, I will be long gone before anyone misses the guard, he thought. Then he walked back to the tractor trailer and checked on his target, who was now passed out, handcuffed, and zip-tied in the rig's sleeper. Joey had also used an old pair of underwear and some duct tape to seal the man's mouth shut.

He got into the driver's seat, started the rig up and headed north for Chicago.

"Maybe this job ain't so fucking easy," he said as he tried to find a rock and roll station on the radio.

***

The sun was setting as he pulled into the warehouse district. Joey steered slowly and carefully through the maze of shipping containers and industrial equipment. He was headed toward a familiar place where he'd gotten rid of more stolen goods than a dozen large discount box stores had in their inventory at any given time. As he rounded the corner of a warehouse with a large gantry crane parked between it and the water, he saw that his underground connection had followed through with their promise.

There were half a dozen new, black GMC SUVs parked next to the edge of the pier. Next to the warehouse, Warehouse 68, he saw a large Cadillac limousine and, behind it, two black Mercedes Benzes. Joey shook his head. He'd never known Nails to have anything but American cars in his fleet of vehicles. Hell, the man even refused to have anything to do with the expensive Italian super-cars that were all the rage with his cousins in New York. "Well, maybe times are changing," he said to no one.

A tall, thin man with a full beard stood next to Nails' limo, smoking a cigarette. He noticed Joey driving the rig toward him, stepped away from the limo, and started walking straight in front of Joey's path.

Joey stopped as the bearded mobster climbed up on the driver's side steps.

"You Joey?" the man asked with a medium baritone voice. As he spoke, the smoke of his cancer stick blew into the cab. The kid couldn't have been more than twenty-six, and while he had a full beard, the hair on his head was thinning quite rapidly. Joey guessed he'd be bald in two years.

"Yeah, that's right. I'm here to see Nails," he answered, waving the smoke away from his face.

"'Kay, just pull up to the doors. Everything is set."

"Thanks," Joey responded, but the Beard was already walking away.

The warehouse door began to open as Joey approached. He waited a few moments until it was fully open, then he drove in to park the rig. He checked on his passenger, who was still passed out. Joey even pinched the man's nipple and twisted it really hard to make sure he was completely out, then shut the rig down and climbed out of the cab after the warehouse door closed.

There were about fifteen men standing around. Joey scanned the crowd for Nails. Then the Beard ordered everyone to get to work. Two forklifts appeared out of nowhere. The men opened the trailer doors and began to remove the pallets of tires. Other men quickly uncoupled the trailer and jacked it up as a couple of other men chocked the wheels and started using pneumatic impact wrenches to tear the trailer apart.

A deep bass voice filled Joey's ears. "Quite a sight, ain't it?"

Joey turned around and saw Nails. He was a large man, maybe six foot three or four, his long sandy blond hair pulled back in a ponytail, face covered with the same colored hair. His beard was down to his chest. He wore a plain white t-shirt and a leather vest full of outlaw biker patches. *Fuck*, Joey thought, *how long has it been since I've seen Nails? A year? Two?*

"You fuckin' outlaw! How ya been? What's it been? A year?" he said as he reached out and hugged Nails.

Nails returned the hug and Joey felt his ribs protesting as the big man tried to crush him. "Nah, man, it's been eighteen months. You fell off the grid. Didn't think I'd ever hear from you again." Then he released Joey and held him at arm's length.

"Shit, man, I've been working off continent. Lots of jobs in South America and Africa."

"Really? Anything that will affect us?" Nails asked, referring to his organization's drug and hooker trades.

"Nah, just some human trafficking, kidnapping jobs. Been keeping me in the green and the pink."

"Hope it was good pink."

"Only the best."

The men stood there for a minute, assessing each other's strengths and weaknesses and then pushed each other away.

"So, you got a rig full of tires? That ain't like you. Usually you have something a bit more valuable."

"Hey, at eighty bucks a pop minimum, a trailer full of tires is worth at least fifty large. I'm giving it to you for ten. That's a steal."

"Ten plus a clean SUV. Which ain't cheap. What angle you working here?" Nails asked. He was always able to see more in a situation than was apparent.

"Fuck, man, Nails, I'm on a case. Got a real piece of shit tied up in the sleeper. Need to have him moved into the bed of the SUV so I can deliver him to my contract. Unfortunately, this guy is a real fat bastard. Took me almost an hour to get him into the damn rig by myself. And, he's a fighter."

"We can get him moved. Besides, the price of the parts of this rig will more than make up for the cost of the SUV. I'll get Otter to help you."

"Otter?"

"Yeah, the fuzzy-faced dude that's been barking orders for the last five minutes. That's Otter," Nails said pointing at the skinny, balding guy who had directed Joey into the warehouse.

"Damn, I thought he was some FNG or something."

"Well, he is, sort of. He's my nephew. Been trying to make a name for himself for a couple years. He took out a couple US Marshals last year. Got promoted. The Marshals got buried in the swamps of Louisiana."

Joey nodded in complete understanding. Never fuck with the club; never fuck with the family. An unwritten yet important rule.

"So, ten large and a clean SUV."

Joey turned and saw Nails holding a set of keys in his hand. He took the keys and looked around the warehouse. No other vehicle was inside. "Where's the ride?"

"Outside. Give the keys to Otter. He'll get it for you and help you move your… cargo."

"Thanks," Joey said, and he walked off toward Otter, who was standing a few feet from the men tearing apart the trailer. He handed Otter the keys and told him what he wanted. Otter nodded and disappeared.

Ten minutes later, Otter parked one of the SUVs near the rig's cab. When he got out of the SUV he approached his boss and Joey.

"So… what's with the Mercedes?" Joey asked Nails.

"Gift from the Apple. Supposed to diversify."

"Thought you hated Europe."

"Only when Europe doesn't fill my pockets."

"So? What do you think of them?"

"Boss, we're all set," Otter interrupted.

"Okay, help Joey with whatever he needs. If you don't, your ass is mine. Consider me number one and him number one A!"

"Yes sir."

Nails turned to Joey and said, "I'd love to hang out, but I've got two other deals going on tonight. Otter will do whatever you need him to do. The money is in the SUV. The rest is up to you."

"Thanks, brother," Joey said.

"Think nothing of it," Nails said as he walked away.

Joey turned to Otter. The man-boy was in the process of lighting up another cigarette, "Otter, I need to get my cargo out of the sleeper and into the back of the SUV without any hassle. Quick and easy. I checked him not fifteen minutes ago. He was passed out but I don't trust the son of a bitch. He could be faking it. I want him loaded and ready for transport in ten minutes."

"Relax. I got this. I'll get a couple of my boys and we'll get him moved. You just sit back and enjoy the show."

Joey didn't trust Otter or his boys but he didn't really have a choice. He stood to the side as the three men pulled the body from the sleeper and began to carry him over to the back of the SUV.

"Ugh, what the fuck is that smell?" one of the henchmen said aloud.

"He's covered in filth," Otter replied, struggling with the unconscious man's upper body.

"It's his feet," Joey shouted. "They're all fucked up."

One of the mobsters looked down at the leg he was holding and his face turned slightly green. "Gross. That shit is nasty!"

Halfway between the vehicles, everything went to shit. Rob kicked out with his legs, forcing the two henchmen to drop him, leaving Otter to carry the rest of the weight of the dirty, naked, bloated man.

As Joey watched, time seemed to slow down. Rob's feet hit the ground as Otter lost his balance and fell backward, taking Joey with him. As they tumbled, Otter started to scream and the cigarette that had been dangling out of his mouth dropped onto Rob's back. In a couple of seconds, the air was filled with the acrid smell of burning hair. Otter's screams faded when he hit the ground, the obese man on top of him. The sound of Otter's rib cage collapsing and breaking between the stiff concrete of the floor and the fleshy weight of his load filled the warehouse.

Joey saw several ruby-red blossoms appear under Otter, and he knew the young mobster had no chance of drawing another breath.

He leapt, his Taser held high above his head, knees tucked under him. His scream filled the air of the warehouse and caused all workers to stop and look toward the affair of life and death.

***

"Make sure he is securely locked to the cage and unable to talk," Joey said to several well-dressed mobsters.

He sat with his back resting against one of the rear wheel-wells of the SUV he'd negotiated as payment for the rig and its components. However, the loss of Otter might have some repercussions he'd not planned for. "Fuck it," he said aloud, moving toward the driver's side of the vehicle.

"Sir, we have him secured and he shouldn't give you any trouble for at least three hours," a voice said in Joey's ear.

"Three hours? How do you figure?"

"We gave him a sedative," the man said, miming injecting a needle into his own arm.

"Okay. As long as I can get him to Wisconsin, then all will be all right."

"You need to leave now. We have to clean this mess up and I've no idea what I'm going to say to Otter's mom. We need you to get in the wind. Now."

"I'm gone," Joey said as he climbed into the SUV and headed out of the Chicago Port Authority as quickly as he could.

***

"Fucking Portage, Wisconsin," Joey said to the empty SUV cab. "Why here? Because no one expects bad shit to happen in the Midwest? Shit, most of the bad shit in America happens in the Midwest. 'Course, no one would ever believe it. But shit, most serial killers are located where no one expects them to be."

Joey looked into the back of the SUV and was greeted with a severely complacent and unconscious pervert. "Good," Joey said aloud. "Not too long now. I'll collect a good payday, you'll be transferred to your captors, and I'll be on my way to my next job. I can't wait. I've worked too fucking hard for this payday and all I want to do is spend a week or two in the Caribbean without any questions. I just want to forget this job," he said in anxious conclusion.

Joey drove straight to the coordinates on the GPS. He ended up sitting in the middle of a field, surrounded by cows and a beat-up pick-up truck. Some of the cows had taken to rubbing up against the old rust bucket. A couple had even lain down in the grass next to it.

His phone rang and he answered the call.

"You in the middle of nowhere?" an electronic voice said in his ear.

"Yeah, and I ain't happy about it. And what's with all the cows?"

"Good. Get out of your vehicle, take your stuff and leave the cargo. There are keys in the truck along with your money."

"You better not be jerking me around."

"I don't do jerking around." And with that the phone call ended.

Joey gathered up his stuff and was about to leave when Rob started thrashing around. He turned and looked at the man. He was dirty and covered in his own piss and feces. Half of his body hair was burnt off and he stank to high heaven. "Sorry, man, my job is done and I think you're done too."

Rob grunted and yanked on his restraints harder.

"Ain't no getting out. Have a good life… what little there is left of it."

Joey got out of the SUV, walked over to the pick-up and tried to shoo the sleeping cows away. They didn't move. One large bovine was actually blocking the driver's side door. "Fuck. Could this shit get any more fucked up?" he yelled as he trudged his way around to the passenger side.

No cows blocked the passenger side. Joey opened the door and found a large brief case sitting on the passenger seat. He smiled. "Yes. Finally. Payday." He tossed his duffel bag and back-pack into the back of the truck and crawled into the driver's seat. "Fucking Wisconsin," he said as he reached for the brief case and opened it, which was the last thing he ever did.

***

Rob watched as Joey tried in vain to get the cows to move away from the truck. He was yanking and tugging as hard as he could to get free from his restraints when the truck exploded, and soon the vehicle he was in was pelted with bits and pieces of cow and metal.

Just when he thought he'd never get free, the back half of a cow crashed onto the roof of the SUV, crushing it in, breaking out the glass in the doors, and devastating the metal cage Rob had been handcuffed to. He took the opportunity to crawl out of a broken door. In doing so his chest and belly were cut with broken glass, metal shards, and some splintered cow bones. He didn't feel the incisions when they occurred; his adrenaline was pumping and everything was covered in blood.

As he crawled away from the wreckage through the sawgrass, mustard weed, and dirt, he muttered prayers to a God he didn't believe in. He was so consumed with escaping he failed to see the three figures walking toward him. "Please, God, if you're out there, help me. I'm sorry. I didn't mean it. I'll change. I'll…"

"Praying ain't gonna help you, you sorry piece of shit," a familiar voice said.

Rob stopped his hobbled crawl and looked up towards the voice. "Mary! Thank God! You can help me. Please. Wait. What are you doing here? How'd you know…" Then everything fell into place in his starved, beaten, and electrified mind.

"You really are a stupid asshole, ain't you?"

"But, but, I didn't – "

"Save it. I know what you've been doing. I've known for years. You think my kids don't talk to me? You think I didn't know about your overseas trips? You think I don't know what you do on the road all across this country? You think I'm some sort of dummy?"

Rob hung his head, and tears began to stream down his face uncontrollably, revealing pale, white, clean flesh beneath the blood and grime. "You planned all this? The kidnapping?"

"I had help," Mary said. She turned on a flashlight, shining it toward Rob's right.

He followed the beam and saw a young man in his early thirties. The man stood tall in his camouflage clothes, and in his right arm he held a hunting rifle. Rob noticed a pistol in a military holster on his hip.

"Son… you?"

"Yeah. Me," the man said in a deep baritone. "But you ain't been my dad in a long, long time. Far as I'm concerned, you were just a sperm donor. Nothing else."

And with that said, the young man stepped forward and Rob tasted the freshly polished leather of his boot.

***

"Girls," Mary commanded, "make sure he is ready to move. Sweetie," she said as she looked toward the young man in the military garb, "please go get our truck."

"Yes, my dearest." He trotted off into the darkness.

Mary's two girls stepped forward, each wielding a cattle prod, and began to zap the living consciousness out of the man who'd abused them. Their gleeful laughter was louder than the burning wreckage not twenty feet away.

When Mary was sure Rob was unconscious, she called the girls back. The truck, driven by her real husband, Larry, arrived and they quickly loaded the unconscious sack of meat into the back. Mary took the wheel and the girls sat next to her in the cab. Larry rode in the back with his father.

Minutes later, Mary parked the truck inside an old barn. Well, the outside was old. Inside, Larry, Mary, Jordan, and the girls had converted it into a modern slaughter house. They'd spent months getting everything together and practicing their techniques on deer, pigs, and cows. They'd even been able to supplement their income by selling the meat to local farmers.

Larry had even had the forethought to offer their butchering services to local hunters who didn't want to get their hands dirty. Then he'd built a smokehouse behind the barn so they could smoke the meat for customers who wanted that service. They'd been in business not eight months, but they were becoming quite successful.

With the efficiency of a journeyman, Larry quickly strung Rob up by his heels, then secured the man's hands to the floor. He then grabbed a hose and began to spray the man down. Mary was busy getting all the tools out of the sanitizer. The girls sat on stools, eating chips and drinking soda. Their eyes never once looked away from the preparations.

"Where's Jordan?" Larry asked Mary.

"Oh, he's in the house monitoring the police channels. If anything comes across about what's going on he'll let us know. He is also checking the internet to make sure there is no chatter about Joey and his antics in Chicago. The internet and social media have exploded with what went down at the docks. 'Course, the police are clueless."

"Yeah, that was a real mess."

"His own fault. I warned him about Rob."

Larry shrugged. "He's clean enough – for now. We gonna do this like we planned?"

"Yeah, except I want him awake. He needs to know this ain't gonna be quick and easy. I want him to suffer for what he's done to my kids and all the other people he's hurt."

"It's your scene," Larry said with a shrug. He pulled some smelling salts out of his pocket, cracked the ampule, and shoved it into one of Rob's nostrils.

The immediate effect was quite comical. Rob started thrashing and cursing like a veteran sailor. The girls laughed.

"Now, now, hubby. You know all this struggling ain't gonna help," Mary said. She stepped forward with a pair of pruning shears, grabbed ahold of his manhood, and, with the swiftness of a barber, cut it clean off. She held the flaccid piece of meat in her hand, knelt down, and shoved it into Rob's open mouth. "Shut up, you piece of shit." She turned to Larry. "Cauterize the wound, my love. Can't have him bleeding out before we all have our fun."

The air filled with the searing scent of flesh. Mary took some duct tape and wrapped it around Rob's head to help quiet the screams and to make sure he didn't spit out his own penis.

"He's not going to choke on that?" Larry asked

"He may, but I don't care," Mary said and turned to the girls. "Ladies, it's your turn. Have fun."

The girls stood up, smiled at each other, and stepped over to the bench where Mary had carefully placed all the tools. They each picked up implements of destruction and approached the man who'd made their lives miserable.

"This is fun. Can we do it again?" one of them asked their mother.

"Maybe," Mary replied, beaming as a proud mother should.

WRETCHED ANNIE
RICH HAWKINS

Even above the sound of the rain, Ray heard the corpse rolling about in the boot of the car. His mouth tasted of metal and nervous tension. He didn't risk moving his trembling hands from the steering wheel, in case he lost control of the car and it veered into the ditch at the roadside. Thin sticks and bare hedgerows scraped at the rain-pelted windows. In the dimming light of dusk the windscreen wipers worked at their limit to keep up with the downpour.

In the passenger seat Huntoon watched the road ahead and sipped from a bottle of supermarket brand vodka. He hadn't said a word since they'd passed the last ramshackle village. Ray tried to think of something he'd done to displease the older man, but he couldn't remember. His throat tightened as he tried to think of something to say, so he decided to leave it and concentrate on the way ahead.

The country roads were neglected and twisted into serpentine forms – black tarmac and wet gravel, potholes and weeds, winding through silent villages seemingly lost in time. Flanked by fields and meadows. Tall trees grasping for the starless sky. Ray couldn't wait to get back to the city, to solid concrete and familiar streets, fast food and tower blocks.

All this effort to dispose of a police informant.

"You're scared, aren't you?" Huntoon said.

"What?" Ray asked.

"You're scared. You're nervous."

"Is it obvious?"

"To anyone with eyes."

"Oh."

"Is that all you have to say?"

Ray cleared his throat. "I think so."

"Look like you're about to shit your pants."

Ray wiped beads of sweat from his upper lip. "This is my first time dumping a body."

A half-smile played across Huntoon's mouth, revealing the gold tooth where his lateral incisor should have been. "I know. That's why I'm here. Mr Cobb wanted to make sure you did the job properly."

"I'll do the job properly."

"I hope so. That prick in the boot has to stay hidden, because if he's ever found it'll lead straight back to Mr Cobb. And if that happens, he'll have our fucking heads on sticks."

"I won't let Mr Cobb down," Ray said.

"You won't while I'm around."

After a moment of silence Ray asked, "How many times have you dumped a body for Cobb?"

"*Mr* Cobb."

"Mr Cobb, I mean, of course."

"Many times."

Ray squinted at the rain. "You're from around here, aren't you?"

Huntoon sighed. "Born and raised. When I first moved to the city I was mocked all the time for my accent."

"You haven't got an accent."

"Not anymore. I lost it after a few years in the city. And, anyway, the last man who took the piss out of my accent ended up with a butter knife sticking out of his eye."

Ray turned the wheel as the road curved to one side. He switched the radio on, but there was only the hiss of static. "Can I put a CD on?"

Huntoon lowered the vodka from his lips. "No. The last one you put on was shite."

"Dr Dre?"

"You think you're from South Central? Compton?"

"I like it."

"Shite. Absolute shite."

"Okay."

"Turn the radio off," Huntoon said. "We're nearly there."

***

A few miles on they found a place to stop, and Ray pulled over to the side of the road under the dripping bough of a tall oak tree. When Ray turned the headlights off, such was the darkness around the car that his breath stuck in his throat.

Huntoon, ape-like and slouching, took one last swig from the vodka bottle.

Ray climbed out of the car and switched on the torch he'd taken from his jacket pocket. He pulled his hood over his head and grimaced up at the drizzle. Rainwater dripped from the leaves and branches of the great oak, pattering on the road like a hundred tapping fingers bidding him welcome.

Huntoon opened his door and stepped outside. He swept his torchlight over the roadside hedgerows and shadowy thickets, then down both directions of the road.

The black trees sighed with the passage of the winter wind.

"It's fucking freezing," Ray said, shivering as he glanced around. "I hate the rain."

Huntoon pointed the torch at him, and he flinched from the light. "Stop moaning. Get on with it."

"Sorry. I was only saying."

"Well, don't. We've got a job to do. Sooner we get it done, sooner we can fuck off out of here."

Ray took out his cigarette lighter and pack of Marlboros.

"What are you doing?" Huntoon said.

"I thought I might have a smoke while we shift him."

"You can wait until we've finished."

"Really?"

"Yes."

"Okay."

They walked to the rear of the car, opened the boot, and lowered their torches to the corpse wrapped in blue tarpaulin and bound with thin rope. He was a small man but Ray wasn't looking forward to carrying him across the field.

"We should have chopped him up."

"Be my guest," said Huntoon. "There's a hacksaw somewhere in the boot. If you're up to it, of course."

"I'm good, thanks."

"Thought so. Let's get this done."

***

The starless sky was the only witness to their passage through the metal gate into the sodden field. They struggled with the weight of the corpse. Ray carried two spades in a bag over his shoulder. His arms were aching and he had to keep blinking the rain from his eyes.

Huntoon moved in silence, glancing around them. Ray couldn't see the boundaries of the field, and the sky was only a shade lighter. The rain, which had worsened since they'd left the road, only helped to obscure their surroundings.

"How much farther to the woods?" Sweat beaded at the nape of Ray's neck and trickled down his back. "I can't see anything out here."

Huntoon spat. "Nearly there."

"Okay."

After what seemed like hours spent traversing the field, the woods loomed ahead. The trees were like a wall that had recently emerged from the ground to meet the approaching men.

Ray wheezed a sour breath through gritted teeth. "How far will we have to go into the woods?"

"Will you stop asking questions?"

"You just asked a question."

"Don't get clever, boy, or you'll end up in the same hole as this poor bastard."

"Sorry."

"We won't have to go too far."

"Okay. Sorry."

"Stop saying sorry."

"Okay."

"You're a fucking idiot, Ray."

***

They moved through and below the trees, stepping lightly. Shadows rose and fell from their torchlights, then retreated into the deeper dark of the woods. Rain slipped through the skeletal canopy. Water dripped from branches and trickled down gnarled trunks.

"Did you remember the spades?" said Huntoon.

Ray nodded, then realised that Huntoon couldn't see him in the dark. "Yeah."

"Good. Because if you forgot, I'd make you go back to get them."

"I know."

"You don't know anything, boy."

"Sorry."

***

They found a patch of ground between some trees and set the body down. Ray pressed one hand to his back and winced.

Huntoon directed his torch about and prodded the damp earth with his boot. "This will do. Seems mostly clear of tree roots. Should be able to dig fairly deep enough to keep animals away."

Ray's legs ached and heat prickled the backs of his thighs. His throat was dry and scratchy like he was coming down with an infection. When he realised he'd forgotten his bottle of water he turned his face to the falling rain and opened his mouth. Huntoon watched him and shook his head. Once Ray was done gulping at raindrops, Huntoon threw him a spade, and then they set to work on the ground, backs bent towards the treetops and the pitch black beyond.

***

It took well over an hour to dig the grave. They lowered the corpse into the earth then refilled the hole with the loose dirt and patted down the topsoil. They covered the ground with leaves and fallen branches. When it was done they stood in the rain and looked down at the grave beneath the woodland detritus.

"Should we say some words?" Ray asked. "I know he was an informant, but we still knew him."

Huntoon spat and looked as if Ray had suggested a naked dance about the trees. "Don't be so soft. He got what he deserved. We all get what we deserve."

"Do you believe that?"

Huntoon hefted his spade and laid it on his shoulder. "Let's get out of here. Fucking heartburn's giving me gyp, and I left my pills back in the car."

Ray nodded, wiping his mouth with his sleeve. "Okay."

***

The men started back through the woods. Ray tried to make conversation but Huntoon responded with grunted answers or just ignored him completely. Eventually he gave up and just kept his attention to where he placed his feet upon the sodden woodland floor.

They pressed on in silence, back the way they had travelled into the woods, but Ray felt a cold prickle of unease and anxiety in his chest. He found himself glancing about at the low sounds drifting from between the trees – the rustle of movement from the small mammals that scurried in the night. Something brushed through the treetops above him. When he looked to his right he thought he saw the silvery gleam of fox eyes from within a briar patch.

"Are we going the right way?" Ray asked.

"What do you mean, boy?"

"We should be out of the woods by now. Fuck, we should be back at the car by now."

Huntoon halted and wiped his brow. Ray stopped beside him. In the pale light Huntoon's face was severe and defined by thin shadows. And from his expression, Ray could tell he'd been thinking the same. Then Huntoon looked around into the surrounding trees stretching away from them, past the rain and the constant dripping.

"The woods can play tricks on you. Nothing more than that. We'll soon break through the trees."

Ray nodded, but his sudden feeling that they were being followed was difficult to ignore.

As they moved on, Huntoon murmured words under his breath.

Ray thought he'd said: "These are old, old woods."

***

Farther on, no more than a hundred yards through the trees, their torchlights found a strange symbol carved into the wide trunk of an oak.

"What is it?" said Ray.

Huntoon didn't answer as he stepped towards the tree. Ray stood beside him. The symbol was a vertical crescent, like a sliver of the Moon. Two narrow lines ran through the crescent at a forty-five degree angle. Ray noticed the lines looked like they'd been scored by sharp claws, but he chose not to speak of it.

Huntoon reached out and ran his fingers over the symbol, then drew them away, as if suddenly aware of his actions. Then he looked to the ground, lost in thought, his face caught in a frown that made him appear older than even his advanced years.

"Do you know what it is?" said Ray.

Huntoon looked up and regarded him. His mouth was partly open. He blinked. "Let's keep moving."

"Do you recognise it?"

"We need to get out of the woods."

***

They went on. The rain didn't stop or lessen. Shadows moved in Ray's peripheral vision. Huntoon scanned ahead and to their sides, as if waiting for something to appear.

They found the torn remnants of blue tarpaulin and broken rope on the ground. Dark bloodstains on the plastic. Left directly in their path, like an offering for them to stumble across.

They froze and stared down at the shredded remains.

"Is that what I think it is?" Ray said.

Huntoon exhaled. "I think so."

"Someone dug the body up and removed the rope and tarpaulin, then left them here. But where's the body?"

Huntoon toed the tarpaulin, then stepped away like it was something distasteful. He looked at Ray. "I think we're in trouble."

Ray shivered, and not from the cold. "Who did this?" He noticed the pistol in Huntoon's hand. "Where did that come from?"

"I've had it all along. You can't be too careful. Plenty of psycho farmers out here."

"You think a farmer did this?"

"No."

"Then who?"

"That symbol we found – I recognised it. I wasn't sure at first, but then I remembered some old stories my grandfather told me when I was a boy. I never thought they were true. Always assumed them to be myths and folk tales. All that bullshit. Now I'm not so sure. I felt we were being watched as soon as we entered the woods."

Ray almost laughed. "Are you talking about goblins and ghosts, for fuck's sake?"

Huntoon shook his head. He opened his mouth and began to talk, but was interrupted by a wailing scream from deep in the woods behind them. They turned to look back into the trees from which they'd travelled. Huntoon raised his pistol. A sound of mourning or rage followed the wail. It seemed neither human nor animal. Something Ray had never heard before, and didn't want to ever again.

"We've angered her," said Huntoon. "It was a mistake to bury the body in these woods."

"I don't understand," said Ray, staring into the dark.

"You're not supposed to understand, boy. You're not from around here. You never heard the stories."

Ray's voice was boyish and weak in the rain. "The stories your grandfather told you? What are you talking about?"

"It doesn't matter. It's too late."

"So what do we do now?"

Huntoon turned to him. "We're supposed to run, boy."

***

And they ran and stumbled, kicking through bracken and the carpet of stinking mulch and moss. The lowest branches of trees impeded and stabbed at them; it made Ray think of hands with sharp fingernails.

He dropped one of the spades and did not go back for it.

Their torchlights flashed past gnarled trunks and shadowy nooks between the trees. In his panic he thought he saw faces emerge from the patches of darkness and then retreat with gleeful light in their eyes. He spat each breath through a mouth filling with bile-sour saliva. He was certain he could hear something behind them. Something closing in, moving quicker than was possible through the scratching thickets. Something that walked forever in the woods.

Huntoon stumbled and fell against a tree. He grunted, cried out. Ray went to him and held him up. Huntoon grimaced, clutching his chest, breathing through gritted teeth. His eyelids fluttered.

"You okay?" Ray said, crouching beside him.

"Need my pills."

"We'll get them. Come on."

Huntoon looked up, and then his eyes fell on something past Ray's shoulder. His mouth fell open. He paled. Ray didn't want to turn around, but he did, and he saw what had reduced Huntoon, a man who'd killed men in cold blood, to frightened silence.

The pale form of a woman coalesced from between the trees. She looked too old to be out on such a night. Her crooked shoulders bent to the right, head cocked to the same side. A skeletal thing from the heart of the woods, clad in what seemed to be a tattered old gown made from stained cloth. Her arms and legs were bare and spindly, with the suggestion of brittleness about them. Her hair fell in wispy strands about her gaunt face, over her gold-yellow eyes and the wrinkled cartilage of her nose and her gnashing black-gummed mouth.

Ray realised she was almost seven feet tall. He couldn't speak, and didn't try to, in case it became a scream.

"It's her," Huntoon whispered between shallow breaths. His hand pawed at his chest. "Oh God, it's her."

The old woman's face held such an expression of rage that Ray had to look away for fear of losing his wits. And when he found his nerve to look again, she was already loping towards them with her eyes blazing and her long limbs splayed like some great gangling insect. Then Ray did scream, and fell back against the tree with Huntoon gasping beside him.

Huntoon raised his pistol and fired three times at the woman, and when the report of the gunshots had faded to a ringing silence, she had vanished. But Ray heard something rushing away through the treetops. He put one hand to his mouth and bit down on his knuckles.

***

Later, after traipsing in silence for over an hour through the endless woods, they found shelter under the thick bough of an old oak. The rain seemed to never stop. They squatted and huddled together like fugitives. Huntoon held the pistol close. His mouth was opening with little breaths. Ray kept watch with the remaining spade and his torch. Adrenaline broiled in his limbs and empty stomach. He felt sick.

"Do you know what that thing was?" said Ray. "Are you going to tell me?"

Huntoon exhaled and looked down at the ground. Ray had never seen the man so scared and morose. "Do you really want to know, boy?"

"I think it's for the best."

"For the best?"

"Yes."

"All that matters is we're going to die out here."

"Then I want to know the name of the thing that's going to kill me."

Huntoon rested the back of his head against the tree. "Wretched Annie. That's been her name for centuries, perhaps more."

"Wretched Annie? Who the fuck is she? *What* is she?"

"Something out of ancient folk tales and myths. A demon from pre-Christian times."

"Pagan times," said Ray.

Huntoon nodded. "Some sort of spirit; was said to haunt the woods in this area of the country. She would snatch anyone passing through the woods, and they'd never be seen again. No one knew how the story began. It was claimed she was some kind of elemental creature or some shite like that. She had powers, to make people become lost in the woods, to make the woods seem endless. And then she would snatch her prey and take them away to her nest."

"Her nest?"

"That's right."

"I wish you hadn't told me now."

"You did ask, boy."

"How are we going to get out of here?"

"We won't."

***

They walked through the never-ending woods. There were sounds of snapping branches far behind them. Ray thought he heard his mother calling to him, calling his name. He ignored the voice.

"She's been calling me, too," said Huntoon. "Imitating the voice of my ex-wife."

"Does she think she can fool us?"

"She's just taunting us. She'll soon be after us again."

Ray said nothing more and looked away.

They struggled onwards.

***

Huntoon stopped and sat down on the ground. He bowed his head to his chest. His shoulders rose and fell, then trembled. He was clutching at his heart.

Ray ran back and crouched beside him.

"This is where I stop," said Huntoon, spittle on his chin. He winced and squeezed his eyes shut. "I can't go any farther."

"Heartburn?" Ray said.

"My pills are for something a bit more serious than heartburn. Fucking stupid of me to leave them in the car."

"We have to keep moving."

"We're not going to get out of here, boy. She won't let us escape. We're going to die, if we're lucky. She might have something worse in store for us. I can't face it. I can't go on. I suggest you do the same as me after I'm gone."

"What are you going to do?" Ray asked. He glanced at the darkness around them, and then turned back to Huntoon.

The old man had the pistol barrel in his mouth. His eyes were dull and sad, glistening with tears. And before Ray could reach for the pistol, Huntoon pulled the trigger and shot the back of his head out.

***

Ray left Huntoon behind, and a few hundred yards on he heard a wailing cry beyond the trees he'd recently ventured through. He travelled with the pistol in his coat pocket, and the spade and torch in either hand. The dripping woods around him. Endless night. Endless rain. Hours spent walking, tripping, stumbling and falling. He twisted his ankle in a hidden divot, and when he slumped upon the ground, gritting his teeth in pain and desperation, that was the closest he came to following Huntoon's lead.

He limped onwards, dragging his feet, gasping at the aches and pains in his exhausted, drenched body. Several times he thought it would be easy to take the pistol and put it in his mouth, but he couldn't do it. Didn't have the nerve. Lacked the will. It was no surprise to him.

And, finally, after realising he couldn't go on, he succumbed to the cold exhaustion and slumped to his knees. He dropped the spade.

There was the sound of a quick rustling behind him. He grabbed the pistol and turned awkwardly on his knees and fired at the lurching form of Wretched Annie until the gun was empty. When the smoke cleared she had disappeared, but Ray could hear her somewhere in the trees, whispering old curses. He struggled to his feet to stumble away, glancing back to see her vague shape far behind him, and heard her mewling and throaty coughs in the dark.

The ground fell away below him to a steep wooded slope, and he realised this too late to slow down. He flailed as he tumbled head-over-heels and hit the dirt and slimy mulch. The breath was knocked out of him, and only when he rolled to the foot of the slope did he stop, his limbs and torso prickling with scrapes, cuts and bruises. His vision blurred from hitting his head against a stone on the way down. A few teeth felt loose. He lay on his back and gulped at the air, his heart squeezed by the white-hot terror in his chest. He had lost the pistol and the torch, and now he waited in the darkness for Wretched Annie.

***

She galloped down the slope to find him. And then she fell upon his shivering body, nuzzling his neck with her terrible wet mouth. He felt her teeth at his throat, and he waited for them to clamp down, but the killing bite never arrived. She withdrew from his neck and moved her face close to his own and began mewling and cooing. His groin warmed with the release of his bladder, an acrid stink that was paltry compared to Annie's musk. She sniffed at the air, but thankfully ignored the spreading patch of piss on Ray's trousers.

"Please don't kill me," he said. "Please don't..."

She looked at him with her yellow eyes, full of animal cunning and malevolence. Ray whimpered and started to cry like a child. She made a low sound in her throat. Ray couldn't look at her; he thought it best to avoid eye contact, in the hope she would lose interest.

Wretched Annie seized the sides of his head with her great hands and planted her mouth upon his. He tried to scream, but she nuzzled and licked and bit at his lips, then withdrew from his bleeding face.

Ray fell onto his back and made little sounds of terror and shock, his hands pawing at his ragged lips. The taste of her mouth lingered within his, all sulphurous and yeasty. He gagged, leaned to one side and retched until he spat blood.

"Please...please." His voice was barely a whisper, pushed past teeth broken by Annie's explorations.

Mercifully, he was barely conscious when she grabbed his ankle and pulled him along the ground toward a place only the dead had seen.

***

Damp ground beneath him. The stink of rotten meat in darkness. He knew deep in his gut where Annie had taken him. He stifled a sob and drew his limbs inwards as he sat up with his back against wet stone. He put one hand to the pain of his wet mouth, and with the other hand pawed through things that felt like bones or sticks. Then he remembered the cigarette lighter, and sighed with relief at its weight in his pocket. He grasped it, turned it in his fingers. The small flame reared up before his face. He shielded it with one hand, praying for it to stay alight.

The flame showed him the remains of those who'd been here before him. Human and animal bones were scattered about, most of them splintered, broken or smashed. Skulls and jaws brown from the passing of decades or even centuries. Torn clothing, filthy rags. Children's shoes that belonged in a museum, all blackened and warped by age. Dead leaves, twigs, moss, feathers. Colonies of black toadstools flourishing in dark, dripping corners.

He was in a deep cave. He had never felt so hopeless.

Nearby, propped against the wall of the cave, Huntoon's corpse glistened slick-red in the light of the flame. He'd been skinned. His eyes were gone. All the epidermal layers were peeled away and his mouth was fixed in a death-grin. His gold tooth glimmered.

"I'm sorry, Huntoon," Ray said, his voice muffled from the ruin of his mouth. He looked around, hoping for a glimpse of daylight and a way out, but he realised he was too deep inside the earth, and there was only the waiting darkness ahead of him.

Ray cried for a short while, thinking of all the things he'd never do again: watch a football game, eat an Indian takeaway, or drink a pint of lager. He slumped against the cave wall across from poor Huntoon and waited for Wretched Annie to appear.

And soon she came loping out of the dark to stand over him, staring down at his shivering and distressed form. He looked up at her, the cigarette lighter close to his chest, and felt his wits slipping away. Her dark pubis and what remained of her shrivelled breasts were visible under her filthy gown. She eyed him through wet strands of lank hair across her face, but she made no attempt to snatch the lighter from his hands. Instead she turned away and skittered over to Huntoon and began to eat him, ripping away bits of flesh and pawing them into her slavering mouth. Ray watched and cried. Occasionally she would throw scraps of meat at his feet. And when she'd finished with Huntoon and he was no more than a scattering of smashed bones and red pulp, she crawled over to Ray, purring in her throat.

"No, please, no," he muttered, cowering from her.

With one clawed hand she reached out and started stroking one side of his face, gazing into his eyes. As he cringed and whimpered, she moved her hands lower, fussing at his trouser buttons. He was too numb with terror and revulsion to resist. She grabbed his flaccid cock, and as she started to caress and stroke, he went hard in her hands.

Annie made an excited sound.

Ray vomited onto his lap, even as his erection trembled. She pushed him onto his back and mounted him forcefully, almost crushing his ribs with her squeezing legs. He felt himself enter her cold wetness and he vomited again. She didn't seem to care as she moved upon him, grunting and sniffling like an animal.

Ray screamed, but it only served to increase her excitement. Her eyes rolled back, her grunts quickened, and she opened her awful mouth to gasp and scrape her black tongue across her lips.

Ray looked away from her face and noticed a shaft of bone just out of reach. He stretched his arm towards it, crying and whimpering, shaking from Annie's ecstatic thrashing. He grabbed the bone, snatched it up without Annie noticing. One end was jagged from where it had been snapped. He looked up at the monster raping him, lunged with the sharp bone, and stabbed Annie in her right eye with all of his remaining strength.

She screamed in great pain and fell away, sliding from him with a horrid wet sound. She writhed and kicked. Her scream was so loud it brought to Ray such terror that he was barely aware of his undressed crotch. He dropped the lighter and rolled away from Annie, still holding the bone shard, buttoning his trousers as she reeled about the cave floor and slapped against the walls with her hands.

Annie collapsed to her knees. Ray brought the sharp end of the bone down upon her until her face was a pulped and shredded bowl. Then he punched into her brain to finally still the movement of her limbs.

He fumbled for the lighter, found it after much panicked pawing. He sparked it and then lay on the cave floor, panting and wheezing in the meagre glow of the flame. There was a sharp pain across his stomach, and he looked down to see that Annie's claws had slashed at his navel. It was bleeding, but the cut wasn't deep enough for his guts to spill out.

Holding one hand to his belly, he struggled to his feet and went to find daylight.

***

It was morning when he finally staggered outside. The rain had stopped. The woods were busy with birdsong and the sounds of mammals. The sun was rising over the trees. A plane left vapour trails in the blue sky.

Ray glanced back at the dark of the cave and then set off into the trees, hoping to find their end.

ABOUT THE AUTHORS

Alice J Black lives and works in the North East of England with her partner and slightly ferocious cats! Alice has always enjoyed writing from being a child when she used to carry notebooks and write stories no matter where she went. She would be the girl in the corner scribbling away while everything went on around her. She writes all manner of fiction with a tendency to lean towards the dark side. Dreams and sleep-talking are currently a big source of inspiration and her debut novel, *The Doors*, is a young adult novel which originally came from a dream several years ago. Several of her short stories have been included in anthologies with Burning Willow Press, Dark Chapter Press and JEA and she is always working on more. When she's not writing, she always has a book attached to her hand and will read from whatever genre suits her that day.
alicejblack.wordpress.com

Dawn Cano began her writing career in February, 2016 when she wrote *Sleep Deprived* on a dare. Since then, she's released Amazon best-selling stories such as *Bucket List* and *Violent Delights*, and she really gets a thrill from talking about herself in third person. When she's not writing sick and twisted stories, Dawn likes to write articles and reviews for The Ginger Nuts of Horror, the UK's largest independent horror website, spoil her mastiff, Penelope, drink plenty of wine, and give people a hard time on Facebook.
facebook.com/dawn.cummings.716

Sarah Dale is an author, mom, partner, daughter, step-mom, friend, dog-walker, cat-appreciator, library book-balancer, word lover, think-thinker and picture-taker living in Lincoln, Nebraska, and just generally trying to get things done.
facebook.com/wecouldbeheroesnovel

Author of her own misfortunes, also known as *Carnalis*, first novel in the Dead Central series (Strigidae Press, 2016), **Rose Garnett** is now unfortunately engaged in the creation of other hideous monstrosities in the hope of making the world a more terrifying place.

Rich Hawkins hails from deep in the West Country, where a childhood of science fiction and horror films set him on the path to writing his own stories. He credits his love of horror and all things weird to his first viewing of John Carpenter's *The Thing*. His debut novel *The Last Plague* was nominated for a British Fantasy Award for Best Horror Novel in 2015.

Stuart Keane is a horror/suspense author from the United Kingdom. Currently in his third year of writing, Stuart has started to earn a reputation for writing realistic, contemporary horror. With comparisons to Richard Laymon and Shaun Hutson amongst his critical acclaim – he cites both authors as his major inspiration in the genre – Stuart is dedicated to writing terrifying, thrilling stories for real horror fans. He is currently a member of the Author's Guild, and co-director/editor for emerging UK publisher, Dark Chapter Press. Stuart is the author of several works, and has featured in a number of #1 bestselling anthologies, including his Dark Chapter Press editing debut, *Kids – Volume 1*. Stuart was born in Kent, and lived there for three decades. A major inspiration for his work, his home county has helped him produce numerous novels and short stories. He currently resides in Essex, is happily married, and is totally addicted to caffeine.
stuartkeane.com

Chad Lutzke lives in Battle Creek, MI. with his wife and children where he works as a medical language specialist. For over two decades, he has been a contributor to several different outlets in the independent music and film scene including articles, reviews, and artwork. Chad loves music, rain, sarcasm, dry humor, and cheese. He has a strong disdain for dishonesty

and hard-boiled eggs. He has written for *Famous Monsters of Filmland*, *Rue Morgue* and *Scream* magazine, and is a regular contributor to Horror Novel Reviews, Halloween Forevermore and Heavy Planet. In 2016, several more releases will be added to Lutzke's body of work, including *Car Nex: From Hell they Came* and the *Cadence in Decay* anthology as well as two secret projects. Stay tuned!
chadlutzke.weebly.com

Rhys Milsom has a BA in Creative Writing from the University of South Wales and a MA in Creative Writing from the University of Wales: Trinity Saint David. His fiction and poetry has been published in *Wales Arts Review*, *Litro Magazine*, *The Lonely Crowd* and *The Lampeter Review*, amongst others. His debut poetry collection, *Amnesia*, is published by Onion Custard Publishing and has been described as "*…a frank comment on increasingly important conversations: youth lethargy, drink, drugs and notions of masculinity*" and "*the voice of the poems is a raw, transparent and open one throughout.*" Rhys runs a quarterly literature and art night called Milieu. Held in Cardiff, Milieu is a night of spoken word, art, photography and visual concepts, and aims to give established and emerging writers/artists space to showcase their work. Rhys lives in Cardiff with his partner and daughter, Ivy.
twitter.com/rhys_milsom

Jonathan Moon is a dark fiction writer living in Moscow, Idaho. He is the twisted mind behind *HEINOUS*, *Worms in the Needle*, *Hollow Mountain Dead*, *Stories To Poke Your Eyes Out To*, and several other nasty and terrible things from epic fantasy to hardcore horror to poetry. Recently accepted into the Anthropology program at the University of Idaho, Mr. Moon plans on spending his life studying the human animal. He wears masks, carries knives, and tells lies. Lots and lots of lies.

Skip Novak is a 48-year-old mid-western boy who now lives on the eastern seaboard of America. For his full time job he gets paid to play with toy trains. In his off time, he writes, smokes

cigars and tells tall-tales of his days serving in the U.S. Navy. You can find him on Facebook and Twitter under the name "Skip Novak", I know, how original.
aloysiousthoughts.blogspot.com

Duncan Ralston was born in Toronto and spent his teens in small-town Ontario. As a 'grown-up,' Duncan lives with his girlfriend and their dog in Toronto, where he writes dark fiction about the things that frighten, sicken, and delight him. In addition to his twisted short stories found in *Gristle & Bone*, the anthologies *Easter Eggs & Bunny Boilers*, *Death By Chocolate*, and the charity anthologies *Burger Van* and *The Black Room Manuscripts*, he is the author of the novel, *Salvage*, and the novellas *Every Part of the Animal* and *Woom*, an extreme horror Black Cover book from Matt Shaw Publications. He also co-hosts the horror podcast Screen Kings, dedicated to dissecting Stephen King movies and miniseries.

Jack Rollins was born and raised among the twisting cobbled streets and lanes, ruined forts and rolling moors of a medieval market town in Northumberland, England. He claims to have been adopted by Leeds in West Yorkshire, and he spends as much time as possible immersed in the shadowy heart of that city. Writing has always been Jack's addiction. Whether warping the briefing for his English class homework, or making his own comic books as a child, he always had some dark tale to tell. Fascinated by all things Victorian, Jack often writes within that era, but also creates contemporary nightmarish visions in horror and dark urban fantasy. He currently lives in Northumberland, with his partner, two sons, and his daughter living a walking distance from his home, which is slowly but surely being overtaken by books...
jackrollinshorror.wordpress.com

Craig Saunders is the author of over thirty novels and novellas, including *Masters of Blood and Bone*, *RAIN* and *Deadlift*. He writes across many genres, but horror, humour (the 'Spiggot' series)

and fantasy (the 'Rythe' tales) are his favourites. Craig lives in Norfolk, England, with his wife and children, likes nice people and good coffee.
craigrsaunders.blogspot.com

Tamara Fey Turner is an American writer. She currently lives in southern California with her favorite grey tabby, Gus.

Hidden in a remote location in California lives a man that responds to the name **Peter Oliver Wonder**. Though little is known about him, several written works that may or may not be fictional have been found featuring a character of the same name. Devilishly handsome, quick witted, and as charming as an asshole can be, Peter has come a long way since his time in the United States Marine Corps. Making friends wherever he goes, there is never a shortage of adventure when he is around. The works that have been penned under this name are full of horror, romance, adventure, and comedy just as every life should be. It is assumed that these works are an attempt at a drug-fueled autobiography of sorts. Through these texts, we can learn much about this incredible man.

ABOUT THE EDITORS

David Owain Hughes is a horror freak! He grew up on ninja, pirate and horror movies from the age of five, which helped rapidly install in him a vivid imagination. When he grows up, he wishes to be a serial killer with a part-time job in women's lingerie… He's had several short stories published in various online magazines and anthologies, along with articles, reviews and interviews. He's written for *This Is Horror*, *Blood Magazine* and *Horror Geeks Magazine*. He's the author of the popular novels *Walled In* (2014) & *Wind-Up Toy* (2016), along with his short story collections *White Walls and Straitjackets* (2015) and *Choice Cuts* (2015).
david-owain-hughes.wix.com/horrorwriter

Jonathan Edward Ondrashek loves to spew word vomit onto the masses. He's had an array of poetry, reviews, articles, and interviews published in the past decade. One of his short stories recently appeared in the anthology *Fifty Shades of Slay*, and his first book in 'The Human-Undead War' series debuted in April 2016. If he isn't working at his day job, reading, or writing, he's probably drinking beer and making his wife regret marrying a lunatic.
jondrashek.com